About t

Sophie Pembroke has b̶e̶e̶n̶ writing romance ever since she read her first Mills & Boon novel as a teen, so getting to write romance fiction for a living is a dream come true! Born in Abu Dhabi, Sophie grew up in Wales and now lives in Herfordshire with her scientist husband, her incredibly imaginative daughter and her adventurous, adorable little boy. In Sophie's world, happy is for ever after, everything stops for tea and there's always time for one more page.

Kimberly Lang is a Southern belle with a trouble-making streak and a great love of strong heroes and even stronger heroines. A former ballet dancer and English teacher, she now does yoga and writes the kind of books she always loved to read. She's married to her college sweetheart, is mum to the most amazing child on the planet, and shares her office space with a dog named Cupid. Visit her website at BooksByKimberly.com

Sharon Kendrick started story-telling at the age of eleven and has never stopped. She likes to write fast-paced, feel-good romances with heroes who are so sexy they'll make your toes curl! She lives in the beautiful city of Winchester – where she can see the cathedral from her window (when standing on tip-toe!). She has two children, Celia and Patrick, and her passions include music, books, cooking and eating – and drifting into daydreams while working out new plots.

Christmas Nights in the City

SOPHIE PEMBROKE

KIMBERLY LANG

SHARON KENDRICK

MILLS & BOON

First Published in Great Britain 2024
by Mills & Boon, an imprint of HarperCollins*Publishers* Ltd,
1 London Bridge Street, London, SE1 9GF

www.harpercollins.co.uk

HarperCollins*Publishers*
Macken House, 39/40 Mayor Street Upper,
Dublin 1, D01 C9W8, Ireland

Christmas Nights in the City © 2024 Harlequin Enterprises ULC.

A Midnight Kiss to Seal the Deal © 2021 Sophie Pembroke
The Million-Dollar Question © 2014 Kimberly Kerr
Christmas in Da Conti's Bed © 2014 Sharon Kendrick

ISBN: 978-0-263-36261-9

MIX
Paper | Supporting
responsible forestry
FSC™ C007454
www.fsc.org

This book contains FSC™ certified paper and other controlled sources to ensure responsible forest management.

For more information visit: www.harpercollins.co.uk/green

Printed and Bound in the UK using 100% Renewable Electricity at CPI Group (UK) Ltd, Croydon, CR0 4YY

A MIDNIGHT KISS TO SEAL THE DEAL

SOPHIE PEMBROKE

To all the New Year's Resolution makers out there

CHAPTER ONE

CELESTE HUNTER GRIPPED the phone in her hand a little tighter and whispered the words she'd never thought she'd say into it.

'What if I'm not good enough?'

On the other end of the line her agent, Richard, laughed. 'I don't believe it. Are you actually *nervous*?'

Celeste scowled, even though he obviously couldn't see her. 'Isn't that a perfectly natural response to appearing on television for the first time?'

'I didn't think you *had* natural responses, darling.' Richard sighed. She could just picture him shaking his head, his hand already hovering over his computer mouse as he moved on to more important things.

'I am human, you realise.'

'You're basically a walking encyclopaedia. Or history textbook, I guess.' She could hear his dismissive shrug. 'You're on a quiz show that is quite literally called the *Christmas Cracker Cranium Quiz*. I hardly think any of the questions are likely to stump you.'

'You're right.' Celeste knew she was intelligent. She'd had an excellent education and had a phenomenal memory for detail. Those were the things that had taken her as far as she'd gone in her academic career so far. She was a great historian.

That wasn't the part she was worried about.

'You're thinking about the new show,' Richard guessed, correctly.

'*Possible* new show,' she corrected him. The TV show they'd pitched for was very much still at the discussions stage, and Celeste just knew that the production company would be watching her appearance on the quiz to decide if she really had what it took to front a history show by herself. 'No counting chickens, remember?'

'Where does that saying come from, anyway?'

'Aesop,' Celeste answered absently.

'See! You know everything!' Richard yelled gleefully. 'Now stop worrying. I have to go deal with an actress with a secret lovechild with a politician. *That's* real problems.'

Celeste laughed. 'Good luck with that.'

'And you break a leg on that show, you hear me?' He paused, just for a second. 'But not literally. You know that, right? It's just a saying. Like the chickens.'

'I know that.' Poor Richard. He still hadn't quite adjusted to having an academic for a client, rather than actresses and pop stars. She'd never been entirely sure what had made him take her on in the first place—she didn't think he was, either. Curiosity, maybe. Or boredom.

Whatever, it seemed to be working out so far.

'Seriously, Celeste. Go sit in the green room with your laptop, and work on that book of yours. Not the academic treatise on whatever it was. The fun one. The popular one.'

'Two things I've never been in my life,' Celeste joked, but even she could hear the edge to it.

'That's what you're worrying about?' Richard sighed again. He was a big guy, in his late fifties, with a bushy beard that was more salt than pepper. When he sighed, his whole body moved, like a sad-faced dog. Even though she couldn't see him, just imagining it made Celeste feel a little better.

'If Tim and Fiona from the production company watch this...what if they decide I'm not enough? That I don't have...whatever it takes to be *good* at this.' That elusive X factor, she supposed.

'Have you ever *not* been good at something before?' Richard asked.

'Not really.' Apart from making friends and not boring people. Her best friend, Rachel, was the solitary exception to the rule. Even her brother, Damon, who she was pretty sure at least loved her, found her dull, she was sure. And her parents...well. They were pleased by her academic successes anyway. She hoped.

They certainly weren't pleased by any of her media successes. Apparently, she was *'dumbing down important research until all you have to say is derivative and reductive'*.

'Then have faith that you'll be good at this, too. Theo Montgomery's hosting, yeah? Follow his lead if you feel lost. He's good at charming a room, whatever the papers are saying about him at the moment.'

Celeste pulled a face. She didn't know what the papers were saying particularly, but she knew of Theo Montgomery. The sort of guy who got where he was because of his name, his face, and surface charm—but nothing underneath it. No substance.

Whereas she was nothing *but* substance.

Yeah, she really couldn't see Theo Montgomery being her new role model, whatever Richard thought.

Sighing, Celeste looked down at the Christmas jumper the wardrobe department had forced her into—worlds away from her usual, safe black outfits. Maybe that was the trick—to pretend this wasn't her here at all. She could be TV Celeste, instead of University Celeste.

Except she'd never really been very good at pretending to be something she wasn't.

Perhaps it was time to learn. If she wanted that show...

And she did. She couldn't explain why—especially not to her academic parents, who would be horrified she was contemplating something so...pedestrian. But she loved teaching history at the university, loved sharing her knowledge about her specialist area—women in classical literature and ancient history. And the idea of spreading that knowledge further, of getting people who might never have even thought about the subject before excited about those historical and mythical figures she loved, that excited her.

She just wasn't sure that she was the right person to do it.

'You're right. I'll go work on the book.' Working— whether it was researching or writing or teaching—always calmed her down. She knew what she was doing there.

It was only outside that safe world where she had all the answers that she struggled.

'Good. And, Celeste?' Richard said. 'Try to smile, yeah?'

Celeste scowled again, an automatic response to being asked to smile, honed after years of men telling her how much prettier she'd be if she did. And then she hung up, since her agent was clearly out of useful information.

She was just going to have to do this her own way. Starting with mentally preparing herself by focussing on something she *knew* she was good at. Writing her book.

And woe betide anyone who interrupted her.

Theo Montgomery was on a mission. Or a dare. A bet, perhaps. No, mission sounded better. More exciting, yes.

But also more…official. As if it gave him a reason for being there, sneaking around the green room instead of hanging out in his private dressing room as he normally would for a show like this.

And there had been a lot of shows like this. Well, not *exactly* the same—the *Christmas Cracker Cranium Quiz* was definitely a one-off. But he'd presented a lot of special occasion quiz shows, or entertainment specials. Apparently his was the face the network liked to trot out for this kind of thing.

He wasn't going to complain about that—especially right now. He knew that, after everything that had been published about him in the papers lately, he was lucky to still have the show. Even if it might be nice, every now and again, to be wanted for something other than his face, or his family name, Theo was under no illusions that the combination of both were what had got him where he was—TV darling, never short of work, or a date, or someone asking for his autograph.

Or where he'd been, before this mess of a break-up with Tania that was all anyone seemed to be talking about lately.

But overall, he had what he'd always wanted. What his family wanted for him, after a fashion. And he wasn't so bloody ungrateful as to complain about it now. Not when he had a lot of viewers to bring back on side, too. Viewers who'd listened to Tania's side of the story and jumped to the wrong conclusions.

The break-up had been amicable enough, Theo had thought. They hadn't even been together all that long. But the British press had loved the whole alliterative relationship, Tania and Theo, the reality TV star and the presenter, so they'd earned a lot of column inches.

And Tania had been a lot happier to tell her side of the break-up—with embellishments—than he had.

His agent, Cerys, had made it clear they were on a mission to salvage his career now. It was hard to be the nation's sweetheart when the same nation was tutting at him and saying 'that poor girl' behind his back.

Or, as Cerys put it, *'They want to be wooed, Theo. Charm them back onto your side again. Remind them why they love you.'*

So Theo would smile, and be charming, and ask the questions and laugh at the poor jokes attempted by the semi-famous contestants, and hint at the answers when they got stuck because it was *Christmas*, and nobody really took this sort of quiz seriously, right?

And talking of the contestants, that brought him right back to his current mission.

Because this was supposed to be a 'cranium quiz,' something a little harder than the usual *Who was Christmas number one in 1989?*—'Do They Know It's Christmas?' of course—the producers had also trotted out a higher intellectual calibre of celebrity guests.

There was the astrophysicist who did all the shows about the solar system, the kids' presenter who made Shakespeare accessible for primary school children, the morning TV doctor who treated the nation's bunions and STDs, the mathematician from that other quiz show, the guitarist from that band who also had a PhD in psychology and, last of all, the rising-star historian, an academic who was starting to make a name for herself, bringing the ancient world to life in guest slots on radio show interview and history podcasts.

Everyone except the historian he'd met on things like this before, or at some party or another after an awards ceremony. He'd actually been clubbing with the kids' TV presenter, David, while the guy was still in Shakespearean dress. And he and the mathematician, Lucy, had even had a bit of a thing, for a few nights, a couple of years ago.

No, his mission didn't involve any of them. It was centred firmly on the historian.

Celeste Hunter.

Before the show started, he was going to find her, introduce himself, maybe even charm her a little. Because he was pretty sure that Celeste Hunter was someone he was going to want to get to know.

He might not have met her, but that didn't mean he wasn't aware of her. He'd heard her speaking on plenty of podcasts and radio shows over the last few months, in that way that often happened in the media. Rumour had it she was lined up for her own series, soon. Once a person got a little bit of attention from one show, suddenly they were everywhere.

Like him.

And in this case, Theo thought it was a good thing. Celeste Hunter was *interesting*. Engaging, even, when talking about subjects that mattered to her—like ancient history.

But she wasn't just a specialist, he knew. He'd heard her talk about periods of history throughout the ages. She was a *brilliant* addition to today's quiz, and he was a genius for suggesting her to the producers. They'd joke about history, riff off some of the questions, and she'd make him look really good again for the cameras. Because, although no one would guess from his public profile, Theo liked history. He even knew a bit about it—although nowhere near as much as Celeste. He was interested though and engaged—and, knowing there was a fair smattering of historical questions in the stack for Celeste, he was most excited about that part of the show.

Theo eased his way into the green room, past an assistant carrying a tray of coffees, and smiled at the various inhabitants. There was so much festive filming going on in the building today that all the contestants had been shoved together in one of the green rooms, after hair and make-up. Luckily they all seemed in good enough spirits about it.

He greeted all the celebrities he knew, exchanging quick pleasantries and jokes, and even a hug with Lucy the mathematician.

'It's so great that you could all be here for this today,' he said, filling the words with his trademark enthusiasm. 'I really think this is going to be a "cracker" of a show.'

There were good-humoured groans at that, and he flashed them all a smile before turning to find the one person in the room he didn't know already.

She was sitting at the other end of the green room, as far away from everyone else as it was possible to get. He'd only ever heard her on the radio, but Theo had to admit his first look at Celeste Hunter didn't quite match up to his imagination.

She'd sounded so self-assured, so confident on the radio, he'd assumed she'd be older—older than him, at least. But the slender, serious woman tapping away on her laptop in the corner looked younger than him, if anything. Her dark hair was artfully waved around her face, something he assumed Sandra in Hair and Make-up was responsible for, given the way Celeste kept pushing it out of her eyes in irritation. She was wearing black jeans and heeled boots, her ankles crossed in front of her as she stretched out her long legs, the laptop resting on her knees. The jeans were paired with a sparkly festive jumper that he thought might actually light up, given the dimmed bulbs dotted around the Christmas tree design.

It was so at odds with her serious, concentrated face, it made him smile as he approached, moving into her space and waiting for her to notice him there.

It took about a minute longer than it usually would.

Finally, Celeste Hunter tapped a last key on her laptop, looked up at him, and scowled. 'Can I help you?' She didn't sound as if she wanted to help him. Maybe he shouldn't have interrupted her work.

'Hi there! I'm Theo Montgomery, the host of today's show.' He gave her his most charming smile, and hoped for the best.

'Yes.' Her gaze flicked back to her computer screen, then up to him again.

Right. 'Since you're the only contestant today I haven't met before, I thought I'd come and introduce myself.' Like a normal, friendly person.

This usually worked a lot better than this.

She stared at him. 'Okay. Do you need me to introduce myself too?'

She sounded reluctant. Theo took a seat beside her anyway. 'You're Celeste Hunter. I liked your piece on the Roman Empire in Britain on the radio last week.'

That earned him a surprised look, but a scowl soon settled back across her face, as she looked back at her screen. 'Apparently it was derivative and reductive.'

He didn't contradict her, even though he hadn't thought that at all. His opinion wouldn't matter to her, he guessed, and even on five minutes' acquaintance he was sure she wouldn't hesitate to tell him so. He had enough experience of being told that his job was meaningless or didn't qualify him to talk on any subject except charming people. He suspected Celeste would say the same about him, and he couldn't imagine that tonight's quiz was going to change that.

Shame. This was one guest he'd actually been looking forward to meeting, had lobbied to have included because he'd assumed she'd be as fascinating and engaging in real life as she was when presenting on the radio. He'd hoped he'd be able to talk to her about his own interest in history, his own studies and hopes to move more into that sphere.

Apparently not. This was why people should never meet their heroes.

Theo got to his feet, fairly sure Celeste wouldn't notice or care if he just left now. Still, the good manners his mother had ingrained in him long before his agent had insisted on them meant that he couldn't just walk away. So he smiled, and said, 'Well, I'd better go and get ready—we'll be starting filming soon. I'll see you out there. Break a leg!'

Celeste winced at his words, then nodded at him in acknowledgment, before beginning to type again.

Right, then. Clearly not a people person—which was a shame, since apparently charming people was the only thing Theo was qualified to do. Celeste Hunter was uncharmable, though, it seemed.

Which was fine. After all, once they got through filming tonight's show, he'd never have to see her again anyway.

Whistling to himself, Theo waved goodbye to the other guests and headed back to his dressing room to perform his traditional pre-show routine.

This was going to be a great show, a great night, and Celeste Hunter wasn't going to ruin that for him.

Where the hell are Damon and Rachel?

Celeste paced the corridor outside the green room, waiting for her brother and best friend to *finally* show up. She'd tried working on her manuscript to distract her from her growing nerves and her mother's voice in her head, telling her that this show was an insult to her PhD, but then Theo Montgomery had interrupted her with that charming TV-star smile, and reminded her all over again that this sort of show was *not* what she'd studied all these years to do.

God, her parents were going to be so disappointed when they found out about this. A TV series of her own, she might have just about been able to swing. Well, probably not, but she could dream… The *Christmas Cracker Cranium Quiz*? No. She'd tried mentioning it before, in rather vague terms, but the look on her mother's face had stopped her even considering going into details.

Normal parents would be excited for her. Proud, even. But then Jacob and Diana Hunter had never pretended to be normal. Never wanted to be, either.

Which was why she needed Damon and Rachel to just *get here*. They were normal people. They'd remind her that, actually, this was fun and festive and a boost to her career. The chance to show that production company that she had what it took to front her own show. It was the kind of opportunity most people would be hugely grateful for, even if she had no idea who at the network had dredged her name out of the halls of academia to take part.

She had a feeling it wouldn't happen again, not after that moment in the green room.

She'd been rude to Theo Montgomery. She hadn't *meant* to be, exactly. She just didn't deal with interruptions well. And since she'd already been freaking out a little bit about the company she was keeping in there—people her *parents* would probably recognise, and they didn't even own a television—well, she'd sort of just reacted, without thinking about it. Damon had been trying to break her of that habit for most of his life, but it never seemed to take.

She should probably apologise. Later.

First, she needed to get through the filming.

Celeste had never done anything like this before. Radio, sure, where she just had to answer a few questions she definitely knew the answers to—that was why they asked her to come on the show, because she knew about it. They were always pre-recorded, and usually she had an idea of the questions the presenter was going to ask before she even showed up, so she could prepare.

She liked being prepared.

But this…as she'd looked around the green room it had been obvious that this was a general knowledge quiz, ranging from science and maths to literature and arts, and hopefully history somewhere in between. She would be expected to know things *outside* her area of expertise.

The exact opposite of what she'd been training for her whole life.

'You have to specialise, Celeste,' her parents had been telling her, ever since she was in her teens. *'If you don't know exactly what matters to you, then you won't matter at all. Generalists never get anywhere. You need to find a niche, squat in it, and defend it with your life.'*

Her parents were academics. She'd wanted to be an academic. Of course, she'd listened to them.

Her brother, Damon, meanwhile, had rebelled, gone completely the opposite way, and become the quintessential Jack of all trades. While she had settled into her niche—women in the ancient world—and only dabbled in other areas of historical research as a bit of a hobby.

A well-rounded view of world history was generally encouraged in the Hunter household. A well-rounded view of anything else was generally not.

And appearing on a Christmas quiz show that reduced human knowledge to questions about Christmas number ones was *definitely* frowned upon.

She'd swotted up on a lot of festive history, ready for the occasion, though. Just in case.

'We'll be starting soon, Ms Hunter,' a production assistant told her as she hurried past.

Celeste's heartbeat jumped, and she fumbled for her phone in her pocket. She needed to remember to switch it off. Or leave it in the green room, probably.

But first… She hit autodial for her last number and tapped her foot impatiently as it rang and rang.

'Where are you?' Celeste asked, as soon as her best friend, Rachel, answered. 'We're starting filming any minute!'

'We're here, we're here,' Rachel replied soothingly. But Celeste could hear a car door opening, which suggested they weren't, actually, inside the building or anything. 'We'll be there any second now, I promise.'

'Okay. Hurry!' She hung up. Hopefully that was Rachel getting *out* of the car, rather than into it, or they'd never make it. And Celeste wasn't at all sure she could do this without them. Actually, she wasn't sure she could do it *with* them there, either, but the odds seemed slightly better, so she was going with it.

Three endless minutes later, Damon and Rachel tumbled through the doors into the lobby, and Celeste's whole body seemed to sway with relief. Only for a moment, though, because really they were very late.

'What took you so long?' she asked, grabbing Rachel's arm and pulling her into step with her. 'Let me guess, Damon was flirting with your stepsisters?' She should have predicted that. Allowed time for it. Historically, adding extra time to any schedule to compensate for Damon flirting was never a bad idea.

'Actually, it was my fault. I had to fix a window display before we left.' Rachel sounded apologetic, and Celeste felt briefly guilty for being so cross. She was sure that Rachel's stepmother would have been the one nagging her to fix it. For reasons Celeste only kind of understood, Rachel was reluctant to break the fragile peace that existed in her family, so of course she'd have risked being late to make her stepmother happy.

She still reckoned that Damon would have been flirting with Rachel's stepsisters in the meantime.

'Are you ready?' Damon asked, all charm and confidence and totally at ease with himself, as usual. How her little brother had got *all* the charm in the family, Celeste wasn't sure, but it did seem rather unfair. He always joked that it was because she got all the brains, but his highly successful business argued otherwise.

'Not really,' she admitted.

But it was too late. It was showtime, and there was already a production assistant hurrying down the corridor towards them ready to usher Celeste onto the set, while Damon and Rachel slipped into the audience.

'Break a leg,' Rachel whispered to her as they headed for their seats.

'Hopefully not,' Celeste muttered to herself. But she felt better for knowing that Damon and Rachel were out there anyway.

This would be fine.

CHAPTER TWO

THIS WAS HORRENDOUS.

Maybe if Theo broke some sort of minor bone he could get out of doing the rest of the show. There was bound to be someone else in the building who'd be happy to take over from him. Let *them* deal with the quiz show guest from hell. Because he was pretty sure this festive televisual outing was going to do nothing to repair his fractured reputation.

As Celeste explained—not for the first time—why the answer card he'd been given was actually inaccurate, Theo could see the producer, Derek, glaring at him from just off set. Damn. Apparently, Derek remembered exactly whose idea it had been to invite Celeste on the show in the first place. He'd been kind of hoping everyone would have forgotten about that.

The worst part was, under other circumstances, the stuff she was saying would be interesting. And she was passionate and engaged as she talked about it—far more than she had been during that awkward meeting in the green room. Theo found he genuinely wanted to know more about why the story about Prince Albert bringing Christmas trees to Britain from Germany was wrong. Just…not right now. Not in front of a studio audience that was clearly getting more uncomfortable by the second. Not when they had to finish another three rounds of this damn quiz, and the other celebrity contestants were getting restless.

Had she finished? He thought she might have done. To be honest, he'd stopped listening, and focussed instead on his inner panic about his career circling the drain.

Theo grabbed the next card from the pile and prayed that it would be about anything other than history. Thank God, children's literature. That should buy him a minute or two. He was sure there was a question in the stack somewhere about who sent the first ever Christmas card, and he had a feeling the answer was going to be wrong.

Had she been reading up about festive history, ready for tonight? She must have been.

'*Move it along, Theo,*' the impatient voice came in his ear, and he tried to focus on the words on the card.

'In your teams now, can you name all eight of the reindeer that feature in the classic Christmas story, *The Night Before Christmas*?' That should be safe enough, right? For starters, Celeste wasn't a team captain. David would have to give the answer to this one. And then it was the end of the round, and Theo was pretty sure they would call a break after that. They'd been at this for hours longer than they should have been already.

David buzzed and gave the correct answer, while Celeste sat silent beside him. Had she even weighed in on that question? Theo didn't think so. Obviously, she didn't know *absolutely* everything, then. That was kind of reassuring.

A break was called, and Theo jumped out from behind the presenter's desk, desperate to move. He'd never been good at staying still, one of the reasons he'd rejected any kind of office job as a career option. He needed variety, and the ability to wander about and chat to people.

He veered left, away from the production team, though, when he realised they were in a serious-looking huddle, presumably discussing this disaster of a show. The rest of the contestants similarly had gathered around the red team's side, leaving Celeste sitting alone behind her team's desk.

Theo sighed. This kind of was his fault. He'd suggested bringing her in when, clearly, this wasn't a good fit for her. She must be hating every minute.

He'd never been any good at letting a situation fester—not at work, anyway—so he moved towards her, ignoring the part of his brain that told him that, on past evidence, this was a stupid idea. She looked up as he approached, and Theo could see the resignation settle on her face.

'Hey, how are you doing? Do you need more water?' The jug in front of her was full, and Celeste just gave it a pointed look before returning her gaze to meet his, with a slight smile.

It was a disturbingly direct gaze, and Theo shifted uncomfortably under it. There was none of the charmed expression and delightedness he usually tried to inspire in people in that smile.

Celeste Hunter's eyes said, *I am here, you are here, why is this?* And nothing more.

Theo bit the inside of his cheek to stop himself automatically confessing all the reasons for his existence and—more pertinently—her presence on his quiz show.

'Did you need something?' Celeste asked, eventually, having obviously concluded that he was too stupid to continue this conversation on his own after his ridiculous water statement.

'I just wanted to see how...how you thought this was going.' Over Celeste's shoulder, he could see the production team watching him. He was pretty sure the other contestants would be doing the same behind him. All waiting to see if she was about to tear him to shreds again.

'I think your question team need to be a little more thorough in their research,' she said, folding her hands neatly on the table in front of her. 'But otherwise, fine.'

Fine. She thought this was fine. 'Have you ever actually seen a TV quiz show?' The words were out of his mouth before he could stop them, and he heard an audible gasp from Lucy the mathematician.

Celeste's expression didn't change. Her hands didn't move. She was completely and utterly still and in control.

'Of course, I have. Well, once or twice. Maybe just once, start to finish. They weren't exactly required viewing for my PhD. But I did my research and watched *you* on some of those shows. Clips of you anyway.' She tilted her head to study him. 'Your face is less shiny on TV.'

His face was less shiny when he wasn't so stressed.

'Why did you agree to do this show?' he asked desperately. He couldn't be the only one to blame here, right? Yes, he'd suggested she take part. But *she'd* agreed.

'I wanted to…' For the first time, she flinched, and looked away. 'My agent thought it was a good idea. He said it would build my profile.'

Of course. Even if Celeste clearly had no showbiz instincts, her agent would. He wondered if the poor guy was sitting out there watching, seeing all his dreams of discovering the next big docu-star going up in the smoke coming out of Celeste's ears as she argued with the answer card.

Come to that, he hoped his own agent wasn't out there tonight. She hadn't said she'd be coming, had she? He'd rather delay the inevitable tongue-lashing until after the thing had been aired.

He glanced out towards the audience and frowned. Was it less full out there than it had been before? He turned to the door and saw a queue of people leaving the studio. Surely it hadn't been that bad?

'Hang on a minute,' he said to Celeste, and crossed the set in a few long steps, collaring a young production assistant called Amy, who coloured prettily when he asked what was going on.

'They're needed in another studio,' she replied.

'There's another show *stealing* my audience?' He tried to sound outraged, but it came out rather more petulant, he thought. Damn, he was tired.

Amy glanced towards where Celeste was now disagreeing with David, her team captain, about something. 'To be honest, I'm pretty sure they all went willingly.'

Theo sighed as the studio doors closed and the call went up to resume filming. 'I don't blame them. Come on, let's get this over with.'

Oh, that had been horrible. Whose idea had this been anyway? Why on earth had she ever thought that she could do a show like this anyway? She wasn't built for it. She couldn't smile prettily or charm people as Theo could. She could educate them, correct them. But make them like her? No.

She was never going to get her TV show after this. But what else was she supposed to do? This was who she was.

Okay, maybe she hadn't needed to get into that argument with Theo about who sent the first Christmas card. And she probably shouldn't have told him his face was shiny; TV guys were sensitive about that sort of thing, right? But in truth, she'd been flustered. And nervous. And lots of other things she wasn't used to being.

In her confined, academic world, she was in control. She could be calm, collected and sure, safe in her knowledge and her education. Out here in the showbiz world… not so much.

There had just been so much she *didn't* know. Oh, not so much the specialist stuff, where the questions had clearly been put in to cater to individual contestants' knowledge base. She didn't care about them; they weren't her speciality, why should she know the answers?

It was the general, everyday Christmas knowledge that got to her. Like the quick-fire round at the end, all about silly Christmas traditions that everyone was clamouring to answer because they were so easy.

She'd hardly known any of them. And the ones she did, she'd only learned from watching TV with Rachel.

Her family had their own, unique traditions, she supposed. Just another way that they weren't like everyone else. Her parents had always implied it made them superior, in some way. But right now, Celeste wasn't so sure.

The other contestants had all left by now—she'd heard them talking about going to a bar together afterwards, but she hadn't been invited. Not that she'd have gone if she had. The crew were clearing up and the audience filing out—a lot fewer of them than there had been, Celeste admitted. The filming had gone on much longer than planned.

She supposed that was probably her fault.

No, not just her fault. Theo Montgomery's fault, too. He was the one who had kept arguing back at her, who couldn't accept that she was *right*. She knew history. It was the one thing she *did* know. So why wouldn't he let her tell him he was wrong?

Maybe he was just one of those men who had to be right all the time. Like her father.

There was no sign of Damon and Rachel in the thin-ning audience so, figuring that the coast was probably clear by now, Celeste headed back to the green room to gather her things, changed out of the miserably spar-kly light-up Christmas jumper and handed it back to the wardrobe people. Then, resigned to chalking the whole TV thing up to experience and never trying it again, she headed out to find her missing brother and best friend.

The first half of that proved to be easier than she'd ex-pected: Damon was waiting for her in the corridor outside the green room. Celeste tried not to show how relieved she felt to see a friendly face.

She and Damon might be as different as siblings could be, but he *knew* her. Understood her, at least more than most people.

Celeste didn't have many people in her life who mat-tered to her, but Damon and Rachel were the heart of them.

She showed her love by scowling at her brother and stomping towards him.

'Where on earth did you go? And where's Rachel?'

Damon's easy smile made her feel a little less stressed, at least. 'We got dragged in to film this New Year party show. They didn't have enough partygoers because of some issue on the Tube, and your filming had already gone on longer than it was supposed to any-way.' Of course they had. Because wherever Damon went, he always found the coolest room to be in, the best party to attend. And it was never the same one that Celeste was in.

Celeste rolled her eyes as she pushed past him to con-tinue stomping down the corridor and decided to focus on the second part of his statement. Yes, the filming had run long. But it wasn't *her* fault. 'Only because *that man* kept getting things wrong.'

She didn't need to look back to know that Damon was laughing at her. Silently, but still laughing. 'In fairness, Theo Montgomery was only reading out the answers on the cards.'

'Because he's not bright enough to actually know any-thing himself,' Celeste shot back over her shoulder. Then she winced and felt the colour flooding to her cheeks as she saw the man emerging from the room behind Damon into the corridor.

Theo Montgomery, of course. And from his raised eyebrows, he'd heard everything Celeste said.

She hadn't meant it, not really. She was just off kilter, and that made her defensive. Damon knew that, because he knew her. Theo didn't.

Damon stepped towards him, hand out for Theo to shake, which he did. Because he was a nice guy, like her brother, who knew how to be polite and charming in a way Celeste was never going to manage.

'Mr Montgomery. I'm Damon Hunter, Celeste's brother—we met earlier? I just wanted to take this op-portunity to apologise for my sister.'

Great. Rub it in. Yes, I'm rubbish with people and you're not.

Why did she like her brother, again?

'No need,' Theo said, just as jovially. 'Trust me, I've heard worse. You stayed for the whole filming?' He sounded amazed at the prospect. Celeste didn't blame him.

Damon shook his head. 'No, I just follow my sister around to make the necessary apologies. And now that's done, I'm heading home.'

Wait. They couldn't go home. Because they were still

missing someone. Celeste might not have the interpersonal skills of her brother, but at least she kept track of her best friend. The people that mattered to her, Celeste understood and cared for.

Everyone else...not so much.

'Where's Rachel?' Celeste asked again, ignoring Theo. 'I said we'd give her a lift home.'

'She, uh...she left early,' Damon said.

Okay, that was a lie. If her brother knew her, she knew him too, and she knew when he was lying. Besides, he sounded guilty as hell.

Celeste narrowed her eyes. 'What did you do?'

'What makes you think I did anything?' He turned to Theo. 'Does it make you feel any better that she treats *everyone* this way?' he asked, as if she weren't there at all.

'A little,' Theo admitted. Celeste continued ignoring him.

'You always do something,' she said to Damon, instead. 'Let me guess, you were flirting with some other woman at the bar and leaving her all on her own?'

'I can promise you that absolutely was not the case. I was attentive, friendly, we even danced together.'

'Rachel *danced*?' Well, that was a red flag if anything was. 'I have never once, in ten full years, seen my best friend dance. There is something else going on here, and you are going to tell me all about it on the way home. Come on, let's get to the car.' Then, suddenly remembering his existence, she turned to Theo. 'Thank you for having me on your show, Mr Montgomery. I'm very sorry that the question team screwed up so many of your answer cards.' Okay, it probably wasn't exactly what the etiquette guides would recommend, but she'd made an effort. That counted for something, right?

'Once again, apologies for my sister's attempt at an apology,' she heard Damon saying as she walked away.

She was out of earshot before Theo replied, which she decided was probably for the best.

'Did you skip the year at school where everyone else learned how to make friends?' Damon asked as Celeste settled into the heated front seat of his overly fancy car.

'Actually, yes.' Her parents had insisted that she be put up a year, since her birthday was so early in the year anyway, and she'd already known everything they'd be teaching her in reception. Until recently, that had always been a point of pride for her.

Suddenly, she wasn't quite so sure it should be.

Damon rolled his eyes and started the engine. 'Right, of course you did. Well, maybe it's time for some sort of catch-up lesson. Starting with, if you want to make friends you have to actually let people in, rather than automatically pushing them away.'

'I don't know what you're talking about.' She crossed her arms over her chest, happy to be back in her own plain black V-neck sweater again. Sparkly festive-wear was really not her thing.

'Did Theo Montgomery try to be nice to you?' Damon asked patiently.

'Maybe.' She supposed that was what he'd been doing when he'd interrupted her in the green room. At the time, she'd only registered that he'd disturbed her work and heightened her nervousness, not why he'd been doing it.

'Was he, in fact, friendly?' Damon pushed. 'Because he seemed like a friendly guy to me.'

'I suppose.' Celeste scowled out of the car window. 'What does it matter now? I never have to see the guy again.'

Damon sighed. 'Call it a lesson for next time. When someone is pleasant to you, try being pleasant back. You might actually make a friend. Or something more.'

'You're assuming that I want more friends,' Celeste pointed out, ignoring the pang inside her chest at the idea. Yes, maybe she sometimes wished she were better with people, as Damon was. And yes, it would be nice to meet someone. Someone special. But that wasn't how her life went. She'd accepted that long before now. 'I have too much research to do—and a whole book to write—to have time to spend with new friends. Besides, I have Rachel.'

'Yes, you do,' Damon said, his voice suddenly soft as he spoke about her best friend.

Celeste turned to study his face in the glow of the streetlights they passed. Yep, there was definitely something going on there.

'What really happened with Rachel tonight?'

'I told you.' Damon reached out and pressed the button to turn on the radio, and a Christmas number one from before she was born filled the car. 'Nothing happened.'

He was lying. But then, so was she.

So Celeste let it go. For now.

Four days later, Theo woke up too early on Saturday morning to his phone buzzing. And buzzing. And buzzing, until it buzzed its way off the bedside table and crashed onto the floor.

He lay back, buried in the pillow, listening to it vibrate against the hardwood floor of his London flat, and weighed up the merits of ignoring it against answering it.

On the one hand, his phone lighting up the moment his do-not-disturb ended at—he squinted at the clock—six-thirty in the morning had never yet turned out to mean anything good. On the other, he wasn't going to get any more sleep with this racket going on, and his downstairs neighbours would be banging on the ceiling soon if he didn't stop it. His apartment building might be in one of the most expensive areas of London, and security was excellent, but someone had definitely skimped on the soundproofing.

The phone stopped. Theo held his breath.

Buzz.

He sighed as the device began its journey across the floor again, powered only by its own vibrations. Then he swung his legs out of bed, swooped down and picked it up.

'Hello?' He suspected that there were a hundred notifications waiting for him, from the way it had been behaving, but right now the immediate call was his priority. Especially as the caller ID read Lord And Master, after the caller had nabbed his phone in the pub one night and changed it. He really should change that back some time.

'Where the hell have you been?' Cerys, his long-term agent, snapped the moment he answered.

'Sleeping. Like normal people. It's the weekend, Cerys.' He forced a loud yawn, just to prove the point.

'Theo, you forget that I know you're not actually the lazy, artless aristocrat you pretend to be. So quit acting with me and pay attention.'

Damn. With anyone else he would have got away with that. People saw what they expected to see, in Theo's experience. And when they looked at him they saw someone who had all the advantages of life, all the education, money, looks and privilege it was possible to have, and used it to entertain people on telly on a Saturday night. So they expected him to be equally frivolous with his brain, his time, his money, his life.

In a lot of ways, they weren't wrong.

In others...well. Theo hoped he'd prove them at least premature in their judgement, eventually.

But not Cerys. Cerys knew exactly who he was, what his ambitions were and how damn hard he worked to get there. Which meant there was no fooling Cerys.

And since he was already in her bad books for the whole Tania mess, he'd better play nice.

'What's happened?' he asked, sitting up a little straighter, and reaching for the tablet on his bedside table. Despite being in silent mode, it was managing to convey a sense of dramatic urgency through constantly flashing notifications from every social media or news site he'd ever signed up to.

'Did you watch the show when it aired last night?' Cerys asked, sounding calmer, at least.

'The *Christmas Cracker Cranium Quiz*?' Theo enunciated carefully; that name was a total tongue-twister, one he almost suspected the producers of coming up with as punishment for him for something, as he'd had to say it repeatedly through the show. Maybe one of them was friends with Tania. That would explain a lot.

'I don't know, Theo, did you spend twenty minutes mansplaining festive history to an actual *historian* on any other show this week?' Cerys snapped.

'What?' That wasn't what had happened. Was it? Theo ran through the filming again in his head. Celeste had argued with all of the history questions, of course, but that was just a small segment of the show. And he'd just explained what he'd had written on the answer cards...

Or *mansplained*. Apparently.

'I didn't—' he started, searching for a defence, but Cerys cut him off before he had time to find one anyway.

'I've seen the show, genius. Whatever you think happened isn't what the great British public watched last night, and that's all that really matters. *As you already know!*'

Theo winced. 'I need to watch it.'

'Yes. And while you're watching it, you need to read what everyone else who watched it is saying about it. About you.'

'I'm not going to like that part at all, am I?'

'Not even a little bit.' Cerys was a great agent, but she didn't believe in all that 'babying the client along' nonsense. They'd known each other too long anyway, Theo reasoned. If she suddenly started being nice to him, he'd know his career was over. 'You thought the Tania stuff was bad? This is worse. That was just you being an arsehole over a personal break-up—'

'I told you, it was amicable!' he interrupted.

Cerys ignored him. 'This is you being a patronising, superior arse on prime-time television.'

He hadn't been. Had he?

Theo shook his head. Cerys was right: it didn't matter what had actually happened. It mattered what the viewers *thought* had happened. He'd definitely learned that since the split with Tania.

Since Cerys was still being blunt and shouting at him, there must be a way out of this mess.

Travel back in time and not suggest Celeste Hunter as a guest on the quiz? Or just erase all knowledge of Celeste Hunter from my brain?

Hopefully a more practical way than anything he could come up with right now.

'Okay. I'll watch the show. I'll read the comments. And then what do I do?' he asked plaintively.

Cerys paused. Oh, that wasn't a good sign. Not at all. 'Cerys?'

'Shh. I'm thinking.'

Theo sat in anxious silence, willing his own brain to give him the answers. But then, he'd never been employed for his brain, had he? And even if he had, this kind of problem required the sort of strategic thinking that he'd never been good at.

That was why he'd hired Cerys.

As the silence stretched on Theo allowed himself to glance at the notifications on his tablet, taking in just the first lines of the many, many comments about him as they filled the screen.

Nation's sweetheart or nation's misogynist?

God, typical man. Has to be right about everything.

Privilege on show.

Well, of course he went to Eton, didn't he? So he thinks he knows everything.

It wasn't worth pointing out that he'd actually gone to Winchester, Theo knew. He put the tablet aside, although he was itching to read more—and to watch the actual show. Because as far as he remembered, he *hadn't* pretended to know better than Celeste. Because he didn't. Obviously. At least, not when it came to history.

He'd just had to give her the actual answer that was written on the card, as the director had been telling him to through his earpiece.

Had something happened in the editing room to make him appear a total arse? Or had he been more arsey in the first place than he'd ever realised? He wouldn't know until he watched it back.

God, he hated watching himself on television.

'Okay, here's what we're going to do,' Cerys said suddenly, and he tuned back into the phone call. 'We need to fix this—and quickly. Your reputation was battered enough before now; this really won't have helped. I don't think the Powers That Be will be planning on making any panicked changes before New Year, but we don't want to take that chance.'

'You mean, before I present the *New Year's Eve Spectacular*.' Live, in Central London, the biggest event of his career so far. The last thing he needed was protestors showing up to shout insults up at him or throw tomatoes or whatever. Or even just fewer people tuning in than normal to watch it in the first place, because he was presenting.

Or the Powers That Be deciding not to take the risk and instructing him to come down with a strategic case of laryngitis before December the thirty-first, so someone else could take his place.

Television was a precarious career, he'd always known that. But until now, he'd never realised quite how easy it was to slip and tumble down the slope from the top.

Cerys had always assumed it would be a sex scandal that would bring him down. So far, he was in trouble for *not* wanting to have sex with Tania any more, and for arguing about history. She must be so disappointed.

'Exactly,' was all she said. 'We need to fix this before anyone starts talking about making any changes. So right now, I'm going to make some phone calls, and get a number for you. While I'm doing that, you watch the show.'

'And then?'

'Then I'm going to call you back, give you that phone

number, and you are going to follow my instructions *to the letter.* Okay?'

'Yes, ma'am,' Theo answered. Because although he already knew he wasn't going to like whatever Cerys's plan was, he liked the idea of losing his career even less.

CHAPTER THREE

Have you watched this yet? Call me when you have.

THE INNOCUOUS EMAIL had come through from her agent, Richard, that morning, but Celeste had been buried deep in the research for her next chapter, so had put it off until she was ready for her scheduled mid-morning break. Now, as the final credits on the *Christmas Cracker Cranium Quiz* rolled, she smiled to herself.

That hadn't actually been nearly as bad as she'd expected. She'd avoided watching the show when it had aired the night before, partly because she was nervous about how it would turn out, and partly because she'd been having dinner with her parents and some of their department colleagues, and there was no television in the Hunter family home.

She clearly had a friend in the editing suite. Celeste remembered the actual filming as being more confrontational on her side—the way she always got when she was nervous or feeling intimidated. But in the final cut, Theo came across as far more superior, more patronising, than in real life.

Which, she supposed, wasn't entirely inaccurate, as he hadn't given her *any* points for all the questions she'd answered far more correctly than his bloody answer cards had.

Finishing the last gulp of her cup of tea, Celeste turned to her other breaktime indulgence—checking her social media accounts. While she didn't tend to post much, she kept up with the world outside her office through them—they were sort of her guilty pleasure. She mostly followed other historians, archaeologists, researchers and writers—as well as a few university and academic accounts, plus the odd political or news website or reporter. She'd actually had to turn off the notifications on her phone and computer, to stop herself getting distracted when she was working. And she *never* let herself check them first thing in the morning. That was a slippery slope she didn't want to fall down.

Which was why she had no idea she'd become an overnight Internet sensation until she checked her phone.

She blinked at the number of notifications showing, and tapped through to them, scrolling slowly as she took in the words.

Celeste Hunter doesn't need Theo-bloody-Montgomery mansplaining history to her.

There were screenshots, too. Oh, God, she'd become a meme.

Celeste: I have a PhD in this.

Theo: I have an answer card written by an inadequate researcher. So I must be right!

Celeste: I'm an actual professor of history.

Theo: Yeah, but I have generations of white male

privilege on my side. Who do you think they're going to listen to?

There were more. So many more.

Then she remembered the second part of her agent's email. *Call me.*

'So are we thinking the show went well?' she asked, weakly, when Richard picked up.

'For us? Very well.' She could practically hear his grin down the phone line. 'For Theo Montgomery, not so much. Not that that's our problem.'

'I feel kind of bad about that,' Celeste admitted. 'The way the show was edited… I mean, yes, I *was* right. But he wasn't actually so patronising about it in person.'

'Nobody cares what *really* happened, Celeste. You know that.'

'Yeah.' She'd learned, a little, over the past year. After the first radio slot she'd done, as a favour for a friend who'd had to drop out at the last minute, it seemed as if she'd got her name on some sort of list. Suddenly she was every producer's pet historian, trotted out to offer an historical perspective on current events, on school history exams, on latest discoveries and research. No matter that her official area of expertise was ancient history, she'd become a knowledgeable semi-pro on the whole span of human existence. At least it was the one thing her childhood had prepared her for.

And it had led to the talks about her own TV show, looking at women through history—starting with Ancient Greece.

She supposed something like this could only be good publicity, and production companies definitely loved good publicity. No wonder Richard was sounding so thrilled.

'So, we need to capitalise on this,' he went on. 'We need to show that production company that your series is a sure bet. We could have it commissioned by January! Get you on display a bit more, now you've stepped out from behind the radio mic and people know what you look like.'

Celeste pulled a face at that last bit, glad that Richard couldn't see it. On display wasn't exactly her favourite place to be, she'd learned. Especially when it wasn't on her terms.

'What's your calendar like between now and the new year?' Richard asked.

She looked at the stack of research materials, liberally spotted with sticky notes, that were supposed to form the basis of her book. Not even the popular history book she was supposed to be writing to support the case for the TV show, but the *other* one. The proper, serious, academic text that would cement her career at the university—the one her parents would approve of.

The one that was going nowhere at all.

'I have some time,' she told Richard. 'Term ended yesterday, so I don't have any more lectures or seminars to give until January.'

'Great! I'll see if I can get some appearances set up for you, then. Keep in touch!'

And he was gone. Celeste sighed, and put down her phone—until she noticed the new message notification, the one notification she allowed herself, since hardly any-one ever messaged her, was flashing.

Fancy lunch? My treat. Seems like I owe you. Theo Montgomery.

Cerys had been right. He *hated* this idea.

He especially hated the part where he was sitting in

a restaurant, alone, with people staring at him, whispering behind his back. He didn't need to be able to make out the individual words to guess what they were saying. Exactly the same things as everyone on social media—and the morning TV shows, apparently—had been saying since the *Christmas Cracker Cranium Quiz* aired. Plus, all the older gossip about Tania and the break-up, probably, just for good measure.

He'd watched the show. He'd read the comments. He'd watched the show *again*.

Then Cerys had called back, given him Celeste's phone number, and told him exactly what he needed to do.

'Make it right, Theo. And quickly.'

He hadn't honestly been sure that Celeste would respond when he texted her. He should have called, probably—Cerys had told him to—but Theo remembered what had happened last time he'd interrupted Celeste, in the green room, and decided that it might go better if he allowed her to respond in her own time, rather than ambushing her with a phone call.

Perhaps it was the right move, because she *had* texted back. And she'd agreed to meet him, here, in a neutral restaurant, ten minutes ago. He checked his watch; no, fifteen now.

Celeste didn't seem like a habitually late person to Theo, but, apparently, he was wrong. That happened a lot. Just ask his parents. *They* still hadn't forgiven him for 'losing' Tania—a rich, beautiful, famous prospective daughter-in-law they would have embraced willingly, despite her 'unfortunate start' on reality TV. His parents always claimed to have incredibly high standards for their social circle, but as far as Theo could tell they mostly all came down to 'money' and 'fame'.

God, what if this debacle lost him both of those? Infamy, he knew, was not the same thing.

Maybe his father would take some comfort in the fact that he'd been right all along, and Theo really would never amount to anything worthwhile. If Celeste didn't show up for this lunch, it might be the best he was going to get.

Finally, after another five minutes, the restaurant door flew open and Celeste Hunter strode in, wrapped in an elegant white wool coat, black boots clicking on the tiled floor as she crossed towards him. Her dark hair was twisted up on the back of her head, her lips painted a bright Christmas red, and she seemed completely unaware of the way every person in the restaurant turned to look at her as she approached him.

Theo was not unaware. He could hear the whispering, the *'Isn't that her?'* that hung in the air behind her.

'I'm sorry I'm late,' she said, stripping off her coat and hanging it on the back of one of the empty chairs. Underneath it, her black jumper matched her black jeans. Her lipstick, Theo realised, was the only colour about her. 'There were all these...people waiting outside my office at the university. Apparently last night's show was a bit of a thing.'

A bit of a thing? Did she really just describe my career-crippling disaster as 'a bit of a thing'?

She had. Because, of course, that was all it was—to her. *Her* career was the university, her academic life. TV was merely a bit on the side.

Whereas it was all he had.

'Apparently so,' he said drily, although she didn't seem to pick up on the faint hint of sarcasm in his voice. 'In fact, some of the rumours online are starting to get a little outlandish. And nasty.'

She had the good grace to wince at that, at least. 'If only you'd just admitted I was right at the time, huh?'

Theo honestly couldn't tell if she was joking or not. Why was this woman so hard to read? He was *good* at people, usually—it was what had got him as far as he'd come. But this woman? He had no idea what was going on inside her head—or how she was going to react when he put Cerys's plan to her.

She might go along with it. Or she might verbally eviscerate him while pouring hot oil onto his chest on the restaurant table while the crowd cheered her on. It was hard to tell.

He was just going to have to take his chances. But he could at least improve them by softening her up first.

'Thank you for coming, despite everything.' He flashed her his best 'love me' smile, and she looked a little taken aback. Fortunately, the waiter arrived at that moment with the wine he'd ordered, and poured them both a glass.

God, he hoped she liked Viognier, or this would be off to a worse start than ever.

He held his breath as she took a sip, then started to let it out when she smiled at the waiter, only to have it catch in his chest again.

That smile, he thought, as he half choked on his own breath.

She hadn't smiled like that when they were recording the show. And she definitely hadn't smiled at him like that ever—not even when he'd done nothing beyond politely introduce himself. Yet the waiter got that smile— all bone-deep pleasure and gratitude.

He supposed it was reassuring to know that she *could* smile like that. It might make the next phase of Cerys's plan easier.

Theo took a sip of the wine to soothe his throat after the coughing fit Celeste had totally ignored. It was nice enough wine. But not worthy of that smile.

'This is delicious, thank you,' Celeste said to the waiter. 'Did you suggest it?'

The waiter—young, spotty and obviously impressionable—blushed. 'Um, actually your, uh, companion chose it.'

The smile disappeared as she turned back to Theo. 'Oh, well. It's still nice wine.'

Theo decided to let that one pass while they ordered— Celeste asking the poor waiter what most people ordered, then going with that.

'So.' Celeste folded her hands on her lap, over the napkin the anxious waiter had placed there, and looked Theo dead in the eye. 'I imagine you invited me here to apologise?'

He had, of course. That was step one of Cerys's master plan. But being asked to do so outright like that…it made him want to, well, not.

Theo lifted an eyebrow. 'You don't think there's any reason you should need to apologise to me?'

That earned him a flash of a grin. Nothing like the smile she'd given the waiter for the wine, but still. Better than anything he'd managed from her so far.

'Of course,' she said, her tone heavy with sarcasm. 'I'm so sorry that your mansplaining and patronising behaviour got you into trouble with your adoring fans.'

Theo rolled his eyes. 'Come on, I was actually there too, remember? I haven't just watched the edited footage. I know what really happened.'

She raised both eyebrows, and sat back in her chair. 'Enlighten me, then.'

He wanted to. He wanted to fight his corner, wanted

to stand up for what he felt had really happened. But he also wanted all the other people sitting in the restaurant to stop listening to their conversation.

This was never going to work. Cerys hadn't met Celeste, or she'd never have imagined for a moment that it *could* work.

But what other option did he have?

Theo took a deep breath, and started again.

'You're right. I *did* ask you here to apologise. Let's start over, shall we?'

One step at a time, that was all he had to focus on. If this went well, he might not need all the other steps of Cerys's absurd plan.

He just had to keep the conversation civil for one lunch.

How hard could that be?

Why on earth had she agreed to this lunch? Curiosity, Celeste supposed. The curse of the academic. She just couldn't help but want to know what happened next, and why.

Plus Richard had been pretty insistent, when she'd called him back to ask what to do. Apparently, being seen with Theo Montgomery again, even if she wasn't sure why he wanted to see her at all, was a Good Thing, publicity-wise.

'Keep them talking,' as Richard put it. *'Doesn't matter what they're saying, as long as they're talking about you.'*

But Celeste was pretty sure Theo *did* care what people were saying. Was it just that he was so used to being the Nice Guy he couldn't handle people thinking otherwise? Or was he concerned about the effect on his career?

Or—and this seemed the least likely—was he genuinely sorry about how things had gone down at the filming?

That last went out of the window as he asked if perhaps she should be apologising to *him*, of all things. But then he pulled himself together and she saw something she hadn't expected to see from Theo Montgomery.

Authenticity.

He immediately hid it again, behind that charming smile and smooth words, suggesting they start over. But for a second there, Celeste almost believed she saw the real human behind the TV persona.

And he looked just as baffled and annoyed about this lunch as she was.

Interesting.

She'd pegged him as a faker straight off—she'd had enough students who tried to pretend they'd done the work to know how to spot a faker at a hundred paces. Besides, wasn't that the whole point of TV? To show a faked-up version of reality? Even her own appearance on the quiz show hadn't been authentic—she'd never be caught dead in a Christmas jumper outside that studio.

Some people, she knew, had been faking so long they'd forgotten how to be real. She'd assumed Theo would be one of them.

Apparently, there was still some hope for him after all.

'I'm sorry that the research on our show wasn't up to your own standards,' Theo said, which she noticed wasn't actually a real apology on his own behalf. 'I could tell that you'd prepared well for the show, and to a level that our researchers clearly weren't expecting.' A flash of that charming smile. 'And I'm sorry that I couldn't accept your—obviously correct—answers. I hope you didn't feel that I was mansplaining to you. On the contrary, I had the producer in my ear telling me to read out the official answer—but *I* was far more interested in the answers you were giving.'

Did she believe him? Celeste wasn't sure. But then he went on, 'Is it really true that Prince Albert wasn't responsible for bringing Christmas trees to Britain?'

So, he'd been paying attention. Or he'd just watched the show again in preparation for this lunch.

'Are you questioning me now?'

He held up his hands in surrender. 'I swear to you I'm not. Is it so hard to believe that I might be interested in the answer?'

Yes. Not just because he hadn't been the other night— she could understand that, under the constraints of filming and with his producer talking in his ear, hurrying him along, he might not have had the time or mental space to care about the real answer then. But in her experience, even when she stripped away those problems, most people weren't all that interested in the real answers anyway.

The simple, familiar stories were more interesting. Prince Albert had brought the Christmas tree. Thomas Crapper invented the toilet—except he didn't. Santa Claus was designed by a popular drinks company in the thirties—also not true.

People didn't want the complicated, multi-layered truth—the same way that people didn't want to bother with her, and her difficult to understand nature. They wanted the straightforward historical anecdotes that made sense and that people nodded along with—exactly how they wanted Theo Montgomery and his bland smiles, rather than her, on their TVs every night.

Except…the people who'd posted on social media about the show *had* been interested in her answers. They were cross that Theo had cut her off before she'd fully explained them.

They hadn't said she was boring, unlike most other people outside her family. They'd been *interested*. In her. And maybe it was because it was Christmas, and lots of people were interested in Christmas, right? But if she could get them interested in that—if she could get *Theo freaking Montgomery* interested in that—maybe she could get people interested in the lives of women in the ancient world, too. Maybe she really could pull off her own show.

It had to be worth a try, right?

'Queen Charlotte, the wife of George III, put up the first one in 1800,' she said, watching to see if his eyes glazed over. They didn't. 'Where she grew up, in the duchy of Mecklenburg-Strelitz, Germany, the tradition was to decorate a single yew branch. She brought the tradition over with her in 1761, and the whole palace started getting involved in it. Then in 1800 she was planning a children's party at Windsor and decided to pot up a whole yew tree and decorate it with sweets and baubles and load it with presents. The kids were enchanted, of course, and Christmas trees became all the rage in English high society.'

Theo smiled, looking genuinely charmed at the information. 'I did not know that. Thank you.'

'You're welcome,' she replied, suddenly awkwardly aware that she was basically lecturing her lunch date on British history.

Well, it wasn't as if she had much else in the way of small talk, was it? That was always the problem with her dates, or interactions with people outside the history department. She bored them quickly. Hell, sometimes she even bored herself. She wished that she could just let things go, not feel she had to correct people all the time. But it was as if there were an itch inside her, whenever things were factually lacking. And the only way to scratch it was to present the true facts.

No wonder it had been so long since she'd had an actual date.

The rest of the meal passed pleasantly enough. The waiter brought their meals, which were fine, although Theo questioned her choice of the chicken Caesar salad in the depths of winter.

She shrugged. 'The waiter said it was their most popular dish.' She always ordered the most popular dish. She knew nothing about food, really, and, beyond it being the fuel her body needed to keep functioning, she'd never really thought about it much. So it seemed much more sensible to her to let the consensus of others decide what she should eat.

Theo obviously didn't agree. 'What if the most popular dish was something you didn't like?'

'Then I'd order the second most popular dish. Obviously.'

It was only by the time they'd reached dessert—which she'd declined in favour of coffee, as had Theo—that she got the feeling that there was more to this meal than just a simple apology.

'I have to admit, I had a secondary reason for inviting you to lunch today,' Theo said, as he toyed with the foil wrapper of the mint that came with his coffee.

Wow. Her intuition was actually correct, for once. Delayed, of course, but right. That didn't happen often. At least, not with people she didn't know. Damon and Rachel she could read in an instant—she'd been studying them both for years. She'd *learned* them, the same way she learned everything else. Strangers, not so much.

'I suspected as much,' she said.

Theo smiled. 'I imagined you would. You're an intelligent woman.'

She liked the way he said that. She shouldn't, because she was sure he was just buttering her up for the next part. But when Theo said, 'You're an intelligent woman,' she didn't hear it as an insult. He wasn't saying: 'You have brains, why can't you understand people?' Or: 'You're smart, but don't think you're smarter than me.' Or even: 'You're intelligent, why won't you just agree with me, when I'm obviously right?'

He was just saying that she was intelligent, and that it was a good thing.

She liked that.

'So? Why am I here?' Celeste asked.

Theo drew in a breath, then looked up and met her gaze with his own. She made herself hold it, look for the truth, even though she wanted to look away with every fibre of her being. She didn't look people in the eye like this, not unless she had a point she needed to hammer home and wanted to be sure they had it.

But now she was just...listening. And looking for the truth in Theo's eyes.

'Because the show that aired last night was edited to show me in a bad light. I don't know why, or by who. And I need you to believe that I didn't intend to dismiss you or disregard the points you were making about historical accuracy.'

'Why?' That was the part she didn't understand. Why did he care what *she* thought?

'Because I'm going to need your help to fix it.'

CHAPTER FOUR

CELESTE DREW BACK a little at that. 'What do you need me to do?'

'Exactly what you are doing,' Theo replied, as reassuringly as he could. 'Just being seen with me today, showing that you don't actually hate me, that will help.'

She looked around her. 'You mean, you've got someone here to photograph us together? This was all a trick to get me to pretend to like you?'

Ow. 'I was kind of hoping that if we had lunch together you would *actually* like me. Most people do, you know.'

'I'm not most people.' As if he didn't know that. 'So, where is he? The photographer, I mean? I haven't seen anyone taking photos of us. Does he have one of those long lenses?'

'I didn't hire a paparazzi with a tele-focus lens,' Theo said patiently. 'I didn't hire anybody. I didn't need to.'

Celeste's eyes narrowed. 'Explain.'

'Celeste, people have been taking photos of us on their phones since the moment you walked in. They've been talking about us, while we've been sitting here eating. There's hardly a table in this restaurant where at least one person hasn't turned to watch us, to try to listen to what we're saying.' He was used to it, after years in the TV spotlight. Normally when he dined with someone from outside the industry they found it distracting, disturbing to be watched all the time.

But Celeste hadn't noticed it at all.

'Why? Because you're so damn famous and popular?' She was glancing around now, furtively, obviously trying to catch someone with their phone out. It was kind of almost cute—if anything about Celeste Hunter could be called cute.

And she obviously didn't realise how unpopular he was right now. He supposed she didn't really follow celebrity gossip online.

'Because our faces were all over their social media feeds this morning,' he said, with a sigh. 'Because if other people are talking about us, they want to be able to talk about us, too. And if they can say something new, something their friends haven't heard yet, all the better.'

'So this morning the story was that we were mortal enemies after a stupid quiz show,' Celeste said slowly. 'And you're trying to change that narrative. Show people that actually we're friends.'

'Exactly.' He'd known she'd get it, once she got past the part where people she'd never met cared about her life. As he'd said, she was an intelligent woman.

'I probably shouldn't tip my cup of coffee into your lap for manipulating me into lunch, then, should I?' she asked sweetly.

Theo winced. 'Ideally not, no. And I didn't intend to manipulate you. I kind of thought it would be obvious.'

'Yeah, well. You might have noticed I'm not entirely up to speed on things that happen outside my field of expertise.'

It was the first admission of anything approaching a fault or weakness that she'd given, and it made Theo like her all the more.

That was the strangest part about this lunch, he realised. He was actually enjoying it. Even when they were bickering or she was threatening his lap with coffee, he was having *fun*.

Huh. He really hadn't expected that.

'So, what do you say?' he asked. 'Do you want to pretend to be my friend and help rehabilitate my reputation, so the Great British Public can stop calling me a patronising, mansplaining bastard?' Amongst all the things they'd already been saying about him before, about him being a careless, unfeeling abandoner of women.

She looked at him thoughtfully. 'You realise there's also a cohort of your defenders calling me an uppity bitch who thinks she knows better than everyone?'

'Yeah, but you *do* know better than everyone—when it comes to history anyway.'

'Not everyone. Just most people.'

'And you're not an uppity bitch. In fact, I think I might actually like you if you'll let me get to know you.' She looked surprised at that, and he laughed. 'Yeah. I wasn't expecting that, either.'

Although he *had* been—until he'd met her. When she was just a voice on the radio, he'd thought he would like to get to know her. He'd been drawn to the passion in her voice when she'd talked about subjects she cared about—that he cared about, too. So yeah, he'd wanted to get to know her. He just hadn't expected it to be under these circumstances.

'Maybe we can prove them all wrong, then,' she said slowly. 'Or at least teach them not to judge people or their motives on first appearances.'

Theo rather thought she was crediting them with too much power over social media in general, and the Great

British Public in particular. But if that was what it took to get her to agree…

'I say we could give it a damn good go.'

Celeste looked up at him and smiled. 'Then it's a deal.'

She stood up, holding out a hand for him to shake, and the movement jogged the table. The tablecloth caught between her and the surface, twisting as she moved, tugging it up, off balance and…

Tipping Theo's coffee right into his lap.

A gasp went up through the restaurant, and Theo heard the click of a dozen fake camera shutters on phones.

He looked up to find Celeste with one hand over her mouth, looking as though she was trying to stop herself from laughing.

'At least it wasn't *my* coffee,' she said as she handed him her napkin.

'That makes it all better,' Theo grumbled.

Apparently, making people believe they were actually friends was going to be even harder than he'd anticipated.

It looked like Theo and Celeste were a story that wasn't going away.

On Sunday morning, Celeste woke up to a lot of social media notifications, and a sense of impending doom. The doom part was easy enough to fathom—it was the first Sunday of the month, which meant it was Hunter family dinner day. Which was cause enough for doomy feelings in itself, but made worse by the fact that she wasn't properly prepared for it.

It wasn't enough for her parents to get the four of them around the dining table once a month for a nice catch-up and a roast. Diana and Jacob Hunter had to make it a competition. One with themes and decorations and complex menus—and one that Celeste always tried hard at but seldom ever won.

She definitely wasn't going to win anything today, having spent all her prep time yesterday either having lunch with Theo or on the phone with Rachel, who'd sounded very peculiar when she'd called. Celeste might not be the best at reading people normally, but *Rachel* she understood. They'd been best friends since university and she was, as Damon put it, Celeste's social proof that she could actually manage human interaction outside the lecture theatre.

She had a strong suspicion that her brother might be behind her best friend's strange mood. Damon, unlike her, was excellent with people—all people. Often too excellent. Women, in particular, tended to fall fast and hard for him—only to be heartbroken when he let them down, however gently he tried to do it.

Rachel had known Damon for almost a decade, so Celeste had hoped she was immune. But after her disappearance from the TV studios, plus that call last night… Celeste was starting to have suspicions.

Which were definitely still on her mind as she went shopping for ingredients for an emergency starter she could whip up in a hurry in time for lunch. Salmon, perhaps. Damon hated salmon.

Queueing at the supermarket checkout, she scrolled through the notifications on her phone. Gone were the usual links to journals or news items about archaeological digs she had come to expect. Instead, there were at least four different photo angles of Theo getting covered in coffee, plus a few other shots of them just eating lunch together. Opinion seemed to be divided over whether they were arguing or having a nice time.

Both. Which she supposed was why people were so confused. It was baffling the hell out of her.

Normally, when she argued with a person, they got annoyed and left her alone. But Theo seemed to want to spend *more* time together. Which was definitely not normal.

It's only because he's trying to save face, improve his image, that sort of thing.

She needed to keep reminding herself of that. He was a faker, and he'd fake liking her for as long as it served his purpose—then drop her. In some ways, Theo was like Damon—too charming for his own good. Luckily Celeste, unlike Rachel, *was* immune to that sort of charm.

And it wasn't only Theo's career and image that stood to gain from this association, it turned out. Richard was thrilled that their continued association was only drawing more attention to her—and increasing the odds of the production company they were talking to taking a chance on her. As a cloistered academic, she knew he'd been at a bit of a loss on how to market her—especially since her love of *reading* social media didn't extend to remembering to post regularly, or even having any idea what to post. Rachel kept offering her tips. Maybe she should just hire her best friend to pretend to be her on social media. She had no doubt that people would like her better if she wasn't, well, actually her.

'Excuse me. Are you… Oh, what's your name? The one from that quiz show. The Christmas Cracker one.' The woman behind her in the queue, gripping a TV listing magazine with Theo Montgomery on the front, smiled up at Celeste.

'The *Christmas Cracker Cranium Quiz*? Yes, that was me.' Celeste waited to see if that was a good thing or a bad thing.

The woman's beaming smile grew wider. 'I thought it was you! I said to my husband—where's he gone? Fred? Honestly, men. Anyway, I said it was you!'

'And it is, actually, me,' Celeste confirmed, just in case that had got missed somehow.

'Can you sign my magazine for me?' The woman brandished a pen towards Celeste, and she took it, mostly because she was at a loss as to what else to do with it. As she signed her name just to the left of Theo's sharp cheekbone, the woman kept talking. 'I love Theo Montgomery as much as anybody, and I never really believed all that rubbish his ex put about, but, I have to say, it was quite nice to see him put in his place for once! He always has all the answers, doesn't he? Such a charmer. My Fred says he's *too* smooth, but, really, what would we watch if he wasn't on? He hosts all the best shows these days, doesn't he?'

'I suppose he does.' Celeste handed the signed magazine back.

'And he *is* lovely, don't you think?' the woman said wistfully.

'I'm sure I wouldn't know.' Celeste turned away, relieved to see it was her turn at the checkout at last.

All this thinking about Theo Montgomery couldn't possibly be good for her.

She managed to forget about him, more or less, over lunch with the family.

The Hunter Family Monthly Lunch was, as most things were in her family, deeply competitive. Each month, she, her mother and her father were assigned a course of the meal to prepare and serve. Whoever was in charge of starters was also in charge of decorating the dining room in a suitable historical theme. Damon was only ever in charge of bringing the wine, because he refused to compete.

The aim of the dinner was to produce the most interesting dish. Not necessarily the most delicious—Celeste had once won almost a full score from everyone for an authentic Greek dish with a great historical backstory that had unfortunately tasted like rotten fish. Mostly because it almost *was* rotten fish.

On that basis, she knew she'd have failed today. The only saving grace her salmon terrine possessed was that it would annoy her brother, and her decorations were decidedly sub-par.

And sadly, none of that distracted her mother from more important matters at hand.

'I saw some of that festive TV show you were associated with, Celeste,' Diana said, her frown disapproving over the fluttering of her authentic replica regency fan, to match her dress. The Hunters always believed in dressing for dinner, even if they weren't always from the same era.

'Uh…really? Where did you see that?' Stalling for time, Celeste reached across the table for the wine bottle and refilled her mother's glass, as well as her own. At least her father was out of the room, fetching his main course from the kitchen. She'd hoped against hope that her parents' TV ban would mean they'd have missed the whole debacle, but apparently she wasn't that lucky.

'A colleague sent me a web link to a clip from it.' Diana's fan fluttered a little faster. Across the table, a wicked smile spread over Damon's face.

Celeste knew exactly what he was thinking. Discovering that Celeste was taking part in a lowbrow, populist TV quiz was one thing. Being told so by a colleague was far worse, because that meant that Other People knew. People that mattered to their parents.

She wondered who had sent it to them. Someone who thought it was a bit of festive fun? Or a colleague with a grudge? It didn't really matter which, she supposed. The Professors Hunter didn't *do* fun—at least, not when it came to things that mattered, like history or archaeology, their respective specialist subjects.

'Um, which part?' Celeste asked, desperately hoping that the clip would be one of the tamer ones she'd seen around the Internet. Maybe the introductions, or something.

'You, arguing with some gameshow host about how Christmas trees came to be a British tradition.'

So, not a nice tame bit. That was the part that had the Internet most riled up. Of course.

Damon was apparently unable to hold his laughter in a moment longer.

'That link is everywhere, Mum,' he said as Celeste glared at him. 'Have you seen what they're saying about it on Twitter?' He leaned across the table towards Celeste. 'Did you *really* have a make-up lunch with Theo yesterday? The whole of social media is aflame, wondering what's going on between you two.'

Celeste felt the heat flood to her cheeks as she remembered the lunch—and how it had ended. Then she remembered why she was cross with Damon in the first place, and turned the tables.

'Never mind my lunch. Did you *really* take Rachel for afternoon tea at the Ritz?'

'It was for work!' Damon protested, far too quickly for Celeste's liking. 'She's helping out on my latest project.'

'Isn't Rachel an English graduate?' Diana asked. 'How is she going to help with your...what was it? Cinema project?'

'The cinema project was two years ago,' Damon said. 'This is a new one.'

Of course, it was. It was always a new project with Damon. Always the next shiny thing.

Celeste didn't want him treating Rachel that way. And while she was pretty sure he wouldn't, pretty sure wasn't enough when it came to her best friend. 'Just…be careful with Rachel, please? I'd hate for you to, well, give her any ideas.'

'It's work,' he repeated, his voice flat. 'That's all.'

Work was good. Rachel had been stuck in her job, working for her stepmother, for too long. Doing something new and fun with Damon could be good for her. As long as it really was just work.

Rachel didn't date much, and, after a nasty experience with one of her stepsisters' friends the summer before, Celeste couldn't see her jumping into anything new. But it *was* Damon. And Rachel had always been just a little bit misty-eyed when it came to Celeste's brother.

She had to warn him about that. He'd be careful if he thought he might hurt her. He wasn't a bad guy, just… not the settling-down type. With anything.

'Good,' Celeste said, looking away as she spilled her best friend's secrets for her own good. 'Because, to be honest, I think she's always had a bit of a crush on you. I'd hate for you to lead her on, even accidentally.' Urgh, she hated doing this. 'Just don't break her heart, okay? I know what you're like.'

The double doors to the dining room swung open and their father appeared, the white of his Roman-style toga backlit by the hallway bulbs against the dim candlelight on the table. In his arms was a large platter with what looked like an entire pig on it, apple in mouth and all, surrounded by jellies with apple slices and spices inside.

'Dinner is served!' Jacob announced, holding the platter high, a smug smile on his face.

Celeste laughed, and turned her attention back to lunch, happy to forget all about Damon's love life—and her own fake one—for the afternoon.

Having hot coffee dumped in his lap wasn't, in Theo's opinion, the best way to spend a date. But by Monday morning, his lunch with Celeste seemed to be having the desired effect, at least.

'She's good for you,' Cerys announced, when she'd finished cackling at the photo of Celeste trying to hide her own laughter as he mopped up the coffee with a napkin, which was doing the rounds on social media that morning. 'If you can convince people she actually likes you—or, even better, wants you—it'll help give the impression that there's more to you than just a pretty face.'

Theo didn't ask if *Cerys* believed that there was more to him than his looks. He wasn't sure he wanted to hear the answer.

But the ultimate confirmation came as he walked into a meeting late on Monday morning with all the bigwigs involved in the *New Year's Eve Spectacular* he'd hopefully still be hosting in just a few weeks.

It might have been hard to think about the new year with Christmas still around the corner, but after the debacle of the *Christmas Cracker Cranium Quiz* Theo was more than happy to just skip the festive period altogether and start fresh on January the first.

'Good to see you keeping your face in the spotlight ahead of the big show,' one of them told Theo as he took his seat.

'I heard it wasn't his face, so much,' another murmured, loud enough to be heard around the table. Theo ignored them and reached for the coffee pot. 'Careful with that, old boy. Heard coffee's a bit of a sensitive issue for you right now.'

That caused a wave of laughter that cascaded through the room. It irritated him, but Theo had learned many years ago not to let that show. His father loved to see the effect of his jibes and would keep needling if he thought he was close to getting a reaction. Making Theo blow up had been easy when he was a boy, harder as he became a teenager and learned not to play the game.

These days, one of his bestselling points was his easy-going nature, his ability to take a joke at his own expense and keep smiling. Something to thank his father for, he supposed.

Always smiling. That was the job.

'Well, at least I got lunch with a beautiful woman first,' he joked, pouring his coffee without spilling a drop.

That, of course, just opened up a new flood of questions.

'What really is going on with you two?' Matthew, from Finance, asked. 'I read online that you've been secretly dating for months. And Fran said it was you who suggested getting Celeste on the show, so...' He left it hanging, an open question.

Theo considered how best to answer, Cerys's words still echoing around his head.

'If you can convince people she actually likes you—or, even better, wants you—it'll help give the impression that there's more to you than just a pretty face.'

Wasn't that what he wanted people to believe? He'd asked Celeste to help him rehabilitate his reputation—but now he wondered if she could do more. Could being seen with her help him persuade his bosses, and maybe even the Great British Public, that there was more to him than just the ability to smile on cue?

Maybe that was asking too much. But it could be a start…

'You know me, Matthew,' he replied, with that smile he was so famous for. 'I don't kiss and tell. Now, what's on the agenda for today?'

There was still plenty to discuss before the filming date, so he managed to keep the group around the table more or less on topic for the rest of the meeting. But as they all filed out, Mr Erland, one of the real bigwigs, held Theo back.

'I just wanted to say—I was worried, after Friday night. I thought we might have to look at replacing you for New Year, if the country was against you. But you seem to be turning it around.'

Theo's heart thumped in his chest. 'I'm certainly trying, sir.'

Mr Erland slapped him on the back. 'And I always back a trier. Keep it up, Theo, and we'll see you right.'

Hands in his suit pockets, he headed out after the others, whistling a Christmas carol Theo remembered singing in school.

Once he was sure he was gone, he reached for his phone, and scrolled through for the latest name added to its memory.

Celeste answered promptly, but, from the click-clacking he could hear in the background, she didn't stop typing while she spoke to him.

'Yes?' No messing around with unnecessary words for Celeste. It was kind of refreshing, after a meeting that had seemed to be seventy per cent waffle.

'Are you free this afternoon? Well, this evening, really, I suppose.' It was already almost two, and he needed to eat lunch and deal with some emails before anything else.

'Which is it, Theo? Afternoon or evening?' The typing sounds paused for a second, while she waited for his answer. Theo smiled.

'Is your answer different depending on which one I pick?' Dropping into one of the abandoned chairs, he kicked his feet up onto the meeting table and leaned back on two chair legs.

'No. I just like a little precision in my scheduling.' Of course, she did.

'Four-thirty, then. At Hyde Park.' He grinned as the plan came together in his head. 'I want to show you a Winter Wonderland.'

'You mean *the* Winter Wonderland, I assume?' she corrected him. 'Fairground rides and stalls and such? For kids?'

'Not just kids,' Theo countered. 'It's actually one of my favourite things about London at Christmas.'

'Of course, it is.' She sighed. 'Fine, I'll meet you there at four-thirty. Which gate?'

Theo considered, mentally reviewing the map of the place in his head. He'd been there often enough to know the basic layout. 'The Green Gate,' he decided. It was closest to the Bavarian village, and he had a feeling he'd need a glühwein by then. 'I'll see you there.'

He was about to hang up, when he realised that Celeste hadn't. He waited and, after a moment, she spoke again.

'So…we're really doing this? Pretending to be friends?'

Theo thought back to what he'd told his colleagues earlier. At some point, he'd have to break it to Celeste that he was hoping they could pretend to be *more* than friends. At that point, he figured he'd either get a glühwein to the face, or maybe, just maybe, a kiss for the cameras that were bound to be hanging around the Hyde Park winter attraction.

He'd much, much rather the kiss, he decided. And not just because he'd had enough drinks thrown over him lately.

'I told you,' he said, after too long a beat. 'Most people end up *actually* liking me, once they get to know me.' Silence from the other end of the line. 'But if you have to pretend, yeah, I'll take that, too.' He knew when to admit defeat.

'Then I'll see you at four-thirty,' Celeste said, and hung up.

CHAPTER FIVE

'*MOST PEOPLE END up* actually *liking me, once they get to know me.*'

Theo's words were still fresh in Celeste's mind as she hopped off the Tube at Hyde Park Corner, wound her scarf a little tighter around her neck, and headed in the direction of noise, lights and Christmas music.

She hadn't wanted to tell him that actually liking him was exactly what she was afraid of.

Lunch with him had been fun, apart from the coffee incident. And even that had been kind of funny, if she thought about it. Most people she knew would have been furious to find themselves suddenly doused in hot coffee, but Theo had merely rolled his eyes and mopped up the mess. At least it hadn't been boiling, she supposed.

And yes, they'd bickered for most of the lunch, but even *that* had been fun. It turned out she didn't mind people disagreeing with her quite so much when they actually listened to her reasoned arguments and, sometimes at least, changed their mind off the back of them. She was so used to arguing with people who held such deeply entrenched opinions they'd never change them, whatever evidence she presented, that Theo was a lovely change.

He even seemed genuinely interested in her historical

knowledge—something she definitely hadn't expected after the *Christmas Cracker Cranium Quiz* debacle.

But none of that meant that she should start liking him, for one, very good reason.

He didn't like her.

He was pretending to, obviously, to convince the Great British Public that he wasn't a mansplaining, patronising, patriarchal idiot. He was a faker. Pretending was what he did. But he didn't actually *like* her. Very few people did. Rachel, possibly Damon. Maybe one or two of her colleagues or students, from time to time. She wasn't honestly sure about her parents. She'd always worked more on winning their respect, professionally, than worrying about whether they *liked* her.

It had never bothered her before. She had the people that mattered to her, and she had her work. Everything else was basically surplus to requirements. She knew she wasn't always easy to get along with, that her priorities weren't always the same as other people's. But she had the respect of the people who mattered, who made decisions about her career and her future.

What else could she want?

Except suddenly, ridiculously, she wanted Theo Montgomery to like her, the way she liked spending time with him. And that was stupid, so she was going to push it aside and focus on the fact that they were *pretending* to like each other for reasons entirely to do with their careers and nothing to do with them as people.

'Easy,' she said, out loud, gaining an odd look from a small girl in a princess costume who was walking along the path towards the Winter Wonderland with her parents.

Celeste ignored that, too.

Hyde Park's Winter Wonderland was quite the spectacle. Celeste had never been before, although she knew groups of colleagues from the university had organised trips in past years. It would be easy to get lost, especially with only the poorly drawn and not-to-scale map she'd printed out before leaving the university to guide her. She was glad that she'd insisted that Theo specify which gate they should meet at, as there were four, all leading to different areas of the fair in which to start their exploration. She was relieved to see that Theo had chosen the one nearest the Bavarian village, rather than the ice-skating rink. She'd never actually been skating, but she was willing to bet she'd fall over a lot. She wasn't clumsy, usually. But she made a point of sticking to what she was good at, rather than risking being bad at something new.

Another reason not to try and be friends with Theo. Making friends was most certainly something she wasn't good at.

She spotted Theo almost instantly, leaning against a lamppost, his expensive-looking wool coat and what had to be a cashmere scarf lit by the soft glow. His face was as ridiculously perfect as on the telly, and for a moment Celeste was thrown back to that moment in the green room when he'd interrupted her work. She'd looked up and seen the most attractive man she'd ever met in real life smiling down at her, and panicked.

So she'd done what she always did, and gone into what Damon called her 'superior professor' mode.

Apparently, it took more than abject rudeness to drive Theo Montgomery away when his career was on the line, though. As she approached, he looked up and smiled as he saw her. Pushing away from the lamppost, he headed straight for her.

'You came!'

'You thought I wouldn't?' Maybe she shouldn't have.

Maybe she should have stayed safe in her small office, her small, contained and organised life.

No. She was overthinking this. Hadn't she spent yesterday reminding herself that she was immune to charm, and all that stuff? This was a career decision, pure and simple.

She pasted on a smile, and Theo recoiled.

'What?' She let the smile drop.

'That's better,' he said, looking relieved. 'I was afraid you were going to throw glühwein over me before we even got inside.'

Celeste held up her empty hands. 'No glühwein.'

Grinning, Theo grabbed one hand and held it in his own. 'Well, that will never do. Let's go find you some. You can drink while we explore, and then we can talk.'

'Talk?' Everything was moving so fast. Theo's words, his long stride, the spinning lights of the Ferris wheel in the distance. 'We need to talk?'

'Absolutely. And I'd definitely like to do it once we've both *finished* our drinks this time.'

She couldn't help but laugh at that.

Theo slid her a sideways look as they strolled into the Winter Wonderland. 'That's better.'

'What's better?'

'That smile,' Theo replied. 'That's a real smile—not whatever that terrifying thing at the gate was.'

'Yes, I suppose it was.' A real smile. A real laugh. How long had it been since she'd had those things with anyone who wasn't Rachel or Damon? Too long. Way too long.

Still gripping her hand in his, Theo led her towards the Bavarian village, with its cosy wooden chalets and strings of lights illuminating the crowds.

'Come on,' he said. 'Glühwein waits for no one.'

Maybe this wasn't such a terrible idea, Celeste thought as they approached the nearest stall. Maybe this was just what she needed.

Maybe it was the glühwein, or maybe the intrinsic excitement of the Winter Wonderland experience, but Celeste seemed charmed by the evening. Even Theo's ego wasn't big enough to assume that was due to his company. But she'd laughed at his jokes and hardly complained about the accuracy of the Bavarian-ness of the village—low—at all.

Okay, it had to be the glühwein, because Theo was actually having fun.

'How do you feel about ice skating?' he asked as they passed by the outdoor rink.

'Faintly panicky,' Celeste admitted, a show of weakness he hadn't expected from her.

It seemed the more time they spent together, the more she relaxed and showed him the woman behind the prickly, know-it-all exterior.

'We'll save that for another day, then. Ferris wheel?' She gave him a doubtful look. 'Want to just drink more glühwein and maybe find some roasted chestnuts?' he tried again.

Celeste looked relieved. 'That sounds good.'

'You're not much for doing things outside your comfort zone, are you?' Theo asked, as they found a table outside one of the pseudo-Bavarian chalets to enjoy the glühwein.

'I went on your stupid gameshow, didn't I?' she countered. 'Although who possibly thought that I'd be a good guest, I can't imagine.'

Theo winced. 'That…that might have been me, actually.'

'Oh.' Celeste blinked a few times, her eyes round in

the glow of the fairy lights. 'I…wait. How did you even know I existed?'

He shrugged. 'I'd heard you on the radio a few times. You know how it goes, you've never heard of a person before but suddenly, once you've heard them once, they seem to pop up all over the place.' It was all down to the Baader-Meinhof Phenomenon, Theo knew. A frequency illusion, that owed everything to the brain's predisposition to patterns and nothing to fate.

See? He knew stuff, too.

'I've only been on the radio half a dozen times,' Celeste said slowly. 'And only on historical or political programmes. I wouldn't have thought they'd be your cup of tea.'

'I'm interested in lots of things,' Theo replied vaguely.

He wasn't about to tell her about the part-time history degree he'd been studying long distance for the last couple of years. His first attempt at university had ended in failure when he'd dropped out in his second year, and lucked into a TV gig through a random acquaintance. He hadn't been prepared to study then, at eighteen and nineteen, and he hadn't been at all interested in his course—it had ultimately been the subject with the least competition to get into his chosen university. Or rather, the university his parents had expected him to attend, all while telling him he wasn't really bright enough to be there. Looking back, *of course* he'd dropped out—and his father would never let him forget it.

Now he was older, well, he had more respect for and interest in learning. It was fascinating to be studying again, something that really held his attention this time. And he *definitely* hadn't told his parents—or anyone else—that he was doing it.

But he knew his tinkering around the edges of academic study was nothing compared to Celeste's career, so he didn't mention it.

She still looked suspicious, though. Time to change the subject.

'What do you think of the Winter Wonderland?' he asked.

Celeste studied their surroundings thoroughly before answering the question, so Theo found himself doing the same. He took in the busyness, the noise, the lights, the music, the kids, the stalls, the rides... He had always loved the chaos of it all, but, seeing it through Celeste's eyes, he found he could only see the things he knew people complained about in reviews.

Still, when he turned back to Celeste, she was smiling. 'I like it,' she said simply, and Theo felt something inside his chest relax. Then she turned that studious, assessing gaze onto him, and he tensed up again. 'Now. You said we needed to talk?'

He had said that, yes. He was regretting it now, though. It was one thing to *imagine* that Celeste might toss another drink over him when he confessed that he'd hinted to his colleagues that they were actually dating. It was another entirely to facilitate it by confessing.

But it was the right thing to do. Well, the right thing was probably not to lie about it in the first place, but since that ship had sailed...

Theo took a long gulp of his glühwein and tried to think about the best way to broach the subject.

Celeste got there first.

'Is this about all the theories about us online?' she asked. 'My brother tells me that his favourite is the one where we've secretly been dating for months, and were having a lovers' tiff the day of the filming. And, I suppose, when we had lunch. Given the coffee incident,' she added thoughtfully.

He watched as she finished off her glühwein. Perfect. He'd buy her another, if she wanted, after this. But first…

'Is it so bad if people think we're dating?' he asked innocently.

Her gaze turned sharp, apparently totally unaffected by the alcohol. 'Who did you tell that we're dating?'

How did she know? 'I didn't *tell* anyone. I just…might not have corrected people when they assumed.'

Celeste tilted her head to the side as she studied him. Theo shifted uncomfortably, feeling like an artefact in a museum that she was trying to puzzle out. The Rosetta Stone, perhaps. Or one of those carvings that made no sense until you looked at them upside down.

'Why?' she asked finally. Apparently, she couldn't read everything about him, after all. That was strangely reassuring. 'I mean, I know you wanted people to think you were a nice guy again and everything, but that doesn't mean you have to let people think you're actually interested in me. It's not like anyone is genuinely going to believe that I'm your type.'

Theo blinked at that. 'Why wouldn't they believe that? I mean, I'm not sure I really have a type. But you're beautiful, intelligent, funny—'

'I am not funny.'

Of course, *that* was the one she objected to. Theo grinned. 'Yes, you are. You might not always mean to be, but I find you hilarious.'

It was just as well her glass was empty, he decided as she gave it a meaningful look.

'The point is,' he went on, reaching over to take her hand—partly for comfort, partly so she couldn't make a grab for his still-half-full glass, 'anyone would believe I'd want to date you.'

'Even after that show?'

'Especially after that. Did you watch it back? You positively sparkled that night. You were fiery and authentic—and you were right.'

'I was wearing a Christmas jumper.'

'That didn't make you any less right. Or less passionate.' He stroked his finger across the back of her hand, absently. As if it was the most natural thing in the world. And she was watching him do it, he realised. Not stopping him, just watching. 'You had confidence in your knowledge, and in yourself. Trust me, that's very sexy.'

Her gaze shot up to meet his at that, and he saw the astonishment in her eyes. He got the impression people didn't call Celeste Hunter sexy very often. Probably through fear. Because whatever else she was, with those long legs and heeled boots, that dark hair pinned back to reveal her bright, smart eyes...she was definitely sexy. Or maybe Theo had some sort of academic fetish. That wasn't impossible.

'You think I'm sexy?' she asked, in disbelief.

'Who wouldn't?' he countered. 'In fact, the much bigger problem is going to be convincing the Great British Public that you're interested in *me*.'

She smiled at that. Then, without looking down, she turned her hand over under his, so their palms touched. 'We're really doing this, then? Pretending to date, just to improve our professional reputations?'

Theo lifted her hand to his lips and kissed it. 'You know, I think we are.'

Sitting in her office on Tuesday morning, Celeste stared at the photograph on her phone screen. Apparently, they'd been observed together at the Winter Wonderland, and by more than one person if all the different camera angles she'd seen on social media were anything to go by.

She wasn't surprised they'd been photographed, not any more. Theo was a big name in the country, a national boyfriend, almost. People were interested in what he was up to—and, after their fight on TV, together they were a curiosity.

What surprised her was herself. Or rather, her image in the photograph.

She looked happy. Not in an 'all her students turned in their essays on time' way. Not even in a 'knowing exactly how to end this next chapter' or a 'finding the primary source evidence to solidify her case' way. But in an unguarded, relaxed, 'having fun' way.

It was weird.

Oh, she had fun, of course—but only with people she knew well. Which basically meant Rachel, Damon, and a few acquaintances from the university. She'd expect to see herself looking that way at a conference dinner, perhaps, where she was surrounded by people who cared about the same things she did, who were interested in what she had to say because of her reputation, her academic successes.

This wasn't that.

The photo in question showed them sitting outside one of the Bavarian village chalets, drinking glühwein and chatting. But Theo's hand was resting on hers, and he was leaning towards her as if what she had to say were the most interesting thing he'd ever heard.

It's all an act, she reminded herself. *He's an actor. A faker.*

But she wasn't. And she knew the joy on her face was real.

She liked spending time with Theo, in a way she hadn't enjoyed a new acquaintance's company since…she couldn't remember when. And that could get dangerous.

Celeste shook her head. She'd be careful. Besides, almost everyone in the world started to irritate her after a while; Theo would be no different, she was sure. Right now it was fun, but they didn't actually have anything in common, beyond the fact they both wanted their TV projects to be a success. That was all.

And so, when her phone rang again, and Theo's name flashed across the screen replacing the photo of them together, she took a breath, answered, and said, 'So, what's our next move?'

Of course, Celeste reflected a few days later, she hadn't expected the next move to include wearing a swimming costume, outside, in mid December.

'Are you sure about this?' she asked, pulling the fluffy bathrobe she'd been given at the entrance tighter around her.

'Absolutely!' Theo's own bathrobe was tossed over his shoulder, as if the cold didn't bother him anyway. His surf shorts couldn't be much warmer than her one-piece, but they did show off his lightly muscled chest and broad shoulders nicely.

Not that she was looking.

Or was she supposed to be looking? If she was really dating him, she'd be looking, right?

She peeked over at him.

Yeah, she'd definitely be looking. There was a reason Theo was such a favourite on Saturday night TV, and it wasn't all to do with his smile.

He wasn't looking at her, though. He was striding ahead, along the deck of the boat he'd brought her to. It was more of a floating platform, really, Celeste decided. With a bar in the middle, some high cocktail tables, a sturdy rail around the outside, and, of course, the hot tubs at either end.

Celeste followed Theo as he stopped and spoke to people he passed, even posing for a selfie with a group on girls on a hen night. Then, as he reached the far end, he turned back to take her hand, his gaze not leaving her face for a moment.

Good. That was good. She didn't want him ogling her anyway, even if she was mostly covered by her bathrobe.

Although it probably meant she should stop ogling him. Damn.

'Ready?' Theo asked.

'As I'll ever be.' She paused by the edge of the hot tub.

'You realise you have to take the robe off, right?'

'Unfortunately.'

It wasn't that Celeste was insecure about her body. It was just that it wasn't something she often flaunted like this. Usually she was safely tucked up in her personal uniform of black jeans and boots, with a black top. She went a little different with her winter coat—that was white. But otherwise, her only colour tended to come from her bright lipstick. She wanted people looking at her lips and the words she was saying, after all, not her clothes. Plus, it made getting dressed in the morning a whole lot simpler when she didn't have to worry about things going together.

She swallowed. It wasn't as if anyone would be looking at her anyway. And her swimming costume was basically an extension of her normal wardrobe—boring and black. Nobody would even notice it next to the highly coloured and patterned bikinis on show.

Celeste let the robe fall from her shoulders and turned

to place it over one of the loungers beside the hot tub. When she turned back, Theo's gaze remained focussed firmly on her face, although she couldn't help but notice that his jaw was clenched. Was that with the effort of not looking at her swimsuit-clad body?

God, I hope so. The thought caught her by surprise, and she slipped into the water quickly to try and wash it away.

She didn't want Theo looking at her that way—unless it was to make her feel less bad about looking at *him* that way.

'So, what on earth made you think that an outdoor hot tub on the Thames in December was a good idea for our next "date"?' she asked as Theo handed her a glass of champagne.

Settling into the ledge seat around the edge of the hot tub, Celeste let the bubbles pop against her body, the warmth of the water welcome after the chilly winter air, and took a sip of the champagne, letting *those* bubbles pop against her tongue. Somehow, her shoulders already seemed less tense, as if the stress of hunching over her computer all day getting nowhere were seeping out of her into the water.

'That.' Theo sounded smug as he spoke. 'That's what gave me the idea. Wanting to put that look on your face.'

'What look?' Celeste scowled, but it only made him laugh.

'Not that one. The one you had before, when you took your first sip of champagne. You looked like the worries of the world were lifting from your shoulders.' He smirked at her. 'You're too tense, Celeste. I knew that the first moment you snapped at me in the green room.'

'You interrupted me while I was working,' she pointed out. 'So what, now it's your mission to destress me?'

'Perhaps.' Something changed in his smile. She couldn't figure out what exactly, since she wasn't even sure that his lips had moved at all. But suddenly it felt more secret, more private—and warmer, somehow. Maybe it was his eyes, or the lighting on the boat. That was it, just the lighting. Nothing to do with him, or her, at all.

Faker, she reminded herself, silently. *He's a faker.*

She looked away—and in doing so, noticed that they were being watched.

It was hard to whisper to Theo without getting closer; making herself heard over the bubbles was a challenge, and doing so without the guy sitting on her other side hearing even harder. So she shifted a little under the water until she could feel Theo's thigh pressed up against her own.

Glancing up, she saw him swallow, and his gaze flashed down, just for a moment, in the direction of her cleavage before it found its way back to her face.

'Don't look now,' she murmured, 'but there's someone over by the railing with their camera out. I think they're taking a photo of us.'

Of course, he looked. And then he waved. Because that was the sort of irritating man he was.

'I said don't look,' she grumbled.

'Ah, but if I don't look, how can I be sure they've caught my best side?' Theo asked. 'Besides, they're probably the fifth or sixth person to take photos of us since we got here. I've seen at least three.'

'Is that including the hen-party selfie you posed for?'

'Ooh, no, add that one in.'

Celeste shook her head. 'You love this, don't you?'

Theo shrugged. 'It's just part of the deal. It's not why I got into it, if that's what you mean.'

'Why did you, then?' she asked, suddenly curious. 'Did you always want to be a TV star?'

He laughed at that. 'Not a star, no. I suppose…maybe I did do it for the attention, a bit. I just wanted to do something that made people smile, made them stop in their busy lives and have a laugh, perhaps. Plus it was basically the only thing I was qualified for. Smiling and asking people questions like, "Where do you come from?" It's an aristocratic thing.'

His smile was self-deprecating, but somehow Celeste got the impression that he wasn't actually joking.

She wanted to ask him more about that, but she didn't know how. Damon would have; he was the sibling with all the conversational ability. She'd never needed it before.

But now, she wished she'd spent a little more time on it.

Before she'd found a way to phrase her question, Theo had already moved on.

'So. What are we doing this weekend?'

'Together?' Celeste furrowed her brow as she looked at him. 'I'd sort of planned on staying in and working on my book…'

'As fun as that sounds, it's not going to get us seen.' Theo shifted closer still, a conspiratorial smile on his lips. 'Have you seen the press this thing is getting us both? My agent is over the moon.'

'So is mine,' Celeste admitted reluctantly. 'Apparently raising my profile before the producers make a decision about my new show next year is vital, and *this*—' she waved her hand in the tiny space between them, being very careful not to touch any of those wet, firm abs he was showing off '—is doing that nicely.'

'There are still a few people on social media claiming we're faking the whole thing, though.'

'Which we are.'

'Which is why we need a plan to convince people. Starting tonight, and continuing this week.' Theo settled back against the edge of the hot tub, resting one long arm around her shoulder. He was only touching her ever so lightly, but Celeste still had to force her body not to shiver in response. To the rest of the boat—and the all-important cameras—he probably looked as if he were whispering sweet nothings in her ear.

He wasn't.

'I'm filming Monday and Wednesday evenings, and there's a few meetings I need to attend during the week-days, but there should still be plenty of scope for us to get together and be seen. I'll send you some calendar in-vitations once I don't need to worry about submerging my smartphone in bubbly water. What have you got on this week?'

Celeste shook her head as she tried to remember. It was hard to focus when Theo's warm voice was rumbling so close to her ear. 'I have to take my brother Christmas shopping on Thursday,' she replied. 'Other than that… I'm mostly just working on my own. Term is over, you see.'

'Ah, your brother. Maybe it's time to meet the fam-ily—properly this time. What do you think? Lunch?'

CHAPTER SIX

THEO WAS STARTING to regret his suggestion of lunch with Celeste's brother.

It wasn't just that he was, yet again, sitting alone in a restaurant, being watched by people with camera phones, waiting for Celeste—who was late. Again.

It wasn't even that he'd belatedly realised that an over-protective brother might not be all that keen on his plan to pretend to date Celeste for publicity—although that wasn't making him feel any better about the lunch ahead, he had to admit.

No, his biggest problem was his own motives.

Yes, being seen with Celeste had gone a long way to rehabilitating his reputation: if *she* didn't hate him, it made it slightly harder for everyone else to. There'd even been a couple of pieces about how Tania had moved on very quickly with her new fiancé for someone who'd been supposedly heartbroken and torn up by his abandonment. Oh, there remained a vocal minority complaining about him on social media, but those following his supposed romance with Celeste were happily drowning them out.

And yes, Cerys was thrilled. So thrilled, in fact, she'd told him he could ease up now. Let something else over-take them in the news cycle, until their romance was forgotten and nobody really noticed they hadn't been seen together in months.

Except he'd done the opposite. He'd invited himself to lunch with her brother. Because he'd seen her in that plain, boring swimsuit and known he'd wanted to see more. Not just that; he'd had fun. Real fun, on a fake hot-tub date.

What was it about her that drew him in? Part of it had to be the passion she showed when she talked about history, or anything she was knowledgeable about. But it was more than that. The way she let him see under that prickly exterior sometimes. Or how much fun it was to ease her out of that comfort zone she loved so much. Or even just the simple way she made a decision about how she felt about things based on what she thought, not on what anyone else said.

Whatever it was, Theo was too far into this, and he knew it. He just didn't seem to have any inclination to get out again.

And then there was the text message he'd received from his mother that morning.

Looking forward to seeing you for dinner on Sunday. We understand—from social media, I might add—that there's a new woman in your life. Your father says you should bring her along to see the old pile. Let her know what she's getting into.

He wasn't entirely sure how he was going to persuade Celeste to have Sunday lunch with his parents—or how he'd explain it to them if she didn't come. Or which was the worst of the two outcomes, to be honest.

But he was going to have to worry about it later. The restaurant door swung open and Celeste strode in, flanked by a tall, handsome guy in a dark coat, and a woman Theo hadn't seen before. She had her dark hair clipped back from her face, and wore a sweater dress under her coat. She was pretty, in a curvy, petite way—but his gaze was quickly drawn back to Celeste, slipping out of her white coat to reveal her customary black clothing underneath.

God, she was beautiful.

Her companions paused just inside the door, looking faintly astonished. Apparently, they hadn't been following Celeste's social media mentions lately, then.

Celeste said something to them both that he couldn't make out, then smiled—her painted red lips wide, although Theo could tell even from the distance between them that it wasn't one of her *real* smiles—and headed towards him.

This was it.

Theo stumbled to his feet as they approached, trying to return Celeste's smile. As she reached him, he did what he always did on dates: he embraced her, then pressed a kiss against her mouth.

Oh. Ohhh.

It was only meant to be a quick brush of the lips, maybe only at the corner of her mouth, even. But somehow it was suddenly more. Nothing deep—no tongue, as Cerys always warned him about kisses in public. But still.

Their first kiss.

And suddenly Theo was very sure that there needed to be another. And another. And…

Celeste pulled away after a moment, colour high on her cheeks. Good. At least he wasn't the only one affected by that kiss.

She pulled herself together more quickly than he could though.

'Sweetheart, you remember my brother, Damon? And my best friend, Rachel?' Celeste said, looking meaningfully towards their lunch guests.

Rachel. Celeste's best friend, Rachel. So he was doing lunch with the brother *and* the best friend.

He really hoped they were both in a good mood.

Switching into TV-host mode, Theo turned on his smile and reached out to welcome Rachel with a hug—*without* kiss—and shake Damon's hand. Neither of them looked as if they were about to bite his head off, but they did both look a little baffled by the whole situation.

Theo knew how they felt.

Pulling out Celeste's chair for her, he ensured she was comfortably seated before taking his own place at the table. Across the way, Damon was doing the same for Rachel.

Theo frowned. Had Celeste mentioned that her brother was dating her best friend? He was pretty sure she hadn't. That was weird, right?

But he couldn't worry about that now. He'd already clocked the paparazzi stalker at a table in the corner, thinking he was being surreptitious as he snapped away, taking photos of the four of them destined to be on the front page of every gossip site tomorrow.

The important thing was to make this seem like a perfectly normal lunch. That was all. So he smiled, and he laughed, and he made small talk. He let Damon pick the wine—who, in turn, got Rachel to choose—and shared mouthfuls of his main course with Celeste from his own fork. The latter prompted an odd look from his lunch date, and frankly astonished ones from their companions. But it looked like a real date, and that was all that mattered.

The only concerning part, really, was the feeling in

his stomach that it *was* a real date. Because that was how it felt.

And a big part of him wished that it were.

Huh. That was definitely new. And worrying.

Finally, as they polished off the puddings, Theo glanced casually over at that table in the corner, not for the first time since they'd started eating, and realised that the photographer had left at last.

Leaning around Celeste to peer out of the window, Theo watched the guy wandering off down the London street, waiting until he was around the corner before he collapsed back into his seat with relief.

'He's gone?' Celeste asked, shifting her chair away from Theo's to a more normal distance. Ridiculously, he missed her immediately.

Theo nodded. 'Finally.'

Across the table, Rachel frowned. 'Who's gone?'

'Our reporter-stalker,' Theo said tiredly. 'Come on, let's grab after-dinner drinks in the back bar, where it's more private. Then we can explain.'

The back bar was cosy, warm and empty. Theo spoke briefly to the head waiter on their way in, and he nodded, then shut the door behind them, returning moments later to enter, after knocking, with a tray of coffees and liquors. Then he departed again, leaving them in peace.

Finally.

Celeste sank into a chair a strategic distance away from Theo, and tried to think.

She needed to get things straight in her head again because that lunch had felt uncomfortably like a real date. Not just lunch; hugging Theo hello—*kissing* him even— had felt normal. Natural. Even eating his food from his fork had been fine, despite the fact it was something she'd never even done with her last boyfriend, and they'd been together for almost a year.

She knew it was all fake, of course—intellectually. Knowing things intellectually had never been a problem for her.

It was the emotional side that stymied her, every time. And after a week and a half of pretending to date Theo Montgomery…her emotions were starting to scream at her.

Maybe it wasn't her emotions. Maybe it was just her libido. *That* at least would make sense. He was an attractive guy. She was a sexual being. Didn't everything in history always come down to sex, one way or another?

Glancing up, she found her little brother glaring at her, and promptly decided to stop thinking about sex.

'What the hell is going on here?' Damon demanded.

Wish I knew, brother.

Rachel sat down beside her, and Celeste heard the unspoken message her best friend was sending.

I might have come here with him, but I'm on your side. Always.

That was something. She'd been…worried, to say the least, talking to Damon about Rachel as they'd shopped for Christmas presents for their parents that morning. And seeing them together at the Cressingham Arcade where they were both currently working hadn't made her concern lessen any.

She'd tried to talk to Rachel about Theo that week, but her friend had ducked her calls—probably, Celeste suspected, because she was in bed with Damon. In a way, she'd almost been glad when Rachel hadn't answered because, really, what was she going to say?

At least she'd shamed Damon into inviting Rachel to

their parents' Christmas Eve party. That was the least he could do.

And he was still waiting for an answer to his question.

'Do you want to explain, or shall I?' Theo asked Celeste, his upper-class tone lazy. That had irritated her a few days ago—the laziness, more than anything. It should irritate her now.

'I'll do it,' Celeste replied, sharply, pushing the thought aside. 'You'll get it wrong.'

'Probably,' Theo agreed easily. He was just *so* laid-back. That was annoying, wasn't it? She was sure it used to be annoying. 'I'll pour the coffees, then.'

She tried to focus on the matter at hand: explaining her relationship with Theo. Maybe it would even start to make sense to her, too.

'So. Damon, I know you watched the car crash that was our festive TV quiz. Rachel, I assume you did too?'

Rachel nodded.

'It didn't go down particularly well with the Internet fans. Or my agent,' Theo said.

Celeste shot him a look to say, *Who is telling this story, you or me?* Theo shut up and let her continue. *One point in his favour. Still so many against.*

Except it was getting harder to remember those points against, when everything felt so natural when she was with him. So easy, in a way personal interactions rarely were for her.

'So Theo called me and asked me to help him rehabilitate his reputation,' she said.

'And yours,' Theo interjected.

Celeste rolled her eyes. 'My reputation is based on my research, my publications, my education and my brain, not my ability to be pleasant on television. Unlike yours.'

'Your reputation with TV companies, however, is

based *entirely* on that,' Theo pointed out, apparently un-ruffled by the accusation that he was just a pretty face.

Celeste ignored him. Mostly because he was right.

'So what happened next?' Rachel asked, obviously well aware of how Damon was glowering at them both.

'We agreed to a few public appearances together, as friends,' Celeste said, trying her hardest to make it sound as if it were the most normal thing in the world.

'It got a little bit out of hand from there,' Theo admitted. 'There were these stories online…'

'People thought we were faking it,' Celeste explained.

'Which you were.' Damon was still glowering as he spoke.

'So we had to prove that we really *were* okay with each other,' Celeste went on, ignoring her brother. 'By pretending we were in love.'

'So you're mortal enemies pretending to sleep together for the cameras,' Damon said drily. 'The miracle of modern love, huh?'

'Like you can talk,' Celeste scoffed, then turned to Theo. 'This one spent all morning telling me how he and Rachel are just colleagues who sleep together. Apparently, they're having a "festive fling".'

She regretted the words the moment they left her mouth. Of course, that was *exactly* what Damon had said, but, watching Rachel's face as her smile stiffened and the light in her eyes seemed to dim, she knew it was a mistake.

'Sorry, Rachel, that came out wrong,' she said, wincing.

'No, it's true.' Rachel reached for her liquor. Never a good sign. 'He's my festive fling. Right, Damon?'

'Right,' Damon said, although he sounded just as dubious as he had that morning when he'd said it.

Oh, Damon. Oh, Rachel.

She couldn't get her best friend out of this one, or her brother, either. They'd have to figure it out themselves. *She* couldn't even figure out what the hell *she* was doing, pretending to be in love with Theo Montgomery until it almost felt real.

But Celeste had a feeling there were going to be a lot of broken hearts, come the new year.

Theo didn't know what was going on with Damon and Rachel but, to be honest, he wasn't totally sure he *wanted* to know, either. Things were confusing enough to deal with just pretending to date Celeste.

'What do you want to do now?' he asked her as they strolled out of the restaurant together. Damon and Rachel had left, their stalker cameraman had got all he needed, and, really, it was the perfect time for them both to get back to their regularly scheduled lives.

Except he didn't want to. He wanted to spend more time with Celeste. And Theo was almost certain that was going to become a problem, sooner or later.

'Isn't there somewhere we need to be seen together?' Celeste asked.

Every other night, he'd managed to find some sort of event or place he'd been invited to, and convinced her to make an appearance with him for the publicity. Today, for the first time, he had nowhere he was supposed to be, and no ideas.

Celeste rested her head against his shoulder for a second, as if the rigmarole of the lunch had exhausted her. She had her arm looped through his, close against his side, and Theo had an overwhelming need to keep her there.

It was that thought that sparked the idea.

'Ice skating.' It was perfect; he could hold onto her, in public, with perfect justification.

Celeste, however, looked sceptical. 'We're going back to Winter Wonderland?'

Theo shook his head. 'There's a rink at the Tower of London—well, in the dry moat anyway. Come on. It'll be fun!'

'I do like the Tower,' Celeste said tentatively, and he knew he'd got her. History always was the way to her heart.

Not that he was trying to get there. That was absolutely not what this was about.

He just…needed to hold her close. Was that so bad?

There was a queue at the box office when they arrived. He probably could have used his smile and his face to get to the front of it, but he didn't. Whatever Celeste thought, this wasn't actually another publicity date. This was about spending time with her, like a normal couple.

Even if they categorically weren't.

Did she even *like* spending time with him? He had no way of telling. She was the one person in his life he couldn't read. Everyone else was easy—even Damon and Rachel had been obvious in their own way. He wondered if Celeste realised how much trouble there was going to be there, very soon…

But he wasn't thinking about them. He was thinking about Celeste—which seemed to be one of the few non-work things he *did* think about these days.

He'd never imagined, after their first meeting, that he'd enjoy her company so much. And, in fairness, she was still blunt and impatient, and had given him a real earful the one time he'd called and interrupted her train of thought *just* when she was getting a handle on the chapter she was writing.

But she was also fascinating, full of facts and observations he'd never have imagined if he hadn't met her. There was a passion there he so rarely saw in anybody—

one he suspected she only showed when she was talking about history, or perhaps about the things that mattered to her most. He loved listening to her talk—when she wasn't snapping at him. And he loved to watch her think.

Like now, standing in the queue at the Tower of London ice rink, as she stared up at the majestic castle. Her dark hair was swept back from her face as usual, giving him the perfect view of her porcelain skin and the thoughtful look in her eyes.

He couldn't resist. 'What are you thinking about?'

'Do you know, there's been a fortress here since just after the Norman conquest?'

'I did, actually.' She looked at him in surprise, and he shrugged. 'School trip.' It was a lie. He'd come here on his own, as an adult, and read the guidebook cover to cover. Why didn't he just tell her that?

He knew the answer to that too, deep down. Because he was afraid. Afraid that this highly educated woman would laugh at his pretensions to knowledge. What did he know, really? He'd flunked out of university and made his career in a field that just required him to smile and look pretty.

Theo shook the thought away. 'It was a prison too, right? Weren't the Kray twins held here?'

'They were, actually. The last execution here was during the war though—a German spy.' Her smile turned mischievous, and Theo felt his heart skip a beat at the sight. Oh, he was in trouble.

'They say the place is haunted, you know,' she said, and Theo laughed with surprise.

'You believe in ghosts?' he asked incredulously. She was so logical, so academic—so determined to see the evidence and the proof that she'd required dozens of social media screenshots from him to even believe that people were interested in their relationship.

Celeste shrugged. 'Not really. But the stories are always interesting—and the people who claim to have seen them sound terrified. One of them is said to be a grizzly bear, from when the Tower was a zoo.'

'Well, if we see a bear out on the ice, I promise we'll skate in the opposite direction,' Theo said. 'Come on, we're up.'

Celeste bit down on her lip, obviously nervous, as Theo stepped out onto the ice a short while later. He held out a hand to her and she took it, gingerly.

'You've not done this before,' he remembered.

Celeste shook her head. 'Never.'

'Because you didn't want to, or…' He trailed off. If she genuinely hated the idea of ice skating she'd have said, right? He didn't want to be that jerk who dragged her into doing something she didn't want to, just because he thought it would be romantic. Especially since any romance between them was all for show anyway.

'It just…never really came up as an option.' She shrugged. 'My parents weren't big on non-academic activities. And by the time I left home and went to university, well, I was usually busy studying anyway.'

There was something in her voice, a loneliness Theo hadn't heard from her before, and it made his heart ache. She'd been locked away in her ivory tower, learning every dry fact and opinion she could. But when had she actually experienced the world she was learning the history of? He got the impression, not nearly as much as she should have.

'Come on.' He squeezed her hand and led her slowly out onto the ice. 'Don't worry. I won't let go.'

He could have got her one of the plastic penguins kids

used when they were learning to skate, he supposed, but he got the feeling that Celeste hated looking incompetent or unknowledgeable as much as he did. But where he laughed his inferiority off and pretended not to care, she got prickly and defensive. He didn't want that. So instead, he kept her close against him and held her up when she started to lose her balance.

They made their wobbly way around the outside of the rink, ignoring the people watching from the cafe and bar at the end, hot chocolates in hand.

'See?' Theo said. 'I told you you could do it.'

Celeste beamed up at him. Unfortunately, she also stopped focussing on her feet, and her skates slid away underneath her. Theo grabbed her and tried to keep her upright. His stomach lurched as he felt his blades sliding, too. He could grab for the edge, but that would mean letting go of Celeste—

They both crashed to the ice with a jarring crunch.

'I knew I should have used a penguin,' Celeste said, staring up at the night sky above them.

'I reckon it would have been harder to land on than I am,' Theo pointed out from underneath her.

'True.' She looked over at him and he was amazed to realise she was still smiling.

'You don't mind that you fell?'

She blinked. 'I…guess not. I mean, it was fun, even if I wasn't very good at it.'

'It was fun,' he agreed, looking into her eyes and wondering at their depths.

For a long moment, Celeste stared back. Then she blinked and said, 'Come on. I think we deserve a hot chocolate.'

'I reckon they agree.' Theo nodded towards the crowd

that had gathered at the side of the rink nearby, all clapping and cheering.

Celeste froze for a moment, then relaxed as she said, 'They recognise you.'

'And probably you.' Theo levered himself out from under Celeste, and back to a standing position. Then he reached down to pull her up beside him, bracing himself against the side of the rink.

One arm wrapped around her waist, he bowed to their audience, pulling Celeste down with him, laughing as she did the same. He liked her like this. Close and carefree. Not caring that she looked like an idiot.

He cared, of course he did. But he knew that the best way to deal with it was to pretend that he *didn't* care. That, and a little bit of distraction...

Swooping around, he swept Celeste into his arms, so her breasts were pressed against his chest, and her skates were barely touching the ice. God, he hoped he didn't fall again now. That really *would* be humiliating.

'What are you doing?' she asked, her voice a low murmur.

'Giving our audience what they really want,' he replied.

Lowering his lips to hers, Theo finally did what he'd been wanting to do since the moment they met at the restaurant, and kissed her. Properly, this time. With tongue.

Somewhere, Theo decided, as whoops went up from the crowd and cameras flashed, Cerys would be having an apoplexy.

Then he lost the ability to think about anything at all except kissing Celeste.

He didn't miss it.

CHAPTER SEVEN

THEO MONTGOMERY WAS kissing her.

Not like that perfunctory hello kiss at the restaurant; this was a real, no-holds-barred kiss. The sort that would *definitely* send her sprawling over the ice again if he weren't holding her up. Since that brief, hello kiss at the restaurant had scrambled her brains for a good half an hour, she dreaded to think what this one would do.

It's all for show. Remember that. He's just playing up to his audience.

But it *felt* real. That was the problem.

The aches and bruises that covered her body from her fall were rapidly being replaced by other, far more pleasant, sensations. Tingly ones, that reminded her it had been far, far too long since she'd had anyone but herself to keep her company at night. Warm ones, that drove away the chill of a winter night. Hopeful ones, that never wanted these other feelings to end…

Theo pulled away, and Celeste just about resisted the urge to grab his head and pull his mouth back to hers. Mostly because if she let go of his body even for a moment she was pretty sure she was going to fall over again.

The crowd gave up one last, loud cheer, and then dispersed.

'Hot chocolate?' Theo asked, as if nothing had happened at all. As if he hadn't just rocked the foundations of her happy, solitary life by reminding her of all the good things that happened in pairs.

And no, she wasn't talking about the ice skating.

'That would be great,' she managed. 'And I think I'd like my real shoes back, please.'

She needed solid ground under her feet again. Literally *and* metaphorically.

The bar and cafe at the end of the rink were packed with people, but Theo managed to smile their way to a window seat just as another couple were leaving. He disappeared, leaving her looking out over the ice and the castle alone, until he returned with their hot chocolates. It was enough time, at least, for Celeste to bring her brain back down to earth, which she appreciated.

'So, how did you like your first ice-skating experience?' Theo placed her steaming mug, topped with whipped cream, a flake, *and* mini marshmallows, on the counter in front of her.

Celeste beamed at the sickly sweet concoction. Hot chocolate was, in her opinion, the best part of the festive season.

'Worth it for this,' she answered, because she wasn't about to tell him that the *other* best part of this particular festive season was kissing him.

All a show, she reminded herself. She really couldn't afford to forget that.

They drank their hot chocolates in companionable silence as, outside, visitors spun around the rink on their skates, all in the shadow of the ancient castle looming above them. Even Celeste had to admit it was pretty magical.

'You're thinking again,' Theo said, his voice low and

rumbly and incredibly distracting. 'More ghost stories about the tower?'

Celeste shook her head. 'I was just thinking how nice it is to see the modern world interacting with history this way. I didn't think it would be, somehow.' She'd assumed that using historical places this way would diminish them, somehow. Probably because of a lifetime of her parents stressing the value and importance of historic and archaeological sites in their own right, for research and learning, for academics who would publish long, often boring papers on them.

And they *were* important, of course. Those historical sources and places were how she'd built her career. She wanted them to be treasured and looked after.

But she wondered now if they couldn't be used, too. Tourists traipsing over the Acropolis in Greece might not do much to preserve it or improve the experts' knowledge of the ancient world. But they *would* increase those tourists' knowledge. And they'd share that knowledge with their kids, their families.

Her father might grumble as another historic site opened its doors to people who hadn't studied the period as he had, didn't understand what they were seeing. He might claim it was all for the money, but the money was what paid for the research to happen.

More importantly, the interest had to be there. If people didn't care about the history of a place, why would they pay for it to be preserved and studied?

All stuff she'd known academically. But here, watching history meld happily with the modern world, she felt that she understood it, rather than just knowing.

There was the world of difference.

This is what I want to do with my TV show. Bring history to life.

'I like it,' Theo said, simply. 'I like that our city has such a fascinating past, and I like most that it's not locked away there. That we can see it, experience it every day, just living here.'

She'd lived in London her whole life, but she wasn't sure she'd ever just enjoyed the place. She'd either been studying *or* living. Never both at the same time.

She thought she might want to, though. With Theo.

'I think…this is what I want my new show to be,' she said, slowly. 'A way of bringing history beside the modern day. Of making it real to people, not abstract.'

That was the part her parents didn't, couldn't understand. For them, it was another world—one they'd rather live in than this one.

But Celeste wanted both. She just hadn't realised it until now.

'I think that sounds brilliant,' Theo said. 'I can't wait to watch it.'

'If they commission it,' Celeste replied. 'It's still not a sure thing.'

'Ah, Aesop's chickens, huh?' Theo grinned. 'Not counting them before they hatch.'

'That's right.' She tilted her head as she studied him, a surprising thought coalescing in her brain.

'What?' he asked, his expression suddenly nervous.

'Tell me the truth. You're a bit of a history buff, aren't you?'

His gaze slid away from hers. 'It's an interesting topic. I'm interested in lots of things.'

Celeste knew she couldn't read Theo the way she read Rachel, or even Damon. But she was starting to get a feel for him—and not just in the kissing way. There was something more here. He couldn't fake his way out of this, not with her.

'You'd heard me on history shows on the radio often enough to ask me onto that quiz show.'

'I thought you'd be an interesting addition.' He tossed her a smirk. 'Look how right I was.'

'Did you really come on a school trip to the Tower of London?'

Theo paused for a second, then shook his head. 'No. I came as a tourist last summer.'

'Because you're a history buff.'

'Because I was writing an essay about it for my history degree.'

Celeste blinked. Okay, maybe she couldn't read him at all, because she definitely hadn't seen that one coming.

'You're studying history?' she asked.

'Part-time.' He shrugged. 'It's no big deal.'

But it was, she could see that in the tension of his shoulders, the way he wouldn't look at her.

This was Theo behind the smile, behind the fakery.

'Does anyone else know you're doing it?'

His gaze shot up to meet hers at that. 'No. And...I'd appreciate it...'

'I won't tell anyone.' She smiled. 'But I think it's wonderful.'

'You do? For all you know I could be rubbish at it.'

Celeste had had rubbish students before. Ones who didn't show up for lectures, or never turned in essays. Ones who only cared about the university experience, not the studying.

If Theo was doing this in his own time, on top of a full-time job, when he really didn't have to...he was doing it for the love of the subject.

And *that* she most definitely understood.

She smiled at him, and lifted her half-empty mug for him to toast with his own.

'What are we toasting to?' he asked.

'To you, and your studies.'

'How about to you, and your new show?' he countered.

'Fine. To bringing history to life, and into the present.'

'Works for me.' He drank, leaving a hot chocolate moustache on his upper lip, which he licked off. Celeste tried to pretend that the action didn't make her heat up again.

'Now,' he said, when he'd finished. 'Important question for you. How do you feel about Sunday lunch with my parents?'

It was hard for Theo to express quite how much he didn't want to be here. From the way Celeste was watching him, though, her bottom lip caught between her teeth, he had a feeling she understood, at least a little.

Taking a breath, he opened the door of the car. 'Ready?'

'As I'll ever be,' she joked, but he could barely bring himself to smile in return.

Why had he done this? The only thing he could think was that the kiss on the rink had addled his brain to the point where he'd not only told her he was studying history, for heaven's sake, but also forgotten all the perfectly good reasons why he *shouldn't* take Celeste to meet his parents.

Starting with, if *he* didn't want to be there, why should she?

But it was more than that, of course. While he had no doubt his parents would be nice enough to Celeste, he couldn't hope to say the same about how they'd be towards him.

Still, he forced himself not to actively grimace as he helped Celeste out of the car and took her arm. Her dark hair was down today, for once, and it moved in the winter breeze before settling on her white coat.

Any other woman of his acquaintance, coming to meet his parents for the first time, would have asked him what to wear. Not Celeste. He had no doubt that under that coat was an all-black outfit—although a dress or skirt rather than jeans, given the tights she was wearing with her boots today. Her lips were bright red, like Snow White's, and he wanted to kiss them. For courage, perhaps.

Or just because he'd been dreaming of them since he last touched them with his own.

Celeste stared up at Sorrelton House, its many chimneys jutting up into the grey winter sky. 'This is where you grew up?'

Theo tried to imagine seeing the place for the first time. He couldn't remember when he had, of course. He'd been born within its walls, and some days it felt as if he'd never left.

It was a large house. No, that was an understatement. It was unnecessarily huge, for the three of them living there when he was a child, and for his two parents now. Even if he added the live-in staff, which was down to only a few long-standing employees, it was too big. He remembered them closing up the East Wing when he was a child; he didn't think it had ever been opened up again since.

'Yep,' he said, succinctly. 'Come on.'

It was because they didn't have a real title, he supposed, that his parents insisted on all the grandeur. They were minor, minor aristocracy, but even that small amount made a difference. They couldn't live like *ordinary* people, could they? But they didn't have the land or inheritances to live like lords, either.

Theo wasn't sure anyone could afford to live at Sorrelton House these days, the way it had been designed to be lived in. After so many years, the place was a complete money pit.

He didn't bother ringing the doorbell; it would only risk giving Jenkins a heart attack, and it took him forever to get up to the main door from the kitchen, where he spent most of his time gossiping with Mrs Harrow. So instead, he led Celeste around to the side entrance, the one nearest the stables, and slipped in that way. At least he knew that Celeste wouldn't be the least bit interested in the pomp and circumstance of the main entrance hall anyway.

Except in her very own Celeste-like way, of course.

'It's Georgian, right?' she asked, pausing to examine the brickwork as they rounded the corner to the side entrance.

'I believe so.' His voice sounded tight, even to his own ears. Celeste didn't seem to hear it, though.

'Do you know much about the history of the place? Before your family came here, I mean?' She paused. 'Unless it's *always* been in the family? Are you one of those families?'

'No. My great-grandfather bought it, I believe. Before that, I'm not sure. I imagine my father could tell you, if you really want to know.'

He didn't—want to know, that was. He never had— not since he was a child. His father had made clear that the house was a responsibility, and obligation—one he never expected Theo to be capable of fulfilling to his satisfaction.

So, no. He didn't want to know about the history of Sorrelton House. He wanted to get through this lunch and get back out again, as smoothly and as quickly as possible. That was all.

Celeste was watching him now, curiosity and maybe even concern in her eyes. Theo turned away, fumbled open the door and strode into the house proper. If he moved fast enough, maybe the memories wouldn't hit him so hard.

'Theo? Is that you?' His mother's voice echoed down the empty hallways; she might be getting older, but her hearing was still as sharp as it had ever been. Maria Montgomery had always been able to hear a whispered insult or a secret from a good hundred yards. Apparently, it was still her super power.

'Yes, we're here, Mother.'

Reaching out blindly behind him, he somehow found Celeste's hand and gripped it firmly in his own. They'd agreed on the drive out of London how they'd play this. A new couple, yes, but nothing serious. He didn't want his parents getting any ideas about marriage or anything— not least, because he knew that Celeste wouldn't be their first choice for him. Or second or third, come to that.

After all, she was only beautiful, intelligent, funny and, against the odds, mostly a nice person.

'Where's the money, Theo? Or at least a title? Come on, boy, try harder. That was always your problem—you just never tried hard enough.'

He could almost hear his father saying the words in his head.

Really, what was the point of coming home to be berated by him, when he could do it perfectly well for himself?

'There you are!' Maria burst into the main hall at the same time Theo and Celeste reached it. 'We were starting to think you'd got lost. Or forgotten.'

'Are we late?' Celeste asked, confused. 'I thought you

said one, Theo?' He saw her glance at the grandfather clock, as it chimed quarter to one.

Theo didn't answer. Maria didn't bother either as, of course, they were actually early. Five years ago, maybe he'd have second-guessed himself, thought he'd got the time wrong. He knew better now. But how could Theo explain to Celeste that his mother just liked to start with them at a disadvantage, any way she could?

He should have warned her in the car. Shouldn't have brought her at all. But somehow, when he was away from this place, he always believed that it couldn't be as bad as he remembered. That he was building it up in his head, somehow.

It was only once he returned that he realised the truth of it all.

'Come, come. Your father is already in the dining room, Theo, and you know he doesn't like to be kept waiting.' Maria turned away and bustled down the passageway to the dining room at the back of the house.

'I'm sorry,' Theo whispered as they followed.

'What for?' Celeste asked.

'Everything that happens in this house.' That should probably just about cover it.

He braced himself, and headed for lunch.

Forty minutes later, Celeste had a new respect for Theo Montgomery, and his ability to keep smiling and stay polite in the face of abject rudeness. She'd thought he'd done a good job at being pleasant to her, even after she'd spent their first meetings arguing about everything.

Now she knew his secret. He'd been training for this his whole life.

His father, Francis Montgomery, was easy enough to figure out. Perpetually disappointed by life, as far as she could see, and passing that disappointment onto Theo. He was every historical figure who'd ever lost a kingdom, or power, or influence, and blamed everyone but himself. Even the way Theo passed him the gravy wasn't satisfactory.

It was much easier to understand people when you thought of them as historical figures, she decided. Maybe that was the trick she needed, and hadn't realised until now. Something else Theo had given her.

'*He* dropped out of university, you know,' Francis told Celeste, apropos of nothing, over dessert.

She hadn't known. It had never come up. She wasn't entirely sure why it had come up now. And Theo clearly had no intention of telling them about his current studies, so she wouldn't. 'Well, it doesn't seem to have stopped him,' she said cheerfully.

Really, a dinner at which *she* was the cheerful, pleasant, upbeat one was a definite first. And not a good sign.

She glanced across at Theo, who sat staring sullenly at his syrup sponge pudding and custard. She'd never known him go so long without smiling before.

'I think it was the expectation,' Maria, his mother, said, almost as a secret aside, as if Theo couldn't hear them.

'*I* think he was too stupid,' Francis interjected. Maria ignored him.

'Oxford does come with certain expectations, don't you think?' Maria went on. 'And really, all that pressure on young minds. Some people just aren't cut out for that kind of life, are they? But he so wanted to go… *I* always knew my Theo wasn't really going to set the world aflame. It takes a special something for that, don't you think? And we knew early on that Theo didn't have it. But he's found his niche, and that's something,' she added, sounding doubtful.

'He never wanted to work hard, that was the problem,' Francis opined, leaning back in his chair, wine glass in hand. 'That's what happens when people get everything handed to them on a plate, like Theo has. They don't know how to work for it. Born lazy.'

'Well, Theo does actually have a job,' Celeste pointed out. She stared at Theo, waiting for him to say something, to defend himself, but he barely even looked up from his pudding. 'I've seen him do it—that's how we met, in fact. He works hard.' She thought of all the meetings and filming he'd had scheduled at odd times that week, all the time spent making sure everything was in place for the *New Year's Eve Spectacular*. All the emails and calls. Theo was properly involved in the projects he took on; he did a lot more than show up and smile, whatever people thought.

Whatever *she'd* thought, before she got to know him.

When you added in his studies, plus his fake dating her, Theo was anything but lazy.

But his parents didn't look convinced.

'And now, of course, he associates with all these women who are only interested in his name, or his money—no offence, of course,' Maria went on.

'None taken,' Celeste lied, her voice mild. *That*, at least, made Theo look up and give her a tight smile. She wondered when he'd learned to read her so well.

Maybe around the time she'd learned to read him.

His mother was a harder read—but Celeste was pretty sure she was toxic, one way or another. She reminded her of Rachel's stepmother, the few times they'd met, and that was *definitely* not a good thing. Maybe it was just living with Francis that had soured her, until she couldn't find a good thing to say about her own son.

'I always tell him to bring them home to see the old place,' Francis said, with a wheezy laugh. 'That'll put them off! He can't afford to marry a poor girl, not unless she's at least got a decent title they can trade on.'

There was an awkward pause. Were they really waiting for her to tell them if she had money and/or an aristocratic family?

'Of course, he never does bring anybody home,' Maria said, looking wistfully at Theo. 'I would like to see him settled—with the *right* girl, of course.'

Celeste didn't need the sharp look Theo's mother sent in her direction to get the message there. She might not always be great at reading the subtleties of human nature, mostly through lack of experience, but really, there was no subtlety here.

And Celeste didn't have the patience for death by a thousand insults.

'Well, I think we can all agree that's not going to be me!' Smiling cheerfully, she placed her spoon in her bowl, pushed away the stodgy pudding, and got to her feet, smoothing down her plain black dress. 'And now, I'm afraid, Theo and I really need to get back to London. Don't we, sweetheart?'

'Afraid so.' Were those the first words Theo had spoken since they sat down at the table? 'Sorry, Mum, Father.' He didn't hug them goodbye. She wasn't surprised. The Montgomerys were even less affectionate than her own family, which she hadn't really thought was possible.

'Thanks so much for having me,' Celeste said, as she backed out of the room, because if nothing else she'd managed to learn *some* manners over the last twenty eight years of her life. Even if she wasn't sure these people were really worthy of them.

Neither she nor Theo said anything else until they were in the car, down the driveway and back on the main road again, speeding away from Theo's childhood home.

'Well,' Celeste said, finally.

'I'm sorry.' He sounded so miserable, so tense, that she almost wanted to tell him to pull over so she could kiss him again, just to try and cheer him up.

'It's okay,' she said. 'I mean, it's not. They're awful. But honestly, I'm used to dreadful family dinners, so it was almost nice to sit through someone else's for a change. It's a good job I got to know you first, though.'

'Why's that?'

'Because otherwise I might believe some of the things your parents said about you.' She looked over at him and wished he weren't driving, so he could see the truth of her words in her eyes. 'As it is, I know you're nothing like the man they seem to think you are. So that's good.'

Was that the start of a smile, curving around his lips? She hoped so.

'Nothing like, huh?'

He was fishing for compliments now, but, after meeting his parents, she decided he probably deserved a few. 'Nothing at all. You're definitely not lazy, and you're proving with every essay you submit, every online seminar you attend, that you're capable of studying when you want to.' She'd talked him into showing her some of his modules and marks after a few more drinks after the ice skating. From his online tutor's comments, she could see that he was a conscientious and dedicated student, with interesting opinions and interpretations of events and sources that weren't just a repetition of someone else's analysis.

She almost wished he were one of her students. Except then she definitely wouldn't be able to think about kissing him, so it was probably best for all of them that he wasn't.

He was smiling now. She'd made him smile, just by telling the truth as she saw it. She liked that.

'I'm still sorry you had to sit through that lunch,' Theo said.

'That's okay,' Celeste said cheerfully. 'I know exactly how you can make it up to me.'

He raised an eyebrow at that. 'Oh? How's that?'

'You can come to *my* parents' Christmas Eve party with me.'

CHAPTER EIGHT

SPENDING CHRISTMAS EVE in a room full of people who were categorically proven to be brighter and better educated than him wasn't exactly in Theo's plans when December started. But then, nothing in his life seemed to have gone to plan since he'd met Celeste, so maybe it was all par for the course.

The Hunters' town house in central London was worlds away from his own family seat in most ways, but from the moment they'd arrived Theo had sensed something familiar. Something he didn't like. Celeste, however, seemed perfectly comfortable, so he'd pushed the feeling aside and tried to enjoy the party. She'd been there most of the day, helping prepare for the party, and by the time he arrived—with the obligatory bottle of wine for the hosts, or for himself, in case he got really desperate—there were already half a dozen people milling around the living spaces of the house, including her brother, Damon.

'You okay?' Celeste asked as she drifted past holding a tray of interesting-looking hors d'oeuvres. She was wearing a different dress from the one she'd worn for lunch with his parents a few days before, although it was, obviously, still black. This was cut high in the front but fell low on her back, then swished all the way to the floor, only just revealing that her usual boots had been replaced with high heels.

Theo wanted to pull down the shoulder straps and watch it fall to the floor. Although probably not in the middle of her parents' party, he supposed.

'Fine.' He looked around the room. From the few introductions he'd made, everyone here had several more degrees than him, and mostly wanted to talk about their research with other people who would understand how impressive it was.

He was not that person.

Celeste rested a hand against his arm for a moment. 'Sure?'

She'd been like this since she'd met his parents—more sensitive, more concerned. Less Celeste-like. As if seeing inside his secrets allowed her to drop a little of her own armour. And she was letting him in here, too. Showing him her world.

As if this thing between them *meant* something to her.

Or as if she wanted company at a boring family party. That was the more likely answer.

'I'm feeling…a little out of my depth here,' he admitted reluctantly. He'd worked so hard over the years to fit in anywhere, to win people over, to make them smile in a way he'd never been able to achieve with his own parents. But here…he felt inferior again, just like at home.

He didn't like it.

Celeste reached up and pressed a soft kiss to his cheek. 'Just stay away from my mother and you'll be fine,' she told him.

Well, that was encouraging.

'Keep me company for a few minutes?' he asked, trying not to sound desperate. 'I've barely seen you tonight.'

She flashed him an amused smile. 'You know the people here aren't likely to be posting photos of us on social media, right? Some of them might not even know who you are...'

Theo faked horror at that idea, although actually, right then, it seemed like the better option. He didn't want to be singled out and identified here. Didn't want to be highlighted as the know-nothing TV star.

He wanted to be here as Celeste's date. Nothing more, nothing less.

'That's not why I want to spend time with you.'

'I know! You want my feedback on your latest essay, right?' she guessed. 'I've told you, I'll do it, but only if you give me tips about not appearing scary on television.'

'You don't need them, but I'll give them to you, sure. But not tonight.'

She gave him a speculative look. 'Is it because I've already lectured you on my research and books and you figure I'm the only person in the room who won't bore you again?'

'I'm never bored listening to you.'

'Ah, so it is that,' she said, with a grin. 'In that case, try and avoid my dad, too.'

'Celeste...' She started to move away, and he snaked an arm around her waist to keep her closer. 'Is it so hard to believe I might just want to spend time with you? Because I like doing that?'

The surprise in her eyes hurt, a little. It so obviously hadn't occurred to her that he *might* want to do that—which suggested that she didn't want it.

Then he looked a little closer, as she bit down on her lower lip and met his gaze. '*Do* you? Because generally most people don't.'

'I'm not most people,' he told her. 'And yes. I do.'

A small smile spread across her face, a real one, one

he believed. She opened her mouth to respond—until someone called her name from across the room and, with an apologetic look, she slipped away.

Theo sighed, and reached for another drink. He had a feeling that the evening was going to be a very long one.

An hour later and Theo was still looking pretty miserable. Celeste wished she could stop and stay with him for a while—especially since it seemed he actually *wanted* her company, and not just for appearances—but she had bigger concerns tonight. Mostly around her brother and her best friend. She couldn't afford to be distracted by the thought of kissing Theo again.

However tempting that was.

Her conversations with Damon during the day hadn't made her feel any better about whatever was happening between him and Rachel, although she suspected they couldn't keep pretending it wasn't an issue for very much longer. And Rachel still wasn't here…

Celeste's phone buzzed in her pocket. God, she loved a dress with pockets.

I'm outside. Come meet me?

It was Rachel, of course. Dumping her tray on the nearest flat surface, Celeste headed for the door—wincing as she realised that her father had cornered Theo and looked to be practising his latest lecture on him. At least Theo was still managing that polite, TV-star smile. When that started to slip, that was when she'd worry.

'Why didn't you come in? It's freezing out here,' she said as she opened the door, looking around for her friend. Then she spotted her, at the bottom of the steps that led to the town house's front door.

One look, and she knew. She stared, speechless for a moment.

Then, 'Oh, my God, you're in love with my brother,' she blurted.

'I wanted to speak to you first,' Rachel said, with a small smile. 'Before I talk to him.'

Oh. Oh, she'd been right. Everything *was* coming to a head tonight.

Celeste shut the front door behind her and stepped out into the biting cold of the December night. Descending the steps carefully in her heels, she sat on the second from the bottom one in the freezing cold with her best friend.

'Tell me everything,' she said.

And Rachel did.

Some of it she already knew from her conversations with Damon, or the double-fake-date lunch they'd shared. Some of it was new.

And all of it boiled down to one thing—the same thing Celeste had known from the moment she saw her.

Celeste waited until Rachel had run out of steam and words before she spoke.

'So like I said, you're in love with my brother? Is that right?'

Rachel nodded. 'And I'm hoping he feels the same about me.'

Celeste thought back to her last conversation with Damon, in the kitchen before the party started. He'd seemed...conflicted.

'I think he does,' she said slowly. 'The thing will be getting him to admit it.'

She didn't want to give her friend false hope, because her brother was basically a lost cause when it came to love. But on the other hand...

'If anyone can do it, I reckon you can,' she said.

Rachel flashed her a quick grin. 'Do you know, apart from my mother before she died, you were the first person in my life who ever listened to what I had to say without talking over me, or telling me what I should feel. Damon was the second.'

No wonder she'd fallen for him. Celeste knew what a rarity that was in Rachel's life; she'd often assumed that her listening skills were the only reason her best friend put up with her at all. She might not agree with her all the time, and she'd most definitely tell her when she'd got something factually wrong, but she would at least listen first.

'It's one of the most useful things our parents ever taught us,' Celeste said lightly. 'You see, you can't brutally demolish another person's argument or theory without listening to it properly in the first place.'

Rachel laughed, but it sounded more desperate than amused.

'What's he going to say when I tell him?' she asked quietly.

Celeste had no idea. But her friend needed to know the answer, one way or another. 'Let's go and find out.'

Rachel stood up, smoothed down the beautiful wine-red dress Celeste had helped her pick out at the Cressingham Arcade, and nodded.

Inside, the party was still…well, mildly happening, rather than raging. Across the room, Damon stood with their mother, but he turned away from her as Rachel entered, and Celeste almost *felt* the moment his gaze met her friend's.

Whatever Damon told her tonight, it was clear to her that this thing between him and Rachel was no festive fling.

Rachel's heel skidded on the parquet flooring, and

Celeste gripped her arm a little tighter, as Theo had hers on the ice rink.

'You okay?' Celeste murmured.

'No.' Rachel held onto Celeste while she found her balance. 'But I will be.'

'Do you want me to come with you to talk to him?' Not that she was sure what she could do, but she could tell her best friend was scared. Rachel was the one person in the world she'd *always* been able to read right. She'd learned her, the same way she learned dates and names and sources. Because from the moment Rachel had become her friend, she'd known she had to work as hard to keep her as she did her grade average.

'No,' Rachel said. 'I need to do this alone.'

'You're sure?'

Rachel's gaze skittered towards Damon, and Celeste's followed. He looked as if he was bracing himself for Sunday lunch with the parents—or, worse, Christmas Day. Maybe he was.

Oh, she had a feeling this was going to go very badly.

'Sure,' Rachel said, sounding more certain than Celeste felt. 'Besides, I need you to do something else for me.'

'Anything,' Celeste said. She couldn't fix this for her friend, but she could help her through it.

'Distract the rest of the room?'

Huh. She hadn't been expecting that, but she supposed it made sense. There weren't so many people at the gathering that any argument between Rachel and Damon would go unnoticed. In fact, it would probably be the most exciting thing that had happened at one of the Hunters' Christmas Eve parties in years. Of course, Rachel wouldn't want a gaping audience—unlike every time she and Theo went out in public.

'Just while I get Damon out of here. I don't want an audience for this,' Rachel went on.

Celeste tried to smile, although she wasn't sure she managed it very well. 'On it.'

She didn't look back as she crossed the room; Rachel had to do this alone now. And she had a job to do.

Unfortunately, the only way she knew to draw the attention of the masses was by kissing Theo Montgomery.

The things she did for her friends...

Celeste's father was obviously a very intelligent man, Theo decided, but he was no storyteller. He'd been talking—at length—about his research and discoveries for the last fifteen minutes, and Theo was still no clearer what he'd actually been doing.

Celeste would have made the story exciting. He'd have listened to her explain anything. Partly because he was stupidly in thrall to her, but mostly because, despite what she believed about herself, she was actually good at making history interesting. At telling the stories that made the past come to life.

He'd known that about her before he'd even met her, from listening to her on the radio. It was how he knew her new TV show would not only be picked up, but be a success. And it was, now he thought about it, probably why there'd been such uproar after the *Christmas Cracker Cranium Quiz* had aired. People weren't just cross because he'd been mansplaining to her, but because they'd wanted to hear what she had to say, and he'd been following the producer's orders to cut her off.

She'd asked for tips on being on TV but, in truth, she just needed to be herself. She needed to see herself the way *he* saw her—as a passionate, engaged, fascinating historian who made stories of the past feel real and immediate.

He didn't know what her history with men, or other people generally, was like—he hadn't asked and he wouldn't—but he got the impression that others might not have always taken the time to see her that way. Maybe they'd been put off by her sometimes prickly nature—something he suspected now was more down to social nerves than anything else. Or perhaps the people she met simply didn't like being told they were wrong, even when they were.

But she'd let him see beyond the prickles. And he'd been told he was wrong his whole life. It was actually a relief to be told it when it was true. At least Celeste also acknowledged when he was *right*.

She hadn't laughed at the idea of him studying for a degree; she'd encouraged him. And she'd put up with lunch with his parents without flinching, then told him they were wrong about him.

Something he'd been waiting to hear his whole life. Not from fakers like him, who lied for a living.

From someone who told the truth no matter how inconvenient. From Celeste.

And that was why he'd been politely listening to her father drone on for the last thirty minutes, without excusing himself and leaving this travesty of a party. Because if he left, he wouldn't see her again tonight—and, God help him, he wanted to see her again.

He tuned out Jacob Hunter completely as Celeste returned to the room, arm in arm with Rachel—looking stunning in a wine-red gown that had Damon, across the room, standing gawping at her like an idiot. Huh. Obviously things were afoot there.

Suddenly, Celeste broke away from her friend and

headed towards him, a determined glint in her eye. Her father didn't seem to have noticed, as he was still continuing a run-on sentence that had been going on for half a glass of wine now. Theo put his glass down on the nearest table, and braced himself for whatever was about to happen.

Celeste grinned. Oh, but he had a bad feeling about this...

She ignored her father as much as Mr Hunter was ignoring her, her gaze not leaving Theo's as she approached. And then she was in front of him, almost pressed up against him, in fact, that slippery black fabric sliding against the front of his freshly pressed shirt.

'Just follow my lead on this one, okay?' she murmured.

And then she kissed him.

It was like the ice rink all over again, with a similar chance of him falling over, just out of shock. Theo froze for less than a second, before the feel of Celeste's mouth on his let his instincts take over, pushing his brain to the back of the queue.

He knew how to do this, whatever her reasons. Hell, he wanted to do this, had been dreaming of doing this, ever since the last time. His baser instincts weren't going to let his brain ruin this for him now.

Around them, there were murmurs, comments, and he happily ignored all of them. If Celeste didn't care what her family and friends were saying about their public display of affection, he sure as hell didn't. Instead, he sank into the kiss, holding her close and wrapping his arms tight around her as if he never intended to let go.

Maybe he didn't.

Celeste, however, had other ideas. Apparently oblivious to the way her kiss was changing his whole world around him, she pulled away, and glanced over her shoulder.

'Okay, they're gone.' She let him go, flashed a smile at her father, and headed out into the hallway.

Theo blinked, then followed.

'What was that about?' he asked as the door to the living space swung shut behind him, and they were alone at last.

'Rachel needed to talk to Damon, without an audience.'

'So you drew the audience's attention our way instead,' Theo surmised.

She smiled. 'Exactly.'

Theo watched her, watched as her smile started to waver. 'Did I do it wrong?'

He laughed, not at her but at himself. 'Sweetheart, trust me. I don't think you know *how* to do it wrong.'

Celeste gave a one-shouldered shrug. 'Oh, you'd be surprised. Guys are generally with me for my brain, or my university connections, rather than my lips or my body. Which, you know, is a good thing, I suppose.' He'd sworn to himself he wouldn't ask about her past romances. It was none of his business—especially since this wasn't even a real relationship. But if she was just telling him, that was okay, right?

'Not if they're just using those parts of you.' He frowned at her. 'Wouldn't you rather have someone who wanted *all* of you? Brains and body, your soul *and* your sexuality?'

Tossing her hair back over her shoulder, Celeste barked her own laugh this time, too sharp and short to contain any actual humour. 'You can talk. You only want me for my publicity.'

God, if only she knew the truth. How much he *did*

want her, just as she was. Except for her, this was still about her career, and his. She'd never hinted at wanting anything more. And he could only imagine how people would laugh if he even pretended to be smart enough to have anything more with her. Half a distance-learning degree wasn't going to match up to her PhD and academic credentials any time soon.

But if she honestly thought he wasn't attracted to her, that he didn't dream about her lips, her body under his... then she really hadn't been paying attention.

The question wasn't whether he wanted her. It was whether *she* wanted *him*.

He waited, just a moment, until her gaze settled back on his again. He didn't laugh off her comment the way he would have done before that kiss. Didn't make a joke, and let the moment pass. Didn't hide anything, for once.

He let her see the heat in his eyes. And, because he was watching oh-so-carefully, he saw the answering flare in her own, before she blinked and tried to bury it.

'Celeste.' Theo stepped closer, relieved when she didn't move away. 'Do you really think this is still all about the publicity?'

'Isn't it?' Her tone was defiant, but he heard the hope behind it. 'What else could it be? We had an agreement...'

'And then I kissed you on that ice rink and nearly lost my mind with wanting you.'

A sharp intake of breath was the only response she gave him.

He stepped closer. Her back was already up against the bannister, and he was so close now he could reach past and rest one arm on the wood right beside her head. If she gave him the slightest hint, he'd back away.

But she didn't. That heat was back in her eyes, and he could feel it growing between their bodies, too.

'Celeste, I don't know what this is between us. But it's sure as hell not about the publicity right now, okay? There's no one watching. No cameras. And I still need to do this.'

He ducked his head to capture her mouth with his own, loving the small sigh she gave as their lips touched. She wanted this as much as he did. Needed it, even.

He'd worry about what the hell that meant tomorrow.

It was long moments before he pulled away, panting slightly, and rested his forehead against hers. 'How long do we have to stay at this thing?'

Celeste shook her head, as if she was trying to clear it. 'I told my parents I'd stay here tonight. It's Christmas Eve, Theo.'

He swore. Christmas Eve meant he needed to drive back to Sorrelton House tomorrow morning, to brave the festivities with the family. Christmas Eve meant Celeste would have her own family stuff to do.

'That means I have a bed upstairs,' she pointed out, and all the blood in his body rushed in one direction.

But before he could sweep her into his arms and carry her up the narrow town-house staircase, Rachel came barrelling through from the kitchen, her face blotchy with tears.

Celeste broke away from him instantly, taking her best friend into her arms and whispering with her. Then she turned back to Theo, her face thunderous.

'Can you get Rachel a taxi, please? I need to go and speak with my brother.'

CHAPTER NINE

HER HEAD STILL swirling from that kiss, Celeste stormed out into the back garden to find Damon.

'I warned him,' she muttered to herself. 'I *told* him to be careful with her heart, and now look. Honestly. *Men.*'

The fact wasn't completely lost on her that she was avoiding thinking about the man she'd just walked away from inside. Had she really been just about to lead Theo Montgomery up to her childhood bedroom and let him seduce her? Or seduce *him* if it came to it?

Yes, her mind replied. And her treacherous body added, *And you still might.*

Focus, Celeste.

She needed to deal with Damon first. Then she could figure out what the hell was going on with Theo.

She found him, eventually, sitting forlornly on the swing at the end of the garden. Her steps faltered for a moment, when she saw how heartbroken he looked.

This is what love does to you. Where lust can lead.

She shook her head. This wasn't about her. And she wasn't Rachel, and Theo wasn't Damon. They both knew what they had was fake. They lived different lives in different worlds that had only intersected for this brief, wonderful time. In the new year, it would all be over, and as long as she remembered that she'd be fine.

'You are the biggest idiot known to man,' she said, sitting down beside him.

'I know.' God, he sounded miserable.

'Let me guess.' Celeste kicked off the floor with one foot, making the old swing seat sway forward and back. 'She asked you to commit and you said no.'

'Basically.'

'Why? Because you wanted to be free to sleep with as many other women as possible?' If that was the case, she was walking out of here right now and leaving him to be miserable on his own.

'No!' The horror in his voice surprised her into silence. 'Because I'm not that guy. I'd let her down, in the end, when she realised that.'

Oh. *Oh, Damon.*

His head was bowed, his hands clasped between his knees, so she saw clearly the moment his spine stiffened, as if someone had walked over his grave.

'Damon?' she asked, concerned.

'I'm okay.' A lie, but she let him have it. If he was having a come-to-Jesus revelation moment, she didn't want to ruin it. Especially if it might just set him on the right path again.

'For what it's worth? I don't think you'd let her down, little brother.' Standing up, she pressed a quick kiss to his hair, something she couldn't remember doing since he was a child. 'In fact, I think you've got a better handle on this love thing than most of us. You just need to be brave enough to go after it.'

She was as surprised by her words as he obviously was, but she knew they were right, deep down. Damon was a good guy, and if he loved Rachel then he'd do everything in his power to make it right.

Celeste headed back up to the house, her head still

whirling. The whole thing was just a reminder how distracting and distressing love could be. She'd never been sure if her parents really loved each other, or if their academic goals were just so neatly aligned that they'd decided they might as well team up. Either way, they'd made a good enough go of it, but they weren't exactly role models for affection and romance. Or parenting, come to that.

It seemed she'd spent her whole life trying to prove to them that she was as good as they were, earning their love through academic achievements—while Damon had gone the opposite way entirely and followed his own path, never trying to impress anyone at all, never committing to anything.

Celeste had already heard her mother's opinion about her choice of date for the evening; she imagined that it was probably about as favourable as Theo's parents on her. She didn't have a title or money. And Theo didn't have a PhD or a research grant or publishing history. He didn't even have an Oxbridge degree, it turned out.

She reached the back door and stared through the kitchen to where Theo was standing in the hallway, alone. He leaned against the bannister where he'd kissed her, running his hand through his hair. Was he having the same second and third thoughts as she was? Probably.

They weren't a match, that much was clear. But did they need to be, really?

Only if it's for ever.

And it wasn't. It was just for now. And right now… Celeste's body knew what she wanted, even if her mind was still spinning.

She let the door slam shut behind her, and Theo looked up instantly, his gaze locking with her own.

'I put Rachel in a cab,' he told her as he moved closer. 'She was heading to the Cressingham Arcade.'

'Good.' If Damon wanted to go after her, he'd find her easily enough there, right? Those two could figure things out on their own from here.

She had her own love life to sort out.

No, not love life.

Her *sex* life. Something that had been dormant for far too long—not a problem that she imagined Theo having. Which meant maybe he could help her get over her drought, with both of them clear that was all this was.

She stepped towards him, closing the gap. 'In that case, where were we?'

Theo's eyes were dark. 'You were telling me about the bedroom you have upstairs. And how it's Christmas Eve.'

The way he looked at her, she felt like his Christmas gift, waiting to be unwrapped.

Maybe she was.

Do I really know what I'm doing here?

No, she admitted to herself. She hadn't got a clue. But she'd lived her whole life so far knowing exactly where she was going—which degree, which research project, which professor she wanted to study under.

Perhaps it was time to take a leap into the unknown, for a change.

In the other room, she heard her mother laugh, and her father clink some silverware against a glass, ready to make his customary Christmas Eve speech. She didn't need to hear it to know it would be the same as the year before, and the year before that.

She was ready for something new.

'Come upstairs with me?' she asked softly.

Theo hesitated, and she almost took back the whole thing. 'Why?' he asked.

Celeste swallowed. But she'd come this far, she wasn't going to stop now. And besides, having a clear overview of her objectives was a positive thing, right? That was what her PhD supervisor had always said anyway.

'Because I want you, and I think you want me. Not just for the publicity, but for the fun of it, too. So I think you should make love to me tonight, because I can't imagine going another minute without kissing you again.'

Theo surged forward at her words, sweeping her into his arms and kissing her the way he'd wanted to all night. She kissed him back, with all the passion she put into the things that mattered to her: history, proving people wrong, and kissing him.

God, he loved a woman who had her priorities in order.

'Upstairs,' he murmured against her lips.

He could hear Celeste's father droning on in the other room, but there was no way his guests were going to put up with that for very long, and he wanted to be secluded away in her bedroom before any of them escaped out to the kitchen and found them half naked.

Because he was going to have Celeste half naked—no, totally naked—very soon, wherever they happened to be at the time.

'Yes,' she gasped back. 'Upstairs.' She looked back through the door into the garden. He followed her gaze, and saw a figure approaching in the darkness. 'And fast, before my brother gets here.'

They ascended the narrow staircase together, still touching and kissing at every step, hiding their ebullient laughter as Damon stormed through the hallway below and straight out of the front door. And then they were at a dark wooden door, and it was opening, and all Theo could see was a bed and Celeste, and suddenly the laughter faded.

'You're sure about this?' he asked softly, wanting her to know she could change her mind, at any point.

But she nodded, firmly. 'Very.' She bit down on her lower lip for a moment, the telephone-box-red lipstick she'd been wearing almost all gone now, probably smeared across his face.

He kicked the door shut behind him and swept her up into his arms.

Theo wanted to take it slow, to make it worth the wait, to make it better than she could imagine. But as with all things, Celeste had her own ideas, too. Not that he was complaining about them.

In no time, his jacket, shirt and tie had been stripped away, and her hands roamed across his chest, followed by her lips. Swallowing the lust that coursed through him at her touch, he pushed the straps of her dress down her arms, kissing every inch of creamy skin as it was revealed. Her shoulders, her collarbone, the curve of her breasts...

She arched against him, pressing her softness up against all the parts of his body that were anything *but* soft right now, and Theo almost lost his mind.

'On the bed,' he said, his voice desperate and rasping, even to his own ears.

'Yes,' she replied. Then she grabbed his shoulders and, twisting them around, pushed him down onto the mattress so she landed on top of him.

Theo gazed up at her. Her dark hair was loose around her bare shoulders, tousled and wild. Her eyes were huge in the moonlight, her creamy skin almost glowing as he ran his hands over it, from her shoulders, down her arms, skirting her bare breasts, to where her black dress was pooled around her full hips.

She looked like an ancient goddess—Aphrodite or

Venus—come to enchant him. Or a queen, perhaps. Anne Boleyn, seducing her Henry and changing history.

All Theo knew, in that moment, was that whatever she asked for, he would give.

Another time, another place, the thought would terrify him. But right now...

'Are you going to have your wicked way with me?' he asked, the familiar smirk on his lips giving him courage.

This could be just like every other meaningless encounter in his life. Just because it was *Celeste*, didn't mean it had to, well, mean anything.

She grinned down at him, her hair brushing against his chest as she dipped her head to kiss him. 'Definitely.'

'Good.' He grabbed her around the waist and pulled her flush against him as he kissed her again.

He'd worry about everything else in the morning. Right now, he intended to enjoy every minute.

Celeste awoke on Christmas morning in her childhood bed, with Theo's arm resting heavily on her waist, his breath almost a snore in her ear—and her bedroom door crashing into the wall behind it as Damon and Rachel burst in.

'We're getting married!' they announced, in gleeful unison. Celeste blinked at them. Their eyes seemed feverishly bright with happiness or lack of sleep, their cheeks pink from the cold, and their hands clasped tight together.

Grabbing the sheet to her chest, Celeste struggled to a sitting position, which was harder than it should be since apparently Theo slept like the dead.

She should probably cut the guy some slack. She couldn't exactly blame him for being tired after all their... exertions, the night before. Heat rose to her cheeks at the memory of him declaring it was his turn, after she'd, well, had her wicked way with him, as he put it.

They'd stopped keeping track of whose turn it was, after that, but suffice to say the night had not been exactly *restful*. Thank goodness for solid Victorian walls, and the fact that her parents' bedroom was on the next floor up.

She forced her mind back to the present. The room was still mostly in darkness. If she was lucky, maybe they wouldn't notice that she was naked. Or that she wasn't alone in the bed. It could happen.

Then their words caught up with her.

'Wait. Married?'

She'd hoped her brother and her best friend would be able to sort things out. But *married*? How had Damon gone from a confirmed commitment-phobe to a husband-to-be in just one night? That seemed a lot to chalk up to Christmas magic.

But perhaps that same magic was responsible for what had happened with Theo, too. Because in the cold morning light it seemed more like an impossibility than ever. Apart from the bit where he was still snoring in her bed beside her.

Damon shrugged. 'We just figured…once you know you want to spend your life with another person, why wait?'

'Plus, you had to come up with something really good to make up for being such an arsehole,' Celeste said, reading between the lines.

Rachel thrust her left hand towards her, showcasing a glittering diamond. 'You get to be maid of honour, of course. And you can't wear black.'

'Black is very chic for bridesmaids these days,' Celeste said automatically, with no idea at all if it was true.

'I'm more worried about the "maid" part,' Damon said,

a small frown appearing between his eyebrows—yet still utterly failing to completely hide his happy glow—as he gazed past her to the lump under the sheets beside her.

Celeste rolled her eyes. 'Little brother, my sex life is none of your business.'

Of course, Theo chose that moment to wake up, rolling over languidly onto his back before sitting up, his chest bare as he rested against the headboard.

'Merry Christmas, everybody. What did I miss?'

'Damon and Rachel are getting married, and you and I are having the most awkward morning after known to history.'

'And you know history,' Theo replied. 'Congratulations, guys. Damon, I'd shake your hand, but I'm not entirely sure where my trousers are.'

'I think they're over by the window.' Rachel squinted in the semi-darkness of the room. 'I can see the belt buckle shining in the moonlight.'

'How romantic,' Damon said drily. 'So, you've heard our news. Care to fill us in on yours?'

'No news!' Celeste said brightly. 'Just, you know, carrying on the charade that Theo and I are madly in love and together. All for show.'

'Except you're both naked under there.' Damon did not look entirely pleased at the idea. She supposed she didn't blame him. She had made it very clear that there was nothing real between her and Theo, and the guy did have a bit of a reputation. Celeste frowned. Except so did Damon, and his relationship with Rachel had been equally iffy to start with. Her brother had literally no moral high ground to stand on.

Plus, as she'd already pointed out, her sex life was none of his business.

Rachel, thankfully, was slightly more subtle than

her new fiancé. 'Anyway, we just wanted to share our news...'

'You don't know that we're naked. We could have clothes on,' Celeste said, because apparently she just didn't know when to stop digging. Beside her, Theo was smirking. She could feel it.

'I can see your underwear hanging from the wardrobe door handle,' Damon replied.

'And now we'd better go and tell the rest of our families,' Rachel said, bundling Damon towards the door again. 'Happy Christmas, you two! See you both later.'

'Merry Christmas,' Celeste called after them. 'And, uh, congratulations!'

The door crashed shut behind them, and then it was just her and Theo.

Naked.

In her bed.

'So, that was an exhilarating way to start the day,' Theo said. 'What do you say we take another nap to get over it? Or something.' His hand crept up her bare side at the 'or something', leaving her in no doubt what he was hoping that something might be.

And she wanted that, too. She could feel her body already starting to respond to his touch, her nipples tightening under the thin sheet that covered them, the ache that pulsed through her. How could she want him this much when, to be fair, she'd already had quite a lot of him last night?

Christmas Eve magic, that was what it had been. And, oh, it had been magical.

But in the cold light of day, this desperate need to touch him left her with more questions than she liked.

Hang on. Cold light of day. Cold, yes, but there still wasn't much light pushing its way around the curtains.

'What time is it?' she asked, pushing his hand away.

Theo grabbed his watch from the nightstand. 'Urgh. Four-thirty. No wonder it still feels like the middle of the night. We should definitely get some more sleep.'

Celeste wriggled back down under the covers. Maybe if it was still last night, she could enjoy this—enjoy him—a little longer.

Because she knew this couldn't, wouldn't last—that had never been the plan. But maybe it didn't have to be over just yet.

She reached out and ran her hand up *his* side, just as he'd done to her, from thigh to chest, before bringing it back down his front instead. 'Sure about the sleeping part?' she asked.

'Not in the slightest,' Theo replied, and kissed her.

CHAPTER TEN

HE'D DEFINITELY HAD worse Christmas mornings, Theo decided, as he left the Hunter town house a little later that morning, whistling to himself in the cold, still dark air. Yes, he was knackered, and slightly hungover, and certain muscles ached in pleasurable ways after the kind of workout they'd only dreamed of for the last few years, but still. *Definitely* worse mornings.

Celeste had tried to convince him to leave quietly, by the back door preferably, without being seen. He'd given her a look and reminded her that the whole *point* was that he should be seen. This was the perfect addition to the story they were weaving for the press—and it seemed important to remember that this morning. Otherwise, a guy might start to get ideas.

Except there were no press waiting for him outside the town house as he left—although he did bump into Jacob Hunter on the stairs, which was more than a little awkward.

His good mood lasted all through his walk home, while he showered and dressed and loaded the car— taking an extra coffee to keep himself awake on the drive—and right up until he pulled his car into the driveway of Sorrelton House.

Christmas with the family. He'd wish he could have

just stayed with Celeste for the day, except then he'd have been spending Christmas with *her* family, which, after last night, he wasn't sure was demonstrably better.

Except he'd have been with Celeste. Touching her. Kissing her. As if they really *were* a couple, and not just pretend.

She'd been quick enough to denounce that anything had changed between them to her brother, but it *had* changed, hadn't it? Surely it had to, after a night like that?

The only question was, what had it changed into? He'd have to wait until he was back in London, back with Celeste, to answer that one.

He killed the engine, but stayed sitting in the car on the driveway for a moment, staring up at Sorrelton House. He wished Celeste could be with him again this time. For all his duty visits to his parents drained him, it had somehow seemed less awful when she was beside him. Not that he imagined she'd be volunteering for another visit any time soon. Just as he wouldn't be attending one of her father's lectures.

Different worlds.

But in some ways they intersected. She didn't laugh at his studies. He didn't tell her she should stick to academia, not TV. She made him think that maybe, just maybe, there really was something more to him than his name and his face, after all. And he hoped he'd shown her last night that he knew she was a hell of a lot more than just a brain and the ability to recite facts.

Although, to be honest, he could sit and listen to her recite facts all day. Because they weren't just facts, just history, when Celeste said them. They were stories, a new way of looking at the world. The way *she* saw the world. And he was a little bit worried that he'd never get enough of that.

Theo sighed, and hoped that her confidence in him might help him make it through Christmas Day with his parents, without him starting to believe everything they said about him again.

He didn't notice the unfamiliar car on the driveway until he'd already dragged his overnight bag and box of gifts up the front step to the main door. He frowned at the vehicle as he waited for the door to be answered; Christmas was, of course, a formal occasion, and he knew he wouldn't be forgiven for using the side entrance on such a day.

Who could possibly be here?

Other than his aunt Gladys, who always joined them for high days and holidays, and perhaps the widowed vicar from the church at the edge of the estate, he couldn't imagine *anyone* choosing to spend Christmas Day at Sorrelton House.

He got his answer quickly enough, however, as the door was yanked open, not by Jenkins, but by a vaguely familiar blonde in a green and red tartan dress. She was a good few years younger than him, as best he could guess, and Theo had the horrible feeling that he really should be able to place her. Especially if she was spending Christmas with his family.

He forced himself to smile instead of frown as he tried to buy time while he figured it out.

'Merry Christmas!' he said cheerfully. 'How are things going here this festive morning?'

The blonde smiled wanly at him. 'Happy Christmas, Theo. It's lovely to see you again.'

She pressed a dry kiss to his cheek, then moved aside to let him enter.

'Ah, the prodigal son returns, eh?'

That voice, Theo recognised. And the portly figure it belonged to, waddling into the hallway. Hugo Howard, his father's long-term friend and sometime business partner. Which meant the blonde had to be his daughter, Emmaline. Theo didn't think he'd seen her since she was about twelve, so he didn't feel quite so bad about not recognising her.

The family tableau was completed as Hugo's wife, Anna, a tall, thin woman who towered over her husband and glared at everything because she refused to wear her glasses and blamed poor inanimate objects for her not being able to see them, joined them.

'Hugo, Anna. Merry Christmas,' Theo repeated. 'Not that it's not lovely to see you all, but are my parents here too?'

Hugo laughed uproariously. 'You always were the funny one, Theo. Like your dad says, at least you found a way to make people laughing at you a good thing. They're through in the green sitting room. Come on, now.'

Theo shook off the only vaguely veiled insult without comment. But what did it say about his presence here that the unexpected Christmas guests were more likely to greet him at the door than his own parents?

'It's a good job I got to know you first, though. Because otherwise I might believe some of the things your parents said about you.'

Celeste's words, after their last visit. She knew him even better now, of course. But even then, even after only a few fake dates and an acquaintance of less than three weeks, she'd seen him more clearly than his own parents had. She'd understood him, in a way he knew now his own family never would. She made him see himself through her eyes—not the TV-viewing public's, or his father's critical gaze. But Celeste's clear, unwavering, uncompromisingly honest view.

And he saw her, too. She was becoming all he ever wanted to see.

He dumped his overnight bag at the foot of the grand staircase and fell into step beside Emmaline as they all headed for the sitting room.

'This is a surprise,' he said amiably. 'Is your joining us today a last-minute thing, or did my parents just forget to tell me again?'

'Fairly last minute, I think,' Emmaline said, with a smile that barely reached her lips, let alone her eyes. 'I think your father called mine last Sunday and asked us to join him. We were supposed to be going to my brother in Hampshire, but...' Shrugging, she trailed off.

Last Sunday. After he'd visited for lunch with Celeste, then. Suddenly, Theo was very suspicious about the presence of his unexpected guests.

'Didn't my mother tell me you were recently engaged?' He glanced down at her ring finger, and found it bare. Ah.

'It got called off.' No smile at all this time, understandably, just a tight, pinched look.

'I'm sorry.'

'No need to be sorry!' Hugo said, from in front of them. 'All for the best, I say. Plenty more fish in the sea, after all, right, Emmie?' He shot his daughter a significant look, then moved his gaze onto Theo.

Right. Of course.

The sequence of events was falling into place perfectly in his head now. He'd brought Celeste to lunch; his parents had been horrified. So, of course, they had to find someone more 'suitable' for him. And who could possibly be more suitable than the recently dumped daughter of his father's richer-than-sin best friend? The Howards had no title, or pretensions to one, but they had a lot of money. While Theo and his family had the cache of being on the fringe of the aristocracy.

He was sure his father would have preferred he marry someone with money *and* a title, but needs must. And they were obviously very set against Celeste.

It almost made him want her more.

But most of all, it made him want to take a stand against his parents. To step outside the toxic circle they surrounded him with whenever they were together. To tell them, finally, that enough was enough.

He was himself. *He* was enough. And he'd fall in love with whoever the hell he wanted, regardless of what they thought about it.

Not that he was in love with Celeste Hunter, of course. But the principle remained.

And for once, Theo didn't think his usual survival tactics of staying silent and trying not to care were going to get him through Christmas Day with the family. Because he saw things differently now. More clearly.

Thanks to Celeste.

'I really am sorry about this,' he murmured to Emmaline as they entered the sitting room.

She shrugged thin shoulders. 'Could be worse,' she said. 'My brother's wife has eight dogs, and only half of them are house-trained. At least I don't need to worry about that here.'

A ringing endorsement of their Christmas, Theo thought.

At least he wasn't standing in dog muck. Yay him.

It wasn't enough for him, any more. He was done being grateful to be part of the family, to have the name and the face that had put him where he was. He was worth more than that. He wasn't a disappointment—not to himself. At least, he *wouldn't* be, if he kept going after the things that mattered to him. He had more to give than just a charming smile and a posh accent. He could do more than marry money or fame.

And he had to tell his parents that. Today.

Celeste's parents were not, by nature, early risers. But since Damon and Rachel appeared to be fuelled solely by love that Christmas morning, by the time she'd shooed Theo out the front door and ventured into the kitchen in search of coffee, it seemed the whole house were up and ready for the day.

They were also all staring at her.

'What?' Did she have her dressing gown on inside out? Or were Theo's pants stuck to it, somehow? She'd thought this morning couldn't get more embarrassing, but she was willing to be proven wrong.

'I met your young man again on the stairs this morning,' her father said, over the rim of his coffee cup. 'He seemed to be leaving in a hurry.'

Celeste winced. 'Well, it's Christmas Day. He had to get back to his own family.' Poor sod. 'Did Damon and Rachel tell you their happy news?'

'They did.' Her mother poured her a cup of coffee— steaming hot and black, no sugar, the way they all took it. Damon joked it was the only thing all four of them actually had in common.

'Are you ready to reconsider the whole black for the maid of honour thing yet?' she asked Rachel. At least if her best friend was marrying in, she'd always have someone on her side in family debates.

Unless Rachel took Damon's side, of course. Hmm, maybe she hadn't thought this through well enough, when she'd encouraged Damon to follow his heart.

Rachel shook her head and turned her attention back to her coffee—milky white and loaded with sugar, just as she'd drunk it at university.

'Celeste, we're worried about you,' Damon said. Her parents nodded in agreement.

Wait. What?

'The three of you are worried about me?' She kind of needed the clarification. After all, she couldn't remember the last time it was Damon and her parents against her, instead of her and their parents against Damon, when it came to family disagreements.

She was the one who did everything her parents expected of her, followed the path they'd walked first, became what they'd hoped for in a child.

But apparently her sleeping with a TV star was where they all drew the line.

'Possibly for different reasons,' Damon said, giving her a look she knew all too well. It was his 'our parents are ridiculous' look. 'But all *four* of us are concerned.'

Oh, God, he was bringing Rachel into it now. He'd be talking about them as a pair *constantly* now, saying 'we think this' or 'we like to do it that way' as if they were so fused together it was impossible for them to have different thoughts or opinions on anything.

She hated it when people did that. She'd never imagined her brother would be one of *them*.

But then, she'd never imagined he'd agree with their parents about anything, but here they were.

'You too?' she asked her best friend.

Rachel gave her an apologetic smile and a small shrug. 'I don't want you to get hurt, that's all.'

Celeste raised her eyebrows. 'Seems to me I was saying the same thing to you not so long ago…'

'The point is, darling, that you need to think seriously

about how this looks.' Her mother rested her hands on the kitchen table and looked earnestly at Celeste.

'How it…looks?' Had she just not got enough sleep, or was this really as weird as it felt?

'For your career,' her father put in. 'How it looks to the university.'

'It's bad enough doing those puff pieces for those podcasts.' Diana shook her head at the very idea. 'But doing seasonal novelty television as well—and now cavorting around with that TV presenter, too!'

'Nobody is going to believe that you're serious about your research if you're peddling history-lite to the masses,' Jacob said firmly. 'And really, being seen with That Man is just another sign to everyone that you've made your choice—and it's not the right one.'

Celeste could feel strange emotions bubbling up inside her. Ones she wasn't used to feeling. This went beyond irritation or frustration. Yes, she snapped at people all the time when they interrupted her, and she got frustrated when people wouldn't just see that she was right. But those feelings were nothing like the anger that seared through her now.

'Let me get this straight,' she said, her voice clipped. 'Damon, you and Rachel are concerned because you think I'm going to get my heart broken by a TV heartthrob who is only dating me for the publicity, right?'

'Pretty much,' Damon replied.

'And Mum, Dad. You're worried that I'm sabotaging my academic career by taking on TV projects, and that associating with Theo will affect my position at the university.'

Jacob beamed. 'Exactly! See, Diana, I told you she'd understand.'

Celeste's smile felt wicked on her lips. 'Oh, I understand. I understand that you're all very, very wrong about me. And maybe I've been wrong about you, too.'

She spun towards Rachel and Damon. 'I appreciate your concern, guys, but, trust me, everything is fine. Theo and I have an understanding. This isn't like your festive fling, or whatever. That was always just a stupid excuse for you two to have sex without thinking about the consequences. Theo and I know exactly where we are— and it's not leading to flashy diamond rings on Christmas Eve. He's using me for the publicity, and I'm using him for that too—ready for the new TV show I've signed up to hopefully present next year.' Her mother gasped at that. Celeste didn't turn her head, but out of the corner of her eye she could see Diana resting her head dramatically against Jacob's chest. 'The sex,' she added, for impact, 'is just for fun. Nothing more.'

'Now hold on a moment. What is this about a TV show?' Jacob asked.

Celeste moved to face her parents now. 'And you two. You don't care at all that the guy I'm sleeping with is using me. You don't care about my heart, at all. You're just worried that I might show you guys up on the lecture circuit, that your colleagues will think you produced a lightweight, right?'

'Darling, *we* know you're a perfectly adequate historian,' Diana said.

Behind her, Celeste heard Damon smother a laugh.

Perfectly adequate. That wasn't, surprisingly, the part that got to her. It was the way they thought of her as a historian first. That really was all she was ever going to be to them, wasn't it? Or rather, she mattered more to them as an academic than as their daughter.

Suddenly, she had a feeling she knew how Damon had felt all these years.

She was more than just an academic or historian. She was a storyteller. She could bring history to life and share it with others, help other people to feel the same passion and enthusiasm she felt for the past. Show them how the present, the world they all lived in, was built on events that had happened decades or centuries before. How knowing the *truth* about the past made understanding the present—and the chance of change for the future—possible.

Why it mattered—not just to her, but to society.

Theo had shown her that.

'I don't want to talk about the TV show today,' she told them, calmly. 'We're not going to agree on it, I can see that. I believe that history belongs to everyone, and it's important to share it with anyone willing to learn it. I don't want to lock it up in academic texts—I want to live it, to show how it connects with the everyday.'

Her parents stared at her. They didn't get it. She'd known they wouldn't.

She took a deep breath. She'd said her piece about Theo. It was Christmas Day, and Damon and Rachel had just got engaged. And she needed to do a hell of a lot more thinking before she was sure what any of this meant for her future.

But she could see a conversation—no, an argument—with her parents in her future, about her career. And for the first time in her life, she realised that it didn't matter what they wanted or expected from her. She was never going to win their respect the way she'd always dreamt of.

But she could respect herself, and her own achievements. And maybe that would be enough.

'Come on,' she said. 'It's Christmas. Let's…let's just forget all this, just for today. Who wants a Bucks Fizz while we open presents?'

Damon squeezed her shoulder as she headed for the fridge to find the champagne and orange juice, and Rachel gave her a sympathetic smile.

But it didn't stop Celeste wishing that Theo were there, too.

Christmas Day seemed to go on for ever.

From the strategically placed mistletoe that somehow he and Emmaline kept being directed towards, to the barbed comments at dinner, and the discovery that the Howards would be staying until Boxing Day, Theo was exhausted by the time the clock chimed ten, and his mother yawned for the third time, and he figured he could reasonably excuse himself to bed.

To bed, but not to sleep. He had a call to make, first.

Celeste had never been far from his thoughts that day. In some ways, it had felt as if he were watching the whole scene through her eyes. He could hear her sharp comments and smart observations in the back of his mind, all day long.

Now he wanted to hear them for real.

He made it as far as the stairs before his father caught up to him—a surprise in itself. Normally he preferred to demand that people come to him.

'Theo. Son,' he said, and Theo turned, already on the fourth step, to face him.

'Yes?' Maybe this was a Christmas miracle, after all. Maybe his father was about to tell him he was proud of him—and even if it was all down to the whisky, Theo knew he'd take it.

But, no.

'I hope you appreciate the effort that everyone here has put in today to helping you,' his father said. 'And what you need to do next, in return.'

Theo blinked, slowly. 'I'm sorry?'

'I know you're not the smartest tool in the box but damn it, Theo, I thought even you'd be able to figure this one out.' Francis Montgomery's face grew redder with frustration, as well as alcohol. Theo just watched.

He felt strangely detached from the situation. He could see his mother coming up towards them now, carefully closing the door to the room where the rest of their party sat, to spare them hearing this, he supposed.

'Why don't you tell me, Dad?' His voice was calm, too. Calmer than he'd expected he'd manage. There was none of the energy he displayed on camera, and no smile, either. As if he felt nothing at all. 'What is it, exactly, that you're expecting me to do to win your favour?'

'As if you don't know!' Francis blustered, taking a step up the stairs. 'All you've ever needed to do was bring some sort of good to this family. We weren't expecting much from you, but really! Just marry a girl with money and save the family estate, how hard is that? We even *gave* you the girl today, gave you every opportunity, and you didn't make the smallest effort with her! If we have to sell this estate, it will all be your fault.'

Theo was glad of the calmness that flowed through him, wherever it came from. As his father grew angrier, the calmness only increased, letting him see the man before him more clearly than ever.

'No,' he said simply. 'It won't. *You* couldn't save it, Dad. *You* weren't good enough, not me.'

'Theo, don't you speak to your father that way! He's never said you're not good enough.' An outright lie from his mother. It didn't surprise him. She always liked to rewrite events to suit her own narrative.

But Theo was done believing it.

'I want you both to listen to me, for once,' he said. 'I

am not going to marry Emmaline, not least because she doesn't want us to get married any more than I do. In fact, I'm not going to marry anyone just because they have money, or because you approve of them. That's not the world we live in any more, in case you haven't noticed.'

His parents were uncharacteristically silent, so Theo carried on, amazed at how good it felt to say the words at last.

'If you want to save this house, save it. Don't expect me to do it for you. Because honestly? I'd rather you sell the place anyway.' His mother gasped at that, and his father's face turned an even more extreme shade of puce. But Theo didn't care. Because it was true. He didn't want Sorrelton House and all its memories—especially since so few of them were good ones.

He wanted his own life. His own decisions.

He wanted to find out for himself who he was and what he could achieve—not what his parents had always told him he couldn't.

'I don't need anything from you any more,' he said, feeling the truth of the words as he spoke them. 'Sell the house, do whatever you want with the money—I have my own. I have my own life, my own career, and you know what? I've worked damn hard to get where I am, and I'll keep working for the life that I want. Away from here.'

Then he spun round and jogged up the stairs, whistling a Christmas carol as he went.

He'd leave this place tomorrow, and he wasn't sure he'd ever come back. Wasn't sure he'd be welcome, even if he wanted to.

But that was okay.

He could find his own future now.

Theo changed out of the dinner jacket and bow tie he'd been expected to wear for Christmas evening at Sorrelton

House, and into a comfortable pair of sweatpants and a faded and worn T-shirt. Then, leaning back against the headboard of his bed, he relaxed his shoulders for the first time in hours, and called Celeste.

'Hey.'

'Hey. You in bed?' She picked up far too quickly to be in company. Or maybe he just liked the idea of her in bed. Preferably his.

'Yeah.' A rustle of sheets as she stretched out. He could imagine her there, in the bed they'd shared the night before. He liked that he could picture it perfectly. That he could see her in his mind, if not in reality.

Careful, Theo.

He was treading a line here, one he'd been teetering on for so long he'd almost stopped noticing it. It would be oh-so-easy to slide over to the other side.

Except he had a feeling that the line might actually be a cliff edge, and he didn't want to fall.

Theo pushed away the thought that it could already be too late.

'How was your Christmas Day?' he asked, settling himself down more comfortably against the pillows.

'It started with a family intervention about my sex life, but after the fourth Bucks Fizz things started to improve. How was yours?'

'My parents hustled me up a rich and recently dumped date for the occasion. She cried every time she saw the mistletoe they'd hung around the place.'

'Ouch.' He could picture her wincing, but also trying not to laugh. 'They hated me that much, huh?'

She was so quick, his Celeste. 'Apparently so.'

'Well, the good news is, my parents hate the idea of you just as much. Apparently, you're going to ruin my career prospects.'

'Probably true,' Theo admitted. 'You start hanging around with a lightweight like me for too long, they'll assume your brains have rotted out your ears.'

'Hey,' she said softly. It was a voice, a tone he'd not heard from her before. Gentle. Caring. 'Don't say that.'

He could get used to that voice.

'How are the happy couple?' he asked, shifting the conversation somewhere more comfortable. 'Did they at least get to celebrate in slightly more style than when they woke us up?'

'They're worried you're going to break my heart.' The mocking edge to her words told Theo exactly how ridiculous she thought that was. 'I reminded them that we had an agreement, and that this was all for show anyway.'

'Exactly,' Theo said, pushing away the part of his brain that had just been hoping for more. 'I mean, we could probably stop it now, if you wanted. Can't imagine anyone is going to be paying much attention to us over the festive period anyway, and we've kind of achieved what we set out to do.' Except then he'd never get to see her face as he told her how he'd stood up to his parents. Never get to see that small smile as she nodded and told him he'd done the right thing.

'The world no longer thinks you're a hideous, mansplaining arse-wipe,' Celeste said eloquently.

'And the TV-viewing public knows who you are, now,' he replied. 'So we're kind of done.'

'Yeah. I guess we are.'

The pause that followed was just about long enough to give him a tiny bit of hope back. Enough to say, 'Of course, if you wanted a last opportunity to laugh at me, I'm doing a freezing cold Boxing Day river swim in Henley tomorrow morning. I could pick you up on my way, if you wanted. Regale you with my Christmas Day recap—including a last-minute showdown with my father in which his face turned a shade of magenta not found in nature.'

It was, of course, completely out of his way, but he didn't feel like mentioning that.

'A wild swim?' Celeste laughed. 'Yeah, okay. I'd like to watch that. And hear about your showdown. Although I think nature really does have most shades of magenta, you know.'

He ignored that last bit, still smiling about the first. 'And then I'm supposed to be showing my face at some cocktails in igloos thing on Sunday,' he added.

'I've never had cocktails in an igloo before.'

'Apparently it's something everyone should try at least once in their lives.' Theo wondered if she knew how much he was making it up as he went along now. Talking absolute rubbish just for the excuse of seeing her again.

Probably. She was the smartest woman—smartest person—he'd ever met. She knew. And she was letting him get away with it. Why?

Maybe because she wants to spend more time with me, too. He hoped so anyway.

'Then how could I pass it up?' she said, laughing. 'Pick me up in the morning, and we can discuss whether swimming in the freezing cold Thames in December is better or worse than Christmas with our families.'

CHAPTER ELEVEN

IT WAS STILL dark when Theo picked her up from her parents' town house the next morning. They'd barely got off the phone six hours earlier, so she hadn't had time to go home to her flat for fresh clothes, but fortunately her personal uniform of black, black and more black made it easy enough for her to dress from the stash she'd left in her childhood bedroom when she moved out, and still not look out of place.

'Why are you doing this, again?' Celeste settled into the passenger seat of Theo's sports car, while he dumped her bag in the back.

'Same reason I end up doing most things that seem like a bad idea at the time,' he replied, starting the engine.

'Publicity,' they both said, at once.

'Are you comparing sleeping with me to swimming in the freezing-cold Thames?' She shifted sideways in her seat as he pulled away from the kerb. The position had two advantages: one, she could watch him better, and two, she could curl up here and get some more sleep while he drove.

'I'm comparing dating you in public to the Boxing Day Swim,' he corrected her. 'Sleeping with you was an added bonus.'

'I'm glad to hear it. And I want to hear about your showdown with your father, too.' Celeste yawned.

'Later,' Theo said. 'Get some more sleep for now.'

'Okay.' Her eyes fluttered shut as the motor purred, lulling her back to sleep.

When she awoke again, the built-up streets and buildings of London had given way to a gentler countryside—although Celeste knew they weren't far from the city centre, really.

Henley-on-Thames was only an hour's drive from London, and, given the early hour and the bank holiday emptiness of the roads in the pre-dawn, Celeste was pretty sure Theo had made it in considerably less. The Oxfordshire market town was famous for its Royal Regatta in the summer, which she could imagine Theo having to attend as part of his social obligations. It seemed *just* the sort of thing his parents would want to be seen at.

Somehow, a wild swim on a December morning seemed much more Theo-like, to her.

She hoped that his conversation with his parents would help him find more things that were more Theo-like, too. She liked Theo-like. And she was definitely still too tired to think properly if that was an actual sentence in her head.

Theo parked the car and they headed out together to find the other swimmers. There were more of them than Celeste had imagined would think this could possibly be a good idea, all lined up in swimsuits and blue-tinged skin.

'You don't even get to wear a wetsuit?' she asked Theo, incredulously.

'Apparently not.'

'There you are!' A young guy in a thick fleece coat hurried over to them, pushing through the crowd of warmly dressed bystanders who'd come to watch the spectacle. 'I was starting to think you weren't going to make it. Now, the camera crew is standing by to film the whole thing, but they'd like to get a quick chat with you before *and* after the swim, okay?'

Theo nodded. 'Fine. Remind me, how far am I swimming, Gaz?'

'Just seventy metres or so,' Gaz said. Celeste shivered in sympathy. 'From the hotel over there to some club down river, where they'll fish you out. The camera guys are going to follow you in the boat.'

'Great.' Theo looked as if he was starting to seriously reconsider his life choices. Celeste didn't blame him.

'I'll get you some coffee ready at the other end?' she suggested.

Gaz had other ideas. 'We definitely want to get some footage of you cheering on your man too, Celeste. And a kiss at the end would go down a treat, yeah?'

He turned away, heading back to where the camera guys were waiting, leaving Theo and Celeste alone for a moment, before the insanity of the Boxing Day swim started.

'Guess I'm still a publicity asset after all,' Celeste said, unable not to watch as Theo stripped down to his swimming shorts. *God, he looks cold.*

'Guess so.' He flashed her one of those TV smiles. How he could smile like that, half naked in the frost, she had no idea. Must be level one TV training, or something.

It occurred to her, not for the first time, that she might never actually know what Theo was thinking. He was so good at hiding it all behind that made-for-TV facade of his. She'd pegged him as a faker their first lunch together, but knowing he was faking was only part of it. Being completely certain when he *wasn't* was much harder.

How much of their fake relationship was really fake and how much was really real? And how could she ever be sure?

The dark thought clouded her tired brain, and she couldn't seem to shake it away. So she tried a little fakery of her own, instead.

'Well, I'll have your coffee *and* your kiss waiting for you, then,' she said brightly. Then, pressing a swift kiss to his cheek, she headed off down the bank to where the other spectators were gathering to watch the swimmers set off.

'I don't think I'm ever going to be properly warm again,' Theo lamented, several hours later, as they headed back towards London in his convertible, heating on full.

'Well, if you hadn't fallen back in, after you got out in the first place, you might have warmed up sooner,' Celeste said, unhelpfully.

He shot her a glare. 'If you hadn't been doubled over with laughter, you might have helped me out.'

'I'd have spilt the coffee,' she countered.

Theo shook his head. All he knew was that there were going to be photos of him floundering around in the water like a drunken duck, and his supposed girlfriend laughing uproariously at him, all over the Internet by teatime. So much for regaining his dignity yesterday, by finally standing up to his parents. At least he didn't have to deal with what his father might have to say about the whole debacle debasing the family name any more.

'Want me to see if the photos have hit the Internet yet?' Celeste asked, reading his mind, as always.

He sighed. 'Might as well, I suppose. I'm sure they've been on social media for ages. See if they've hit the news pages yet, though.'

Her winces as she scrolled through her phone told him everything he needed to know.

Well, so he looked like an idiot. Again. It was all people really expected of him anyway. He was that nice but dim TV presenter, the unthreatening boy next door, the safe crush for teenage girls and grandmas alike.

Pretending to date Celeste might have actually given him some intellectual and personal cache for once, but nobody expected it to last. Least of all him.

He knew his place in the world up to now. A rich kid without *quite* enough money, an aristocrat without *quite* enough connections, an average learner with a wasted education, one he couldn't even quite see through. The only thing that would impress his parents was if he married someone who'd bolster the family finances and/or social credibility—which he'd now told them he had no desire to do. And even if he had gone along with their plans, he was sure that within the year his mother would have been bemoaning the fact that he could have done better, and his father would be accusing him of not trying hard enough.

But where had trying hard ever got him, really?

It got you Celeste.

Not for long.

The victorious feeling he'd felt after standing up to his parents was already draining away like the freezing water he'd swum in. He'd closed one door, but had he really opened another? Yes, he wanted to go his own way, do his own thing. He just wasn't entirely sure what that way, or thing, was. Other than finishing his degree at last, and carrying on with work as always, what would really change?

'How bad is it?' Even humiliating photos had to be better than this train of thought. He could laugh them off, the same way he laughed off every insult and barb from his parents over the years, every time he was told he wasn't good enough. Every person who walked away when they realised that he wasn't quite enough of anything, after all.

'I mean… *I* think the way you're floundering around on the bank is quite endearing, really. Possibly.'

Theo smiled. From Celeste, that was positively a compliment. At least she was trying to make it less awful for him. She wouldn't have bothered to do that when they first met.

'So, hilariously humiliating, then?'

She nodded. 'Definitely going to be the funny story at the end of the news tonight, sorry.'

Theo sighed. He expected nothing less, really.

'Wait, though…'

He glanced across at Celeste and found her frowning at her phone. 'What?'

'There's a link to another article from this morning… Hang on…'

Maybe the bad feeling rising in his stomach had to do with how much of the River Thames he'd swallowed that morning.

But maybe not.

'What is it?' he asked, when she didn't say anything.

'Shhh. I'm reading.'

There was a junction coming up, and Theo took it, swinging off the motorway and into the forecourt of a service station. 'Show me,' he said, parking the car.

Silently, Celeste handed the phone over. Well, that wasn't good for a start. Celeste was seldom without something to say on a subject.

Theo scanned the article on her phone. Oh. Well, he didn't blame her.

'This was from when you took me to the Cressingham Arcade, before Christmas?' he guessed.

Celeste nodded. 'Must have been. Don't know why we didn't see it before now, but I suppose it's only been a few days.'

They'd been shopping for a present suitable for his mother, since he'd left it to the last minute as usual. Celeste had suggested the arcade where her brother and Rachel were working, so they'd popped there after one of their regular 'out to be seen' lunches together.

And apparently someone had snapped a photo of them supposedly looking at engagement rings at the grumpy old jeweller's shop.

Following the links in the article, he traced the story back to its original source—a tweet posted by a random member of the public, four days ago. 'Looks like it was just some normal person posting it, and they misspelt the hashtag, so it took a while for the gossip sites to pick it up.'

'So, the world thinks we're getting married? Our parents are going to hate that.'

Theo chuckled. 'They definitely are.'

'Good thing it's not true, then.'

And it was. A good thing. Because he wasn't looking to settle down and get married, not even just to prove a point to his parents. And if he were... He and Celeste were from different worlds, different expectations, and different ambitions. He was populist, she was highbrow. He was lightweight, she was a walking history textbook.

She'd be bored of him in no time, and he was sure he'd be a disappointment to her the same way he'd always been to his parents.

Except...if his parents were wrong, if he'd stepped out of that toxic family circle and accepted that maybe there was more to him than they saw...what if Celeste could see that too?

As he pulled back onto the motorway, he couldn't help but let a little hope bubble up inside him.

Theo dropped her back at her own flat, and for the first time since Christmas Eve Celeste finally had space to think. To figure out what the hell was going on in her head—and in her heart.

The rest of the journey back from Henley-on-Thames had been mostly silent. And knowing how badly Theo had needed a shower and a sleep, she hadn't even considered inviting him up to the flat with her.

But now she was there, alone with her thoughts, she almost wished she had. If nothing else, Theo was always a pleasant distraction.

Except he was so much more than that. That was the problem.

They needed to talk. They'd gone into this as a fun scheme, a trick to play on social media, almost. A way to rehabilitate Theo's reputation after Celeste's performance on the *Christmas Cracker Cranium Quiz*, and to raise her profile ahead of her potential TV show.

A TV show she'd heard nothing but warnings from her parents about all Christmas Day, even after she'd told them she didn't want to talk about it, to the point where she was starting to wonder if they might even be right. Oh, not about the need to share history with anyone willing to learn it; she still believed that. But was she really the right person to do it? Was she choosing a career in media as a mediocre historian over her academic focus? All her life, she'd followed the path laid out for her by her parents, but now she was standing at a fork in that road, and choosing the one they'd put 'do not cross' tape over.

And that led her right back to Theo.

She and her agent had pitched the show before she'd met Theo, of course, but back then it was just a concept, a possibility. Now, her agent was emailing daily with updates instead of monthly. Apparently, her raised media profile had everyone keen to get moving with the project, and it looked more like a sure thing every day. And while she'd planned to be mostly consulting and narrating, now they wanted her front and centre on camera.

They'd even changed the title of the show to include her name. Suddenly, it was more about her than the history, than the stories of ancient women she wanted to tell.

She wasn't an idiot. She knew all of that was because of Theo, not her. But what would happen when Theo wasn't part of her life—or her image—any more?

Because he wouldn't be.

They hadn't expressly discussed breaking up, but the plan had never been a long-term one. They lived in different worlds, for all that she might be inhabiting his for a little while. She had research to do, a book to finish, a name to make for herself in her chosen niche.

The TV show was one project, one year. What about the rest of her life?

Theo had talked about what might happen next for her over dinner one night, while they had both studiously avoiding looking at the guy seated at the next table taking their photo.

'You've got your foot in the door now, and that's all it takes,' he'd said, while feeding her one of the prawns from his starter. 'Radio appearances was one thing, but once you're on TV once, that's it. You'll be the channel's go-to expert on all things historical.'

'But I'm *not* an expert on all things historical,' she'd

pointed out. 'I have a speciality. *That's* what I'm an expert in.'

'You know more general history than almost everyone else in the population,' he'd countered. 'That's what matters. They'll rope you in for all sorts of historical programmes now—look at that guy who does all the science stuff. What's his name? He's a physicist, but he ends up on shows about all sorts.'

He was right, Celeste knew now. Her area of expertise was women's history, especially women in the ancient world. But already she'd found herself approached to talk on other topics. Topics that fascinated her, sure, but they weren't her niche. They weren't what she was supposed to be talking about.

Like the history of Christmas. She'd spent a week reading up on that before the quiz show, and look where that landed her. At dire risk of falling for a guy who was only in it for the publicity. And who would always belong to a world she wasn't sure she wanted to be a part of.

She pulled her phone back out to look again at the photo of her and Theo at the jeweller's shop. They hadn't been looking at rings, of course. But some strange emotion tugging at her heart kept whispering, *What if you had?*

Stop it. She wasn't going down that road.

She swiped out of the browser and checked her message and email notifications instead.

Eight messages. Two from Rachel, one linking her to the article about the jeweller's and asking if there was something she needed to tell her, and one with a link to a navy bridesmaid's dress with the word Compromise? underneath. One from Damon that was just a picture of Theo falling in the water at the wild swim and a lot of laughing emojis.

Two from her mother, obliquely mentioning Theo's existence and her disapproval of it, and another one from her father doing the same but without any of the subtlety.

One from her agent, with a thumbs-up emoji next to a photo of her and Theo, and a note about a meeting with the production company first thing in the new year.

And one from Theo, of course.

Igloo cocktails tomorrow. I'll pick you up at eight. x

CHAPTER TWELVE

Igloos on a roof terrace in a city centre, with integral champagne bars.

'Only in London,' Theo observed as they stood outside their own private igloo and took in the city skyline.

The igloos themselves had a large window built in—or left open, really—to enjoy the views, but since Theo had a feeling it would be even colder in there than outside, he was putting it off for the moment. He still hadn't fully warmed up since his dip in the Thames, and even the fake fur coats provided by the owners of the establishment weren't doing much except make him feel like an extra in *Game of Thrones*.

'Mmm,' Celeste agreed absently as she leaned against the railings to look out.

She'd seemed mostly absent since he picked her up. As if her body was present, but her mind had gone wandering. When he'd asked her about it, she'd muttered something about her book, and research, and thinking through ideas.

He was glad she was able to think about work. Because the only thing *he'd* been able to think about for days now was her.

Whatever this thing between them had morphed into, it wasn't what they'd agreed at the start. Which meant they had to talk about what happened next. And that meant talking about what had happened on Christmas Eve, too—and if she wanted it to happen again.

Theo had done a lot of thinking the day before, once he'd warmed up enough for proper thoughts, but he wasn't sure he'd come to any sensible conclusions. Despite it being Boxing Day, and a bank holiday, his agent Cerys had been on the phone the moment she'd seen the pictures of them at the jeweller's shop in the arcade, asking what was going on.

'I told you that you could call it off,' she'd said, sounding amused. 'Do I take this to mean you're heading in a rather different direction?'

'It wasn't what it looked like,' Theo had told her tiredly. 'But…but if it was, would it be so bad?'

Cerys had paused at that, and when she'd spoken again, he'd been able to hear the surprise in her voice. 'Well, I guess that depends on your perspective. I mean, getting married to anyone would kind of dampen your crush appeal a little bit, and I'm guessing you wouldn't want to court social media by appearing in public with up-and-coming celebrities on your arm any more, so there's that. But stars settle down and it doesn't ruin their careers or anything, if that's what you mean. But really, Theo…her? Are you sure? She decimated you on that quiz show. To be honest, I thought there was solid chance she'd do worse than throw coffee over you on that first date.'

'She doesn't like it when history doesn't tell the truth,' Theo had replied, automatically. 'And the answers on those cards were wrong. Well, incomplete, at least.'

Cerys had laughed at that. 'Well, that tells me everything I need to know. You've got it bad. Good luck with that, then.' And she'd hung up.

Theo had wanted to call back, to tell her that Celeste wasn't the person people seemed to think. That, maybe, neither was he.

Because when he was with Celeste, he believed that there was more to him than he'd ever been led to believe. More than just a rich kid with every advantage who still couldn't be anything more than a nice smile and a winning personality.

Something more than just the Montgomery name, as his parents believed, or his face, as the viewing public seemed to think.

The question was, did she feel the same way when she was with him? Or, as he feared, did she think he made her less?

Unfortunately, there was only one way to find out. And that meant having a conversation he wasn't at all sure he wanted to have.

The one about what happened next.

He waited until they both had fresh drinks, and had taken their icy seats inside the igloo. Celeste still seemed a little as if she were on another planet, but she smiled at least as he handed her an extra blanket, laying it out across both of them as they looked out of the cut-out window.

'If I interrupt your thinking will you throw a drink at me?' Theo figured it was best to start with the basics and work up.

Celeste turned to him with a smirk hovering around her lips. 'You're tempting fate just asking, you realise?'

'I know.'

She sipped at her drink. 'But luckily for you this cocktail is too delicious for me to waste it on you. And I'm being a terrible fake date, right? Sorry. Am I supposed to be fawning over you more?'

'No one is looking,' Theo said. It felt weirdly uncomfortable to hear her talk about them that way, after everything. 'And besides, I think we're past all that now, aren't we?'

'*Are* we?' Celeste asked. 'Have you seen the photos from the Boxing Day swim? Whoever is in charge of social media over at your channel has been having a grand old time showcasing our relationship right alongside the listings for your New Year's Eve show.'

'That's just coincidence. And that's not about us anyway.'

'Except it is, right?' Celeste pressed. 'I mean, right from the start that's exactly what we were about. Putting forward the right image for you—and for me too, I guess.'

He didn't like where this was going. Something was twisting in his gut, and he didn't think it was the cocktails.

'At the start, sure. But after Christmas Eve—'

She interrupted him with a laugh, high and tinkling, one that barely sounded like Celeste at all.

He was missing something here. She hadn't been like this at Henley, had she? What had changed since yesterday?

The photo of them at the jeweller's. Was that what was bothering her?

'Is this about the photos yesterday? The stories about us getting engaged?'

'Why would it be about them?' She looked down into her glass as she spoke, and Theo knew she was avoiding his gaze. He was right, even if she wasn't going to admit it. 'They were just stupid stories. We know it's not like that between us.'

'Right.' Except... 'Why isn't it?'

Her shocked gaze met his in an instant. 'What do you mean?'

Theo took a breath. This was it. His chance.

He wanted this feeling to last—the feeling he had when he was with Celeste. Which meant being honest with her. Being real. No TV charm and smile, no spin for social media. No faking.

Just him. And her.

'Why isn't it that way between us? I mean, not getting married exactly, but…we've had fun, right? Together? We could keep having fun, maybe?'

No.

She'd thought she could read him, but she'd never seen this coming. She'd known he was a faker, but she'd never though he'd take it this far.

She'd thought she'd known what she was doing, but now she was pretty sure she had no idea at all.

'I think we should break up. Fake break up. Send a press release, whatever it is we need to do to end this.' Celeste started to stand up, pushing the blanket away from her lap, before she realised she was about to bang her head on the rounded ceiling of the igloo, and sat back down.

She wanted to get away, but she didn't want an audience for this, either. So apparently, she was having the most important conversation of her life so far that didn't take place in front of an academic board in an igloo. Because that was the sort of thing that happened when a person hung around with Theo Montgomery for too long.

'You think… Why?' He shook his head as he looked at her. 'You can't tell me we're not good together. Christmas Eve—'

'Was lovely,' she interrupted him again. The only way

she was going to get through this was by not letting him talk too much. That silver tongue of his could probably talk her into anything; wasn't that how she'd ended up in this mess to begin with?

'So what's the problem here, exactly?' Theo asked.

'You and me…it's been fun,' she admitted. 'But it hasn't been real, we both know that. Hell, that was what we agreed! It was all for show. And yes, I'm attracted to you, yes, I had fun with you—'

'Then why—?'

'But that doesn't change the basic facts of this situation,' she shouted over him.

'And those facts are?' His voice was calmer than she thought she'd ever heard it before. He almost didn't sound like himself. Everything about him was always so alive, so full of fun and mischief. But right now he sounded as dry as her last boyfriend, the philosophy student.

As if this wasn't an act at all.

Don't think about that.

'We come from different worlds,' she said slowly. 'Yes, I'm dabbling in TV, but I've spent my whole life building up my academic career.'

'And you think that continuing to be seen with me would undermine your credentials. I'd make you look lightweight.'

'No! That wasn't what I—'

'Wasn't it?' His mouth twisted in an unfriendly smile. 'Or is it worse than that? You've had your fun with me, but I'm not an intellectual match for you, right? You were slumming it with the stupid TV star for a while, having fun looking at my little history essays for my meaningless bachelor's degree, but I'm never going to live up to those professors you meet at conferences, or whatever.'

'You're not stupid,' Celeste said quietly. 'I never said—or thought—you were stupid.'

'Didn't you?' Theo shook his head. 'Then you must have been the first. If you think I don't know what people say about me—' He broke off.

'Look, it's not you,' she said desperately. 'It's me. And, God, I know that's the most overused line in break-up history, but really. Think about it. I'm grumpy and hyper-focussed, I have no ability to connect with people, really. I can't help but tell them when they're wrong. Your parents hate me—'

'Yours hate me, too.'

'True. And maybe…maybe they're right.'

'To hate me?' Theo's eyebrows went up at that.

'No! They think…they think that your lifestyle, your fame, would distract me from my studies. It would lead me away from academia into the sort of history lite you see in bad documentaries on TV. Like you said, the producers don't care about my area of expertise—history is just history to them. I wouldn't be taken seriously as an academic any more.'

'You might have a lot more fun, though,' Theo pointed out quietly. 'You *love* history, Celeste. Not just certain parts of it—all of it. Is it really so important to you to be an expert in one thing, rather than good at lots of it? More than sharing it with the world?'

'Yes.' Because it always had been. That had been the message from her parents from her earliest days. Find what you're passionate about and pursue it with everything you have. Don't look left or right, don't get distracted. Find what matters to you and make yourself matter.

Damon had gone the other way entirely, but she…she'd embraced the philosophy. She'd gone after academia, a professorship, as her ultimate goal. Working to publish her academic tome on women in history, to prove her place in the canon. And if she gave it up now...what did that leave her?

She'd only ever been good at talking to other academics. If she tried to teach the Great British Public about history instead...would they even listen?

What if she was just wasting her time?

This wasn't one fun quiz show where she was a novelty, a festive amusement. And it wasn't being seen around town with Theo, a curiosity. This was trying to be the real thing, and make people listen to her—when the only person outside academia and Rachel who'd ever done that was Theo, and she didn't even know for sure that he wasn't just faking it.

The university was safer. She knew the rules there, had been training for it all her life.

Life with Theo was the opposite of safe. It was people watching her, commenting on her all the time. It was expanding her secure little bubble so much further outside the university than she'd planned.

This wasn't a one-off TV show. This was a career change—a life change—she wasn't sure she was ready for.

Theo's jaw was clenched, as if he was holding in all the words he wanted to say. He always did, she realised suddenly, surprised that she knew such a detail about him. But this was how he'd been at lunch with his parents, too. Biting his tongue, holding in everything he was thinking.

Was that just how he'd been brought up? Or was it part of who he was now? All the years smiling for the cameras, being the nice guy...hell, he'd only fake dated her in the first place to preserve that image.

But Celeste wanted to hear what he *really* thought, not what he believed he *should* think.

He'd said it to his parents on Christmas Day, by all accounts. How much had that taken out of him? To finally speak up to them?

It didn't look as if he was going to do the same for her, though.

He threw down the rest of his cocktail, swallowing it fast, and slamming his glass onto the ice table. Getting to his feet, his head still bowed to avoid hitting it on the ceiling, he gave her an awkward nod. 'Do you need me to take you home?'

'Theo…' She trailed off. What could she say? He'd asked for something she wasn't ready or able to give. How could she now ask him to stay?

She shook her head. 'I'm fine.'

'In that case… I'll see you around, Celeste.' He turned and walked out, leaving her alone in the icy shelter.

She wished her heart were as frozen as the igloo. Then maybe it wouldn't hurt so much.

'Are you sure you're okay to do this?' Cerys asked as Theo had his mic checked for what was hopefully the last time.

'Of course, I'm okay. Why wouldn't I be?' He wasn't even sure what his agent was *doing* here for the *New Year's Eve Spectacular*. She didn't normally come to his filming, but maybe she had nowhere else to be for the biggest party night of the calendar.

Although he supposed he was sort of *hosting* the biggest party on that biggest party night. Other people probably really wanted to be there. Even if he was wishing he were anywhere but.

'Because you've been—how can I put this?—not your charming self over the last few days.'

Days filled with last-minute meetings and planning, and absolutely no Celeste. Except for the photos of her, which were still all over social media, and people asking him about her.

There was even one photo of her leaving the igloo bar, after him. He'd been staring at it for days now trying to figure out if her eyes in it were red from crying or the cold.

Probably the cold. This was Celeste, after all.

As she'd told him, she didn't really *do* people. At least, not ones who weren't dead and were without an interesting backstory or place in history.

He'd known. He'd known from the start that he couldn't fit into her world, that she'd be another person he wasn't good enough for. And yet he'd let himself hope…

She was the one person who'd made him believe he was more than his name or his face, more than his TV-star status, and more than his parents told him he could be.

It just turned out *she* didn't believe it.

'And now you look like you're trying to burn down the Tower of London with lasers from your eyes,' Cerys went on. 'Is this about Celeste?'

He spun away from the Tower to face her. 'Why would it be about Celeste?' And who the hell decided to do the filming here, where he had to look at that place—the place he'd kissed her properly for the first time—all night long?

Probably him, in one of those meetings he hadn't been paying attention in.

'Because you haven't been seen with her in days, you haven't mentioned her name once until now, and you've

practically growled at anyone who mentions it to you.'
Cerys was not a touchy-feely, reassuring agent. The fact
that she felt the need to pat Theo's arm gently was a definite warning sign that he was losing it completely. 'What
happened, Theo?'

'We ended it,' he said, with a shrug.

*She ripped half my heart out with an ice pick, froze it
and used it to cool her cocktail.*

'It was all very mutual and friendly. After all, we
were never *really* together in the first place, remember.'

*Even if it felt like we were. Even if it felt like every-
thing.*

'Right.' Cerys did not look in any way convinced.
'Did you tell her?'

'Tell her what?' he asked, confused.

'That you're in love with her.'

He had enough practice at looking amused when he
wasn't from listening to the poor jokes told on various
shows he'd hosted, but it still took everything in his
power to laugh at Cerys's words, when what was left of
his heart felt as if it were trying to break out of his body.

'Why on earth would I tell her that?' he scoffed.

Cerys rolled her eyes and patted his arm again. 'Just
get through tonight, yeah? Then we can go get really
drunk and you can cry on my shoulder for a while, and in
the morning it'll be a brand-new year and you can move
on. Well, after the hangover subsides.'

He waited until she'd moved out of his line of sight to
let his amused smile drop.

Oh, God, he was in love with Celeste Hunter. How the
hell had that happened?

The worst part was, he knew *exactly* how and when
it had happened, and he hadn't done anything to stop it.

No. The worst part was that she didn't love him back.

But the *second*-to-worst part…he'd fallen for her the moment she'd scowled at him, maybe. Or when she'd thrown coffee over his lap. Or when she'd sat in a hot tub on a boat and looked so adorably baffled by the whole experience. Or when he'd kissed her on the ice rink across the river at the Tower. Or when she'd sat through a hideous dinner with his parents. Or when she'd talked to him about history and expected him to keep up. Or when she'd told him he was nothing like the man his parents thought he was. Or when she'd kissed him in the hallway and taken him to bed. Or when she'd pulled him out of the river, or when she'd sat with him in an igloo…

The truth was, he hadn't fallen for her once. It hadn't been love at first sight. It had been love, inch by inch. With every story about a ghost bear or the truth about Christmas trees. He'd been fascinated from the start, but the love…that had crept in, without him even knowing it was there.

Until it was so much a part of his heart he thought it might stop beating without it.

God, he was pathetic.

But he didn't have time to dwell on that right now. He had a show to present, and a cheery persona to find again. Cerys was right: he could mope once the work was done, and not before.

Turning his back firmly on the Tower of London, Theo took a deep breath, turned to the anxious-looking production assistant hovering nearby, and said, 'I'm ready.'

CHAPTER THIRTEEN

'WHERE HAVE YOU BEEN?' Rachel asked as Celeste eased her way through the crowds of people at the Cressingham Arcade, all there to celebrate her brother and best friend's engagement, and the new year, not necessarily in that order.

'Sorry, I got caught up writing, lost track of time,' Celeste lied. Well, sort of lied. The losing track of time part was real. The writing, less so.

Seemed as though ever since she'd let Theo walk away so she could focus on her academic writing, she'd written less than ever.

Rachel gave her the sort of look that told her she wasn't buying it at all, then led her over to where the bar was situated, at the back of the arcade. Right next to the jeweller's shop, where she'd been photographed with Theo.

That was the real reason she was late. She hadn't wanted to come. Damon had bought her a T-shirt with that on it one year: 'Sorry I'm late, I didn't want to come.' She should have worn it tonight.

She'd only been here with Theo for an hour or so, and yet it was already filled with memories of him. Her parents' house was unbearable, and she wasn't letting herself anywhere near the Tower of London.

She wanted to stay safe, locked away in her office, where there were no memories of Theo to distract her.

Rachel shoved a champagne flute into her hand. 'Okay, time to talk. What's going on? It's to do with Theo, I take it?'

Celeste looked at her best friend—newly engaged, madly in love, with newfound confidence at work and in herself—and burst into tears.

'Right. This way, then.' Rachel bundled her towards a door, hidden away in the wall between two tiled pillars, and pushed her through it. Together, they climbed a metal staircase to a balcony Celeste hadn't ever even noticed from the ground floor.

Sitting with their backs against the door, champagne glasses in hand, the two best friends looked up at the painted ceiling of the Victorian shopping arcade.

'What do you see?' Rachel asked.

Celeste blinked as the ceiling came into focus. 'Butterflies!'

Dozens of tiny painted butterflies, so realistic she almost thought one might flutter down and land on her outstretched finger.

'Damon brought me up here, the first time I visited the arcade,' Rachel said. 'He showed me so many secret things about the place. But that's not why I fell in love with him.'

'Why *did* you fall in love with him?' As much as Celeste loved her brother, she wasn't sure he was an automatic catch for any woman, and she still thought he'd probably got the far better end of the bargain in marrying Rachel.

'Because he showed me the secret places inside me, too,' Rachel said.

Celeste pulled a face. 'If this is a sex thing, I really

don't want to hear it. That's my brother, remember, and I'm having a hard enough time this week as it is.'

Rachel laughed, the sound ringing off the metal railings. 'That's not what I meant! I mean…he showed me who I could be, if I let myself. If I believed in myself, even—believed it was possible, and went after it.'

'And here I was thinking *you* were the one who showed him he could fall in love, and stop jumping from one thing to the next,' Celeste replied, bumping her shoulder against her best friend's.

'Maybe that's the point,' Rachel mused. 'We both changed—or rather, we both found the parts of ourselves we'd stopped believing in, over the years.'

'That sounds nice.'

'It is,' Rachel agreed. 'So, what did Theo teach *you* about yourself?'

'What do you mean?' Celeste started at the question, and Rachel rolled her eyes.

'Come on, it's obvious that you've fallen for him. You're madly in love and, to be honest, I think that was kind of inevitable from the start.'

'Coming from someone who tried to claim that she was having nothing but a "festive fling" and ended up engaged before Christmas morning,' Celeste grumbled.

'So I know what I'm talking about.' Sighing, Rachel rested her head against Celeste's shoulder. 'It's just me, Celeste. Tell me everything.'

Celeste took one last look up at the butterflies, free and wild and unreal on the ceiling, and started talking.

She told her about the kiss on the ice rink, about the way Theo actually listened when she talked about weird historical facts, and didn't mind—even liked it—when she corrected those things that everyone thought they knew. She talked about how his parents hated her, and hers hated him, and how she didn't care. Because her parents only cared about her career, and his parents only cared about their name and their money, so why should either of them care what they thought anyway? And she talked about Christmas Eve, and the wild swim and the jeweller's photos and then she talked about the igloos...

'Why?' Rachel asked. 'Why did you tell him that your academic career was more important than what's between you? I know you better than that, Celeste, even if he doesn't, yet. You're not your parents, even if you think you are. So why?'

'You're not your parents.'

She wasn't sure if she'd ever realised how much she needed someone to say those words to her.

'Because... I was scared.' Rachel would know how much it cost her to admit it. She'd always powered through life, pretending she didn't care when people laughed at her, or rolled their eyes and walked away when she corrected them. 'He's not like me, Rach. People *like* him. He's friendly and nice and gorgeous and popular and—'

'And you didn't think you could have that?'

'I didn't think I could keep it. I still don't. I'm not good at people—everyone knows that about me. So I pretended it was all about work, and my academic reputation, because I didn't want to admit the truth. I'm in love with him and it would hurt like hell when he walked away from me like every other guy in my life has, when they realise that this is just me. I can't not tell them when they're wrong. I can't play nice with their parents. And I'm going to forget about important dinners and stuff if I'm reading something interesting.'

'Or abandon your brother and best friend at a party while you escape to the library,' Rachel added, mildly.

Celeste rolled her eyes. 'It was nine years ago, Rachel. Are you two ever going to forgive me for that?'

She grinned. 'I think we probably will. And I think Theo would too, if you asked him to.'

'If I admitted I was wrong?' That…did not sound like the sort of thing she would do.

'Is he worth it?'

'Yes.' The word was out before she could even think about it. 'But he was talking about a casual thing. We never said anything about love. And I don't think I could take it if—'

'Give him a chance,' Rachel suggested. 'You never told him you loved him, either, right?'

'No.'

'So tell him. Tell him you were wrong and that you love him.'

'And what if he says he doesn't love me back?'

Rachel gave her a sympathetic smile. 'Then you're no worse off than you are now. And at least you'll know, yeah?'

'I suppose.' It still sounded like a risky deal to her.

'Just…trust me, okay?' Rachel said. 'The people we love are worth taking a chance on. Even if it means admitting we're wrong, sometimes.'

'Damon taught you that too?'

'And you.' Rachel flashed her a grin. 'After all, it's hard to be best friends with you for a decade without admitting you're wrong a couple of hundred times.'

'Very true.' Celeste got to her feet, saying a silent goodbye to the butterflies. 'So, this is your engagement party. I'm guessing a good maid of honour would stay until the end?'

'As long as you promise me you're going to find Theo and not run off to the library, I'll cover for you.'

Grinning, Celeste pressed a quick kiss to her best friend's cheek and raced down the stairs.

It was almost a new year. And she had to do something very important before the clock chimed midnight.

He could feel the Tower of London looming behind him, reminding him of everything he was leaving behind in the old year.

Even as midnight approached, and the crowd of revellers along the banks of the Thames grew louder, and more excitable, Theo couldn't get himself in the right mood. Oh, he pasted on the work smile and played the part, but inside, he was thinking. Hard.

While the band of the moment played their last song before the midnight countdown, he used the break to marshal his thoughts into an order—or rather a list.

New Year's Resolutions.
One: Finish my history degree.

He'd been working on it part-time for years now, and it was time to wrap it up. Not least because he knew, deep down, he'd only been putting it off because he still didn't feel he deserved it.

Well, sod that. He'd done the work—or most of it anyway. Even Celeste had said it was good. So he'd finish the rest. He'd earned it. It might not be an Oxbridge first, but it was something he'd worked for himself, without any extra credit for his name or his face, and that made it all the more valuable to Theo.

Two: Figure out what I want to do next.

He'd told his parents it wouldn't be what they wanted. Maybe he needed to say the same thing to the TV studios. Take a break, and figure out what it was that he wanted to achieve. To do something for himself, for a change. He'd made enough money from his TV career—probably even enough to save a money pit like the family home if he wanted to, which he didn't. He could afford to take a break, a step back at least, while he got his head straight.

His whole life, he'd tried to make nice, to keep everyone on side, to earn *someone's* approval at least. Hell, even fake dating Celeste had been about winning back public approval, to start with. And where had that desperate need to be liked got him?

Well, actually, it had got him pretty far in his career, he thought, looking out over the crowd cheering the band up on stage. But in his personal life?

He supposed it had brought him to Celeste, but it hadn't been enough to let him keep her. And it had also brought him to the place where his parents thought it was okay to try and arrange a marriage for him to further their own ambitions.

That was not okay. And he'd told them so. He wanted to keep that feeling of freedom he'd experienced when he'd done it.

New Year, new Theo.

They'd called—well, his mother had, merrily whitewashing the whole of Christmas Day as if it had never happened. And normally he'd let her get away with it.

Not this time.

He'd go and see them again, as they'd asked. But he was standing firm, now. He'd tell them that he had his own life, his own career. That he was happy and successful. That if he ever married it would be because he loved the person, and it wouldn't matter to him what they thought of his choice. Because they'd never really been particularly pleased that *he* was their son. Never said they were proud of him, or that they loved him. Only ever pointed out his faults.

And he had no intention of letting them do that to his wife, or any children that might be in his future.

He'd put up with it his whole life, but that was no reason anyone else had to.

What else could he put on his list for his best year ever?

Three: Fall in love.

Except he'd already done that, hadn't he?

He shook the thought away. The band were coming to the end of the song, and he could feel the atmosphere rising around him as midnight drew closer.

This was why he loved his job; being around so many people at moments like this, connecting with them, helping them celebrate, feeling a part of it all.

He just wished Celeste were there to share it with him.

The last chord rang out across the crowd, rippling over the river, past the Tower of London behind him. The giant video screen they'd set up at the edge of the water switched from showing the band on stage, to showing him again—then split to show a live image of Big Ben, further down the river.

'It's nearly time, guys!' Theo yelled into his mic, earning a roar of excitement from the crowd in return. 'Are you ready to count down with me?' Another screaming affirmative.

He waited until he got the signal in his earpiece, pressing it into his ear and concentrating to make sure it didn't get lost in the noise of the party below.

'Ten!' he shouted, knowing from there on he was almost obsolete. He'd given them their starting line, and from here the crowd would take the momentum he'd built and run with it.

Except there was something happening, just below where he stood on the stage. Something distracting the crowd from the most important countdown of the year.

'Nine,' he yelled, almost a millisecond too late, as he frowned down at the scene. What was happening down there?

'Eight!' There was someone pushing through the crowds.

'Seven!' Someone with dark hair.

'Six!' And a familiar white coat.

'Five!' And bright red lips as she smiled up at him. *Celeste.*

He lost his place in the countdown for a second, as he tried to process the reality of her being there, now.

'Four!' he yelled, slightly behind the rest of the crowd. The people at the front of the crowd were helping her up onto the stage now. Everyone knew who she was, clearly. And who she was to him.

'Three!' She stood before him, eyes hopeful, biting her lip.

'I couldn't start the new year without you,' she shouted, the words hitting his heart.

'Two!' He hadn't moved. He needed to move, to respond, something.

Celeste took a step back, and he reached out to grab her hand and pull her close against his side, as the crowd screamed for them both.

'One!' He looked Celeste in the eye and hoped she could read in his face everything he couldn't say. At least, not without the crowd and millions of TV viewers hearing it too, through his microphone.

The confetti cannons went off, the balloons sailed down river, and Big Ben bonged to mark the end of one year and the start of another.

'Happy New Year!' Theo yelled, to the crowd, to the viewers, to Celeste and to himself.

And then he kissed her, in front of millions of people, and there wasn't anything fake about it at all.

Celeste fell into his kiss as if she'd been waiting aeons for it, not days. She didn't care who was watching, or what anybody thought. She just knew she was where she belonged. Standing in the shadow of the Tower of London, kissing the man she loved.

Oh. She should probably tell him that, shouldn't she?

'I love you,' she murmured between kisses.

'I love you, too,' he replied, just as an almighty crash tore through the air as the fireworks started. They turned to watch as the sky over the Tower was lit up with colours and patterns, and 'Auld Lang Syne' kicked in on the bagpipes over on the other stage.

'I'm sorry.' Now she was here, she felt the desperate need to tell him all the things she hadn't, that night in the igloo. 'I was a fool. I was scared.'

'Me, too,' Theo admitted. 'Think that maybe we could be scared together?'

She smiled up at him. 'If I'm with you, I don't think I'll have to be afraid.'

'Not ever,' he promised.

Celeste snuggled into his arms as the party continued below.

'How much longer are you hosting this shindig for?' she asked.

'We're live for another fifteen minutes. But after that… I'm all yours.'

'For ever?' It was a big ask. Too big. They still hadn't talked about all the reasons she'd pulled away, or why he'd let her. All the things that were holding them back from the lives they could be living, together.

'If you'll have me,' Theo replied, and she knew suddenly that none of it mattered.

Yes, they had plenty of stuff to work through, but it would all be easier with each other by their sides. They had a whole new year stretching out before them—a whole new life, even—in which to work out the details.

'Always,' she replied.

There was an anxious-looking production assistant waving at Theo from just off camera. Celeste waved back and pressed a quick kiss to Theo's cheek before starting to move away.

Theo grabbed her back and kissed her properly, on the lips. 'Don't go far.'

'Promise.'

She slid away, out of camera view, and watched as the live broadcast on the big screen lit up with Theo's face again. She hid her smile behind her hand as she realised he had her pillar-box red lipstick liberally smeared around his mouth. *Oops.*

'And that's it, folks!' Theo said finally, wrapping up the live broadcast. 'The old year has passed, the new one is here. No need to stop celebrating though! And I hope the rest of your night—the rest of your year, for that matter—is as incredible as I hope mine is going to be. Happy New Year, Britain!'

More cheering as the cameras panned out over the crowds, the river and the Tower of London again. Theo shook hands with a dozen or more people as he made his way towards her, but Celeste didn't mind the wait.

He was right. They had a whole year to make special—and, she hoped, a whole lifetime. Together.

Finally, he reached her side and took her hand in his. 'Ready?' he asked.

'For what?'

'Our future.'

Celeste smiled. 'Absolutely.' History was her first love, of course. But even it couldn't live up to the prospect of a future with the man she loved more than anything.

* * * * *

THE MILLION-DOLLAR QUESTION

KIMBERLY LANG

To Marilynn, Terri, Sunny, Angela, Stacey, Marbury, both Melissas, Anna, Andrea, India, Kelly, Buddy, Chris, Susan, Nelson and the whole ASFA dance department for all the stories that start with, 'There was this one time, during Nutcracker…'

CHAPTER ONE

"SOMEBODY'S GOT A hot date."

It was hard for Olivia Madison to both roll her eyes and apply mascara at the same time, but she managed it—just barely. Rehearsals had run long today and she was now running late. She didn't have time for this. "It's not a date."

Her roommate, Annie, flopped across the bed and examined the outfit Olivia had laid out for tonight. "Hmm…Silky top, the 'good butt' jeans and 'take me' boots. You curled your hair, you're wearing makeup, and…" She stopped to sniff the air delicately. "I smell perfume. All signs point to a hot date. And it's about time. I was getting afraid we'd have to get a couple of cats soon and the lease doesn't allow pets."

"First of all, neither of us is in Cat Lady territory just yet. Getting married and having babies is what your thirties are for. Second, it's just dinner. Pretty much a business dinner, at that."

Annie still wasn't convinced. "In that outfit? Please. Did you shave your legs?"

Olivia had, but that was neither here nor there and had nothing to do with the person she was meeting for dinner. "It's with my brother's college roommate, for goodness sake."

"Is he cute?"

Olivia had to admit he was. She'd looked him up online to see if he'd changed much in the past nine years, rather hoping to find that he'd developed a paunch or lost a lot of hair, only to be disappointed in that hope. If anything, the past decade had been quite good to Evan Lawford, maturing his features—and even the attitude he projected in the photos—light-years past the frat rat she remembered. The sun-bleached hair had turned darker, probably meaning he didn't spend as much time on the beach as he used to, but the color offset his blue eyes nicely. The cheekbones and the jawline she remembered quite well, only the two-day stubble look was also gone. The difference between boy and man was stark and startling at first.

Objectively speaking, Evan Lawford was *hot*. Male-model-broodingly-advertising-expensive-suits-in-a-glossy-magazine hot. "It doesn't really matter. He's a jerk."

"Which means he *is* a hottie, and that's just wrong." Annie sighed and rolled to her back. "Why can't the really nice guys be drop-dead gorgeous, too? Is that really too much to ask?" she pleaded to the universe.

"All signs point to *yes*." Olivia tossed the mascara tube back into her makeup bag. *Jerk* was a nice word for Evan. He was a cocky, arrogant, ego-ridden player.

But he was a *successful* cocky, arrogant, ego-ridden player, and that was what was important at the moment. She'd have to suck it up and deal with the rest.

"So why are you having dinner with him then?"

Because I'm forced to sell myself out in order to further my career. That wasn't entirely exactly true: no one at the Miami Modern Ballet Company expected her to actually sleep with someone for their money, but the trade-off still gave her icky vibes. "I need him to sponsor me."

Annie's forehead wrinkled in concern. "Like a twelve-step kind of sponsor? Are you okay?"

Olivia kept the sigh—and the smart-ass comeback—behind her teeth. It wasn't all that unexpected of a speculation, and at least Annie was asking it from a place of concern. Olivia had left home at fifteen to spend the next decade in studios and on stages, driving herself to reach this point: a contracted principal in an established, prestigious ballet company. Therefore, everyone assumed that she had to have something wrong with her—drug habit, an eating disorder, or even just a flat-out psychotic break à la *Black Swan* picked up along the way. She nearly snorted. There probably *was* something wrong with her, only they didn't have an official diagnosis for it yet.

And while she'd known Annie for only a few months—trading the privacy of having her own place for the opportunity to live near the beaches and nightlife of Miami, even with an unknown roommate—they were getting along very well. "Not that kind of sponsor. An actual please-donate-your-money kind of sponsor."

Annie looked confused. "You're fundraising?"

"In a way. Money is tight all over, and the arts are really feeling the pinch," she explained, slipping into her jeans. Annie averted her eyes as Olivia dressed, but Olivia had lost any kind of modesty years ago through one too many quick changes backstage in view of the entire corps and stagehands. "Our state funding has been slashed, ticket sales are down and corporate sponsorship in general is not as strong as it used to be. So nowadays, rich people can adopt a dancer of their very own. In return, they get all kinds of perks—tickets, backstage passes, first dibs on tables at the En Pointe Ball and for the big spenders," Olivia continued, as she pasted a smile on her face and added a chipper tone, "the chance to have their dancer appear at their corporate—or sometimes private—events."

"That sounds cool." Her forehead wrinkled. "But kinda creepy, too."

"Tell me about it."

"And you need one of these sponsors? I thought you had a contract."

Annie, who worked as a Spanish-language interpreter for the city, was getting a crash course in the state of the arts in America these days. "I do, but my contract isn't cheap. And while MMBC has the option to pick up my contract for next season, there's no guarantee that they will—especially if I'm the only one without sponsorship to offset my cost. Sponsorship doesn't guarantee anything either way, but it won't hurt."

"I see. So you're hoping your brother's college roommate has that kind of money?"

"I know he does. I haven't seen Evan in years, but he and Jory are still real tight." Why that was, she didn't quite know. Evan had nearly succeeded in turning Jory into a carbon copy of himself in college, and while Jory had turned out okay anyway, she didn't really understand what the two men could possibly have in common. "He's got the money." She frowned at the mirror as she finger-combed out the curls and sprayed her hair into place. "I just need to figure out how to ask him for it."

"Why can't you just ask him outright? It seems pretty straightforward, and it's a tax deduction to boot."

"Yeah, but it's…" She wasn't sure how to explain it, even if she wanted to. Which she really didn't. "It's complicated."

"Complicated?" Annie's forehead wrinkled again, then smoothed out as understanding dawned. "*Oh. That* kind of complicated."

"Let's just say that it's not complicated enough to keep me from asking, but complicated enough to make me want to handle the situation delicately."

"If it's going to be awkward, why not just call your brother instead? Get him to play middleman."

"No." *No way.* That was a can of worms she definitely wasn't going to open.

"Then maybe your brother or your parents could sponsor you, instead?"

She knew Jory. Telling him she needed sponsorship—or any money, really—would lead him to opening his checkbook. He'd tell Mom and Daddy, and they'd want to do the same. And that was *not* going to happen. Jory needed to be investing his money into his own business, and Mom and Daddy needed to be saving for retirement.

Mom and Daddy were comfortable enough, but they'd sacrificed greatly over the years to support her dream. So had Jory, in fact. She wasn't going to take another blessed dime from them. Any of them.

She shook her head. "They're in Tampa, and the sponsors need to be local." Even as she said it, she had no idea if it was true. The company probably assumed sponsors would be local—and that was how the donor rewards were structured—but she couldn't imagine any company turning down money, regardless of the source. Still, it was a clean and quick explanation, and Annie accepted it at face value.

"That's a problem, then."

"And I've been in Miami for only three months. I don't really know anyone else." She paused in zipping up her boots to look hopefully at Annie. "Unless you happen to have thousands of dollars tucked away and a hidden, burning desire to support the arts in your community?"

Annie shook her head. "Uh, no."

"Then I'm off to dinner with Evan." She took one

last critical look in the mirror, then turned to Annie. "How do I look?"

"Amazing, as always. And, as always, I kinda hate you for it. If you can't win Evan over with logic or reason, you should be able to flirt his checkbook right open." Annie rolled off the bed and got to her feet. With a cheeky grin, she added, "I won't wait up for you."

Olivia had no intention of flirting with Evan at all. She could be polite and friendly, but this was merely business. She'd flirted with him that one time, and the lessons learned stuck with her to this day. But she was older now, wiser, and she could look back on it for the educational experience it was, without feeling the pain or shame.

Much.

The restaurant Evan chose to meet her at was only about six blocks from the condo she shared with Annie, and Olivia elected to walk it. Eventually, she'd have to buy a car—an expense she'd managed to avoid for at least the past five years—but for now, Miami's public transport could get her pretty much anywhere her feet couldn't.

It might be November, but she didn't need a sweater. However, she grabbed a pashmina in case the air conditioning in the restaurant was set on "Arctic." After spending so many winters in more northern climes, it was so *so* nice to be back in Florida, with her winter gear shipped home to Tampa to the storage unit she kept there. The sun had been down for an hour, but the temperatures were still in the high seventies, perfect for a walk, but it was a little jarring for it to be that warm as businesses took down their Halloween decorations and replaced them with a mix of turkeys and Santa Claus.

She could come to really love Miami. MMBC was a highly respected company with a great mix of classical and contemporary in their repertoire. It may be not as prestigious as some in New York, but the trade-off was a lower cost of living and fewer up-and-comers nipping at her heels all the time. She could still do the occasional guest artist thing when the traveling bug bit her or things started to feel stale, but Miami was a great base.

And she needed to start thinking about the future, anyway. If all went well, she could get another six, maybe seven, years in before retiring, but she was feeling the effects of the past two decades already and her chances of injury increased each year. She needed to be building some kind of foundation, and Miami was ideal for that.

Plus, it was only four hours from home.

All this was great. Provided she could keep the job she'd worked so hard to get. The fact she was willing to turn to Evan Lawford proved how much she wanted her contract picked up for next season. That would give her time to build a reputation and network here in Miami and increase her chances of further seasons exponentially.

She just had to get through dinner with Evan and get his agreement first.

Easy-peasy, right?

Oddly, Evan hadn't asked many questions when she'd emailed him, saying hello and asking if he'd like to get together. She'd provided her phone number, but he'd stuck to email, setting up the place and time with the minimum amount of communication necessary. She wasn't sure if that was a good thing or a not.

It had taken courage—more than she thought she'd need for something so simple—to email him in the first place, but he'd accepted so quickly that she'd only had forty-eight hours to figure out how to actually pull this off.

Evan and Jory were friends, practically brothers. Although she'd not been there to see it, she knew Evan loved her parents and had spent a lot of weekends and holidays at their house instead of his own. Her parents loved him. But that had nothing to do with her, and she couldn't cash in on her parents' kindness or Jory's friendship like some kind of promissory note owed to her.

But *they* weren't friends. They were just two people in Jory's orbit, basically little more than strangers.

Okay, they were *more* than strangers. She just wasn't sure where on the hierarchy of relationships to place her brother's roommate when he was also the guy you lost your virginity to in what turned out to be only slightly more than a one-night stand.

Ugh.

While she'd felt hurt and used at the time, perspective could offer the balm that it probably hadn't been personal. And realistically, he'd most likely saved her from making a similar mistake later on—when she would have been alone, surrounded by strangers, and even more vulnerable. Naïveté was a dangerous thing.

The truly embarrassing part was that she'd known exactly what he was going in to it. Hell, he'd taken Jory into his decadent world of wine, women and song, debauching him quite thoroughly. But with the arrogance only a teenager could have, she'd believed she was different. *Special*.

Combined with Evan's combo of charm, good looks and raw sensuality, that arrogance had easily overwhelmed and shouted down anything she'd known merely intellectually.

That was the rational, reasonable part of her brain. The same part of her brain that turned that burn into something useful, allowing her to focus on her training instead of getting wrapped up in messy entanglements that could have complicated her life unnecessarily. So that was good.

Parties, boyfriends…all those things she'd been told she'd have to sacrifice for her career didn't seem like so much of a sacrifice after that. Or at least not an overly painful one.

Her inner eighteen-year-old still held a grudge about it, but she'd need to keep *that* safely hidden away.

Even if *Evan* felt remorse over the whole sorry incident, she wasn't sure that was something she could—or wanted to—play on, either. She'd look foolish and

ridiculous and hopelessly naive—and petty and ma-
nipulative to boot.

Nope. That little lost weekend needed to stay lost.

She was an adult; he was an adult. This was a purely
business transaction, albeit with a personal glaze. But
there was no crime in networking the contacts you had,
personal or not.

Be friendly. Be businesslike. Evan was a successful
businessman. According to Jory, Evan's advertising
agency was growing in phenomenal leaps and bounds,
and he should appreciate a professional approach. There
was no need to jump right in with the request—a little
pleasant small talk always greased the wheels nicely.
She would put the sponsorship out on the table early,
giving him plenty of time for questions and plenty of
time for her to convince him. If all went well, she could
walk out of here tonight with his commitment and the
ballet's business manager could get the good news by
class tomorrow.

If all went well.

And there was no reason why it shouldn't.

"Good evening, Mr. Lawford."

The valet at Tourmaine opened Evan's door and
greeted him with a smile. Tourmaine was his go-to
place for entertaining clients—modern enough to feel
on trend without being trendy, music loud enough to
hear and enjoy without hindering conversations, and,
most importantly, good food and a staff that knew

him—and his tipping habits—well. "Good evening, Brian."

"Enjoy your meal."

"Thank you." A banal, basic exchange of pleasantries, but one that he needed to remind him that the world hadn't, in fact, gone insane.

Because barring that, he had no idea why Olivia Madison wanted to have dinner with him.

He knew, of course, that she'd moved to Miami. Jory had been ridiculously proud of his sister's accomplishment, and they'd had dinner back in the fall when Jory came to see Olivia's first performance with her new company. But Olivia hadn't joined them, and Jory didn't bring up his sister unnecessarily.

Evan hadn't seen Olivia since she was eighteen, and that was definitely intentional. The only thing that had ever come between him and Jory was Olivia, and they'd nearly come to blows over her, doing damage to their friendship that had taken time to repair. He didn't know how twitchy Jory might be about it these days, but it wasn't something he wanted to stir up—not until he at least knew why Olivia had contacted him in the first place.

Miami was plenty big enough for them to never come in contact with each other at all, and he assumed that was exactly how Olivia—and Jory, as well—wanted it.

So an email out of the blue from her with a dinner invitation had to be viewed with some level of suspicion, yet there was no way he could not have come. If only to find out why.

Yep, that was his story and he was sticking to it.

He was a few minutes early, but Olivia was already there, the unusual coppery-blond hair both Madison siblings inherited from their mother easy to spot in the small crowd of people around the bar. She was in profile to him, reading something on her phone, giving him the chance to examine her at leisure.

She'd been baby-faced at eighteen, but far more mature in some ways than others her age—by then, she'd already traveled and lived abroad, a professional in her career when most others were still figuring out their future. She'd said she'd wanted a taste of real college life, the same as anyone else, and there hadn't been a good reason not to indulge her—and himself at the same time.

The baby face was now gone, replaced by chiseled cheekbones and winged eyebrows that gave her a classical, elegant look, emphasized by the impossibly good posture and movements that were effortlessly graceful—even those as simple as ordering a drink or walking toward him…which she was now doing, a hesitant smile on her face.

"Evan. It's good to see you."

While her tone sounded sincere, he doubted it was completely true. There was a moment of hesitation, then she leaned in for one of those air-kiss things. Her cheek touched his accidentally and she jumped back as if she'd been scalded. He wouldn't deny it: it sent a bit of a jolt through him, as well. He cleared his throat. "And you."

The initial pleasantries finished, they stood there in an awkward silence, and he wasn't used to awkward silences. "You look good," he managed.

There was a small tug of her lips that stopped short of a smile. "So do you."

More silence.

Thankfully, the hostess arrived to save them. "Mr. Lawford, we have your table ready."

Following Olivia to the table gave him another chance to study her, and goodness, she was thin. She'd always been on the slight side, a necessity of dancing, but *wraithlike* was the word that came to mind. It was a good thing they were in a restaurant, because the need to feed her something was nearly overwhelming. She was also taller than he remembered, just a couple of inches shorter than his six-two, and only part of that height came from the boots she was wearing.

Long soft curls hung to the middle of her back, and a gold chain belt hung loosely around her tiny waist. Mile-long legs ended at slightly turned-out feet, giving her walk an unusual cadence that was still somehow graceful and smooth. Chin up and shoulders back, Olivia had presence.

He couldn't take his eyes off her. And that had gotten him in trouble before.

He shook his head to clear it. *Of course* the woman was thin and graceful. She *had* to be. That was a job requirement, and from what little he did know, Olivia Madison was good at her job.

Safely seated in the high-walled booth he favored

for its privacy, the awkward silence that had started in the bar was easy to fill with menu discussions and ordering. He couldn't stop his eyes from widening as she ordered a meal almost as big as his, and as the server walked away, she noticed. "What?"

"That's a lot of food."

She shot him a look. "If it's a problem, I'm perfectly happy to pay for my own dinner."

"That's not what I meant."

An eyebrow arched up. "Really? What did you mean then?"

Her tone could be called innocent and inquiring, but he realized the danger underneath just a second too late to pull the words back. "It's…well, you…" He usually wasn't foolish enough to bring up weight and diet with any woman, but he'd already stepped into it. "I guess I expected you to order a small salad with dressing on the side."

She snorted. "Maybe for the *first* course. But I spent six hours in rehearsals today. I'm hungry."

"Okay, a *large* salad, then," he teased.

Olivia folded her hands primly on the table, and as she spoke, her tone clearly said this was a speech she'd given many times before. "I eat. I have to. I work my body hard, and my body needs fuel to do that work. I stay aware of my weight, but not in an unhealthy manner. Since I'm not obsessing over it, I'd appreciate it if you didn't either. Okay?"

Duly chastised, he nodded. "Okay."

Then she leaned forward. "And seriously, they put

blue cheese *cream* sauce on a *steak* here. How am I *not* going to order that?"

"Fair enough." She talked a good game, but he'd withhold judgment until he actually saw her eat something. He worked in advertising, for goodness sake. He knew about models and the things they did to lose weight, but he had to admit that Olivia wasn't skeletal or starving—she was very slim, yes, but she didn't have the hollowed-out sickly look. "It's just surprising."

She inclined her head, and reached for her water.

"But not as surprising as hearing from you."

Olivia's hand froze, making him suspicious all over again. She recovered quickly, though. "I'm just full of surprises then. Honestly, I feel I've been rather rude not getting in touch before now. My only excuse is that I've been unbelievably busy the last few weeks—getting settled, with rehearsals for the fall performance, and then straight into *The Nutcracker* and the winter special that's coming up in January...I haven't had time to even think."

He'd known Jory for over twelve years, and his sister shared many of his mannerisms, making her somewhat easier to read than the average person. Olivia wasn't fully at ease in this conversation, which wasn't surprising. There were many reasons—beyond the busyness of her life—not to have been in touch before now, but there was no sense bringing those up just yet. That piqued his curiosity further, but he found that he wanted to make her comfortable, nonetheless. The past was bound to come up eventually, and it would be better to have a friendly footing before that happened. "But you're feeling more settled in now?"

"Yeah. I'm not getting hopelessly lost every time I leave the house these days, which is good. And it's nice to be home in Florida, where I can go to the beach anytime I want. Even in November."

Via Jory, he knew Olivia had done recent stays in Chicago and Boston, where the snow would be enough to drive any Florida native to the brink of insanity. "Which beach is your favorite?"

Her mouth twisted. "I haven't actually gone, yet. Like I said, I've been busy."

"Are you some kind of workaholic?"

"I believe that when you love your job, it's not exactly drudgery to put the time in."

"That's not an answer."

"I work a lot, and I like it. How's that?"

"That's a good answer. I might have to use that myself in the future." He paused as the server brought their drinks. Then he lifted his glass to her. "And congratulations on landing the new job."

She accepted his toast, a real smile replacing the hesitant one. "Thanks. It's exciting. MMBC—the company—normally chooses its principals from inside, but they decided to open the search this time. I knew one of the company members from years ago when I first went to New York, and he brought my name up to the artistic director. All the stars just aligned perfectly to get me here." She seemed as if she was just winding up, but caught herself instead, reaching for her wineglass and sitting back against the leather seat. "But what about you? Jory says your agency's doing really well."

"I can't complain. We're only three years old, and we still have some growing to do, but we're good."

"That's great to hear. I'm happy for you." Olivia stared at her glass, pondering the depths of pinot gris, and silence settled again. Then she looked up at him again with that smile he was beginning to think was definitely fake. "Jory's coming down with my parents in a couple of weeks to see the performance."

"I know. We're planning to get together while he's here."

"Oh, good."

"He says your parents are very excited."

"They don't get to see me in action very often because I'm usually so far away. I send videos and stuff, but it's not the same for them. And honestly, I'm excited they're getting to come, too. You know," she added casually, "if you'd like to come with them to the show, I can get you a ticket."

"Oh, hell, no." The words slipped out before he could check them. *Damn it. Insult the woman's career. That's always a great dinner conversation topic.* "I mean, no thank you. I'm not really a fan."

"Of *The Nutcracker* or ballet in general?"

"Both. No offense," he added. "It's just not my thing."

"None taken. We like what we like." She was being gracious, but he still felt as though he'd offended her. "Are you into the arts at all?"

He shrugged. "I used to have a membership to the art museum. I like the Egyptian stuff. There are a few local bands I keep up with." Lord, he sounded like a cultural wasteland. He justified it by saying, "Getting the agency off the ground has kept me pretty busy."

"I'm not judging."

Her smirk implied otherwise. "Yes, you are."

She shrugged a shoulder. "Okay, maybe a little. The arts celebrate what makes us human. They are the cornerstone of civilization and the heart of a community."

He nearly laughed, but swallowed it at the last second. Olivia obviously believed what she was saying. "You should work in advertising. That sounds like copy straight from a fundraising brochure."

She inclined her head. "That doesn't make it less true."

"That doesn't make them less boring, either."

Her eyes widened. "No offense intended again?" she asked.

"Of course."

"You could still support them financially, you know."

He shook his head. "Don't look at me like that."

"Like what?" she asked innocently.

"Like I'm some kind of miser. I give to charity. I just lean toward the more practical. You know, like food, housing, medical care…"

"Those are all very worthy causes."

"Is that sarcasm?"

"No. It's hard to enrich the mind and soul when the

body is hungry. I'm sure your philanthropy is much appreciated."

Evan felt as if there was something else that needed to be addressed. An undercurrent he was missing. But they were interrupted by the arrival of their meals.

Olivia greeted the food with a genuine, "That looks amazing." She inhaled the aroma with a blissful look on her face before taking a bite.

The steak with cream sauce was one of Tourmaine's signature dishes, and rightly so. Olivia obviously agreed; chewing her first bite with her eyes closed while making little happy noises. "Oh, man. That's *so* good."

He swallowed hard. He knew that look. Remembered it as if he'd seen it yesterday. But Olivia hadn't been eating steak with cream sauce the last time he'd seen it. *He'd* put that look on her face.

His blood rushed to his lap with a speed that left him feeling slightly light-headed. That one look had opened a floodgate of memories—memories he'd safely locked in a box to forget until just now. But that look...

He could practically feel those long, strong legs wrapped around him.

When she opened her eyes and saw him staring, she looked a little abashed. "I said I eat. I can't eat like this *all* the time, though, so I enjoy it very much when I do."

If she was going to enjoy her entire dinner like that, he'd be dead by dessert.

Thank goodness Olivia couldn't read his mind.

CHAPTER TWO

EVAN FOUND THAT concentrating on his food helped. Some. Tourmaine's owner, Harry, came by, nicely distracting his attention as he introduced Olivia and she complimented everything from the steak to the music. Harry was duly flattered and invited her back to try everything on the menu.

By the time it was just the two of them again, Evan had himself basically back under control, thankfully.

They ate for a little while, the conversation carefully kept to the simple topics of the excellent food, Jory's successes, her parents and the weather. It was oddly easy. Even fun, at times. There was the occasional over-long pause, but they didn't last. He'd nearly forgotten how smart and funny Olivia could be, and that had only improved in the intervening years. They had very little in common—no overlapping tastes in music, TV or movies, and some widely differing stances on politics and social issues—but that worked in their favor, keeping the conversation moving and interesting. And while he might be shallow, *this* was what had actually tipped the attraction all those years ago and made him risk Jory's wrath.

And it was almost enough to let him ignore that little voice nagging him now.

Almost.

When he decided they'd had enough of the small talk, he charged ahead. "Well, you seem to be settling in fine, so you don't need anything from me in that area, everything is okay with the people we have in common, and," he couldn't help but say through a chuckle, "I don't want to buy season tickets to the ballet. Care to tell me why we're actually here?"

She chewed, but he figured that was more of a stalling tactic than anything else. Finally she swallowed. "To eat dinner?"

"Come on, Liv, you've been in town since when? August? If you'd wanted my company for dinner, you'd have called long before now."

"Therefore, I must have nefarious reasons to do so now?"

"I wouldn't necessarily assume your reasons are nefarious, but you must have at least *one* above and beyond a free meal."

She shrugged a shoulder again.

Fine. There'd been two elephants in the room and Olivia had been talking around them both for over an hour now. If she wouldn't address the specific *why* of this dinner, he'd simply address the problem he did know. He leveled a look at her across the table. "After all, the last time we spoke, you called me a cold, heartless bastard."

She blinked, somehow caught off guard by the blunt statement. "True. I was mad and my feelings were hurt."

At least she was honest about that much. "So why would you want to have dinner with a 'heartless bastard'?"

"I'm trying to make my home here. I thought it'd be nice to expand my network of people outside just the dance world, and you are the only person in Miami— outside my roommate and the company members—that I know. Since I'm not the same person I was nine years ago, I'm assuming you aren't either." The corner of her mouth twitched. "I guess I'm hoping you outgrew that."

"Not really," he said, causing her to choke slightly on her wine.

"Wow." She cleared her throat and thought for a minute. "Well, at least you're honest about it."

"Those aren't exactly bad qualities to have in my line of work."

She thought for a moment, and then nodded. "If that's the case, then we just won't do this again. It's okay. You're friends with Jory and that doesn't automatically include me simply by extension. You have a life, and I can't just intrude upon that."

Well, now he felt like a heel. And the one possibility he'd been steadfastly ignoring as implausible was beginning to win out: Olivia had *wanted* to see him. He'd hurt her and yet she'd still gotten in touch after all this time. It was equal parts flattering and mystifying.

It was also extremely complicated. Jory had put his sister firmly off-limits nine years ago. Not that Evan blamed him. He'd been seriously messed up back then, not nearly good enough for Olivia. Hell, he probably still wasn't what someone like Liv needed, and he had to assume that prohibition was still in place. Of course, Olivia didn't know about any of that. It put him in a very awkward situation. There was a huge difference between an eighteen-year-old and a twenty-seven-year-old, but she was still Jory's sister.

Maybe she was just lonely and in need of a friend. Just because *he* was having flashbacks to happier, more naked times, there was no reason to assume she was, as well. And while he'd broken a major tenet of the Guy Code by sleeping with her before, there was an equally important tenet of the Code that required him to look after a friend's sister when she was new and alone in a big city. There were as many possibilities as pitfalls here. "Well, I guess if you're fully aware I'm *still* a heartless bastard and are willing to accept that, then there's no reason we can't be friends anyway."

Olivia's eyes widened at the baldness of his words, but he could rest easy either way knowing she was coming in with her eyes wide open. The ball was in her court, and he was frankly very curious to find out how she'd play.

Because she couldn't say he hadn't warned her.

You're a coward. A fool. A screaming idiot who should be kept on a leash for her own safety.

Olivia stared at herself in the mirror of the ladies' room and frowned. She'd had such clear, simple goals for this dinner, and she'd failed to accomplish even one.

Instead, she couldn't have made a bigger mess if she'd tried.

In a just and fair world, anger and hurt feelings would not fade enough over time to allow the person who caused those feelings to have the same effect on her that had gotten her into the situation in the first place. Instead of being hit with all the things about Evan she'd hated him for, she'd been overwhelmed with all the things that had sucked her into Evan's bed in the first place.

It was easy enough to say he was charming and good-looking, but it was another to face that head-on. The way that baritone slithered through her insides, turning them to jelly; the way those blue, blue eyes could make the most casual glance feel like a caress. It was even more devastating because he wasn't *trying* to seduce her. That was just his default setting, a natural part of his personality that made him catnip to women.

It was humiliating. She might not have Evan's legions of former lovers, but she wasn't an innocent anymore either. She'd taken lovers, had flings and summer romances, so why was Evan able to reduce her to a simpering virgin again?

Mercy.

She'd been rattled and ready to run for the door the minute she'd laid eyes on him. She should have known then that the whole idea was insane, made her excuses and left instead. But *no*, she just had to try.

Wandering up to a random stranger on the street and asking if they wanted to support the MMBC and adopt a dancer might have been less nerve-racking and equally as successful. And she'd probably like herself a bit more afterward than she did right now.

It hadn't been a completely crazy idea, just one that worked much better in theory than in practice. Regardless of how sensible it sounded on the surface, she hadn't been able to shake that uneasy feeling that swirled underneath, and she was now very glad she hadn't followed, though.

Maybe I'm not a coward. She was a decent human being who'd got carried away for a minute, but pulled back in time. Points for that. And she'd made it through dinner without making a complete fool of herself, so bonus points could be awarded, as well.

Thank goodness Evan could be so blunt, or else she might have tried to pull off this stunt—which she was now viewing as pretty gauche and tacky. She was now going to say good-night and go home, thanking her lucky stars she wasn't leaving in shame.

She'd sort out the other confusing stuff later. Much later, and when she was alone. She took a deep breath and squared her shoulders. *Time for a dignified end to this farce of an evening.*

Evan was waiting for her out front. "Thank you for dinner," she said. "It was good to see you." *Handshake? Air kiss?*

"And you. Do you have your valet ticket?"

"I walked."

"I'll drive you home, then."

"It's only six blocks," she protested, but it sounded weak even to her own ears.

"It's about to rain." As if to punctuate his words, a raindrop landed on her shoulder. *So much for dry Miami Novembers.* It felt like revenge for her tackiness.

Was it worth a standoff? Probably not, and she'd look foolish wanting to walk home in the rain. She was just feeling ashamed of herself in general and didn't want to drag this out any further. Of course, they *could* stand here and continue to argue, but the ridiculousness of that would only exacerbate her foolishness. "Okay. Thanks."

The timing bordered on eerie, as the moment the words left her lips, a car coasted to a stop at the curb and Evan was reaching for the door. The man had to be half genie.

This car was a far cry from the beat-up, perfect-for-trips-to-the-beach Jeep he'd driven in college. Black, low-slung and convertible, it looked expensive and classy, and it suited this adult Evan perfectly.

She wasn't surprised that the valet knew Evan's name—she'd gotten the feeling at dinner that he was a regular here—but the fact Evan knew the valet's name did surprise her. Her experience with rich donors had proved that most of them couldn't be bothered with the little people. He couldn't be *entirely* selfish if he remembered the names of valets and servers.

His car proved that Evan *definitely* had money—regardless of his modest "we're still growing" comments and it was almost enough to make her rethink her original, now aborted, plan.

No. Now she had her mother's voice in her head, reminding her that anything she thought might be a tacky or bad idea probably *was*, and she bit her tongue as Evan put the car in gear.

"Which way?"

"Left at the light," she answered absently. The traffic was bad and the streets were crowded, slowing their progress to a crawl. She definitely could have walked home faster than this. Her original refusal seemed less foolish now, as she was trapped in a small, enclosed space with Evan, his hand only inches from her thigh as he shifted gears.

It created an intimacy she wasn't quite prepared to face at the moment, and in the small space, the silence rapidly gained weight.

When Evan sighed, she knew he felt it, too. "Liv…"

No one but Evan had ever called her Liv. Jory called her Livvy sometimes, but Liv sounded more grown-up and more intimate, somehow. And all things considered, "Liv" carried a lot of baggage straight into the conversation.

She tried to keep it light, nonetheless. "Yes?"

Evan turned his head toward her, but his face was unreadable. "Just so you know, I'm sorry for what happened. Particularly the way I treated you."

She had to swallow her shock. *That* certainly was the last thing she'd ever thought she'd hear. She'd given up hope of an explanation or apology years ago. "Thank you," she managed after a long pause.

He seemed genuinely surprised at her response. "For what?"

"For saying that. It means a lot."

He shrugged a shoulder as he changed lanes. "I know it doesn't change anything, but I can still regret my behavior. The apology may be years too late, but it is sincere."

It was oddly much easier to have this conversation side-on, instead of having to look directly at him. She kept her eyes front and said, "For an admitted bastard, that was a nice apology."

She cut her eyes toward him just in time to see the corner of his mouth twitch as if he found that funny. "Thank you."

I won't ask for details. Asking would sound pathetic and whiny. And there was a very good chance she wouldn't like what she would hear. "Can I ask why things ended the way they did between us?" she said, wincing even as she did.

"Beyond the fact I'm cold and selfish?"

This time, she did turn to face him. "You're saying there's *not* one?"

He looked at her as though he was sizing her up and coming to a decision. Then his eyes went back to the road as traffic began to move again. "Not that I'm willing to share."

"Like that's not going to drive me crazy now," she

muttered, really not caring what it might sound like to him.

"If I tell you it was genuinely me and not at all you, would that help?"

He sounded sincere, and something panged inside her, reminding her of the sweet side of him she'd seen and gone cow-eyed over in the past. Jory had been uncharacteristically closed-mouthed about Evan's background, but she'd known his childhood had been difficult and that he spent time at her parents' house because he was estranged from his own family. She easily painted him as wounded, and being naive and smug and influenced by too many romantic movies, she'd cast herself as the woman who'd heal the misunderstood bad boy's heart. "Maybe. But—"

A skater shot out in front of them, nearly invisible in the mist and dark, and Evan jammed on the brakes, throwing her against her seat belt. His hand flew out at the same time, landing painfully on her chest, and the effect of both managed to knock the breath out of her. The skater didn't even look back as he sped away.

Evan cursed, then asked, "You okay?"

"Yeah." She purposely looked down to where Evan's hand was still pressed against her chest, pretty much copping a feel. Evan moved his hand quickly, without comment *and* without the decency to look even a little abashed or surprised at where it ended up. She, however, felt branded, the imprint of his hand seeming to linger. In hindsight, she should have worn a bra tonight whether she needed it or not. "Dude has a death wish," she said to break the tension she felt even if he didn't.

"You were smart to walk. Traffic down here is abysmal."

"It'll clear some once you turn." The sudden stop had sent her purse into the floorboard, and she leaned over to gather the contents back up. Her lipstick, though, had rolled under the seat and she had to contort herself to get to it. Realizing the solution to both her physical and emotional situation, she gave one last stretch and got it, then sat up and said briskly, "I can walk from here, save you some time."

"Don't be ridiculous."

So much for that idea.

As she promised, the traffic was thinner on her street, and Evan pulled up in front of her building a minute later. "These are nice condos. I'm glad you're not doing the starving artist thing."

"I ate half a cow covered in cream sauce for dinner, so I think we've already covered the 'not starving' part," she said with a laugh. "And I have a roommate to help cover the rent. It's a great location for me. It's fifteen minutes on the bus to the studio, and I can walk pretty much everywhere else."

She had her purse over her shoulder and a hand on the door, and that horrible how-to-end-the-evening tension returned. Evan's face was partly shadowed and unreadable, giving her no help there. Not a date, not friends, not business associates…. She didn't know the protocol.

To her ever-loving surprise, Evan got out of the car and walked around to open her door. Her jaw was still hanging open as he extended a hand to help her out.

For someone who purported to be selfish, he'd been raised right when it came to good manners.

That shock, though, caused her to stumble as she climbed out, pitching herself straight into Evan's arms. He caught her easily, his arms strong and solid around her. He was warm, and damn it, he smelled good. Her heart jumped into her throat.

Over her head, she heard Evan chuckle. "That was graceful."

Kill me now.

He set her back on her feet. "You okay?" Evan asked.

"I'm fine. Just clumsy."

His eyebrow went up. "Maybe it was the wine."

"Yeah, maybe." Shaking it off, she rushed ahead with forced cheer and casualness. "Well, thanks again for dinner. And for the ride home."

His lips twitched. "Take care, Liv. And if you ever need anything, give me a call."

Oh, the irony. "Good night."

Evan waited until the security door closed behind her before driving away. It had been a really, really strange evening, where nothing had gone as planned, but it hadn't been bad either. The beginning and end hadn't been fantastic, but the middle part, like the over-dinner chitchat, had gone pretty well, all things considered. Had she not gone into it with a specific agenda, she'd have called the evening a success.

But even with that failure, the evening still wasn't a total disaster. She *did* live in the same city with Evan, and they might run into each other on occasion; having a truce in place made good sense. And when Jory came to town, he wouldn't feel as if he had to divide his time so precisely. *All good things*, she thought, as she climbed the last few stairs to her floor.

Everything else could just be ignored.

Annie was sprawled on the couch, flipping through TV channels, but she sat up when she heard her come in. "How'd it go?"

"Not bad."

"So he's going to sponsor you?"

"No."

"He turned you *down*? Jeez." Annie went to the counter and got a wineglass, filling it and handing it to her. "That sucks."

Olivia accepted the glass gratefully and sank into the cushions on the opposite end of the couch. "He didn't have to turn me down. I didn't ask."

"What? Why not?"

With a sigh, Olivia ran through the evening, all the small things that added up to tip the scales in the direction of keeping her mouth shut. She glossed over her rather disturbing reactions to him, because, for her own sanity, that was best left unexamined.

"I can't say I blame you. I see where you're coming from, and I'd probably feel the same way. But," Annie continued, as she cocked her head, "what, then, did you say to explain why you suddenly wanted to have dinner after all these years?"

"New in town, don't really know anyone…"

"Olivia, really?" Annie sighed. "He's going to think you still have the hots for him."

"What? No. Not likely."

"You said he has an ego."

"He does."

"Then he *will*. It's actually the only logical conclusion he could come to, to explain it."

"He might think I'm insane now, but that's about all." *And he might not be wrong.* She stood and handed her glass to Annie to finish. "I'm going to bed. I've got Pilates at eight tomorrow."

"I'm sorry it didn't work out."

"Me, too."

It was a shame, but there was always plan B. Plan B involved making sure that everyone from the chairman of the ballet board all the way down to the stagehands loved her *and* working her butt off to prove her value to the company. She'd also talk to the business office to see if they had any ideas of how she could land sponsorship—and to suss out how important that sponsorship really was.

That's what I should have done in the first place, she told herself as she got ready for bed. That was a far more sensible idea than a half-baked plan to talk Evan into it. Hell, plan B should have been plan A. Too bad she didn't think of it first.

At the same time, she didn't regret their meeting.

It would make things easier for Jory when he came to town. She didn't know exactly how much Jory knew about her and Evan, but her brother had made it very clear he considered his roommate off-limits to his little sister. He'd been unhappy and grumpy about it. She hadn't asked him to take sides, but he always seemed uncomfortable bringing up Evan around her after that, giving the whole thing a patina of awkward wrongness—at least to her mind. That, as much as anything else, had led to making it a *thing*—which, now at least, she realized it really didn't need to be.

So, in that sense, dinner wasn't such a bad idea, after all.

The wine, the food and a long day—both physically and mentally—were catching up with her, and the bed beckoned.

As she climbed in and pulled the covers up, she realized she'd gotten distracted by the near miss with that skater and hadn't followed up on his mysterious "genuinely me, not you" statement.

What could he have possibly meant?

The next morning, just outside Boca Raton, the sudden blaring of "Born This Way" caused Evan to swerve dangerously in his lane.

What the sweet hell? The news program chattered on from his car speakers, but that was undeniably Lady Gaga coming from…under the passenger seat?

Pulling off onto the shoulder, he searched under the seat until he found the source: a phone that went silent about the time he got hold of it. It had an overly sparkly rhinestone case, and when he pressed the home button to wake it up, Olivia and Jory smiled back at him.

He couldn't figure out how Olivia had managed to leave her phone in his car, but now the question was what to do with it. The screen had a long list of missed calls from "Annie" and "Theo." Presumably those calls were Olivia using her friends' phones to locate her own. But the phone was locked, so he had no way of calling back.

Based on the sheer volume of calls, though, if he waited another thirty minutes or so, Olivia would be calling again. Sliding the phone into his shirt pocket, he pulled back out onto the interstate.

Last night had certainly been odd. And while he still didn't have a good explanation for why Olivia had contacted him, he didn't regret it. He just wasn't sure what, if anything, it meant, and what, if anything, he should do about it.

It wasn't a feeling he liked. In fact, he intentionally avoided these kinds of situations. Everything needed to be up front and clear, without mystery or games or prevarications. Jory was a straight-up, no games, kind of guy, so he'd assumed Olivia would be the same. Why then did he feel so bothered at the idea she might not be?

He snorted. Maybe because he wasn't sexually attracted to Jory.

Of course, the next question was if Olivia was still attracted to him? He'd like to say yes, and there had been moments, but that could be wishful thinking on his part. But she had left her phone in his car…accidentally or intentionally?

He was pulling into the parking lot of Riley Construction when Olivia's phone rang again. "Hello?"

"Hi." There was great relief in her voice that didn't sound fake. "My name's Olivia, and you seem to have my phone."

Accidentally. That knowledge came with unexpected disappointment and made his words sharper than intended. "Because you left it in my car last night."

There was a pause, then a confused, "Evan?"

"Who else?"

"I thought I'd left it at the restaurant or something. I didn't even think to call you." He heard her sigh. "I'm *so* glad you have it, though. My life is in that phone."

"I know how you feel."

"We should be breaking for lunch soon. Can I meet you somewhere and get it?"

"I'm in West Palm Beach for a meeting and won't be back until later this afternoon."

"Oh." She sounded disappointed. "Well, let me know when and where would be good for you."

"I can drop it by the studio later, though, on my way home," he offered for some reason.

"That would be awesome. I'll be here until around five-thirty or so. The studio is in Wynwood."

"Then I can find it."

"Thanks, Evan. I really appreciate it."

He silenced the phone's ringer before putting it in

his briefcase. Although Olivia would quit calling her phone now, other people might, and he really didn't want that annoying song blaring out during the meeting. If he was remembering correctly, the MMBC studio wasn't too far out of his way home, and he could swing by easily.

But, jeez. She was at the studio already and would be there until five-thirty? When Olivia said she worked her body hard, she hadn't been kidding. Granted, he knew next to nothing about the subject, but he would have guessed the job would be part-time at best. How long could it take, really? He had to assume she knew all the moves; putting them in a specific order for a performance shouldn't take all *that* long.

She'd said yesterday that she'd been in rehearsals for six hours. He'd assumed that was either an exaggeration or at least unusual. Six or seven hours in a dance studio couldn't be easy, much less doing that every day. Or maybe she didn't dance the whole time? He had no idea. A six or seven hour workday didn't seem like much, but then Olivia wasn't exactly sitting at a desk.

Regardless of what his father might say, he wasn't averse to hard work. He'd nearly killed himself to get through school and graduated with enough debt to buy a decent-sized house. Honestly, it was one of the things he and Jory had first bonded over—although for different reasons. The Madisons weren't rich—their family restaurant in Tampa was popular, but hardly a gold mine—and Jory's work ethic was rooted in the love and support of a family that wanted him to succeed.

Neither Jory nor Olivia knew what it was like to drive themselves out of spite and desperation, but they drove themselves nonetheless.

He had to respect it.

Jory, though, had needed to learn to let go, to come out of his shell and trust his instincts. Evan liked to think he played a big part in that, even if it had been mostly through bad influence and serving as a cautionary tale from time to time. But being too serious, too focused and too sure had a downside—and all Evan had to do was point in the direction of his own family for an example.

On paper, his family sounded great; in practice, they were insufferable. He far preferred the Madisons; Jory had brought him home like a stray, and Gary and Dee showed him what real families could be—fun, accepting and loving without reservations or conditions. There was very little he wouldn't do for the Madisons. They'd probably saved him from himself.

Which was why he'd walked away when Jory asked him to—and why he'd done it the way he had. He didn't want to cause tension between Jory and Olivia. If Olivia had ever told her parents about it, Jory must've said something to keep him okay in their eyes. He'd taken the blame, been the jerk, hurt Olivia for her own good. But it had all seemed to work out.

But with Olivia back in his orbit, however tangentially at the moment, it made things a little complicated. Again.

He had a meeting in less than ten minutes and he

needed to focus. There was a lot of money riding on this pitch, and he couldn't risk blowing it because his brain was elsewhere. He wanted Riley Construction in his stable.

Three hours later, he had them. He emailed his assistant and his office manager the good news, then stripped off his tie, tossed it into the backseat, unbuttoned his collar and his cuffs, and put the top down for the ride home.

His brain was buzzing, high on the adrenaline rush of success and future plans, and he forgot he still needed to drop off Olivia's phone until he was almost past the exit.

The parking lot was much busier than he expected, packed with cars. He followed a very tall, very slender teenager and her mother to a set of glass doors and inside into an alternate dimension.

Dozens of young girls—from early tweens to just-licensed-to-drive—packed the hallway. All were tall and slim with their hair pulled severely back. They all wore black bodysuits and pink tights as they contorted themselves into various stretches. They looked like a small bun-headed robot army, ready to invade.

The noise was at a level painful to adult ears, with an occasional squeal rising above the din to make him wince.

He waded through the chest-high crowd, dodging swinging arms and flying feet, to a door marked Office. A middle-aged woman sat behind a desk, seemingly unconcerned with the melee right outside her door. "Can I help you?"

"I'm looking for Olivia Madison."

The woman was professionally distant. "She's in rehearsals. Can I help instead?"

"I'm Evan Lawford. I have her phone."

Her voice warmed immediately. "Oh, good. She mentioned you would be coming by. You're welcome to leave it here with me, and I'll see that she gets it. Or you can wait. They should be done in another fifteen minutes or so."

Wait? In that hallway of overly excited children?

The horror must have shown on his face, because the woman laughed. "*The Nutcracker* gives young dancers from the community the opportunity to perform with a professional company. It's a tradition, albeit a sometimes noisy one."

He reached in his pocket and handed over the phone. "I think I'll just leave the phone with you."

She winked at him. "Smart move. I can't say I blame you."

Back out in the hallway, he tried to move toward the door, but was blocked by adolescent Bun-Bots huddled in a pack near a large window he hadn't noticed on his way in.

None of them were taller than his shoulders, so he could easily see over their heads, and he wondered what was so attention-grabbing that it deserved their awe.

The window offered a side view into a studio with painted cinder block walls and a gray floor. Mirrors lined the front wall and metal bars were bolted to the other three. It was frankly depressing. A dark-haired man in street clothes gesticulated wildly with his hands, obviously trying to make a point to the two dancers standing in the middle of the room. The walls absorbed most of the sound, muffling the words but not the volume or the emotion behind them.

It took him a second to realize that the woman dancer was Olivia. Her hair was scraped back from her face, but small tendrils had worked themselves loose and clung to her face and neck—which were flushed pink from exertion.

She was wearing a one-piece black thing that clung to her like a second skin, emphasizing the long, clean lines of her torso and the length of her legs. Yes, she was thin, but street clothes had hid the truth of her body from him last night. At eighteen, she'd still been growing into herself, but now, Olivia was solid, sculpted muscle, more like an athlete than his mental picture of a dainty, fragile ballerina.

Both she and her partner—who had all of *his* attributes on display as well in just tights and a tank top—were dripping sweat. Yet neither of them seemed phased by the other man's enthusiastic diatribe; they both just nodded as he went over to a stereo and started the music.

Olivia took a breath and started to dance.

Seriously, the studio doors *had* to have been a portal to another dimension, as Olivia seemed able to defy the laws of gravity, physics *and* biomechanics.

She could spin like a dreidel on her toes, then melt into the arms of her partner, her back bent over his arm like her spine was made of rubber. Those long legs extended to impossible heights, her foot easily higher than her head, and her jumps would be the envy of NBA players and world-class hurdlers.

He found himself holding his breath as Olivia's partner lifted her high over his head, supporting her with only one hand in the small of her back. An impressed gasp rose from the crowd in front of him. He didn't blame them one bit.

It was truly the most amazing thing he'd ever seen the human body do, and Olivia did it all with a serene smile on her face, making it look easy and effortless.

Something heavy and hot landed in his stomach. He couldn't quite define it, but it was powerful and impossible to ignore. It was different than just desire: he'd wanted her nine years ago, and that want had nudged at him all last night, but this ran deeper, somehow.

He felt himself starting to sweat, and he left quickly, ending up in the front seat of his car. Seeing Olivia in action, even just for those few minutes, shifted his entire perspective about her.

Jory had said she was good, and he'd had no reason to doubt that, but this showed a side of Olivia he never really knew about. No one got that good at anything without hard work—*really* hard work, the kind few people, including himself, would ever experience or understand. He had to respect that level of determination and discipline. It made his own drive seem pale in comparison.

And Jory had been right to expect Evan to leave her alone. Their affair would have ended—and probably badly, too—in quick enough time, only Olivia would have ended up hurt worse. He knew himself too well, both then and now, to think he'd have been a positive influence in her life at that point.

He still wasn't much of a prize. All anyone had to do was ask any of the past ten women he'd dated, and they'd provide a long list of his flaws. Which, again, was well aware of—and even if he hadn't been, those flaws had been listed for him repeatedly, usually at top volume mere moments before the woman stormed out.

He should walk away. Quickly and to a great distance.

But he wasn't sure if he wanted to. And he was not one to always do the right thing when the wrong thing held much more appeal.

And Olivia was definitely appealing.

CHAPTER THREE

BEING SEPARATED FROM her phone all day had Olivia feeling twitchy and disconnected. Getting it back made her feel like a junkie who'd finally found a fix. Not that she'd really missed all that much, but it was the feeling she *could* have that caused detox jitters.

She wished she'd been able to tell Evan thanks in person; after all, he had gone out of his way to return it to her when she'd been silly enough to leave it in his car in the first place. That would just be good manners.

At the same time, it was probably easier this way. All things considered, she'd had a good time at dinner last night. Evan could be funny and quite charming when he wanted to; even with his assurances he was cold at heart. And she had to question her sanity at her willingness to appreciate that charm when he'd treated her so badly. It made her feel shallow, as if she was desperate and able to fall for good looks and flattery over substance.

It had always seemed strange to her that Jory could be so close to someone like Evan, and she'd been horrified to see Jory adopt some of Evan's partying and hell-raising ways, but Jory was a good man, and he wouldn't be friends with someone completely irredeemable.

And it *had* been a long time. She wasn't the same person she'd been nine years ago, so even with his denials to the contrary, Evan probably wasn't either.

Good grief, she was being ridiculous. She was either lonely or insane or sex-starved—or possibly a combination of the three. Why else would she be having this argument with herself?

Evan had dropped her off last night with "Call me if you need anything," which could be loosely translated as "Have a nice life," so it wasn't even an issue worth stressing over. To assuage her inner Miss Manners, though, she emailed him a quick, simple, "Thank you," and then pushed the whole thing out of her mind to protect her sanity.

She wasn't in a hurry, and there was no good reason to fight the masses on the bus during rush hour. So she showered, picked up her shoe allotment, checked the board for photo calls and rehearsal changes, and spoke to a few of the young girls waiting for their turn to rehearse—general dithering.

She'd make a quick trip to the grocery store for dinner supplies, then head home to an evening of TV and sewing.

It wasn't the most exciting of evenings, but her life didn't exactly suck, either. She'd signed on for this life, so she couldn't complain.

Outside the studio, she stopped to get a barrette

to pull her hair back. When she heard her name, she looked up.

Evan was leaned up against his car, arms crossed over his chest. It was so unexpected, she had to do a double take to make sure it was him, and even then she couldn't be sure he'd actually been the one to call her name. But there was no one else in the parking lot, and the chances of him waiting for someone else had to be pretty slim. She changed course and headed toward him.

Evan looked like an advertisement in a magazine. His collar was loose and his sleeves were rolled up, but it was very much the "businessman after hours" look. Expensive clothes, expensive sunglasses perched on his head, expensive car.

His hair was messy, as though he'd been driving with the top down, and just a hint of five o'clock shadow traced his jaw. *Hummina.* He was picture-perfect, and she wouldn't lie to herself by denying it wasn't working on her. A little shiver slid through her insides. Whatever he was selling, she might be convinced to buy.

Down, girl. She wasn't a naive eighteen-year-old anymore; she knew better. And she knew exactly *what* he was, too, but sadly, that wasn't the bucket of cold water her good sense might hope for. In fact, knowing made it *worse.* If she wanted to, she could walk, eyes wide open, right into that place where what he was willing to give met up with what she wanted to take—with no misunderstandings or heartaches this time.

That was a big *if,* though.

Frankly, her brain was twisted to even go there. Hadn't she *just* gotten all this sorted out in her head?

Guess not. Or at least not entirely.

He looked so good that her vanity kicked in. She was quite glad she'd showered, but she wished she'd known he was here so she could have spent a little more time on herself. Maybe at least dry her hair so it wasn't hanging damp and limp down her back.

She'd gotten her phone from the office *before* her shower. *Before* she'd dithered around in the studio. Which meant Evan had been waiting out here for a good half hour or more, at least.

She felt a little bad about that, but also a little flattered, too, and she smiled as she got closer. "Hey. Thanks for bringing me my phone."

"You're welcome. It must have fallen out when I had to dodge that skater last night."

"Yeah, probably. I didn't expect to see you to thank you in person, so I sent you an email."

"I saw it."

This was weird. Evan looked completely comfortable, at ease even, but the conversation felt awkward. Forced. Since he was standing here, though, she had to assume he had *some*thing to say to her, but there was no nice way to ask "What do you want?". Grasping for conversational straws, she said, "And thanks again for dinner. I had a nice time."

"I did, too. We should do it again."

Well, that was an improvement from the "have a nice life" feeling of last night. The wisdom of another dinner could be examined another time; right now, she'd take it as a compliment. "Sure."

"Are you hungry?"

Whoa. Okay. That was fast. "Now?"

"I watched rehearsals for a little bit. It looks like a good way to work up an appetite."

"Well, um…" She paused as the full statement registered. "You watched rehearsals?"

"Just for a few minutes. You're really good."

She examined his tone for flippancy and didn't find any. If anything, he seemed genuinely impressed. "Thanks."

"I don't know much—anything, actually—about it, but it was still pretty impressive."

She wasn't going to play with false modesty—she'd worked too hard for that—so there wasn't really much to say to that other than "Thank you" even if she'd already said it once.

"So *are* you hungry?"

She was, but…she gestured to her outfit. "I'm not really dressed to go anywhere."

He held up his phone. "According to Siri, there's a great deli-bistro-type place just a couple of blocks from here. I assume it's casual."

"Huey's? Yeah, it's a great place."

"Okay, then. Can we leave the car here?" She nodded, and he opened the trunk. "Then drop your stuff."

Flattery had given way to confusion and uncertainty. They had a past, but it was past. Was he just being friendly or was he hoping he might get lucky tonight?

Was it a little of both? Or neither? Or something else entirely? And why couldn't she decide where her feelings on those possibilities fell on the spectrum?

Oh, jeez. How could Evan mess with her head so easily? And what kind of fool was she to let him?

"Liv? Are you okay?"

She snapped her head up to see Evan standing next to his open trunk, his hand out waiting for her to hand him her stuff and a confused look on his face. "Yeah." She handed over her bags, and he locked them inside. "Thanks."

She took two steps, then stopped. This wasn't an ideal time or place, but it would have to do. "What are we doing?"

Evan looked at her as if she'd lost her mind. "Going to dinner? At least, that's what I thought we were doing."

"No. I mean, why? Why *now*? Considering…"

The confusion cleared and he nodded. "I could ask you the same thing. You're the one who made first contact."

He had her there. And she still didn't have a plausible alternative reason for why she did. "Maybe I didn't realize there'd be a second time."

"There doesn't have to be. I'm not going to drag you to the restaurant and force-feed you—even if you do look like you really need a sandwich."

"Evan, be serious."

"I am."

"Do you honestly believe there's nothing we need to discuss? No air to clear?"

Evan sighed, his face the perfect picture of resigned exasperation. "I feel I'm safe assuming the answer you're looking for is not 'yes.'" He shook his head. "I apologized. What more can I do?"

That was a good question, and one she should have answered for herself *before* asking him. She'd beat herself up over it, except Evan was far too good at scrambling her higher brain functions, turning her into a babbling idiot. "So we're going to be friends now?"

"I kind of thought that was the point of dinner last night."

Nothing ventured, nothing gained. "*Just* friends?"

"You're a beautiful woman, Olivia. Talented, smart, charming." He looked her up and down. "I'm not going to deny there's still an attraction."

"So not just friends, then?" Why did that possibility send a little thrill through her?

"That would be entirely up to you." The wicked little half smile held a challenge and that didn't help.

"And if I did want to be just friends?"

"I'd respect that." He thought about it for a second. "It'd be a novel experience for me."

"You're saying you don't have any platonic female friends?"

"I don't have many friends period."

She could relate to that, but still… "So you're telling me you've slept with every woman you know."

He grinned. "Not *all* of them. Some of them are married."

"You are insufferable."

He grinned. "So I've been told."

She felt off balance. "And this is supposed to encourage me?"

"Nope. I'm just being honest."

How could she be annoyed and intrigued at the same time? In fact, it was almost a challenge. But Evan *was* charming, and hadn't she decided that a peaceful coexistence with him would be a benefit all around?

"So are we going to dinner or not?" he asked.

She had to think about it for a minute. She needed to give herself the chance to weigh the pros and cons and decide if she wanted to shake things up a little bit. Because she had a suspicion that being in Evan's orbit—in whatever way—would not be boring. And now she understood what had drawn her bookish brother into his orbit, as well. The man was just irresistible—and not just in a sexual way. His attitude could be grating, but it was refreshing. And his ego, while quite large, made him fun to spar with. And while *she'd* had a problem with Evan and Jory's friendship, Jory never had, which said a lot about Evan as a person, giving clues to facets of his personality she wasn't aware of.

Oh, she might regret this later, but she might not, either. She might decide that they, too, could be friends, and it would be nice to have another friend. If she wanted to cross that line later? Well, she'd know what she was doing. And if, in the process of this new friendship, she decided that Evan was still a jerk, she could get out easily enough.

She nodded, trying to look regal and haughty—which was a little difficult when wearing yoga pants and a T-shirt with wet, wild hair. "We are."

"Then let's go."

Had he really just agreed to be just friends with Olivia? Considering the rather adult nature of his thoughts recently, that bordered on insane. But that seemed to be Olivia's choice. Could he keep her at arm's length? Maybe being friends would make the attraction wane.

Or not, he thought as he watched the sway of her hips as she walked. While Olivia was elegant, she also had a girl-next-door wholesomeness about her—especially right now, barefaced, uncoiffed and yet comfortable in her skin. Normally, that wasn't an attraction for him, but on Olivia it worked. A little *too* well. Oh, he'd created a challenge for himself. He'd have to play this carefully by ear with the full knowledge he might regret it later.

The MMBC studios occupied a converted warehouse on the fringe of the Wynwood Arts District. Wynwood was still primarily a mecca for the visual arts, but the performing arts were getting a toehold in the area, too. He wasn't overly familiar with the district, but Olivia seemed to be, and she pointed out items of interest as they walked. She was passionate about the arts in general, not just dance it seemed, as well as very knowledgeable, and she told him about shows and upcoming artists and the growth of the area.

"That looks like graffiti, not art," he said as she showed him a mural she claimed was a favorite.

"It can't be both?"

"I want to say no, but I'm starting to think that's not the correct answer."

She laughed.

"You must think I'm an uncultured troglodyte."

After a long pause that bordered on offensive, she finally answered. "Troglodyte? No. Uncultured? Maybe." The mock-haughty tone and twitching lips took the sting out of her words.

"You'll have to pardon me then, and blame it on my childhood. There wasn't much in the way of what you'd consider culture of any kind in Arrowwood, Florida."

"What does that have to do with anything? Beyond being an argument for improved arts education in Florida public schools, that is."

Looking pointedly at a sculpture that looked like salvaged bedsprings from a fairy's junkyard, he said, "I'm thinking art may be something that you have to grow up with to truly appreciate."

She shook her head. "No, it's not. It's for everyone. You just have to expose yourself to it. You don't always have to understand it to appreciate it for what it is. As you learn more about it, the more esoteric stuff will start to make sense. But something is bound to speak to you, if you give it time and the chance to."

"Since I'm reevaluating my mind-set about ballet, I just might believe you."

"That's very flattering." She grinned and it lit up her entire face. "I'd be happy to help you in your quest to expose yourself to what's out there. What do you think of this?"

The bedsprings? "It's um...interesting?"

"See, you're becoming more cultured even as we stand here."

"You know, I feel it." He put a hand to his chest dramatically. "It's like a flower blossoming in my heart, filling me with color and joy and wisdom all at the same time. This piece...it shows the waste and futility of society while celebrating the, the *resilience* of um, *springiness*. And purple."

"Smart ass." She shook her head as she led him away from the sculpture. "So where is Arrowwood, anyway?"

"North of Ocala, south of Gainesville, middle of nowhere."

"And your family is still there?"

"Yep." He didn't elaborate, hoping she wouldn't ask.

"Do you get to go home often?"

"No." It came out sharper than he intended. He could tell by the look in her eyes that Olivia caught the hint that time, and while she gave him an odd look, she didn't press further. The ensuing silence was a bit awkward and noticeable after the easiness of the conversation before, and he needed to find another topic before it either got worse or Olivia decided to ask more questions. Thankfully, he found it quickly. "Hey, look at that."

That was a poster-sized advertisement for *The Nutcracker*, featuring a full-color picture of Olivia in a white-and-silver tutu and tiara. The man holding her up looked vaguely as if he might have been the same man she had been dancing with earlier. "Good picture. Cool pose."

Olivia looked a little embarrassed. "Thanks. That's a fish."

"You're a fish? I thought it was a Christmas-type story."

"It is." She laughed. "That *move* is called a fish, but I'm the Snow Queen—in that picture, at least."

He was getting more confused, not less. "So you're *not* the Snow Queen?"

"Oh, I'm the Snow Queen, but I'm also a mother in the party scene and I alternate Sugar Plum Fairy and Arabian in the second act."

"Is that all?"

He meant that as snark, but it seemed it wasn't. "I also had to learn Dew Drop, just in case, but I wouldn't do them all in the same show." Olivia also must have misunderstood the look in his face, too, as she quickly added, "*Nutcracker* is a big show and we're not that big of a company. I'm just lucky we have a large enough corps to cover Waltz and Snow."

Very few of her words made sense, but her tone was easy enough to understand. "You don't sound very excited about the show."

She shrugged. "It's *Nutcracker.* There's no escaping it."

"Escaping?"

"Almost every ballet company does *Nutcracker* at Christmas. It's a tradition, and because so many people consider it part of their Christmas tradition, it makes a lot of money in ticket sales. So that's great and all, and I'm so glad people love it so much, but you have to understand—this is my twentieth year doing this ballet."

Twentieth? His jaw fell open a little bit, causing her to grin.

"When I was eight, I went with a friend to *Nutcracker* auditions in Tampa, even though I'd never set foot in a studio before at that point. I was cast as a Bon Bon in act 2, and all I really had to do was skip around the stage and look cute. I was hooked, though, from that moment on, and my folks enrolled me in ballet classes in the January. I have danced *Nutcracker* someplace on this planet every single year since then."

"Wow."

"Exactly. I did the math once, and when you consider that rehearsals for a December show start in late September or early October, I've spent nearly five *years* of my life preparing for and dancing in that one show." She leaned in and whispered, "Don't spread this far and wide, but I'm kinda over it."

"But…"

She raised an eyebrow at him. "Are you going to tell me that there's *no* part of your job that you don't find boring or monotonous or frustrating? Or wouldn't be after you'd done that one thing for five solid years?"

There were plenty, but he didn't call himself an *artist*, dedicated to his craft. "No, but—"

She lifted her hands as if to say *there you go* and opened the door to the restaurant.

"Wait a second." He motioned her back from the door. "You're telling me you don't enjoy it?"

"Dancing? Yes. Performing? Yes. *Nutcracker?* That gives me hives. Just hearing the music is enough to make me start to twitch, and it's *everywhere* this time of year."

"If your marketing and PR people knew how you felt, they'd put a gag order on you before they let you out in public."

"Hey, now, I can behave in public." As if to prove that, Olivia lifted her head and in an interview-perfect tone said, "I'm so thrilled to be making my first appearance in MMBC's production of this classic and timeless ballet. It's truly a Christmas tradition, enjoyable for people of *all* ages, and I encourage *every*one in town to come see the show."

"That's better," he admitted as Olivia grinned at him again. No one would be able to tell she hadn't been grumbling about it five seconds before. "You're a good liar."

"I'm not lying," she protested. "Every word of that was true."

"You're good at lies of omission, then." A strange look crossed Olivia's face, and he wondered if he'd insulted her somehow. "But I respect that. I'm in advertising, remember? It's all about the image." He opened the door to the restaurant and motioned for her to go in. "Now let's eat."

Olivia's order tonight was far more in line with what he'd expect—a hummus and veggie pita with a side of fruit and iced tea. "I can't eat like I did last night *all* the time," she explained with a shrug. Then, over his protests, she insisted on buying both their dinners. "If we're going to be friends, you can't buy all the time either."

Evan couldn't quite find his balance in all of this. Olivia's grudge had somehow been appeased, but he still felt as if he was on probation with her—regardless of her easy, friendly attitude. It was the quick switch that bothered him. People didn't just adapt like that.

But he saw no danger in enjoying it, as long as he didn't forget who she was.

And there was no danger of *that*.

CHAPTER FOUR

TONIGHT WAS EASIER by far than last night, Olivia thought. Having an understanding—even if she didn't fully understand it—with Evan helped, and she was actually able to relax. His very bald "it's up to you" kept a flirty undercurrent running under the dinner conversation that was actually kind of fun.

Plus, after watching that little bit of rehearsals, Evan suddenly had an interest in ballet and peppered her with questions.

"Have you ever been dropped?" Evan had a keen interest in the lift he'd seen.

"Yes. But not ever from that particular lift and never by Theo."

"So you trust him."

"With my life." She laughed. "I've known Theo since we were really young. He was my partner when we took silver at Nationals. We've done thousands of lifts together."

"But you *have* been dropped before."

"Of course. It's not fun, but it does happen. I even

ended up with a mild concussion once." She took one last sip of her drink and started cleaning up the debris of their meal.

Evan wasn't quite letting it go, though. "You say that like it's nothing."

"It was an accident. Like I said, it happens. Sometimes it's something I did, sometimes it's something he did, but there's no sense assigning blame. You learn from it and go on."

"And if you get hurt?"

"You're much less likely to make that mistake again, that's for sure. But it's his job to do his best to catch me before I hit the floor. Partners who goof around and make it more likely someone's going to fall will soon find themselves without partners at all."

"Are there men you won't dance with?"

She nodded. "But most of the time, I just do what I'm supposed to do and trust my partner to do his part." She stood. "You ready?"

Evan stood, too, and led her toward the door. "But to let some guy hold you upside down with one hand? That's a lot of trust."

"It goes both ways, you know. If I mess up, he could get hurt. I could injure his back or his shoulders or kick him in the head. Or he could get hurt trying to keep *me* from getting hurt from something that was my own fault." It was fully dark outside now, cool, but not cold, and the neighborhood's nightlife was warming up. "We have to trust each *other*, or else we'll both end up hurt."

"How very Zen of you," Evan scoffed, as he fell into step beside her, adjusting his pace to hers.

"I know it sounds cheesy, but it's the truth."

"Trust has to be earned," he said seriously, causing her to do a double take at the emotion in his voice. Before she could answer though, he continued. "It takes time. You just show up and trust that this guy is not going to drop you on your head."

"That's not how it works."

"No?"

"Of course not. It's like sex."

It was a common joke in the studio, and she said it without really thinking how Evan might interpret it. When he stumbled, then looked at her with wide eyes, she regretted saying it. But when he reached for her elbow and pulled her out of the flow of foot traffic next to a Picasso-inspired mural to ask, "*Sex?*" she lost the regret. *This might be fun.*

She couldn't quite name the look on his face—horrified interest? shocked interest?—but it was enough to spur her on. "Just like you shouldn't jump into bed with someone you just met, you don't introduce yourself to a new partner and then do the most complicated lift in the program." She tried to put the right amount of earnestness into her words. "It would be all awkward, you know, feet and hands in all the wrong places, and getting frustrated because it's not feeling right and it's not any good for either one of you. And what's the point of having sex if you're not going to enjoy it? Sex is great, but good sex is *better*, and *great* sex takes an investment. *That* kind of great sex requires a little trust in your partner."

Evan cleared his throat and Olivia felt wicked.

"So you start slow and simple, feeling each other out." She ran a hand lightly over his chest. "You look for quirks that you'll need to adapt to and learn how his body moves." She ran her hands up his arms and squeezed his biceps gently. *Wow.* "You have to find your partner's strengths, learn how his hands feel, and how you'll fit together...that's the foreplay. And you can't rush that, can you?" Evan shifted uncomfortably as she moved her hands up and over his shoulders, but he shook his head. She leaned in, lowering her voice, moving slowly around his body, trailing her fingers. "You've got to get in sync with your partner first, and then...*then* you can trust him to do what needs to be done. *Then y*ou're free to go at it hard, full-out, over and over, until you're sweaty and exhausted, but satisfied with what you accomplished. And that feels *amazing.*"

Evan's breath had gotten shallow as she spoke. More surprisingly, so had hers. She dropped her hand as Evan swallowed hard and gave himself a small shake. "You are evil, Olivia Madison."

"Whatever do you mean?" she protested with as much eyelash-fluttering innocence as she could muster.

When Evan lifted his eyes to hers, she saw heat there. It fanned embers she'd been trying to smother, and they flared with an intensity that rocked her back on her heels. Regretting she'd let bravado lead her into the deep end, she stepped back to let some air between them. The option may have been put out there, but she wasn't ready to decide whether to exercise that option or not.

But Evan certainly looked ready. And, *damn*, that was tempting. "So, anything else you want to know about ballet?" She tried for a light and airy tone and started walking again. "Pointe shoes? Tutus? Turns?" she tossed over her shoulder as Evan caught up.

"As a matter of fact, I do have more questions."

"Ask away."

"I'm curious about positions. Beyond the basics, of course." An eyebrow went up in challenge. "And what about your flexibility? Stamina?"

Jeez, she really was in over her head. She should know better than to play games with a master. "What about them?"

They were back at Evan's car, where her stuff was in his trunk. Figuring he'd have one of those fancy keyless entry things, she reached for the trunk latch and was rewarded when it popped open. Grabbing her bag, she tossed it over her shoulder and turned to face him. *Big mistake.* Evan was close. *Very* close. She could smell him, feel the heat of his body. And she was trapped between him and his stupid fancy car.

His smile was wicked. "Or you could just tell me more about that foreplay."

Over his shoulder, she could see her bus arriving like a gift from God to get her out of this. She focused on the relief of that and tried to ignore the little shiver that went through her. "Another time, maybe." She shim-

mied out and ran toward the bus stop, hand up to signal the driver to save her simply by stopping. "Bye!"

She looked back over her shoulder as she climbed
aboard, only to see Evan leaned against the trunk of
his car, grinning at her. When he saw her looking, he
shouted, "Coward!"

Maybe so, but I'm not stupid, too.

Surprisingly enough, Olivia got in touch a few days
later with an invite to something called "Margaritas
and Melodies," which turned out to be a fundraiser for
the symphony. She was taking his arts education seriously, it seemed.

He'd been torn, unable to decide, when her invite
first landed in his in-box. He recognized danger when
he saw it.

He might have agreed to just being friends, and she
might be on board for that, but it was going to be very
hard. He wanted her; he wouldn't lie to himself about
that, but *three* outings? He either needed to nip this in
the bud, or accept the direction this was heading and
the possible consequences of that.

He wanted to be a better person and a good friend
to Jory, but his big head wasn't exactly in total control.
He'd accepted the invite before he'd really thought it all
the way through and now, here he was—consequences
or no consequences.

It was a casual affair, held in one of the larger gal-
leries in the art district. They had a good-sized crowd
packed in there, and the conversations nearly drowned

out the background music of the symphony playing pop tunes given a classical twist. There were the usual fundraiser things—silent auctions, raffles, light refreshments and an overpriced cash bar.

He knew a lot of the people in attendance, though, and all of them seemed surprised to see him there. It was a good place to make new business contacts. He should have gotten more involved in the arts sooner.

He mentioned that to Olivia, and she gave him a pitying look. "I can't believe you're just now figuring that out. But," she corrected sternly, "you're not here to do business. You're supposed to be absorbing the atmosphere and appreciating the culture."

"The music is nice."

"It is. Our symphony is great and we're lucky to have that talent here. What do you think of the art?"

Frankly, he found it garish and ugly, as if the artist had randomly stuck household trash to a canvas and flung paint at it. "It's…unusual."

"I think it's hideous," she whispered.

"Wait, what? It's art."

"Yes, it's art, but that doesn't make it *good* art. The value in the piece often lies in the eye of the beholder, but I think it's derivative, amateurish and ugly." She leaned in to read the artist's name. "And this Jackson Pollack wannabe is…Damien Hoffman. Ever heard of him?"

"No."

"Looking at this stuff, I'm surprised anyone has."

"I thought you artsy types stuck together. Feeling the muse and all that jazz."

"I work really hard to perfect what I do. This guy rolled out of bed, stuck rubber bands to a canvas, called it art and had the nerve to slap a two-thousand-dollar price tag on it." Olivia sounded personally insulted.

"Ooh, do I hear some interdisciplinary infighting? Paintbrushes versus pointe shoes at dawn," he teased.

She cleared her throat. "The music is nice, though."

"So we said. Here, have a snack. You're getting grumpy." He offered her his plate, piled high with bite-size hors d'oeuvres.

"No, thank you."

"It's not bad stuff."

She wrinkled her nose. "That's okay."

"First you insult the art and now the food? *Tsk, tsk.*"

"If I'm going to load up on carbs and fat and calories, I'm going to go get a piece of cheesecake from the bakery and really make it worth my while. Not all junk food is created equal, and I'm picky about my splurges." She smiled. "But I will take another margarita."

"That, I can handle." He tossed the plate and offered her his arm. They headed toward the bar, only to be waylaid by a couple of his clients.

When they finally got past, she said, "You seem to know a lot of people here."

"I've lived in Miami for six, nearly seven years now. It happens."

"Since so many of them seem to be plugged-in to

the arts community, I'm surprised your friends haven't dragged you to these kinds of things long before now."

"Oh, man, I'm going to be on every mailing list in the city now, aren't I?"

She nodded without sympathy. "Yep. That's what friends are for."

"I know them," he explained, "but I wouldn't say we're friends."

She nodded. "That I understand."

"Really?" Olivia seemed friendly and outgoing. She shouldn't have a hard time making friends. Jory certainly didn't, so he assumed it was just part of the Madison DNA. "I don't like a lot of people. What's your excuse?"

"I just don't normally stay in one place long enough to make a lot of friends."

"You sound like you're on the run from the law or something."

"I have commitment issues," she confessed matter-of-factly. "I've never been able to agree to anything that locks me in longer than a season. And even then, I have small panic attacks before I sign the contract."

"I'm not sure that's healthy. Have you talked to a psychiatrist?"

"I'm not crazy." He looked unconvinced, so she added, "At least not in any clinical sense, thank you very much. But see, when I was accepted into the National Ballet Academy, I realized dance was what I really wanted to do with my life, and I began to believe I could actually make it my career. So, I made a list of all the places in the world I wanted to dance and all the things I wanted to achieve. I've been checking that list off ever since."

"Like where?"

"New York, Boston, San Francisco, London, Paris, Rome, Prague—"

"Prague?"

She nodded. "Great city. They have wonderful support for their ballet companies."

And he'd lived in Florida his entire life. "You're quite the traveler."

"Jory says I have itchy feet, and it's true. I do."

"That's got to be tough, though."

"It can be. It's got its problems, but it makes up for it in other ways. This is the life I chose, and I don't regret it. I've gotten to see and do a lot."

But there was a cost to everything, he knew. "What's your record?"

"My second time in New York. I stayed eleven months, but only because I stayed on to do summer stock."

"And the shortest?"

"Honolulu, six years ago," she answered immediately. "I signed a six-month contract, but broke my foot three weeks after I got there, and they released me from it. I knew some folks in Dallas, so I went there to recuperate and finished out the season with their company as a guest artist once I was well."

He ordered their drinks. "I didn't hear Miami on that list."

"It wasn't, but priorities shift as you get older. I'm ready to slow down a little, start looking ahead to retirement and what happens after that."

The absurdity of that made him laugh. "You're talking about retirement while everyone else your age is just starting their careers."

"Yes, but that gives me the chance to do something completely different if I want—I don't even have to stay in the arts. I could go school and learn about…" she said with a grin, "advertising, maybe."

"I don't recommend it."

"You seem to be doing pretty well."

"Exactly. The Lawford Agency would crush your little upstart biz like a bug." He handed her the drink and lifted his in a mock toast.

"How very pleasant of you."

"Hey, you're not the only one who made a list of things they wanted to accomplish."

"Really? What's on yours?"

"The only one you need to worry about is number two—making my agency the biggest and best in Miami."

"What's number one?"

"Making it the biggest in the world."

"Oooh, I like a man with big plans. Why don't—"

He didn't hear the rest of that statement because he caught sight of Elaine headed toward him like a missile. *Hell.* He hauled Olivia up against his side, ignoring her shocked "What on earth…?" as he anchored an arm around her waist.

"Evan." Although Elaine was pretending to be friendly, she lacked control over her tone of voice.

"Elaine."

"You're the last person I expected to see here."

"Well, I'm full of surprises."

Elaine looked at Olivia expectantly, and Olivia seemed to finally understand the situation, relaxing into him and smiling at Elaine.

"I don't believe I know your friend."

"This is Olivia Madison. She dances with the Miami Modern Ballet Company. Liv, this is Elaine MacDonald. Elaine's a software designer."

Olivia extended her hand. "Lovely to meet you."

"I'm afraid I don't follow the ballet. It's so old-fashioned at times, and I prefer my arts more modern and cutting-edge." Elaine was taking out her jealousy and hostility toward him by insulting Olivia, who didn't deserve it. He bristled.

"Well, ballet's not for everyone," Olivia answered quickly. Although she'd said almost exactly the same thing to him, her tone was different, landing the insult easily, yet without sounding like it. He was impressed, and waited to see where Olivia would go next.

"I prefer the visual arts," Elaine explained condescendingly. "For instance, I've been following Damien's career since the beginning. The energy and innovation in his work is so exciting," she gushed in the direction of the paintings. "It's very avant-garde, and not for everyone."

Olivia nodded in agreement. "I agree it's not for

everyone, because its over-derivative nature shows an immaturity in the artist that concerns me—or maybe it's just a lack of knowledge." She turned to Evan and smiled sweetly again. "What's coming out of New York right now in this medium is incredible. I guess it just hasn't made it to Miami yet."

Boom. That was a direct hit and Elaine's face reddened. Maybe she would think twice next time before picking a fight with someone who didn't deserve it.

Or maybe not. Elaine was taking a deep breath. And he stepped in before things got really ugly. "Good to see you, Elaine, but we must be off. Take care." He steered Olivia to the other side of the room. "I'm liking this friend thing," he whispered in her ear.

"Do you want to tell me why I just got in an Art 101 competition with that woman?"

"Because you are amazing and delightful and I could kiss you right now. That was brilliant and Elaine totally deserved it."

"But I didn't," she reminded him.

"I know, and I'm sorry. That was her way of trying to needle me."

"What did you do to her?"

He hesitated.

"*Oh*," Olivia said, nodding as understanding dawned. "If I'd known *that*, I might not have taken her down like that. After all, I understand where she's coming from."

"It's not the same thing at all. I mean, you just met her. She's not a nice person."

"But you slept with her anyway?"

He could see her estimation of him sliding south even as she spoke. "I didn't know she wasn't a nice person when I did," he said in his own defense.

"I see. But still…"

"It would be one thing for her to take it out on me because I can handle it and I possibly even deserve it."

"*Possibly?*" Olivia snorted and rolled her eyes.

He cleared his throat. "But attacking another woman just because I might be sleeping with her now? That's bad form."

"You should be more careful about the women you get involved with, then."

"We weren't 'involved,'" he corrected. "We went out a few times."

"And you slept together."

"Well, yes. She's beautiful, and I promise I didn't know she was crazy at the time."

"So you were keeping everything casual."

"Yep. Always do."

"And she didn't know that?"

"Guess not."

Olivia cocked her head. "Why?"

"Why didn't she know? Beats me."

"No," she corrected gently, "why do you keep everything casual?"

"So many questions. What difference does it make?" Olivia just stared at him. Finally, when he couldn't stand the silence another second, he said, "Because I make a terrible boyfriend. Ask any of my exes."

"At least you admit it. That's the first step, you know, admitting you have a problem."

"Oh, I'm selfish, unable to commit…"

"Egotistical, a womanizer, smug…" she supplied.

"Gee, thanks."

"If we're going to be friends, I have to be able to be honest with you," she said primly.

"Maybe I should rethink this friend thing," he muttered.

"The truth hurts." She patted his arm. "But think of all the opportunity you have for personal growth. Then you can have a real relationship one day."

"Oh, you're one to talk."

Olivia's mouth fell open. "I beg your pardon?"

"I don't see you in a relationship."

"I told you. I move around a lot. That, in and of itself, is an issue," she explained, "but I'm also very committed to what I do. I love my job and it comes first. A lot of guys can't handle that."

"We're both just doomed to be forever alone, then, huh?"

"Yeah." She sighed. "It's a good thing we're pretty."

He looked at her and they both burst out laughing.

"Come on," he said, "Let's get out of here. I've had enough culture for one evening."

"And I'm hungry," she added.

"Why am I not surprised?" At least he could let go of any worries he might have about her eating habits. "The pigs in a blanket would have at least filled you up, you know."

"Yuck. There's another place I like about three blocks from here. Will you eat falafels?"

Ugh. "Art *and* falafels in one night?"

"Yes. Good brain food and good body food."

He sighed. "Fine. If I must."

She sighed and took pity on him. "There's a pizza truck just down from the falafel place."

"Then lead on."

About a block later, he remembered what else he wanted to ask. "By the way, what *is* going on in the New York art scene right now?

She shot him a look that questioned his sanity. "How the hell would I know? I'm a ballet dancer."

He burst out laughing. This friend thing…it wasn't always easy to remember just to be friends, but it wasn't as bad as he thought it would be, either.

But then, Olivia had never been what he expected anyway.

And he liked that.

A couple of days went by and Olivia didn't hear from Evan at all. She couldn't decide if that was a good thing or not. It was probably the *wise* thing, but still….

They were friends, and those weren't dates, so it wasn't like he owed her a follow-up call. At the same time, there'd been those *moments* which made the lack of contact now seem like a rejection. So while lack of contact seemed the wiser option, it didn't feel like the better option and bordered on slightly insulting.

Evan—or actually his agency's page, but still—had

liked her Facebook page, and she'd returned the "like," but that meant less than nothing.

It was all too weird. Annoying. Of course, then she got annoyed at herself for being annoyed in the first place. So juvenile.

This was definitely a sign that she needed a group, a posse, something. The lack of a large social circle wasn't new for her—because she moved around a lot, she tended to have more acquaintances than actual friends—but the disappointment over it *was* new. Maybe it was because she really did want to put down roots here, and knowing *that* made her more aware of the sparseness of her life in general.

She owned no furniture—another reason why she'd chosen to live with a roommate in a furnished apartment—and very little "stuff." She'd moved her entire life to Miami from Chicago in a rented Subaru Forester with room to spare. Memorabilia and keepsakes and that kind of stuff had always lived in a rental shed in Tampa, waiting for the day she'd settle down or retire.

If Miami was going to be that place, then she needed to start building a life here—one beyond the studio. It was a little scary to contemplate, and the fact she was annoyed at Evan of all people drove home how much she needed to just commit and get started on that. She'd been here three months already; what was her excuse? *Beyond* the niggling worry that her contract wouldn't be renewed next season. She'd never been without a job or an offer before; she wasn't going to be unemployed.

Maybe the fact she wanted this so much was driving the fear she wouldn't get it.

But she also knew that worry was just asking for failure. *If you worry you will fall, you will fall.* It was advice she'd passed on to hundreds of young dancers—and it was *good* advice. She needed to listen to her own platitudes.

She'd just have to work under the assumption that everything would work out the way she wanted and that Miami would become home. The worst-case scenario? She'd have to rent a bigger truck when she moved.

So by Friday, she'd made her first major purchase, and she luxuriated with her laptop on the wonder that was a new mattress and bedding and surfed the internet in well-supported, high-thread-count comfort. She felt oddly grown up.

She'd given up on wondering what kind of friends she and Evan were supposed to be, so she was quite surprised when her phone rang and Evan's name popped up on the screen. "Hey."

"How've you been, Liv?"

"Good. Busy as always. You?"

"The same."

They were the masters of inanity. And she was getting the feeling that Evan did it on purpose, just to throw her off balance. But for someone who'd been wondering if or when Evan was going to call, she was remarkably without a topic of conversation. "So what's up?"

"Do you work tomorrow?"

"I've got rehearsals until three, why?"

"Would you like to go to a party tomorrow night?"

She needed a minute to process that question. Dinner was different than a party. Dinner was simply food, and people had to eat. She was helping Evan expand his arts education. They could make as much or as little out of those as they needed. A party with his friends was a whole other animal. That might be an actual "date" and did she want to go there?

Evan had to be a mind reader because he seemed to pick up on the thoughts whirling through her mind. "It's a business thing. One of my clients is having their holiday party early to beat the after-Thanksgiving rush, and it's so much easier if I bring a date."

So it was a date, but not a "date." She wasn't sure how she felt about that.

She started to ask how a date would make it easier for him, but stopped herself before she asked the single most ignorant question ever. Evan was young, good-looking, successful and single. "So, in reality, you need a beard."

He laughed. "More like a shield."

"Do I get combat pay?" she teased.

"Free food and booze—and this client goes all out, so it should be quality food and booze. Well worth the splurge."

"While I do the arm-candy-small-talk-thing? Um…I don't know."

"One, while I'm sure you'll make great arm candy,

don't feel you need to hang on mine every second of the evening. Two, Matt Abrams is a big supporter of the arts scene, so between him and his family, friends and clients, there's a good chance you'll find some arty and cultured people there to talk to."

That got her attention. "Matt Abrams as in the Abrams Corporation?"

"Yes. Why? Is that a problem?"

The Abrams family were like gods in the Miami arts and humanities scene. A concert series, a lecture series and an entire *wing* of the art museum carried their name. The MMBC ballet board genuflected at the mere mention of the family. They were already donors, of course, but meeting and mingling in a social situation—well, it wouldn't hurt her to be personally known by any of them.

And, a little voice reminded her, she was still in need of a sponsor. An Abrams corporate event *had* to be a good place to find one.

"Olivia?"

She'd been spinning too long again. Evan was going to think she was mentally deficient in some way. "Formal or semiformal?"

"Cocktail is fine. Do you have a dress?"

"Of course."

"Then I'll pick you up around seven-thirty."

"I'll be ready."

Hanging up, she gave herself a congratulatory mental pat on the back. Seems she hadn't been making such bad choices, after all. Her reward for not being tacky and asking Evan for the sponsorship was entry into the very social circle that could provide exactly that.

Being Evan's friend definitely had benefits.

CHAPTER FIVE

OLIVIA WAS A HIT at the Abrams's party, and Evan congratulated himself on his excellent idea. She was elegant and charming, mingling easily with the other guests and a whiz at party small talk. She'd confessed in the car on the way over that meet and greets were as much a part of her repertoire as *Swan Lake*, as they were essential for...*something*. He hadn't been paying as much attention as he should have because Olivia in a little black sparkly number had fried much of his brain. A simple back sheath that looked demure from the front dipped low in the back to show the sculpted muscles of her shoulders and the long line of her spine from her upswept hair to the small of her back. The hem stopped high enough on her thigh to showcase those amazing legs without looking trashy. Although he'd managed to get his tongue off his toes—eventually—every now and then he'd catch sight of her unexpectedly and all his blood would rush south again.

He wasn't sure he'd be able to hold up his end of this "friends" deal—simply because he couldn't guarantee he'd be able to keep his hands off her for much longer. Not and keep his sanity intact, too. He had to be a masochist to even consider it. Olivia's uneven, hot-and-cold flirting was an added stumbling block, as he couldn't quite tell where her thoughts were heading.

But tonight, they were here as "friends," and repeatedly introducing her and explaining their relationship—"my best friend's sister"—*should* be enough of a reminder to keep his hands in his pockets. But since he rarely brought women to business events, questions about the true nature of their relationship were clear in everyone's eyes.

It was probably in his, too.

Olivia didn't require constant attention, which was nice, allowing him to socialize and mix business in as needed. These people were potential new clients for his agency, and he needed to work the room. But she was also usually near enough to function as that all-important shield, keeping enough speculation alive to prevent any other women from making their move.

A couple of hours into the evening, Matt Abrams made his speech, thanking everyone for another great year. Then the band started playing and people headed for the dance floor.

Olivia was chatting with a woman he vaguely recognized as the wife of one of the city managers as he sidled up beside her. They exchanged pleasantries for a few minutes, then the woman made her excuses with a smile and left them alone.

"Having a good time?"

"I am. Thanks for bringing me. And you were right—the food is great."

He hadn't seen her go near the buffet, but that was neither here nor there. Olivia was also going easy on the booze, nursing a glass of champagne while others were starting to feel their buzzes. When he offered to get her another, she shook her head. "I'd rather stay sober. I don't want to make a fool of myself in front of all these people."

He inclined his head toward the dance floor. "Then why don't we go dance?"

Olivia shook her head. "I said I *didn't* want to make a fool of myself."

"No one's expecting any fancy moves out of you, Twinkletoes."

"Well, that's good."

He reached for her hand, but she shook her head. "I don't really dance."

"You don't *dance*?" He was waiting for the punch line.

"Not like that, I don't."

"Wait…you're actually serious, aren't you?" When she nodded, he couldn't stop himself from laughing, which earned him a withering look from Olivia.

"If I go onto the dance floor, people expect a lot out of me," she explained. "Like I'm supposed to be Ginger Rogers or something, even though my idea of a waltz is a lot different than theirs. It's embarrassing when I can't deliver what they expect. All dance training is *not* equal."

"I'll lead then."

Her eyebrows went up. Slightly suspicious and disbelieving, she asked, "*You* can dance?"

"Well enough not to step on your feet." He held out his hand again. She still looked suspicious. "Come on. What happened to trusting your partner?"

She cut her eyes at him, but didn't acknowledge that conversation otherwise. "You'd better not make me look bad," she warned, but she put her hand in his and let him lead her to the dance floor. Once there, he was able to pull her decently close to him in a special sort of torture. She smelled amazing and his hand found warm bare skin above the deep drape of her dress.

At first, Olivia was stiff in his arms, but after a few minutes, she relaxed a bit and followed his lead. It was nothing fancy—he stuck to the basic steps and she picked them up quickly—but Olivia was obviously impressed when she smiled at him. "You're good."

"You sound surprised."

"Because I am. I didn't peg you as the dancing type." The teasing smile took a little of the sting out of her words.

"Ah, well, I like women, and women *love* a man who'll take them dancing."

Olivia laughed. "That explains it, then. I knew there would be a good reason. So where'd you learn to dance like this?"

He led her through an easy turn and into a shallow dip. "The Recreational Dance Society of Jacksonville. Beginners always welcome."

"*Really?* In college?"

"Yes, really. Why the disbelief?"

She shook her head. "I just can't picture eighteen-year-old Evan Lawford taking time out of his partying to take dance lessons."

"Like I said, the ladies like it."

"I believe it, but you need a better story."

"Why?"

In all seriousness, she said, "Because the lady might not like to hear that you only dance in the ongoing quest to get into her panties."

He had to respect her blunt honesty. "Then what story should I tell?"

She really seemed to be thinking about it. "Um... Like your mom teaching you when you were little. Maybe dancing around the kitchen with your feet on hers. It's a sweet image and would work nicely."

He snorted at the idea and Olivia gave him an odd look. "There's no way I could say that with a straight face," he explained. "I come from a very conservative religious household. No dancing allowed."

"None?"

"No. Dancing inspires lust." He said it with snark, but his father *was* being proven partly right even as he spoke. Evan was certainly lusting after Olivia right now. Much more of this and he was going to have to loosen his hold to put more space between them before Olivia felt that lust.

To his surprise, she collapsed into giggles. "What's so funny?"

"You. Taking dance classes to rebel against your parents. That's got to be the strangest, yet most civilized form of rebellion I've ever heard of."

"Hey, there was plenty of other rebellion," he said in his own defense. "And long before college, thank you very much. There was just no place I could learn to dance in Arrowwood."

Her eyes narrowed suspiciously. "A whole *town* of people who don't dance? Did you grow up in that town in *Footloose* or something?"

"Yes, as a matter of fact, I did. Call me Kevin Bacon." When she continued to stare at him, waiting for his response, he finally shrugged and offered, "When your father is a hellfire preacher in the town's biggest church, no one is going to teach you to dance, even if you ask nicely."

Olivia was incredulous. "*You're* a *preacher's* kid? Oh. My. *God.*" She started to laugh, but pressed her lips closed instead, making the sound come out as an unladylike snort. "That explains oh-so-much about you."

Damn it. He'd assumed she knew, but this proved that Jory had kept his promise and that information to himself. But the last thing he wanted was amateur psychology from Olivia. "Actually, that explains nothing about me."

"I beg to differ."

"Well, you'd be wrong." To throw her off-topic and off balance, he led her into a more complicated pattern that had her nearly tripping over her feet to catch up.

She shot him a dirty look, clearly aware of why he'd

done it. But "I thought you said no fancy moves," was all she said about it.

"Sorry. I thought you could handle it."

"You thought wrong. I still don't know what I'm doing."

There was a sigh in her voice that changed the subject nicely, even if she didn't mean for it to. But they'd been dancing—literally and figuratively—long enough.

He leaned close enough to drop his voice but still see her face. "Do you need a bit longer to feel me out, learn how my body moves and how we fit together?"

He felt her stiffen at the reminder of the words that had been haunting him, and she stumbled slightly again. She'd put the idea out there, though, so she had to have been expecting it to come back on her. A pink flush, evident even in the low light of the room, crawled up her chest to her neck. "I'm not sure we're quite in sync yet."

His thumb stroked the soft skin of her back, and he felt the muscle beneath jump in response. "I think we're getting there. You just need to let go and trust me to do my part."

That flush had made it to her cheeks, and he could see her pulse fluttering in the base of her throat. But when she lifted her eyes, they met his evenly. "That's the thing, Evan. I'm not sure I can."

And, that, sadly, was the truth. Even if Evan looked shocked to hear it.

She knew perfectly well what Evan was capable of—

and honestly, it only made it more difficult to make decisions. She had plenty of memories of exactly how they fit together, what his hands felt like and how he moved. And since he'd had nine years to improve on his technique, the possibilities made her knees a bit wobbly.

But knowing what he was capable of cut both ways, because she knew what he *wasn't* capable of, either. *That's* where she'd gotten burned before. And while she could talk a good game this time, she had to be honest with herself, too, and she wasn't completely sure she trusted herself to be okay with where that limit of capability was.

Evan was the scariest kind of womanizer: he genuinely liked women, and he could be caring and sweet—up to an extent. She didn't think it was an act he pulled just to lure women into his bed, because he didn't need to pretend anything to get women to accept a no-strings fling. The fact that easy, sexy charm probably *wasn't* an act was what made him so dangerous. Even knowing what she knew, even after he'd hurt her before, even telling herself exactly where the line would be going in…it still didn't bode well for her in the end.

And she'd be a fool to set herself up for the hurt—however unintentional—this could cause.

"You can't what? Let go? Or trust me?" Evan asked. There was tight humor in his voice—he didn't seem angry or hurt, just curious, surprised and maybe, just *maybe*, a touch offended.

The song changed, and Evan altered his pace, but not the steps—which they'd now repeated enough that she didn't have to think too much about her feet. But it did remind her that they were not alone: a couple hundred of Miami's wealthy and elite surrounded them. "This isn't an appropriate place for this conversation, Evan."

It was a viable, reasonable excuse—and she'd jumped on it for exactly that reason.

"There's loud music and lots of booze. No one's paying any attention to us, sweetheart."

Okay, different tack. She might as well be up-front and honest. "I thought we were going to be friends."

"We are. Look at us. Perfectly friendly."

"Then why are you making a pass at me? I thought you said you'd respect my wishes."

"I said I'd respect it if you said 'no.' I didn't say I wouldn't ask." He pulled her a little closer and the effect was devastating. "And you haven't said 'no,' yet."

And that was a glaring and very telling lack of action on her part. While Evan might be lots of less-than-gentlemanly-things, she didn't doubt he would back down as soon as she said it. Yet somehow the magic word wouldn't make it past her lips. She was a fool, but she'd put herself in this position willingly, knowing she'd have to make the choice sooner or later.

She had weaknesses—plenty of them—and she always had to balance the want against the price she might later pay for the indulgence. Everything was a trade-off: she might have a slice of chocolate cake, but skip the bread, or she'd do extra sit-ups the next day to work off some of the extra calories. As long as she didn't eat cake every night, it wasn't a problem.

Everything in moderation. Splurge occasionally because life was short. You only live once.

Evan was a splurge. And far more tempting than any chocolate cake. The big question, though, was could she enjoy Evan in moderation this time?

Evan hadn't said a word the whole time she went over things in her mind. He'd just kept dancing, kept stroking his thumb over her back and raising goose bumps on her skin, waiting for her to answer.

She took a deep breath and met his eyes. The heat there should have scorched her. "I haven't said no, but then, you haven't actually asked me a question, either."

Evan finally stopped moving. The hand he was still holding shifted slightly, keeping them palm to palm but allowing his fingers to thread through hers and squeeze gently. "Do you want to get out of here?"

Moment of truth time.

She only hesitated for a second.

"Yes."

Evan seemed genuinely surprised at her answer, and for a split second, Olivia wondered if he'd just been messing with her, teasing her and flirting without expectation.

Because if so...well, she'd have to kill him.

But then she noticed the way his fingers continued to tighten around hers and the slow, sexy smile. "Good."

Their exit was hurried and as sly as possible. Evan mumbled something about not wanting to make the entire rounds and Olivia agreed. She grabbed her wrap and purse and tried to look dignified—just in case—as they slipped out the door and into the stairwell headed to the parking deck.

Her heels clacked on the metal stairs and it echoed in the emptiness. Evan kept a hand on her elbow to steady her down the first two flights, but on the next landing, he stopped, trapping her between his body and the wall and causing her heartbeat to kick into double time.

Then his hand was cupping her cheek and tilting her head to his and…

Sweet mercy. This was probably a big mistake. A decision she was going to regret.

But the regret would come later, and right now, she had this. Her purse dropped to the floor, forgotten, as she gripped the lapels of his jacket.

Evan's kiss was everything she remembered and more. Unhurried but hungry, it promised all kinds of pleasures to come, and pure *want* drowned out any cautions from her higher brain functions.

He tasted like the whiskey on the rocks he'd been drinking earlier, only hot and far more potent. Then he leaned into her, pressing her back against the cool cinder block wall, deepening the kiss and blocking out everything that wasn't him.

And his hands…one was gentle against her cheek, but the other was strong against her hip—both of them caressing and stoking the fire kindled by his tongue.

She slid her hands under his jacket to feel the hard muscles of his stomach hidden under fine cotton, then wrapped her arms around his waist to pull him against her.

A groan echoed off the walls, and she wasn't sure

if it was hers or his. Evan's lips were hot against her neck, sending shivers over her skin. Hooking a foot around his calf, she pulled his thigh between hers and squeezed, trying to release some of the tension building inside her.

"Liv." Evan mumbled against her neck as a tremor rocked his body against hers. The hand that had been kneading her hip reached for hers as he pressed another hard kiss against her lips, then he bent down to get her purse and pushed through the door into the parking deck.

Olivia followed on shaky legs. At the car, Evan stopped to kiss her again, and she nearly climbed him like a tree, wanting more. Whispering a promise that made her blush, Evan opened her door. She scrambled inside as Evan went to the driver's side.

Some of her hair had come down—or been pulled down by Evan's hands—and she could feel the French twist now wobbling drunkenly on her head. Not caring or bothering with a mirror, she searched for the other pins and let it all fall loose around her shoulders with a big shake. Evan paused as he put the car in gear to run his hands through the messy curls, then used it to tug her over to his side for another kiss. "I don't know how I'm going to get us home."

"Drive fast."

Evan grinned at the command, and tires squealed as he accelerated. They were both quiet, and Olivia wondered if the pounding of her heart was audible to Evan as his hand landed on her knee and moved up to gently stroke the sensitive skin of her inner thigh. Her nails dug into the leather seat as the muscles began to quiver. She let her head fall back against the headrest and closed her eyes as his fingers moved slowly, maddeningly, *dangerously* higher.

But was it actually dangerous? A little voice inside her was shouting a warning, but it was easy enough to ignore. Dumping old emotions on top of this would be a mistake. She was an adult, not some starry-eyed kid, and *this* was not the same as last time at all.

Evan was hot and sexy and occasionally sweet, and there were far worse reasons to have sex. There was no reason to overthink this. Evan's fingers moved another crucial inch. Hell, why was she even thinking at all when she could just *feel*?

Mercy.

All that attention to *feeling* meant Olivia had no idea how long she'd been in the car or even where they were, but Evan was killing the engine and coming around to open her door. The breeze and the play of the lights told her they were near water, but she had no idea *which* water and she lacked enough knowledge of Miami as a whole to even hazard a guess.

Wherever they were, it was gorgeously landscaped and lush—the building not brand-new, but not shabby either, and the fact it wasn't a high-rise meant they might be off one of the canals, but not right off the bay. She had no idea. But, really, it didn't matter. Evan paused long enough to give her another kiss before leading her up the path to his door.

She half expected Evan to grab her, sweep her off her feet and carry her to the bedroom the second the door closed behind them, but instead, she found herself pulled gently into a long, unhurried kiss. He took her purse and wrap and laid them on a table before tossing his keys on top and shrugging out of his suit coat. She took a deep breath as an anticipatory shiver ran over her.

"Can I get you a drink or something?" he asked as he loosened his tie.

The air rushed out of her lungs. *Was he kidding?* She was so primed that one more touch might do the trick and Evan was playing Gracious Host? Hell, the only thing keeping her from dragging *him* to the bedroom was the fact she didn't know where the bedroom *was*.

"I'm good, thanks," she lied. More accurately, she felt like an idiot, standing in his foyer like an unsuspecting prom date who'd just been friendzoned.

"You sure? Wine? Water?"

"I'm *sure*." She didn't like the tone of her voice, but it couldn't be helped.

In a snap, the Gracious Host was gone, replaced by an almost predatory look that weakened her knees. "Good. That way," he pointed.

"Finally," she said honestly, slipping out of her shoes and following him. "I thought we were about to have a tea party."

"Hey, I was just trying to be nice."

"Noted. Appreciated."

Evan backed into a room, pulling her with him, and she could see the bed just over his shoulder.

"But I didn't come here for nice," she added.

A split second later, she was flat on her back on that bed with Evan looming over her. "Since you put it that way…"

She wasn't sure if that was a warning or a promise, but she was okay either way. Evan straddled her hips, his eyes watching hers as he unbuttoned his shirt and tossed it aside.

Oh yes. Very nice. It might be shallow, but Olivia spent every day in the company of men who, by the nature of their careers, had excellent bodies. *That* set a standard difficult for an average guy to meet. But Evan…oh, he'd do *nicely*. Plenty of definition and strength on display without being overly brawny or muscle-bound. A light sprinkling of hair accented his pecs before narrowing to a trail that bisected a nice set of abs and disappeared into the waistband of his pants. Her fingers itched to trace that line, and she did, following it from his belt buckle to his sternum, loving the way the muscles contracted under her touch.

Evan tugged her dress up over her hips, nearly to her ribs, before pulling her up to slide it up and off. Olivia had that one moment of self-consciousness but tried to push it aside. Evan had seen her naked before; he knew what he was getting. She had no breasts to speak of, no "womanly" curves. She was just as far from the lingerie model ideal figure as any other woman. It was a double standard, she knew, to expect a certain physique from a man while she offered a bony, boobless body in return, but Evan didn't seem to mind any more now than he had then.

If anything, Evan seemed to like it, his eyes hooded and dark as his hands mapped a path for his lips to follow. Her breasts might be small, but they were very sensitive, and the rasp of his tongue over her nipple had her arching off the bed, begging for more.

She'd been a virgin the first time with Evan, too naive to not confuse love and sex, and too nervous to fully appreciate the experience. But tonight...*mercy.*

Her hands were shaking with need, making her attempts at his belt and zipper clumsy. Evan finally took over, shucking his clothes and giving her the skin to skin contact she craved. His skin was hot, his body heavy on hers, his fingers and tongue working black magic on her until she wanted to scream.

So she did.

Olivia's thighs squeezed him like a vise, threatening to crack a rib as she came against his mouth. Evan felt the shock wave roll through her body and redoubled his efforts, working his tongue until she was tugging at his hair, pulling him up and over her and wrapping those long powerful legs around his hips.

The sight of Olivia nearly stopped his heart. That golden-red hair was wild and tangled, and her skin was flushed pink and glistened under a sheen of sweat. She opened her eyes, dark with desire but focused directly on his, and used those legs to leverage him closer.

He knelt between her thighs, indulging his need to

touch her. Her skin was so soft, but it draped over steel-hard muscle that fluttered as his fingers touched it. He'd seen her in action; he knew she was strong and had seen what she could do with her body, and it gave him a primal level of satisfaction to see her body react so strongly because of him.

But that strength put him in a tug-of-war—her pulling him closer, him holding back, wanting to touch and explore with leisure—that he wasn't entirely sure he'd be able to win, even if he really wanted to.

He anchored himself and slid his hands over her ribs to her breasts, tracing light circles around her nipples. Olivia's eyes rolled back in her head and teeth caught her bottom lip.

"Ev-*an*..."

The breathy, exasperated plea made him smile. He squeezed a nipple gently, causing her to groan. "Yes, Liv?"

Her hand grabbed his wrist. "Don't tease."

"But you said not to rush the foreplay, remember?"

"You're evil." A tiny tremor shook her body and she released his wrist. "And you're killing me."

He wanted to feel smug, but Liv's hand had slithered down between them, palming him and working him with gentle, insistent pressure that threatened to snap his control. His hands were shaking as he reached for the nightstand drawer and grabbed a condom. "I know the feeling."

That earned him a smile that turned wicked as she took the condom from him, turning a simple, usually perfunctory action into an erotic one that left him groaning and wheezing for air.

"Now who's teas—?" The question was cut short as Olivia lifted her hips and guided him in.

He lost the ability to speak—the ability to even *think*—as all his higher brain functions shut down, narrowing his focus to one thing, and Olivia's deeply satisfied sigh echoed his own.

He moved slowly at first, taking his time, loving the way Olivia responded—earnestly, wholeheartedly and enthusiastically—the little moans spurring him on. He wanted to savor, prolong it, but he'd been waiting for nine years to have Olivia in his bed again, and that resolve was weakening under the need to lose himself in her completely.

She was thrashing, fisting the sheets and moving her hips frantically, trying to increase the pace. Rolling to his back, he pulled Olivia atop him to let her take the lead.

Her hair fell like a curtain around them, blocking out everything else as she rocked against him, finding her groove and driving him insane. When her eyes glazed over and her rhythm faltered, he grabbed her hips and took over, slamming into her again and again until she arched nearly in half, her whole body shuddering and shivering as her orgasm moved through her.

It was beautiful to watch, but her climax pushed him over the edge, causing him to explode with enough force to make his vision go fuzzy at the edges.

When he was finally able to think again, Olivia was

draped over his chest, her breath still heaving. Carefully, he pushed her hair out of his face and hers, gathering it into a loose ponytail and wrapping it around his fist.

Olivia smiled, but her eyes stayed closed. "Thanks. It was bothering me but I couldn't be bothered to find the energy to move it."

"Well, that was about all the energy I had left. I may be dead now."

Her fingers stroked slowly over his chest, then she opened her eyes. "Pity."

Amazingly, that was enough to stir his blood, if no other part of his body. "Just give me a minute or two."

"Yay." After a heavy sigh, she asked, "Am I too heavy? Do I need to move?"

The woman weighed nothing, and she felt amazing anyway. "No."

"Good." After another sigh, she seemed to doze off.

Since the only remaining option was for him to lie here and think—which he really didn't want to do—he did the same.

CHAPTER SIX

OLIVIA EASING OUT of bed woke him up. Sunshine streamed in through curtains he'd forgotten to close, telling him they'd slept pretty late.

But then they hadn't gotten much sleep before the sun came up, either. He felt wrung-out and sore in muscles he didn't know he had, but the deep, sated satisfaction well made up for that.

Olivia stretched, bending herself into another of those impossible positions. It was kind of sexy, until he heard a sharp crack.

"Ouch."

She started, then looked over her shoulder. "Just wait," she said with a weak smile and proceeded to crack seemingly each and every joint in her body—including some he didn't know *could* crack. "Ah, that's better."

"Good lord, Olivia. It sounds like you're falling apart."

She shrugged. "I'm in pretty good shape for my age, so I'm lucky."

She was in excellent—amazing—shape. "For your *age*?"

"Sadly, I can't be twenty-one forever. A couple of my friends have already retired, but they had injuries that tipped the scale a little early. If I make it to thirty-five, I'll be happy." She reached for the shirt he'd thrown on the floor last night and slipped into it. "I need water. I'm as dry as the Sahara this morning. Do you want anything?" she called as she disappeared down the hallway.

He grabbed a pair of boxers and followed her. "I'll make coffee."

"Oh, that will be excellent. But water first." She poured a full glass and drank deeply as he filled the pot and measured coffee. The initial morning-after awkwardness that they avoided by Olivia's snap-crackle-pop routine settled in belatedly and they stood there silently as the coffee brewed.

Finally, he asked, "Do you need to be home at a specific time today?"

"Not really. I've got some sewing and laundry to do, but I have Sundays off unless we're performing or something. But," she quickly added, setting down her glass, "I don't want to keep you from whatever you need to do today. I can call a cab or…"

"I've got no plans." He paused and reached for the hem of the shirt she wore, tugging her a few inches closer. "Yet."

"Well, all I have is the dress I wore last night. It rather limits my options."

"You don't need clothes for what I'm planning."

"I'm intrigued."

"Good."

Olivia was angling in for a kiss when a loud, fast guitar riff played and her purse began vibrating against the table. She pulled back as if she'd been burned.

"It's okay," he said, "You can answer it."

"I'd really rather not."

In that second he recognized the tune and realized why it was familiar. At that point, he wanted to put even more space between them. There was really only one person Olivia would assign that particular song to on her phone because it was one of his favorite songs: Jory.

He didn't know why she might not feel like talking to her brother at the moment, but it served him up a heaping load of guilt for his behavior. Not for sleeping with Olivia—he had no regrets—but because he knew he *should* feel bad for not staying away from Jory's sister. It was a fine hair to split—but one he'd been splitting all his life. He might be sorry what he did was a sin, but only *because* it was a sin. But he wouldn't be sorry he did it because he'd enjoyed it and would do it again if the opportunity presented itself. His father, needless to say, hadn't been pleased with that bit of amateur theology runaround. Where he and Olivia were concerned, he doubted Jory would be impressed with that logic either, and forgiveness wouldn't be easily given.

"That's Jory's ringtone," Olivia explained unnecessarily, then she shook her head. "Maybe I shouldn't have brought him up right now. You know, all things considered."

"Well, one of us had to."

"But my brother and my sex life aren't really something I like to discuss in the same conversation."

"I'm sure Jory feels the same way. But," he added, "You and me? It's kind of hard *not* to bring him in."

"Ew. Gross."

"Liv," he chided, "You know what I mean."

"I do. I also know that I'm an adult and it's none of my brother's business who I sleep with."

"True."

Olivia looked uncomfortable. "How much does Jory know? About before, I mean."

"You don't know?"

"I know he knows something, but he certainly doesn't talk about it, and he wasn't keen on even the *idea* of us hooking up." She shrugged. "But you two are friends."

Evan had no idea where to go from there. "Does it matter? That's ancient history."

"Except that it's news now, isn't it?"

"Is it?"

Olivia sighed. "Look, I'll be honest with you if you'll be honest with me."

That was almost ominous. "Seems fair," he said carefully.

"Honestly, the less Jory knows about my sex life the better. And as I said, it's none of his business who I sleep with."

"I happen to agree with you on that."

"So, I don't see the need to tell Jory about this. Do you?"

"I can assure you that your brother does not want me anywhere near you, so no, I don't see the need to tell him anything either."

Instead of agreement, he got a surprised look from her. "Why is that?"

"Because as you said, it's none of Jory's business."

"No. Why do you say Jory doesn't want you near me?"

"Because you're his sister." Surely she understood that.

"But you're his friend. If you're good enough for him to hang out with, why aren't you good enough for me?"

Oh, where to begin. "Because."

"Because?"

He poured coffee, stalling, and when that didn't work, he tried to shrug it off. "Yeah, because."

"Is this some kind of weird guy thing?"

"Yes," he said, hoping she'd leave it at that. "It's a guy thing."

"How juvenile. It's like you're still teenagers."

He was beginning to agree. Hell, hadn't he already convinced himself there was a big difference between an eighteen-year-old sister and a twenty-seven-year-old sister? But that might just be wishful thinking on his part.

"So sisters are completely off-limits?" she asked

and waited until he nodded. "That's insane. What if we were to fall in love?"

Evan spit his coffee across the counter, burning his lip in the process. "Whoa, there. Liv, I—um…"

She waved a hand and passed him a towel. "Oh, calm down. It's purely a rhetorical question. It just seems unfair. Does he get to put other, nonrelated women off-limits?"

"No."

"Then that's just ridiculous. Either it's his business who you sleep with or it isn't."

"It's more complicated than that."

"Only because boys are weird."

"Oh, and girls aren't? One of your girlfriends would be okay if you slept with her brother?"

That gave her a second's pause. "I wouldn't know. Unless that girl's brother was also dancing in the same company, the chances of me meeting him are slim. Anyway, dancers are a small community. Chances are whoever you're sleeping with has slept with someone else you know anyway. The grown-up thing to do is to butt the hell out of any sex that doesn't currently involve you."

She had a refreshing, mature approach that didn't help at all in this instance. "I'd agree, but the last time I slept with you, Jory practically broke my nose. Right, wrong or indifferent, Jory *does* have strong opinions when it comes to me and you."

Olivia blinked. "He did *what*?"

He cursed. "Nothing. You want some breakfast?"

"Oh, no, you can't drop something like that and just move on. So Jory does know we hooked up?"

He could lie. It only depended on which Madison sibling he wanted to anger today. From the look on Olivia's face, it was probably safer for him to tell the truth to her. "Yes."

"And he was mad about it."

"Yes."

"Why? And don't give me any 'because of a Guy Thing' crap."

"Aside from the 'Guy Thing crap'—which is not crap, by the way—you don't screw around—literally or not—with someone's sister when you have nothing to offer."

"Every woman is someone's sister."

"Then let me rephrase—"

"No need," she interrupted. "It'll never make sense. But if Jory was so mad about this, how come he never said anything to me about it?"

"Because once it was over and done with, there was no need." He could hope she'd accept that at face value.

"That little…" She shook her head slowly. "I'm going to kill him."

"Olivia…"

"Don't," she warned. "Jory told you to back off, didn't he?" She didn't wait for his answer. "*That's* why you dumped me like that."

"In all fairness, you were leaving for London—"

"New York," she corrected.

"—or wherever in another couple of weeks or so. What difference did it make?"

"It made a hell of a difference to me. *Jory* makes a decision, *I* get dumped and *you* get to be the bad guy. He comes out smelling like a rose. I'm going to *kill* him."

"Liv, be serious. You're getting all worked up over something that happened years ago. And Jory really did mean well."

"Oh, as long as he *meant* well, that changes everything," she snarked. "I'll just forget all the hurt and shame and stuff since he 'meant well'."

Somehow he was the rational person in the conversation. Jory owed him big-time. "How would you going off to New York feeling like you had some kind of attachment to me have been at all good for your career?"

"I wasn't 'attached' to you," she mumbled.

"Really? Then why did it hurt?" Her lips flattened and she looked deep into her coffee cup. His point made, he continued. "But that way, you went off, with nothing holding you back. And being mad at me was far preferable to you being mad at Jory, right?"

"Why are you being so damn reasonable about this?"

"Because I happen to think Jory was right." It had been the right thing—for everyone.

That took some of the wind out of her sails. "Wow. You really are a cold, heartless bastard."

"So you've said."

She lifted her chin. "So what about last night, then?"

"There's a big difference between then and now. Not

only are you an adult, you're established in your career and your life—there's not much for me to screw up for you now. I've been very honest about what I wanted, so if you did make that choice, my conscience could be clear."

Olivia rubbed her temples. "I'm not sure how to process this."

"Then or now?"

"Either. Both. It's going to take a little time for me to make sense of it." She looked at him. "Here's the thing about now, though—*I'm* not worried about Jory or what he thinks. Are you?"

There was a clear challenge there that was impossible to fully answer. "I brought you home last night, remember? But, no, I don't see the need to rub Jory's nose in it. I may not be the best of friends, but I hope I'm better than that."

"If it makes you feel better," she said quietly, the quick change of mood surprising him, "I think you're a really good friend to Jory."

He certainly didn't feel like it. "Yes, because sleeping with his baby sister is the true sign of friendship."

"But you don't want him to be upset, so that says something. Does it make me a bad sister to sleep with my brother's best friend?"

"Well, when you put it like that…"

"The thing is, I can see where the idea of possibly being put in the middle or forced to choose sides comes into this, but that's an issue *any* time two people you know—especially if you know them independently of each other—are involved. It's selfish to demand other people adjust *their* behavior so that *you* aren't made uncomfortable at some point. And it's insane to think you *could* put those demands on people. It's like telling a married couple they can't get divorced because it will mess up the seating charts at your future dinner parties." He started to argue, but Olivia lifted a hand to stop him. "I don't like to think about my brother having sex, either, so you know what I do? *I don't think about it.*"

He couldn't help but laugh. "That's very logical, Olivia."

"Thank you."

"But people, as a whole, aren't logical. Especially about people they love. Or sex."

"Then it's your call. I'll leave now, if that's what you want."

"I didn't say that. But Jory won't forgive me if you get hurt again."

"Your ego is simply astounding." She shook her head.

"It has nothing to do with ego."

She sighed, then shrugged. "Well, if you don't think you can handle me, that's fine." She set her coffee cup on the counter. "I'll go get dressed. Call me a cab, will you?" she called over her shoulder as she headed back down the hall.

He caught her in the bedroom and tackled her to the bed. "Can I handle you? Liv, honey, I thought I proved that last night. *Repeatedly*. The real question is…can you handle me?"

"I think that was proven last night, as well."

He pretended to think as he worked the buttons of her shirt open. "Maybe we should try it one more time. Just to be sure."

"Might take more than *one* more time," she said. "You know, to be *absolutely* sure."

His conscience sent up a small protest, but Olivia was sliding out of that shirt and…

Well, at least he could say he tried.

There was nothing quite like orgasms to completely change a girl's outlook on life.

It was rather silly, actually, as nothing else in her life had changed at all, but Olivia had to admit she was in a much better mood. Like a pressure valve had been opened.

Endorphins, she thought. *Amazing things*.

There was a slight soreness to muscles that hadn't been used like that in a long while, but the little frizzle of energy remaining in her blood was well worth the trade-off. And while Evan had brought her home early last night, the sheer amount of energy expended on what would normally be her lazy day off left her feeling a little tired and hungover as she warmed up at the barre Monday morning.

But even with that, she still felt it was worth it. No regrets at all.

She wasn't sure she could say the same about Evan,

though. She had to respect the level of loyalty to Jory that would make a player like Evan think twice about sleeping with a woman, but it dinged her pride as well—as if she had to talk him into it or something. Her inner femme fatale was a little miffed.

But everyone kept asking her about the smirk on her face, so she couldn't be *too* miffed about it. Or stay that way for very long. After all, once Evan had gotten past the whole Jory's-sister thing, she could make no complaints about his performance.

She even felt a bit better about the way Evan had treated her before. It still stung, and she still needed to kill Jory, but she had to look at it in a different light now. If nothing else, it made it a little easier to reconcile her attraction to Evan *now*. At least she didn't have to feel completely shallow or masochistic about it anymore.

As for what would happen next…possibly the best part of this was that she didn't *need* to worry about "next"—no matter what it might be. There was a very nice freedom in that.

"Earth to Olivia?" Theo waved a hand in front of her face. "Can you move so we can put the barres away?"

She'd spaced out, moving through the warm-up by rote and habit, and now she was busted. "Sorry," she muttered and went to stretch, figuring she'd use the time to get her head back in the studio where it belonged before she hurt herself.

Theo followed her. "You okay?"

"Yeah." She put her foot on the barre and lay over

her leg. "Just a little out of it today," she offered as an explanation.

"Career, money or sex?"

"Excuse me?" she asked.

"It's got to be one of the three. The smirk on your face means it's probably good, so that strikes worries about family and health off the list of topics to space out over."

"I'm putting my money on sex." Tina, one of younger soloists, propped her foot up onto the barre next to them.

"Oh, really?" Theo asked eagerly, totally ignoring the shut-up-please look Olivia shot him. "And why is that?"

"Leslie, that new apprentice—"

"Which one is she?" he interrupted.

"Kinda short, dark hair. Bad feet but pretty turns?"

Nodding, he said, "Okay, go on."

"Leslie works for a catering company that did the big Abrams Corporation party Saturday night and Olivia was there. With a very good-looking guy, too."

Olivia hadn't seen anyone she knew, but then there'd been a lot of people there, and she hadn't been paying all that much attention to the staff. *Damn.*

"How interesting."

"I know. Leslie didn't recognize the guy, though. Then she got busy and forgot to ask."

Good lord. They were gossiping about her as though she wasn't even there. She stood up. "*Ahem.*"

"Shh," Theo said, pushing her back down over her leg. "You stretch." He turned back to Tina. "*And...?*"

"*And* Olivia left early with Mr. Tall, Hot and Anonymous."

"So definitely sex, then. Okay, 'fess up, Olivia," he said, tapping her on the back. "Who is he?"

She didn't even bother to lift her head. "Oh, so *now* I get to be a part of this conversation?"

"Yes, please. We want details."

"The juicy ones," Tina added.

She didn't want to be the subject of dressing room gossip, and demurring to answer all but guaranteed she would be. But that did not mean she was willing to confirm speculations about her sex life for the company to further discuss at their leisure. "He's my brother's college roommate."

"Oh." Tina looked disappointed, and Olivia bit back a smile. While the truth of that statement might be causing *her*—and Evan—problems, she had to love it a little, too. A complete, concise, easy-peasy speculation shut down without any of the "he's just a friend" vague denials that would be met with even *more* probing. "But if he's hot *and* important enough to get an invite to the Abrams's do, give him my number."

Hell, she wasn't sure she had Tina's number even if she did want to offer Evan up like that. "I'll let him know you're available."

"Please do," Tina said and went back to the other side of the room, presumably to tell the others what new info she had.

She smacked him, hard. "Gee, thanks, Theo."

"What?" he said, rubbing his arm.

"Did you really *have* to encourage her? She's still annoyed that I got 'her' contract. Way to give her more ammo against me."

"That contract was only Tina's in her dreams. She's lucky her big butt ever made it out of the corps." He waved it off. "So are you going to tell me about this guy or not?"

"I need to go change my shoes."

"Come on."

She sighed. "I already told you. He's my brother's college roommate. He needed a date for the party, and I had nothing better to do. So I went. And I met Matt Abrams, so that's not too shabby, either."

"And your smug mood today is caused by...?"

"I had a good time." She wasn't going to offer more than that, and Theo could infer anything he liked from it. She trusted Theo not to provide grist for the rumor mill. Of course, it helped that she had some dirt on him, and he knew it.

After a moment, Theo nodded. "Good for you, sweetie. Now, I'll let you go change your shoes, as I'm pretty sure Sylvie is going to want to run through the *adage* first."

Olivia took a second to check her phone while she was at it and found a text from Evan: You busy tonight?

It made her smile and put a sizzle in her blood at the same time she gave it a mental side-eye. There was a definite overtone of booty call to the message, which part of her felt she *should* be offended by. At the same time, the memories of yesterday were fresh enough to make her glad of an encore.

Theo was calling for her, forcing her to make a decision. I'll be done by 5:30, she typed quickly and dropped the phone back into her bag. There was no sense second-guessing herself, and there was no reason not to enjoy herself while she could.

With the decision made and the rationale accepted, she found her mind much clearer and her usual concentration returned. In fact, she almost forgot about Evan all together until later that afternoon when Leslie-the-apprentice mentioned seeing her at the party. That sent her back to her phone during the water break to see if he'd responded.

I'll pick you up at your place on my way home. 6:30-ish.

The rest of the afternoon dragged by.

Broiled chicken and steamed veggies. It wasn't exciting, but Olivia was forcing him to eat better these days. Well, not *forcing*—she actually hadn't said anything about his diet—but a man could only eat junk while his dinner partner ate healthy so many times before guilt set in. He'd buckled under in less than a week. Olivia still hadn't said anything, but she'd smirked when he told her tonight's menu.

"It's ready," he called, setting the plates on the coffee table. Olivia came out of the bedroom in yoga pants and a tank top, braiding her hair as she walked.

"Good, I'm starved. Thank you for cooking."

As she settled beside him, he noticed her bright pink socks. "Are you cold?"

She paused, a forkful of chicken partway to her mouth. "No. Why?" He indicated the socks and she shrugged. "Oh, that. I've just got ugly feet."

He honestly hadn't paid that much attention to her feet before—he'd been too busy focusing on other, more interesting parts of her anatomy. "They can't be that bad."

"Oh, yeah they can. This is yummy, by the way."

He'd seen pointe shoes. There was no way they didn't do bad things to her feet. "Let me see them."

She crossed her legs, tucking her feet under her thighs. "No way."

"Come on," he cajoled. She shook her head and took a bite. "I'm going to see them eventually."

"Maybe. But not now. It'll kill your appetite."

"One of my first jobs in college was at a restaurant. I cooked, washed dishes, scrubbed the grills. It tore my hands up."

"My parents own a restaurant. I'm well aware of what it does to your hands."

He put his fork down. "Well, my first college girlfriend dumped me because she said my hands were troll-like, and she didn't like them touching her."

"What a witch."

"True, but my point is, I understand."

"Look, even *I* think my feet are gross. I'm not showing them off. *No*," she added when he started to protest. "End of subject."

"It's not like I can't sneak a peek later."

"That's up to you. I can warn you, but I can't stop you." She shook her head. "You might regret it, though."

"You've got some weird hang-ups," he mumbled.

She smiled at him angelically. "Everyone's crazy in their own special way. The trick is to find the person who thinks your special brand of crazy is kinda cute."

"You've got a special brand there, that's for sure," he mumbled toward his chicken.

"Where did you work?"

He let her change the subject, since she obviously felt strongly about it. "The Carousel."

"That place on the beach where the waitresses wear bikinis?"

"That's the one. How do you know about The Carousel?"

"Who in Florida *doesn't* know about that place? It's legendary. I never got to go, of course, but I've heard stories from friends and other people who went to Jacksonville for spring break." She shook her head. "Wow. When you decided to rebel against your upbringing, you went all out, didn't you? Dancing, drinking, women, working in a place like that. Were you trying to mark off all seven deadly sins or just break half the Ten Commandments?"

"I had a punch card. Every tenth sin earned me a free ice cream cone to enjoy in my front row seat in hell."

"So much for a 'civilized' rebellion."

"It takes more than a few dance lessons to really rebel."

"What did your parents think?"

"I didn't tell them anything, but this girl from high school was also going to school in Jacksonville and come summer break, she went home and told *everyone* all my sins."

She shook her head in sympathy. "I hate people like that."

"Me, too. My father threatened to disown me, my mother cried because they were so embarrassed I'd turned my back on everything they'd tried to teach me. Big drama."

"But look at you now. You're certainly doing well for yourself. They can't be too upset with how you turned out."

He shrugged.

"They're not? Why?"

"Honestly, I have no idea if they are or not. I don't even know if they know how I turned out. I haven't been back to Arrowwood since the day I left, and I haven't spoken to my parents in ten, maybe eleven, years."

"I'm so sorry."

Of course Olivia would think that a tragedy. She had great parents. "I'm not. It's better this way. Everyone's much happier, I promise."

Carefully, she asked, "So there's no chance for reconciliation?"

He leaned back and studied her. "Show me your feet."

"What?"

"If you want to talk about my parents, you have to show me your feet. It's only fair if we *both* do something we don't want to."

She actually seemed to consider it. "Point taken. I won't pry anymore. But I *am* sorry you have unreasonable and judgmental parents."

"Thanks, Liv. Now you know why I've always preferred yours." That reminded him, especially since Olivia hadn't mentioned it yet. "Speaking of your parents, have you talked to them today?"

She shook her head. "Mom called earlier but I was in rehearsals. She left a message for me to call tomorrow. Wait—why do you ask?"

"I normally go to your parents' for Thanksgiving, you know."

Olivia looked at her plate. "I'd forgotten about that."

"Dee called today and asked me to give you a lift to Tampa."

"You're kidding."

"You don't have a car, Olivia. It makes sense."

"But I've lined up a rental. I *want* to drive."

"They're just worried about you driving Alligator Alley on your own at night."

"I'm an adult. I've been on my own for years. I've navigated foreign cities where no one speaks English. I think I can handle a four-hour drive through central Florida all by myself."

"But the cell reception sucks through there. I see their point, even if you are too skinny for the alligators to bother eating."

She shot him a sour look for that crack. "I'm going up on Wednesday, but I have to come back Friday night. I'm in the Santa parade on Saturday. You shouldn't have to cut your holiday short because of me."

"I've got plans on Saturday myself. It works out fine."

Olivia muttered under her breath.

"Give in graciously to make your parents happy, and I promise I won't look at your feet when you're naked later," he offered as a compromise.

"But I *wanted* to drive. I haven't driven since August."

"Fine. I'll let you drive part of the way. Will that make you happy?"

She grinned. "Oh, I was hoping you'd say that. Deal. I can leave anytime after four on Wednesday."

CHAPTER SEVEN

IT TOOK THEM longer than expected to get to Tampa. They blamed it on traffic, and everyone accepted that explanation without question. Thankfully, no one seemed to notice they were a bit more rumpled than they should be after the drive.

Evan, though, felt a little bad about the delay when he dropped Olivia at the Madisons' and saw the genuine excitement and misty eyes of Olivia's homecoming. They were truly an ideal family, straight out of a greeting card commercial—Dee fussing when she found out they hadn't eaten yet, and Gary offering him gas money for the trip. He declined both the money and the offer of food and left for Jory's place. Olivia thanked him for the ride politely and with the right amount of distance, but she had a small, I've-got-a-secret smile on her face as he left.

He got another helping of guilt when he got to Jory's twenty minutes later. He'd delayed seeing his best friend in order to see his best friend's sister naked—which he wasn't about to admit. He tossed his gear into Jory's "guest room"—which was more of a weight room with a twin bed from Jory's childhood bedroom tucked in the corner—while Jory got them both beers.

Like his sister, Jory chose to live downtown, doing his part to help gentrify an area trying to reinvent itself. It was a stark contrast to his parents' suburban lifestyle, but Jory had taken to it perfectly, all the way down to the local microbrewed beer he offered. A perfect example of a young, upwardly mobile lawyer with a hipster bent.

They caught up on a few things, then Jory said, "By the way, thanks for driving Livvy up."

"Not a problem."

"I told Mom not to ask you, but she still worries about Olivia."

"I was coming this way anyway, so it made sense."

"And it went all right?" Jory asked carefully.

That was probably as close as Jory was going to come to bringing up Evan's past with Olivia. He hadn't mentioned it since the day Evan had agreed to leave Liv alone. "It was fine. It's been a long time—too long for old grudges."

Jory snorted. "You obviously don't know my sister very well. She can carry a grudge with the best of them."

He'd say he was getting to know Olivia pretty well these days. And while Olivia could carry a grudge, she seemed equally capable of letting it go. But there was really no way to offer that information to Jory. "She didn't bring it up today, so I didn't either. I'm pretty sure she's over it." That wasn't a lie. They'd talked the whole way up, but not about that. "By the way, I brought wine for tomorrow," he said to change the subject. "Don't let me forget it."

Jory nodded. "Livvy didn't need that kind of baggage back then. She'd have gotten far more attached to you than you to her, and it would have ended badly. Who knows how that could have thrown her off, and she was just starting out. A clean break was the only way for her."

"In retrospect, I agree with you."

"I appreciate that. And, seriously, I wanted my sister to like you—and you her—just not like that." He laughed. Evan tried, but he was having a hard time seeing the humor. "I'm not counting on you two being friends, but it'd be nice to know you could at least stand each other. We'd all feel better knowing there's someone close by she could call if she were ever in a pinch."

So Jory's ban on Evan and Olivia contact wasn't complete. Just with the assumption they'd remain vertical and clothed. Evan bit back a smile—at least once, they had. It'd been quick, but far hotter than anticipated. "She has my contact info, and I've told her not to hesitate to call if she needs anything."

"Good. And thanks. Did she happen to mention anything about a boyfriend to you?"

Evan nearly choked on his beer. "No. Why?"

"Livvy's been hard to get in touch with lately, so I called her apartment and talked to her roommate.

Annie was a little cagey about her whereabouts, so I'm assuming she must be seeing someone."

Liv was spending a lot of time at his place these days—after all, he didn't have a roommate to make things awkward and she did. She rarely spent the night though, as he had to leave a lot earlier than she did and the bus didn't run anywhere near his place. But it wasn't *every* night. They each had lives they had to live. It *was* a lot of time, though. He'd tell her she needed to quit ignoring her brother every time he called while she was with him. "I wouldn't know."

"Well, could you somehow work it into the conversation on your way home?"

He nearly choked. "Why are you so concerned about your sister's love life? That's a little disturbing—not to mention really none of your business."

"That's what Livvy says, too." He laughed and shrugged. "I'm just curious. I want her to be happy, and I refuse to feel bad about that."

Evan liked to think that Olivia *was* happy—maybe not in the way Jory probably meant, but she certainly seemed happy enough for the time being.

And he liked to think that part of that was because of him.

It struck him that he was happy, too. More relaxed. That was definitely Olivia, he decided. It was a weird kind of thing—more than the average friends-with-benefits, but not a *relationship*—but it worked for them. And he was having a very good time. "I'm sure she's fine, Jory. Leave her alone and let her live her life. You two have always been pretty tight. She'll let you know if she needs you."

"I can hope." Jory went to get another round from the fridge, and by the time he got back he'd moved on to other topics, thank heavens. The weird uncomfortable feeling that settled on his shoulders from talking about Olivia lifted and everything felt normal again.

But when he finally stumbled into bed, bleary-eyed from drinking half the night with Jory, he realized he was missing her.

And frankly, drunk or not, that scared him a little.

Olivia was all smiles and teary hugs goodbye when he picked her up Friday afternoon, but the smiles faded as soon as they turned the corner and she collapsed back against the seat and rubbed her temples. "I love them so much and miss them tons, but *whoa*...I knew there was a reason I moved to Miami and not Tampa."

He laughed. "Beyond the fact Miami offered you a contract?"

She shot him a level look. "You're assuming Ballet Tampa never offered."

"So they did?"

"Of course they did. I just didn't want to go back to Tampa. I've had offers from lots of different companies over the years, and I've been fortunate enough to be able to be picky. I already told you I had a list of places I wanted to dance—both foreign and domestic—and as long as those offers were coming in, I wasn't about to move home." She pointed a finger at him and warned, "But don't tell my folks that or I'll have to kill you."

"I've got no room to talk, so we're good."

"I want to see them and spend time with them, but I can only handle short periods of it before I feel smothered. I know the smothering comes from me being gone, but because I've been gone so long, I'm not used to being smothered. Does that make sense?"

"Yep."

"Good, because I'm not sure I fully understand it."

"You've lived away from home for a long time and you're very independent. It doesn't mean they're not great people or that you don't love them."

"They are, and I do." She sighed. "Ugh. I'm a terrible child."

"No, you're not. You're living your life—which is exactly what you should do. *And* exactly what Dee and Gary *want* you to do. They're so unbelievably proud of you."

"Thank you for that. I feel a little better." She reached over and squeezed his hand. He returned the squeeze. Then Olivia pulled out her seemingly bottomless bag of pointe shoes and ribbons and threaded a needle.

"You just sewed a bunch of shoes the other day. How many pairs of those things do you need?"

"More than you might think." She was quick and efficient, finishing with one ribbon by biting off the thread. Then she tied a new knot and started on another ribbon. "Did you and Jory have a good time?"

"Yep. And I'm supposed to ask you if you're seeing someone."

"*Ouch.*" Olivia pulled the needle out of her thumb and sucked on the wound to soothe it. "Are you kidding me? Why would he care?"

"Hey, your mom asked me the same thing. You know, you could really save me some awkward moments by returning their calls."

"I *do*. Eventually. I've just been a bit busy recently and there are only so many hours in a day. Given the choice between being with you and calling my family…" She shot him a sly smile. "I chose you."

"I'm flattered." And he was. More than he really should be. More than he was comfortable with, actually, for a multitude of reasons.

But it was still kind of nice.

And that was also was also a little scary.

Thanksgiving pretty much marked the end of any kind of normality in Olivia's life—until at least after Christmas. She was prepared, though. She'd done her Christmas shopping in October and had had her Christmas cards addressed and ready to go since Halloween. She was used to the craziness of December—the run outs to various schools, the photo calls, music rehearsals, tech rehearsals, dress rehearsals, appearances on morning shows, the evening news and at half a dozen area events. That was on top of the usual classes, doctors' appointments and the like. Oh, and the sixteen or so actual performances they'd do over the next three weeks, of course. It was nonstop between now and Christmas Eve, but once the curtain closed that night, she could retreat to her bed and not be required to surface again until after the New Year.

It was the nature of the business—especially now that she was a principal—and while the schedule was grueling at times, she loved it.

But she'd never tried to do it before while she was seeing someone—or at least someone who wasn't also doing *The Nutcracker* and keeping a schedule equally as insane as hers. And *that* was a problem.

Evan, bless him, said he understood, but anyone would get frustrated when they were being shoehorned into a schedule—meals had to be grabbed during holes in that schedule, but they weren't exactly leisurely affairs at nice restaurants. Late nights with endless hours of athletic, sweaty sex were out of the question, too. She needed sleep—lots of it. She wasn't complaining—much—as it was still *good* sex, but it was rather like being put on a restricted diet after unlimited trips to the dessert bar.

After a week of rushed encounters and last-minute cancellations, Olivia was sure Evan would be over it. Surprisingly though, he wasn't. She had to give him credit for that.

The real problem, though, was that she was worried about it at all. She'd had more than one guy hit the road when faced with the truth of her priorities—and where they ranked on that list. It hadn't bothered her before.

So while it was sweet that Evan was trying to handle it, the scary part was that she was juggling, trying to create time just for him. It created stress she didn't need, but she couldn't not see him, either.

She had most of today and all of tonight off to rest up before tomorrow's opening. She could make it up to him—at least a little.

Funny, since when did she care?

She left class, ran her errands and went home. After a fast shower, she pulled a T-shirt on and crawled under the covers for a quick nap before Evan got off work.

"Olivia. Liv. *Olivia*."

She fought her way back to consciousness. Evan sat on the edge of her bed, shaking her gently. Groggy and disoriented, she squinted at him. "What are you doing here?"

"Annie let me in. When you didn't show for dinner or answer your phone, I thought something bad had happened to you."

Details came into focus. Her room, which had been flooded with daylight when she lay down, was now dim and shadowy. A glance at the clock told her she was supposed to meet Evan over an hour ago.

"Sorry. I was up at four-thirty this morning to do *Wake Up, Miami!*. I only meant to lay down for an hour or so." She reached for the bottle of water beside her bed—gone warm a long time ago—and drank deeply to wake herself the rest of the way up. "Let me change and we'll go."

"Are you actually hungry?"

"Not really," she answered honestly. "But you probably are."

He shook his head. "Why don't you go back to sleep, then. You look tired. I'll talk to you later." There was a strange, almost annoyed, undertone to his voice.

"I said I was sorry."

"I know."

"This is a really busy time for me. I warned you," she reminded him.

"I know."

"Then why are you mad?"

"I'm not," he insisted.

"You seem like it."

"Olivia, what do you want me to say? No, I'm not loving the situation, but—"

"It's only going to get worse once we open."

"And I said I understand. I can live with it, even if neither of us likes it very much."

And this was where the problems began. She sat up and faced him. "That's the thing, Evan. I *do* like this. I *love* it. I got my dream job, and I don't regret anything I gave up to get here or begrudge anything I have to do to stay here. And I can't have a boyfriend who can't accept that this is who I am and what I do."

Evan looked shocked. "I didn't realize that's where we were."

The comment didn't make sense, and the way Evan was avoiding eye contact and looking distinctly uncomfortable had her mentally replaying what she'd said. "Sorry, I didn't mean *boyfriend* boyfriend. It's just easier and quicker to say that than 'the guy I'm sleeping with'."

"Oh. Okay then."

Was that disappointment in his voice? The moment got really heavy and awkward and tense. She swallowed, sucking up her courage to go out on that limb. "I like you, Evan. I always have—except when I didn't," she corrected. "And I like *this*. What we have and what we're doing. But I'm not in a huge rush for it to be more, and I certainly don't need it to be less."

"I like this, too." He smiled, and it was possibly the sweetest, most vulnerable smile she'd ever seen on his face. She felt her heartstrings twang. "And I like you, too."

This was now officially a *moment*—bed head and all. But should she address it? Was it something she really wanted to explore right now? She didn't even fully understand what she was doing and deep contemplation—much less talking about it—might just screw it up.

She took the easier path. "Sorry I stood you up." She ran a hand down his arm. "But I do feel much better after my nap."

"You do, hmm?" Evan crawled onto the bed on all fours. Once in front of her, he sat back on his haunches and brushed her hair off her face, tucking it behind her ears. Then, holding her chin, he leaned in for a kiss. It was sweet, gentle even, with a new wealth of meaning behind it that caused her heartstrings to twang again.

She deepened the kiss, hooking her fingers in his

belt loops to hold him in place, and Evan's hands eased gently over her shoulders and down her back to gather her shirt in his hands and pull it up and off, leaving her completely naked.

Evan, though, didn't seem to be in any rush. He laid her back, watching her with hooded eyes as his fingers tickled over her skin—cheekbone to collarbone, sternum to navel and hip to hip before reversing course and ending up at her lips. It definitely had the desired effect—revving her engines and causing her breath to shallow. But there was something else, too; something new and unusual and unexpected going on inside her. She didn't want to examine it too closely, but it gave everything an additional buzz.

With Evan taking his sweet time covering nearly every inch of her in hot kisses, that buzz amplified to all-out tremors, leaving her a quivering mess barely able to return his kiss when he finally returned to her lips. In the process, he'd shucked his clothes without her noticing, and skin slid over skin in a hot caress. She reached for him, only for him to move her hands over her head and press them into the pillow. "I got this," he whispered.

That promise was nearly enough to push her over the edge without any additional assistance, but Evan was far from done. It was slow, delicious torture that left her biting her fist and gasping for air as the shock waves rocked her.

When he finally knelt between her thighs, sliding inside her with one smooth thrust, she came hard and fast. Evan didn't let it break, pounding into her, keeping her orgasm rolling longer than she dreamed possible, the intensity nearly causing her to black out.

It took forever for her breath to slow and for her vision to clear, but the sound of Evan's heart beating nearly out of his chest told her she hadn't gone there alone.

Good.

This was new, different and kind of scary. But it wasn't *bad* either, so she wasn't sure what to do...

When Evan pulled the covers up over them both, she figured she'd rest for a little while, then they'd go down to the diner for a late—make that very late, she corrected herself after glancing at the clock—dinner.

She slept straight through 'til morning and woke up alone.

There was a note propped against the clock, though.

When you've got time, I've got time. Have a great show. *E

That afternoon when she went back to her dressing room after warm-up class, she found a huge bouquet of flowers that brightened the room and filled it with the most wonderful smell.

The card read, *And you've got this. Be amazing to-night.*

For someone who said he made a terrible boyfriend, Evan wasn't doing too badly at all.

That freaked her out a little.

The fact she was liking it, though?

That freaked her out a lot.

* * *

Evan didn't expect security to stop him at the stage door. In retrospect, it made sense, but who would have thought backstage crashers would be such a problem at the ballet? The security guard called down to Olivia's dressing room for permission, made him sign in and then *finally* gave him directions down a labyrinth of hallways to a door with Olivia's name and picture on it. She called "Come in," seconds after his knock. "That was fast."

"I brought you your lunch…" He trailed off. Olivia was in sweats, barefaced and reclining on a leather doctor's-office-style couch, one foot submerged in a bucket on the floor, steam rising off the water. "What happened?"

She shrugged. "Stupid new shoes rubbed a blister. I'll be fine by showtime. The hot salty water helps."

Hot salty water on an open wound? "You're insane."

Keeping her foot in the bucket, she sat up. "Actually, I'm *starving.*" She held out her hands for the bag he was carrying. "Please and thank you."

There was another rather ratty-looking chair, and he sat as Olivia tore into the bag. Looking around, he said, "This is not at all what I pictured your dressing room would look like." It was a small room, with the couch and chair on one side, and a table with a mirror surrounded by lights attached to the far wall. A metal bar hanging from the ceiling held an assortment of colorful costumes. The table was cluttered with makeup and the flowers he'd sent last night. But the cinder block walls and painted concrete floor were drab and gray and depressing and he told her so.

"Hey, this is like the Ritz compared to what the corps is in downstairs. At least I have some privacy. And my own bathroom."

"How was the matinee?"

"Good," she answered around a mouthful of hummus and veggies.

"Even with the blister?"

"I've had worse. So what have you been up to? You're kind of dressed up for a Saturday."

He leaned back and watched her carefully. "I went to the ballet."

Olivia paused mid-chew to look at him. When he nodded, she swallowed. "Seriously?"

"Yep."

"You were in the audience? For the matinee?"

"Yeah. You were great, by the way. I couldn't tell anything was wrong with your foot at all."

She looked pleased. "Wow. I thought you didn't like the ballet."

"I like *you*," he clarified. "The jury's still out on the whole ballet thing."

"See, it wasn't as awful and boring as you expected."

"It had a few moments there that were a little tough, but overall, no. And you're just amazing to watch."

Her cheeks turned slightly pink. "I'm impressed. And very flattered you came."

"I thought you were starving."

"That, too." She started to take another bite, but

stopped. "Is that why you were able to get here so quickly?"

"Yeah. I was going to come backstage and surprise you, but you texted me first. By the way, I had no idea the TSA guarded your doors."

"There are some people who like the ballet a little too much, but mostly security's there to keep random people from wandering in just to see what's going on."

She popped the last bite of her sandwich into her mouth and sighed contentedly. "That was perfect and much appreciated. I'll save the fruit for later. Can you hand me that towel?"

Once she'd dried her foot off, she crossed behind him to the door. The click of the lock got his attention and, a second later, Olivia was climbing into his lap, her thighs straddling his.

"Don't you need to conserve your energy for tonight's show?" He asked the question seriously, but his hands were already cupping under her butt to pull her closer. This wasn't what he'd come for, but watching Olivia dance still had a powerful effect on his libido.

"I think I've got *just* enough energy for a quickie *and* tonight's show." She started unbuttoning his shirt as she spoke.

"Good, because I expect my money's worth out of my ticket tonight. It's supposedly a very good seat."

Her fingers paused. "You're coming again tonight?"

"Yep. I wanted to see you do all your parts."

She leaned forward to kiss his neck.

"Is this because I brought you food or because I watched a ballet?"

She grinned. "Both." Her fingers quickly finished with the last few buttons. She pushed his shirt open and ran her hands over his chest. Then she caught his eye. "And, more importantly, it's *neither.*"

CHAPTER EIGHT

OLIVIA HAD CHANGED out of her tutu into a robe and was removing her makeup when the security guard at the stage door called down to get approval for her parents to come backstage. A few minutes later, there was a knock at her door.

Mom was misty-eyed as she wrapped her in a big hug. "You were wonderful, baby."

"Thanks, Mom."

Daddy handed her a bouquet of roses, his big smile saying all that and more as he hugged her. Jory hugged her, too, then made a crack about how sweaty she was. "But you just get better each time I see you. Great show."

"I'm so glad y'all could come." That was true. Knowing that family or friends were in the audience gave her a little extra boost and a real reason to smile.

"They told everyone in the surrounding two rows how talented and amazing you are and how very proud they are of you," Jory said. "It was all I could do to hush them when the Overture started."

"Because it's true," Mom insisted, completely un-ashamed of her behavior.

"Yes," Jory agreed, "but if you keep annoying people around us, they're going to make us start sitting in the top of the balcony."

"Why don't you go change?" Daddy said. "I'm sure you're hungry." Ever since her very first show, her parents always took her out afterward for pancakes. She was too far away for many years for it to happen as often as she liked, but it was something she was definitely looking forward to doing more often now. The family made themselves comfortable as she grabbed her clothes and took them to the bathroom to get dressed.

When she came out a few minutes later, her mom was hanging up her costumes neatly and tidying her makeup table. "You don't have to do that, Mom."

"Old stage mom habits die hard. But now that you're out, I'll get some water for the flowers."

The theater provided a couple of vases just for this reason, and Mom arranged the roses they'd brought as Olivia took her hair down and brushed it out the best she could. Jory and Daddy were flipping through their programs.

"So many pretty flowers," Mom said.

The bouquet she'd received onstage tonight sat in water on the small table in front of Daddy and Jory, ready to be reused tomorrow. A smaller bouquet of violets and daisies from Theo sat on the shelf above her mirror next to the bouquet Evan sent on opening night—which was now looking a little worse for wear, but still pretty. The flowers Evan sent last night were on her makeup table, taking up too much room, but she liked them there.

Mom set the new flowers next to Theo's bouquet. "So who's this 'E' that's sending you flowers?" she asked.

Olivia sent up a silent thanks that Evan signed the cards in the flowers with just the one initial. And while the handwriting was masculine, she assumed Mom wouldn't recognize Evan's handwriting... *Crap, but Jory would easily.* She should have pulled the cards out and hid them away.

She kicked her "getting ready" mode into high gear before Daddy or Jory decided to join this conversation. "Just a friend."

"A *special* friend from the looks of those flowers." Mom smiled as she said it.

"A supportive friend," she corrected. She tied her shoes and stood. "I'm starved. Who's ready for IHOP?"

"Are you sure you wouldn't rather go someplace nicer?" Mom asked. "Evan sent us a list of restaurants that were open late."

Daddy shook his head. "We can't break tradition. Dancers are a superstitious lot."

"Exactly, Daddy. Dinner anywhere else could jinx the whole run of shows."

"Well, I guess we can't have that."

Most of the conversation in the car and after they arrived at the restaurant revolved around the show—the differences between this choreography and the choreography in other productions she'd danced. Her family weren't necessarily experts, but they certainly had a higher than average knowledge of repertoire, thanks to her.

Over pancakes, Jory changed the subject. "We were looking through the program during intermission and some of the dancers have a 'Sponsored by Such-and-Such Company' under their bios. What's that about?"

Just a reminder that she still didn't have one. "It's just another way for the company to raise money." She explained the program briefly, while downplaying its importance and her own need.

"Well, if you need a sponsor, honey," her dad said, "The Bay Café would be proud to. No one needs to know it's your family."

Since that was exactly what she *didn't* want, she was glad that lie she'd told Annie was easily available and believable. "Thanks, Daddy, but the sponsors need to be local. I'm still new in town and people don't know me yet. But after *Nutcracker* is over, folks will know who I am. I'm sure I'll get one in the New Year." *Fingers crossed.*

"So are you thinking you'll stay here for a while then?" he asked.

"That's my plan. I love Miami, it's close to y'all, and MMBC is great. I've decided if they offer me a multiyear contract, I'll take it."

Jory laughed. "*You?* Commit to a multiyear contract? My world is askew at the thought."

She punched him in the arm. "I've even been looking at getting my own place—an actual home where I can have my stuff and grow flowers and things. And when I retire, Miami will be a good place to launch my next career."

"We really didn't realize that when we sent you off at fifteen that it would take you twelve years to find your way back. Not that we're not proud of everything you've accomplished," Mom added quickly, "but it's nice to hear you're wanting to settle down close to home."

"What about your itchy feet?" Jory asked.

She shrugged. "There will always be guest artist appearances or touring troupes, so if my feet get *too* itchy, I can do that. If not, I'm still good. I've checked off most of the dream cities on my list, and that's more than most people can say."

"Most people aren't as good as you."

"Thanks, Daddy. But this decision means that maybe next year when you come and see me dance you won't have to stay in a hotel."

"But it's a tradition," Mom protested, "and you don't need company in your house when you need your rest more. And," she said, looking at her watch, "that's probably our cue to take you home so you can get a good night's sleep. Is it just a matinee or do you have an evening show too, tomorrow?"

"Just the matinee."

"We'd love to see it, sweetheart, but we've got a big party to cater tomorrow evening and need to get on the road early."

"It's that time of year. Busy for everyone. I'm just glad you could come." She meant that.

"I'm staying at Evan's tonight and heading for a meeting in Key West tomorrow," Jory said. "Can I grab you for brunch or a cup of coffee?"

"Maybe. I've got an eleven-thirty call time, so it really depends on how early you get up."

Jory dropped their parents back at their hotel, then took Olivia home on his way to Evan's—which she'd carefully purged yesterday of any of her personal items left there. She didn't like the stealth and deception, but Evan was adamant about it.

It felt juvenile and it annoyed her, but right now was not the time to make that stand. She had enough on her plate at the moment, and there wasn't a rush. She was having a good time with Evan, but for how long? Why stir up a mess if this was just going to spin itself out? If it turned into something else, something stronger, then they'd *have* to address it, and she'd deal with that when the time came.

She waved Jory off, not expecting to see him in the morning. Knowing him and Evan both, there'd be much drinking tonight and hellacious hangovers in the morning—at least for Jory.

Sure enough, a text pinged into her phone as she was getting up the next morning. The lack of capitalization, punctuation and basic grammar skills spoke clearly to the pain of Jory's hangover and his need for more sleep. She laughed, then texted him three more times, twenty minutes apart, just to bug him.

That's what siblings were for, after all.

Evan texted her a couple of hours later, offering to pick her up after the show, which told her Jory had finally gotten up and on the road. It was a nice, bright, sunshiny day, so Jory had to be hurting for his drive down to the Keys. Evan, though, claimed to be fine.

It still sat wrong on her—basically *your brother's gone now, so we can have sex again.* But she told herself there'd be plenty of time to dive into that later on.

After all, this was the biggest, most exciting time of the year for her, job-wise, *and* she had a pseudoboyfriend on the side. Her life didn't suck, that was for sure.

So she should just enjoy it.

Evan left work early on Monday, eager to get home. He'd left Olivia asleep in his bed when he left this morning—which was a new and unusual experience for him—and, according to her, she was going to be lazy all day and he just might still find her there when he got home.

He wouldn't mind that at all, he thought with a grin.

But he had no such luck. Instead, Olivia was on his living room floor, one leg pulled up over her head in a stretch that made his hamstring hurt just looking at it. But, *damn*, she was flexible, and that, as always, stirred up his blood.

She didn't acknowledge his arrival, but then he saw the wires running from the iPod strapped to her arm to her ears. She had a light sheen of sweat on her forehead and chest, and her cheeks were flushed. When he squatted down next to her and nudged her, Olivia jumped—nearly kicking him in the face as she did.

"Sorry," she said, pulling the buds out of her ears. "Didn't hear you."

"I thought you were just going to have an easy day and relax."

"I am." She lay back down and pulled her other knee to her chest, unfolding her leg until her toes touched the ground behind her shoulder.

"And you consider this relaxing?"

"Just some Pilates and stretches so I don't get all stiff. Plus, I can only nap and read for so long before I get bored." She peeked at him around her ankle. "I was planning to shower and get dressed before you got home, but you're earlier than I thought you'd be."

He couldn't help himself. He ran a hand over the thigh displayed so beautifully in front of him. "I gotta say, this is a nice view to come home to, though."

She grinned, releasing her leg and hooking it around his shoulder to pull him closer for a kiss. "You're so easy to please."

He kissed her long and slow, loving the way she wrapped herself around him like a vine. It was a nice thing to come home to. Actually, *she* was nice to come home to. Nice and not at all as awful as he'd always thought it would be. It was something he could get used to. The realization pulled him up short.

Olivia untangled herself with a sigh and a moan. "I'm going to go get cleaned up and changed. I'm hungry."

"For someone so skinny, you eat a lot."

"That's because you keep helping me burn off all the calories. It's excellent cardio." With a wink and a sexy smile, she disappeared into his room. He heard the water running a second later.

There were various bits and pieces of exercise equipment and dance gear lying around, his fridge was full of healthy snacks and the whole place smelled vaguely of Olivia. He liked that, too. Especially how that scent clung to his sheets—and sometimes his clothes—giving him a whiff of her even when she wasn't around.

And he wanted her around more often.

He was man enough and honest enough to admit he was in strange, uncharted waters, but he had no regrets. Things had moved quickly—almost disturbingly so—but it wasn't as if they'd started off five weeks ago as strangers.

Ending things with Olivia nine years ago had been the right thing—he still stood by the intention if not the execution—but neither of them had been in the right place anyway. Now maybe they were. It was worth a shot, right?

As if he'd just tempted the Fates, his phone rang— Jory's ringtone, reminding him of a possible problem ahead, but one he was willing to tackle this time.

Just not at this moment. Not yet.

He took the phone to the patio to answer.

"Hey. How's the head?"

"I don't know what the hell you put in my drink, but

I'm just now feeling human again. I had to go to dinner last night feeling like death warmed over."

"The tequila was your idea."

"Sometimes when I'm around you I seem to forget we're nearly thirty, and I can't drink like that anymore."

"Just keeping you young at heart, my friend."

Jory made a sound suspiciously like a snort. "Anyway…I've got a big favor to ask."

"What kind of favor?"

"It's about Olivia."

Carefully, as if Jory would somehow be able to tell that Liv was currently in his shower simply by the tone of his voice, he said, "Okay."

"She was telling us the other night about some kind of sponsorship thing the company does. Businesses or individuals give money to sponsor a particular dancer and in return, get all kinds of perks the regular donors don't get. Looking at the program I got the other night, Olivia's the only dancer—outside the corps— who doesn't have one of those sponsors. She tried to downplay it, but I think it's something she needs—especially if she's going to get to stay in Miami."

Something crawled over his skin and warning bells went off in his head.

"Dad offered, of course," Jory continued, "but Livvy said it needed to be local businesses."

"How much?"

"I'm not sure exactly and the website doesn't say, but based on what I've been able to research online, several thousand dollars, at least."

"I see. And you're asking me to sponsor her."

"If not you, maybe you know someone who could? She's still new in Miami and doesn't know a lot of people with that kind of money."

But she knew me. "I'll see what I can do." It was all he could manage to say right now.

"I know it's awkward, but…"

"Not at all," he lied.

"Thanks. I'll see you next week when I'm headed back through."

"Yep. Have fun down there."

This was what it felt like to have a bubble burst. He didn't want to believe the dark thoughts creeping in, but they had merit and couldn't be dismissed out of hand. If Olivia needed this sponsorship, why hadn't she mentioned it? The fact she hadn't mentioned it at all—directly or indirectly—seemed glaringly, suspiciously *off*.

All those happy thoughts from earlier slammed into this new information, making him wonder if he'd been a fool.

A few minutes later, Olivia joined him on the patio. She was casually dressed, hair braided back off her face, minimal makeup. She took the other chair and propped her feet—in socks of course—up on a planter. "It's nice out here."

"Yeah."

She looked at him funny, but kept her voice light as she tried again. "We should eat outside tonight. Maybe grill something."

"If you want."

"You could even have a nice steak. Give the chicken a break for the evening." She laughed, then got quiet when he didn't join her. "What's wrong?"

He had neighbors, so he wasn't going to have this conversation outside. "You want a beer?"

"Sure." She followed him inside, leaning against the counter as he opened the beers and handed her one.

"I was just thinking," he started in a conversational tone, "You never did tell me why you got in touch after all these years."

For a brief second—literally a flash he would have missed if he hadn't been watching her so closely— Olivia looked uncomfortable. *Yeah, there was something she was hiding.*

Just as quickly, she was shrugging as if it was nothing. "It seemed weird to be in the same town and not get in touch. And I thought it might make things easier for Jory in the long run if we had a truce in place. And I'm glad I did. Think how awkward Thanksgiving *could* have been otherwise."

"For Jory. Who we're not telling about us."

An eyebrow went up. "That was more your idea, not mine."

But she hadn't fought too hard about it either. He let that pass for the time being, wanting to get his biggest suspicions confirmed or denied. "But why? It's not like we parted on good terms."

"I guess I decided to get over it and let go of a ridiculous grudge."

"Jory says you never let go of a grudge."

"Jory's not the expert on me he seems to think he is." She placed her beer carefully on the counter and met his eyes. "What is this all *really* about?"

Well, he wasn't getting anywhere the indirect way. "I understand you need some kind of sponsorship."

She blinked in surprise. "How do you know about that?"

"Because Jory just called me and asked if I'd do it."

"Darn. I'm sorry. He shouldn't have done that." She shook her head and reached over to touch his hand. "I told him not to worry about it, but I should have known he'd call you."

"Of course he did. He says you need a local sponsor and hey, I'm local."

"I only said that so that my folks—and Jory for that matter—wouldn't try to do it."

"But you do need the sponsorship."

"I don't *need* it," she corrected, withdrawing her hand. "It would be nice to have it, but—"

"And just like Jory, I was the one person in Miami who you knew would have the money. Was that why you contacted me wanting to get together?"

He could almost see the wheels turning in her head as she decided how to answer. Finally, she took a deep breath and exhaled slowly. "Yes, but—"

That hurt worse than expected. "I'd have given it to you, Olivia. All you had to do was ask. You didn't have to sleep with me first."

"*Whoa.* Don't even go there. One has nothing to do with the other." He could tell he'd offended her, but that didn't give him any truths. "I'd gotten myself into a panic thinking I *had* to get that sponsorship if I wanted a contract for next season, and yes, I figured you would be the obvious choice."

"Because of my friendship with Jory? Or because you felt I owed you after what happened with us?"

She didn't address that statement, making him assume he'd scored there, too. "It was a bad plan. I admit that now. I decided—at dinner, after I actually saw you again and talked to you—that it would be tacky to even ask because there was too much other stuff between us. And you made it very clear you had no interest in donating. I let it go and I was okay with that."

"So leaving your phone in my car was just a happy accident?"

"Of course it was." Her eyebrows pulled together. "How conniving do you think I am?"

"Honestly, Olivia, I don't know anymore. I was led blindly into this."

"Oh, *please*. You all but made a pass at me at Tourmaine's. You flat-out propositioned me the very next night. It was clear what you wanted."

"What was I supposed to think? You called me out of the blue. I thought that was what *you* wanted."

"So your feelings are hurt because you feel misled? Or is it because I hadn't been pining over you all these years?" She turned to look at him evenly, and some of the snark and the heat left her voice. "What difference does it make why I called you *then*? It has nothing to do with where we are now."

"It doesn't?"

She pulled back as though he'd slapped her. "Excuse me?"

"Surely you were planning to ask me for it eventually."

Olivia's jaw tightened. "If you don't quit implying that I'm some kind of prostitute, I'm going to kick your butt so hard you'll be coughing up ribbons from my pointe shoes tomorrow."

He'd definitely hit a nerve. "I don't know why you're so surprised I'd think that."

"Maybe because we've spent a lot of time together and you should know me better than that. Or at least be willing to give me the benefit of the doubt."

"My apologies. I'm a little thrown by this. I mean, at least I came into this honestly, with the mistaken assumption you were, too. You know, like mature adults."

Her jaw dropped. "Oh no, don't you dare start tossing out words like 'honesty' and 'maturity' like you have a clue what either one of them means. *I'm* not the one who's lying to my supposed best friend because I don't want anyone to know that we're sleeping together."

"That's different."

"How?" she snapped. "Either you're an adult or you're not."

"You're changing the subject."

"Not really. I may have come into this a little dishonestly, but you're still wallowing in the lies. And you're making me your accomplice when I have nothing to hide." Her eyes narrowed as she crossed her arms over her chest. "Or am I just a convenient bed buddy with an expiration date looming, and *that's* why you don't want to tell Jory?"

"You're not exactly pushing hard to tell him either. I could assume you don't want him to know his sweet baby sister is sleeping with his best friend again when it'll all be over once you get your money."

She slapped him. Hard. The crack echoed in the room. "I'm *not* sleeping with you for money. Right now, I'm not sure why I'm seeing you at all." She stormed out of the room.

There'd been a delay between the sound of the slap and the sensation, but as blood rushed to his cheek, it began to sting. He rubbed it gently. He couldn't get too angry about it, though; she *had* warned him.

He wasn't sure who was in the right and who was in the wrong, but it wasn't pretty either way.

He could hear Olivia talking, but to whom was the question. As he came out of the kitchen, Olivia nearly ran him down in the hallway. She had her phone to her ear and her bags draped over her shoulder. "Thank you," she said and hung up, shoving the phone into her pocket.

Dodging around him without a word, she gathered up her stuff out of the living room.

"You're leaving?"

"Yep," she snapped.

"How? You don't have a car."

"I've got a cab on the way." She didn't have that much stuff, and it didn't take her long to load it up.

"Olivia…"

She spun on him, her eyes hot with anger. "I'm not going to stay here and let you continue to cast aspersions on my character just for the opportunity to be another notch in your bedpost. Not again. It's not worth it." She paused at the door. "And just to be clear… I don't need your money. I'm very good at what I do and *that's* what matters most. But even if I had to choose, I'd rather go home and teach preschoolers at the local Toe, Tap and Twirl than take a dime of sponsorship money from you. Goodbye, Evan." She slammed the door hard enough to shake the frame.

Well, that wasn't what he'd planned for this evening, and it was a big turn from where he'd started just an hour ago.

But what else could he have expected?

CHAPTER NINE

Rage and insult propelled Olivia into the parking lot of Evan's condo, where she paced while waiting for her taxi to arrive. Her eyes burned, but the anger was too strong to let the tears fall.

The fact there were tears at all shocked her. There was so much to be angry about, but tears meant something else. Tears meant she was hurt, and she didn't want to be hurt. She shouldn't even be in a place where Evan *could* hurt her. But those tears threatening to fall meant she was in that place—even if this was the first time she'd realized it—and that knowledge only made everything worse.

But maybe it was better to know now, before she got in any deeper. Evan hadn't changed all that much after all—*the selfish, egotistical jerk.* She'd at least admitted where she was wrong; Evan couldn't even see that he might be, much less admit it.

Maybe Jory had been right all along, trying to keep her and Evan apart. She'd been too caught up in her own infatuation and hormones to realize that Jory might have sound reasons. Maybe Evan knew those reasons were sound as well and *that's* why he'd been so adamant about keeping Jory in the dark. Jory might have told her more than Evan wanted her to know.

Not everything you wanted could be good for you, and sometimes you needed someone else to smack your hand away from the cookie jar.

In a fair and just world, men like Evan would come with warning labels tattooed on their washboard abs. She sighed. There was no reason to think she'd have paid any attention to a written warning when she'd done such a good job ignoring the real-life examples and lessons she had. Man, she was stupid.

She'd walked right into this, honestly believing it would somehow be different just because she wanted it to be. She could pass some of the blame to Evan, but she was equally as responsible for her own hurt.

Maybe a little more so, since he'd even tried to warn her.

The cabbie asked if she was okay, and after a couple of assurances on her part, he finally seemed to accept it and remained silent as he took her home. She tipped him extra, though, for his concern.

It wasn't that late, but the living room was dark and quiet as Olivia locked the door behind her. *Good.* She sighed in relief and went to the fridge for something to drink. She really tried to limit her alcohol during performance weeks, but the wine beckoned and she gave in. Taking a big swallow, she headed down the hall toward her room.

"Olivia?"

She jumped at the voice, nearly dropping her glass. "Annie! I didn't know you were here. Did I wake you?"

"No, I was just…" She changed tacks abruptly. "I thought you were staying at Evan's tonight."

"Not anymore."

Surprised turned instantly to concern. "Is everything okay?"

"Between me and Evan? No. That's pretty much over."

"Oh, Olivia, I'm sorry."

"Thanks, but I'm okay."

Annie put a hand on her arm. "Do you want to talk about it?"

Did she? Just for the sympathy even though justice was out of the question? "Thanks, I—"

"Annie?" That was a male voice. Olivia looked at Annie, who gave her a slightly embarrassed smile and shrugged. The man the voice belonged to stepped into the hallway a second later. He was shirtless and barefoot and oh-*my*-pretty to boot. Belatedly, Olivia noticed that Annie was slightly disheveled herself. "Is everything okay?" he asked.

"Stephen, this is my roommate, Olivia. Olivia, this is Stephen. We met through work."

"It's nice to meet you," she said lamely.

"And you," Stephen said. "I took my mother to see *The Nutcracker* last week. You were very good."

"Thank you." She wasn't as completely stupid as she thought, because she could still tell when she was a fifth wheel. "Please don't think I'm rude not to hang out and chat, but I'm going to go to my room now and listen to some music. Very loud music. I'll use headphones so it won't bother you."

"Good night, then," Stephen said, reaching for Annie's hand.

"Are you sure?" Annie asked. "If you need to talk, I can..."

"No," she insisted. "I'm thinking a long hot bath and an early bedtime is the probably the best thing for me right now. Good night."

Headphones on and music cranked up, Olivia turned the water on and left the tub to fill. In a way, it was good that she and Annie not talk it to death and obsess over Evan or what he did or did not do. It was what it was. Wallowing wasn't good for anyone, now was as good a time as any to let it go. It had been only a little more than a month, so it wasn't as if she was deeply invested or anything.

So why the hell was she crying?

Although Evan didn't like himself much for thinking it, Jory was really the last person he wanted to see at the moment. He already felt bad enough for sleeping with Olivia and lying to Jory about it—which made it a little hard to face him—but now he had the added guilt of wanting to avoid his best friend. It was a big spiral of guilt, and he didn't like feeling guilty about anything.

And Jory made him think about Olivia—they had the same hair color, same features, same mannerisms—

when he was quite determined *not* to think about her. He felt foolish for not realizing her ulterior motives— regardless of when she abandoned those motives, and more than a little annoyed that she'd think his motives were anything more than protection for all of them.

He might be selfish occasionally, but he usually had a good reason why.

If not for Olivia, he'd be happy to have Jory here. It was just difficult to act as if everything was perfectly normal, the same as it was before Olivia decided to walk back into his life.

And while Jory had spent the week on a half business, half scuba diving trip in Key West, *he'd* spent the week working on *not* thinking about Olivia and trying to forget the past month or so. They were in vastly different moods because of this.

They'd gone easy on the booze last night as Jory was still cussing him for the hangover last Sunday, and he'd stated early on in the evening that he would *not* be doing the four-hour drive home today hungover, too.

Evan was drinking coffee and half watching the news when Jory, freshly showered, shaved and not hungover, came in carrying a cup and staring at his phone.

"Mom says to tell you she's moving Christmas dinner to the twenty-sixth this year," Jory said, reading off his phone. "Olivia has a Christmas Eve performance, and Mom doesn't want her to have to rush home on the twenty-fifth. So everything is shifting a day later."

"Actually, I don't think I'll be able to come this year."

"Why not?"

The surprise tinged with disappointment made him feel a little better. "I've had another invitation."

"From who?"

"I do have other friends, you know."

Jory sat. "You've had Christmas dinner at our house for nearly ten years. If you have other friends, they've been stingy with the invites up to now."

Olivia had always been in another city, usually unable to make it to her parents' until after he left. It had worked fine in the past, but this year...definitely not. "Maybe it's a new friend."

Jory snorted. "Because you make *those* so easily and often."

"Hmm, I'm beginning to think I might have one friend too many right now."

"Mom will be disappointed."

He'd rather have Dee disappointed than horrified. Olivia obviously hadn't said anything to her family about what happened—and he was grateful for that—but that might change if she were forced to share her holiday with him now. If he wanted to salvage what he had with the Madison family, he needed to stay away. He should have stayed away from Olivia altogether if for no other reason than respect for Jory and Gary and Dee.

But he was selfish, as usual, and arrogant, as well, thinking he could have his cake and eat it, too.

"Is it Olivia?"

Was Jory a mind reader now? "What?"

"Y'all seemed okay at Thanksgiving, but I realize now that may have been just for Mom and Dad's benefit. If that was all an act, I can understand why you wouldn't be up for another round."

"Look, I had to tell Olivia the truth about what happened. She deserved to know that it wasn't about her." He couldn't tell Jory the full truth, but he should—and could—tell him that much. There were enough secrets in this freaky triangle, and *that* one needed to be put to bed for good.

Jory coughed. "I'm surprised she didn't come after me with the carving knife."

"She wasn't happy about it, but I think I got her to see your point. You weren't wrong, and you did mean well."

"I'm sure the fact I 'meant well' went over splendidly." He rolled his eyes.

"Oh, yes, of *course* that made all the difference to her."

Jory picked up on his sarcasm. "Maybe I'll apologize then. I never really brought it up before, simply because it was easier not to."

Damn it, that wasn't what he wanted. "She's let it go. I've let it go. Why bring it up at all?"

Jory leaned back and rubbed his eyes. "You know, if you'd been *this* guy nine years ago, maybe I wouldn't have minded it so much. You and Olivia, I mean."

Evan nearly fell out of his chair, but recovered quickly. "I am the same guy."

"Nah. You're not as angry or as hell-bent on breaking every one of your parents' rules. Raising hell is fine and good—and something you needed to do for your own sake—but you were taking it to extremes. And seducing every girl that got within twenty feet of you like it was your mission in life..."

"No one wants their sister mixed up with a guy like that. I get it, Jory. No need to beat that dead horse."

"Want to hear something funny?"

"Yes, please." *Anything to change the subject.*

"About five years ago, Mom got this idea that you and Olivia would be a good match if she could ever get you two in the same room."

Evan choked.

"I know, it's crazy, huh?" Jory laughed at the thought. "She just wants you in the family, and since you're too old to formally adopt, that was her next idea. But now that Livvy is finally contemplating settling down in one place..." He let the implication hang.

Evan, though, was still sputtering and couldn't talk, which Jory seemed to read a completely different way. "Don't worry. I don't think Mom will actually push that idea, so it's safe if you change your mind and decide to come for Christmas, after all."

He coughed and cleared his throat. It was all just too much to even process.

Jory, thankfully, didn't seem to need a response. "And unless you need the Heimlich maneuver, I should probably be hitting the road."

Evan walked Jory out.

Jory tossed his overnight bag in the backseat. "Oh, by the way," he said. "I owe you an apology."

"For?"

"Dropping that sponsorship thing on you. When Olivia mentioned it, you were the first person to come to mind, and I called without thinking it through all the way."

Liv and Jory were definitely two peas in a pod. According to her, she'd done the same thing but backed out before actually making the request. "Don't worry about it."

With a nod, Jory got in his car. "And if you change your mind about Christmas, just give Mom a call and let her know. She'll make you the cookies you like."

It was barely noon and he already needed a drink. The entire Madison family seemed determined to drive him insane—but for different reasons in completely different ways.

It was insult to injury. Had he wanted Olivia partly because she was forbidden fruit? Maybe, but now that she might not be so forbidden after all, he wanted her still.

But he still couldn't have her. What had she said about men she wouldn't dance with again because they'd dropped her? Well, he'd dropped her twice. She wouldn't trust him again.

This sucked.

It also hurt more than he liked to admit, but considering the amount of hurt he'd thrown on people in the past... Well, his dear old dad would love to know Evan was reaping exactly what he'd sown, just as warned.

Call it payback, karma or divine justice—it sucked no matter what he named it.

But he'd earned it. Fairly. Olivia had every right to walk, and he couldn't fault her for doing it.

And it was probably better for her that she had.

The real question was whether he could just let her go.

Wednesday afternoon, Olivia was in the studio working on her variations for the winter special. She didn't have to be there—the rehearsal schedule was cut way back during performance weeks—but it was pretty much the only thing she knew to do with herself.

She hadn't heard from Evan in over a week. She'd rather expected—maybe *hoped* was a better word—to hear *something*, but there'd been nothing but silence. It was both good and bad.

If this really had run its course, a clean break was better in the long run—no need to draw it out. Because the past week had proven one thing to her quite clearly: although she'd let her hormones lead the way, sticking around for good sex and good times, she'd gotten in deeper than expected. Deeper than was wise.

She'd obviously learned nothing in the past nine years because she was pretty much right back where she'd been before with Evan: hurt.

Screw it. And screw him.

She'd gotten all attached to the idea of settling down

in Miami and taken it too far, insanely believing that Evan could be a part of that.

Maybe she'd been dropped on her head too many times.

It was horrifying enough to have her trolling websites from other companies, thinking a change of city might be nice.

No. She wasn't leaving Miami. Not because of him. She'd never let her emotions drive her decisions about her career, and she wasn't going to start now. Not over a guy.

She'd never had to live in the same city with an ex before—at least not for very long—but people did it all the time. It had to be possible. Miami was a big place.

Hell, as long as Jory and Evan were friends she'd never be fully away from him anyway. He'd continue to be on the fringe of her life.

She'd gotten over him before, and she'd get over him again.

She stretched and shook her legs out. *This* was what she was good at. Anger and hurt feelings could be pushed down and forgotten for a while when her feet were moving too fast for her to focus on anything else and the details required her full concentration.

This was who she was. She'd made her choice years ago.

She cued up her music.

Olivia always felt a little deflated when the curtain closed on a show for the last time—even when that show was *The Nutcracker*. Months of work and preparation—over. The adrenaline rush of performing, the energy of the audience, the lights and costumes and music—that was her drug of choice and she was a junkie.

And like a junkie who'd been riding on a major high, the crash would come. But she had a couple of hours yet to enjoy the ride. As she left the stage, Theo ran up beside her. "We have a Christmas Eve tradition here at MMBC—a greasy, high-fat, carb-loaded feast at Lucy's Diner. Do you want to come?"

"Sure." Annie had left this morning to go to her mom's in Fort Lauderdale, so she'd be going home to an empty house anyway. "When?"

"It'll take at least thirty or forty-five minutes for everyone to get packed up, but I'll come knock on your door when we're ready."

"Great." In her dressing room, she scrubbed the makeup off her face and started packing up her stuff—well, more tossing it haphazardly into a bag to be sorted later. She'd taken home all but the essentials yesterday, so there wasn't that much to pack.

Loraine, the costume mistress, came in to pick up her costumes, followed a minute later by Richard, the artistic director, who handed her a card and wished her a Merry Christmas.

"And I didn't have a chance to tell you before the show, but we got a call yesterday from a business wanting to sponsor you. That's pretty impressive for someone who's still relatively new in town."

She fought to keep her face still and her tone light. "That's wonderful. Can I ask which business?" *We've done sixteen performances, dozens of public appearances, and the* Times *did a big write-up last week. Any one of those things could have landed me a sponsor.* She realized she was holding her breath.

"The Lawford Agency. It's a newish advertising agency, but it's getting big. They haven't donated before, so extra congrats for landing us a new one."

Evan. As soon as Richard had told her she'd gotten sponsorship, she'd known it would be him. Somehow she managed to keep a smile on her face and make the proper responses, hiding the wave of mixed emotions inside her. Once Richard left though, she collapsed onto the couch and rubbed her temples.

She'd told him she didn't want his money. So why'd he do it? Was it a peace offering? Guilt money? Bribery? Payment for sexual services rendered? That one made her feel a little nauseous.

And while there was a definite feeling of relief that came with the knowledge he'd all but guaranteed that MMBC would offer her another contract, it was riding uneasily on top of the other clashing emotions.

She was still sitting there, trying to sort it out, when Theo stuck his head around the door. "You ready?"

"Yeah." She grabbed her bags and followed him out. A crowd of company members were gathered by the stage door. "Wait," she said, reaching for his elbow. "I'm going to have to pass. I just realized I have something I need to do."

Disbelieving, he blinked at her. "At eleven o'clock on Christmas Eve?"

"I know, but yes."

He gave her a careful look. "Is this something you need help or backup for? Maybe a driver for the get-away car?"

"No, but thanks." She rose up on her tiptoes and kissed his cheek. "Merry Christmas, Theo."

"Merry Christmas, Olivia."

She waved at everyone as she passed them and went to the parking deck where she'd left the car she'd rented for the drive home tomorrow. Halfway to Evan's house, she realized how very, very stupid she was being. Even if it weren't beyond rude to show up unannounced at someone's house after eleven o'clock—on *any* night, much less Christmas Eve—there was no guarantee that Evan would be home. He wasn't heading to Tampa tomorrow to be with her family, she knew that much, but that didn't mean he was staying in Miami over the holiday, either. He could be anywhere on the planet.

But she was already pulling into the parking lot, so she had nothing to lose at this point.

Evan's car was in its spot, so that improved the chances of him being home exponentially. But as she rang the doorbell, she realized that he might not be home *alone*.

Dear Lord, would she *ever* learn to not run off half-cocked on half-cooked plans? But unless she was going to ding-and-ditch, it was a little too late now.

Half an eternity passed before she finally heard

him unlocking the door. The irritated look on his face quickly turned to surprise, though, when he saw her. But he didn't say anything.

He was barefoot and wearing battered jeans and the T-shirt she sometimes wore when she was there because it was extra soft from years of washing. Although his hair was mussed and adorable, he didn't look like he'd been asleep.

At this point, she wasn't sure anymore whether she was angry or curious or what, and since she hadn't given a second's thought to what she actually wanted to say now that she was here, they ended up staring at each other in silence for a long moment.

"Olivia?"

"I told you I didn't want your money." The words just tumbled out, unplanned and very ungracefully.

"Well, it's a good thing I gave it to the Miami Modern Ballet Company and not you, then."

"You know what I mean. I never asked you to sponsor me."

"But Jory did. So I did it for him. And your parents. A small way to pay them back for all their kindness over the years."

"So it had nothing to do with me." He shrugged, and it grated over her last nerve. She hadn't wanted to cash in her family's relationship to Evan like some kind of IOU, yet she'd ended up exactly there. Hell, she should have just stuck with plan A—it would have been tacky and awkward as hell, but it would have been quicker and less painful than the long way around she took to get here. "Well." She cleared her throat, feeling like a complete fool. "Welcome to the MMBC family. Your generous donation is much appreciated, and we hope you enjoy the many benefits your sponsorship includes."

"Why are you here, Olivia?"

Such a loaded question. And one she wasn't sure she had the guts to answer. "I needed to know why you did it."

"It's only money, not arms and legs. And as you said, it's a tax deduction, and it's good PR for the agency."

A reasonable answer, even if she wasn't sure what it meant for her. Hell, she wasn't sure what answer she'd been hoping for, but that one left her feeling like a leaking balloon. "Okay, then. Sorry I bothered you. Good night and um…Merry Christmas."

She turned away before she made this any worse or more humiliating. She wouldn't run, but she could damn sure walk away quickly.

"Olivia, wait." Evan caught up with her and put a hand on her upper arm. When she turned around, he stepped back, hunching his shoulders and putting his hands in his pockets, but he didn't speak immediately. He leaned against his car. "Do you have any idea…" He stopped and thought for a second. "Your parents are better parents to me than my own. And Jory's like a brother to me."

"Yes, I know." She wouldn't mess that up for him or damage that relationship, no matter how angry or hurt she was. She was going to tell him that, but he spoke first.

"Then can you imagine how disloyal it feels to want you? Carnal exploration of their only daughter and sister seems a poor way to pay back that kindness. And wanting any more than that feels like taking too much. I'm a heartless bastard, but even I know that's a step over the line."

"I see."

"On top of that, I know that if screw things up with you, I risk losing it all. Of hurting everyone I care about in one fell swoop. It's a bad place to be in."

Lovely. She'd been doomed to this by her own loving, wonderful family. The same family she took for granted.

He sighed and stared up at the sky. "So, yeah, I tried to play both sides of the game and have it all." He shook his head and shrugged. "But I managed to screw it up anyway, which is pretty amazing even for me. I can't have you and I can't be around them without being reminded of that, so now I can't have them, either."

This was twisted, but she knew too much to not see Evan's logic. And it made her mad. "That's bull."

Another slap would have been far more preferable. In fact, *anything* would be preferable to this Greek tragedy. "No, that's the truth."

"If you won't give me any credit, at least give some to the family you claim to respect so much."

Why couldn't she see that he was just trying to do

the right thing for once? "I do respect them. And you, too, believe it or not."

"Then grow up," she snapped.

"Excuse me?"

"So your parents suck. I hate that for you, and I'm glad mine could be there for you instead. You should know them well enough to know that no matter what, they won't turn their backs on you. So drop the martyr act. Either you want me or you don't."

She made it seem so easy. "I already hurt you once. Wasn't that enough?"

"I like how you think this isn't hurting me now."

"See? You've just proven my point."

Olivia's lips thinned. Then she nodded. "Well, I guess got my answer." She turned her back on him and walked quickly toward a small black sedan.

And there it was. At least it was done and they could move on. It was for the best, really. But his feet were already moving in her direction, catching up with her before she could open the door.

When she turned around, he kissed her, fully expecting her to push him off and slap him again, so Olivia kissing him back felt like a Christmas miracle. It went on and on—desperate, but more sweet than carnal.

He steadied her as he set her on her feet and loosened his grip without letting her go. "No. *That's* your answer."

She smiled. "I like that one much better."

"Me, too, but—"

Olivia put a finger over his lips. "Let's just take this one step at a time."

"Figure out the basics, how we move together, before trying the harder stuff?" he teased.

"Exactly."

He grinned at her and got one in response. "Does that mean you're learning to trust me?"

"Maybe," she hedged.

"Then we'll have to keep working at it."

"Practice makes better."

"And I'm looking forward to it."

EPILOGUE

"IT'S ONLY SIX WEEKS." She stared at the contract. She hadn't gone looking for this. She was happy in Miami. The spring show was only a couple of weeks away, and then she and Evan were going on their first official vacation as a couple. These were exciting, heady times. But now that the opportunity presented itself, her feet were itching to go.

Evan barely looked up from his tablet. "I know. You should sign the contract."

"You could come to Paris and visit me, if you wanted," she offered.

He smiled at her. "Maybe I'll do that. Sign the contract."

She refilled her wineglass, stalling for time. Things had been going so well between them the past couple of months, and she didn't want to screw it up now. Hell, she'd just moved in last week—although that had been partly precipitated by Annie wanting to move Stephen into their condo. He might think she was having second thoughts. "It's just an amazing opportunity and it fell into my lap."

"Which is exactly why you should go." He seemed calm and unbothered by the idea.

"Maybe I shouldn't. I mean, I just signed my new contract with MMBC." *Argh*. The indecision was killing her. "Maybe I should stay here and do their summer stock."

That finally got his attention. "No, you shouldn't. Sign. Go. Summer in Miami versus summer in Paris? Paris wins." He held up the pen, but she didn't take it. "Sign it. You know you want to," he said, waving the pen like a hypnotist.

"Are you trying to get rid of me?"

He rolled his eyes. "If I say yes, will you sign the contract?"

She shot him a dirty look. "Six months ago I wouldn't have thought twice about this. What is wrong with me?"

He grinned at her. "Six months ago you didn't have me."

"And *there's* the ego. I should go just because you said that."

"Exactly. *Go.*" He took her hands. "Yes, I will miss you terribly, but you should still go. I'll be here when you get back. You don't have to choose between me and your career. You can have both."

Both? She hadn't thought she'd wanted both. But now she did.

"I'll probably be ten pounds heavier because I'll

be eating whatever I want for six weeks, but I'll be here."

She leaned in to give him a kiss. "I'll still love you anyway."

Evan pulled back a little in shock. "You love me?"

Ooops. She'd been thinking it, but hadn't worked up the courage to say anything, and now.... But Evan didn't seem panicked or poised for flight, just surprised—and maybe a little pleased. That gave her courage. "Yeah. I'm pretty sure I do."

"Oh. Wow."

"Just 'wow'?" That wasn't exactly a rousing endorsement. Maybe she'd gone too far, too soon.

"I didn't know that you felt that way, I mean."

"Why would I put up with you otherwise?"

"I'm good in bed?"

She pretended to think, then shrugged. "Meh."

An eyebrow went up. "Oh, really?" Evan scooped her up and over his shoulder like a sack of potatoes, carrying her down the hall to their bedroom, where he dropped her on the bed. Climbing on top of her, he said, "That sounds like a challenge."

She was trapped between Evan and the mattress, caged by his arms—not that she was really complaining. He dropped his forehead to hers. "I love you, too."

A happy bubble filled her chest. "Wow."

"So will you go to Paris?"

She felt safe saying, "Yeah. I think so. Will you come to visit me?"

He thought for a second. "I'll come at the end to see your show. And then we'll take a week or so for vacation. How's that?"

"That sounds good." She leaned up far enough to kiss him. "*Two* vacations planned, and it's barely May. What will we plan for the fall?"

This time he didn't stop to think at all. "How about a wedding?"

She couldn't have heard that correctly. But she couldn't think of anything else that sounded like that. "A wedding?"

"Yeah. I'm thinking small and tasteful. Or big and ostentatious, it's totally up to you."

"Wow."

He looked surprised. "Just wow? That's not actually an answer, Liv."

"You haven't actually asked me a question, you know."

He grinned, and it was contagious. And while she wouldn't have thought ten minutes ago she was ready for this, she was sure it was the right decision.

"Do you trust me?"

"Yes."

"Do you love me?"

"Yes."

"Olivia Madison, will you marry me?"

"Yes, Evan, I will marry you." He kissed her then and happiness made her toes tingle. She pulled her head back and made him look at her. "One thing, though."

He pulled back, worry on his face. "What's that?"

"You get to tell Jory."

* * * * *

CHRISTMAS IN DA CONTI'S BED

SHARON KENDRICK

This book lovingly acknowledges the feisty and wonderful McCormick women – and most especially Joan and Eileen.

CHAPTER ONE

NICCOLÒ DA CONTI hated marriage, Christmas and love—but most of all he hated it when people didn't do what he wanted them to.

An unfamiliar feeling of frustration made him bite back a graphic expletive as he paced the floor of the vast New York hotel suite. Outside, skyscrapers and stars glittered against the deepening indigo sky, though not nearly as brightly as the Christmas lights which were already adorning the city.

But Niccolò was oblivious to the party atmosphere, or even to the onset of this most hated time of year. All he could think about was his only sister and wondering why she was being so damned *disobedient*.

'I do not want,' he said, sucking in a ragged breath in an attempt to control his rapidly spiralling temper, 'some tacky topless model acting as your bridesmaid. I have worked long and hard to establish a degree of respectability in your life, Michela. Do you understand what I'm saying? It cannot be allowed to happen, and what is more—I will not allow it to happen.'

From the other side of the glitzy New York hotel penthouse suite, Michela's expression remained unchanged as she looked at him.

'But you can't stop me from having her, Niccolò,' she said stubbornly. 'I'm the bride and it's my decision. That's the thing.'

'You think so?' His mouth hardened and he felt another hot flicker of rage. 'I could refuse to pay for this wedding for a start.'

'But the man I'm marrying is rich enough to carry the cost of the marriage if you decide to take such drastic action.' Michela hesitated. 'Though I'm sure you wouldn't want the world to know that Niccolò da Conti had refused to finance his only sister's wedding, just because he doesn't approve of her choice of bridesmaid. Wouldn't that be a step too far in the modern world—even for a man as old-fashioned as you?'

Niccolò flexed and then relaxed his fingers, wishing there were a nearby punch-bag on which he could vent his mounting frustrations. The world usually ran according to his wishes and he was not used to having them questioned. Bad enough that Alekto Sarantos was acting like some kind of prima donna…without having to cope with the bombshell that Alannah Collins was here.

His mouth tightened with anger as he thought about his sister and the sacrifices he had made. For too long he had fought to keep their tiny family unit intact and he was not prepared to relinquish control over her just yet. Because old habits died hard. He had faced shame and tragedy and had seen them off. He had protected Michela as much as was within his power to do so, and now she was about to enter into marriage, which would see her secure for life. His careful vetting of would-be suitors had paid dividends and she was about to marry into one of the most powerful Italian-American families in New York. She would have the sanctity he had always wished for her and nothing would be allowed to tarnish the occasion. Nothing and no one.

Especially not Alannah Collins.

Even the *thought* of the minxy little tramp made his body react in a complicated way he found difficult to control—and he was a man who prided himself on control. A powerful combination of lust and regret flooded over him, although his overriding emotion was one of rage, and that was the one he hung onto.

'I cannot believe that she has had the nerve to show her face,' he bit out. 'I can't believe she's even here.'

'Well, she is. I invited her.'

'I thought you hadn't seen her since I withdrew you from that appalling school.'

Michela hesitated. 'Actually, we've…well, we've stayed in touch over the years,' she said. 'We emailed and phoned—and I used to see her whenever I was in England. And last year she came to New York and we took a trip to the Keys and it was just like old times. She was my best friend at school, Niccolò. We go back a long way.'

'And yet you told me nothing of this before?' he demanded. 'You maintain a secret friendship and then spring it on me on the eve of your marriage? Didn't you stop to consider how it might look—to have someone as notorious as this tawdry exhibitionist playing a major role in your wedding?'

Michela lifted her hands up to the sides of her head

in a gesture of frustration. 'Are you surprised I didn't tell you, when this is the kind of reaction I get?'

'What does Lucas say about your connection with her?' he demanded.

'It happened a long time ago. It's history, Niccolò. Most people in the States haven't even heard of *Stacked* magazine—it folded ages ago. And yes, I know that a video of the original shoot seems to have found its way onto YouTube—'

'*What?*' he exploded.

'But it's really quite tame by modern standards,' said Michela quickly. 'If you compare it to some of the music videos you see these days—well, it's almost suitable for the kindergarten! And Alannah doesn't do that kind of stuff any more. You've got her all wrong, Niccolò, she's—'

'She is a tramp!' he gritted out, his Sicilian accent becoming more pronounced as his temper rose once again. 'A precocious little tramp, who shouldn't be allowed within ten feet of decent society. When will you get it into your head, Michela, that Alannah Collins is—'

'Whoops!' A cool voice cut into his angry tirade and Niccolò turned to see a woman strolling into the room without bothering to knock and suddenly his words were forgotten. If somebody had asked him his name right then, he thought he might have trouble remembering it. And yet for a moment he almost didn't recognise her—because in his memory she was wearing very little and the woman in front of him had barely an inch of flesh on show. It was the sound of her naturally sultry voice which kick-started his memory and his libido. But it didn't take long for his eyes to reacquaint themselves with her magnificent body—nor to acknowledge the natural sensuality which seemed to shimmer from it in almost tangible waves.

She was wearing jeans and a white shirt with a high collar, but the concealing nature of her outfit did nothing to disguise the luscious curves beneath. Thick black hair like lustrous jet hung over her shoulders, and eyes the colour of denim were studying him with a hint of mockery in their depths. Niccolò swallowed. He had forgotten the pale creaminess of her complexion and the rosiness of her lips. He had forgotten that this half-Irish temptress with an unknown father could burrow underneath his skin, without even trying.

As she moved he could see the glitter of a little blue dragonfly brooch gleaming on her shirt-collar, which matched the amazing colour of her eyes. And even though he despised her, he could do nothing about the leap of desire which made his body grow tense. She made him think of things he'd rather not think about—but mostly she made him think about sex.

'Did I just hear my name being taken in vain?' she questioned lightly. 'Would you like me to walk back out and come in again?'

'Feel free to walk out any time you like,' he answered coldly. 'But why don't you do us all a favour, and skip the second part of the suggestion?'

She tilted her chin in a way which made her black hair ripple down her back, like an ebony waterfall. But the smile she slanted at him didn't quite reach her eyes.

'I see you've lost none of your natural charm,

Niccolò,' she observed acidly. 'I'd forgotten how you could take the word "insult" and give it a whole new meaning.'

Niccolò felt a pulse begin to pound in his temple as his blood grew heated. But much worse was the jerk of lust which made his groin feel unbearably hard. Which made him want to crush his mouth down over her lips and kiss all those insolent words away and then to drive deep inside her until she screamed out his name, over and over again.

Damn her, he thought viciously. Damn her, with all her easy confidence and her louche morals. And damn those sinful curves, which would compel a grown man to crawl over broken glass just to have the chance of touching them.

'Forgive me,' he drawled, 'but for a moment I didn't recognise you with your clothes on.'

He saw the brief discomfiture which crossed her face and something primitive gave him a heady rush of pleasure to think that he might have touched a nerve and hurt her. Hurt her as she had once hurt his family and threatened to ruin their name.

But she turned the look into a bright and meaningless smile. 'I'm not going to rise to that,' she said as she turned instead to his sister. 'Are you ready for your fitting, Michela?'

Michela nodded, but her eyes were still fixed nervously on Niccolò. 'I wish you two could be civil to each other—at least until the wedding is over. Couldn't you do that for me—just this once? Then you never need see one another again!'

Niccolò met Alannah's speculative gaze and the thought of her smiling serenely in a bridesmaid gown made his blood boil. Didn't she recognise that it was hypocritical for her to play the wide-eyed innocent on an important occasion such as this? Couldn't she see that it would suit everyone's agenda if she simply faded into the background, instead of taking on a major role? He thought of the powerful bridegroom's elderly grandparents and how they might react if they realised that this was the same woman who had massaged her own peaking nipples, while wearing a dishevelled schoolgirl hockey kit. His mouth hardened. How much would it take to persuade her that she was persona non grata?

He flickered his sister a brief smile. 'Why don't you let Alannah and I have a word or two in private, *mia sorella*? And let's see if we can sort out this matter to everyone's satisfaction.'

Michela gave her friend a questioning look, but Alannah nodded.

'It's okay,' she said. 'You're quite safe to leave me alone with your brother, Michela—I'm sure he doesn't bite.'

Niccolò stiffened as Michela left the suite and his unwanted feeling of desire escalated into a dark and unremitting tide. He wondered if Alannah had made that remark to be deliberately provocative. He would certainly like to bite *her*. He'd like to sink his teeth into that slender neck and suck hungrily on that soft and creamy skin.

Her eyes were fixed on him—with that infuriating look of mild amusement still lingering in their smoky depths.

'So come on, then, Niccolò,' she said insouciantly. 'Do your worst. Why don't you get whatever is bugging you off your chest so that we can clear the air and give your sister the kind of wedding she deserves?'

'At least we are agreed on something,' he snapped. 'My sister does deserve a perfect wedding—one which will not involve a woman who will attract all the wrong kind of publicity. You have always been wild—even before you decided to strip for the cameras. And I don't think it's acceptable for every man at the ceremony to be mentally undressing the bridesmaid, instead of concentrating on the solemn vows being made between the bride and groom.'

'For someone who seems to have spent all his life avoiding commitment, I applaud your sudden dedication to the marriage service.' Her cool smile didn't slip. 'But I don't think most men are as obsessed with my past as you are.'

'You think I'm obsessed by your past?' His voice hardened. 'Oh, but you flatter yourself if you imagine that I've given you anything more than a fleeting thought in the years since you led my sister astray.' His gaze moved over her and he wondered if the lie showed in his face because he had never forgotten her, nor the effect she'd had on him. For a long time he had dreamt of her soft body and her sweet kiss— before waking up in a cold sweat as he remembered what he had nearly done to her. 'I thought you were out of her life,' he said. 'Which is where I would prefer you to stay.'

Calmly, Alannah returned his stare and told herself not to react, no matter what the provocation. Didn't matter how angry he got, she would just blank it. She'd seen enough of the world to know that remaining calm—or, at least, *appearing* to—was the most

effective weapon in dealing with an adversary. And
Niccolò da Conti was being *very* adversarial.

She knew he blamed her for being a bad influence on his beloved sister, so maybe she shouldn't
be surprised that he still seemed to bear a grudge.
She remembered reading something about him in the
press—about him not being the kind of man who
forgot easily. Just as he wasn't the kind of man who
was easily forgotten, that was for sure. He wore his
wealth lightly; his power less so. He could silence a
room by entering it. He could make a woman look at
him and want him, even if he was currently staring at
her as if she were something which had just crawled
out from underneath a rock. What right did he have
to look at her like that, after all these years? Because
she'd once done something which had appalled his
straight-laced sensibilities—something she'd lived
to regret ever since? She was a different person now
and he had no right to judge her.

Yet it was working, wasn't it? The contempt in his
eyes was curiously affecting. That cold black light
was threatening to destabilise a poise she'd spent
years trying to perfect. And if she wasn't careful, he
would try to crush her. *So tell him to keep his outdated
opinions to himself. Tell him you're not interested in
what he has to say.*

But her indignation was beginning to evaporate,
because he was loosening the top button of his shirt
and drawing attention to his body. Was he doing that
on purpose? she wondered weakly, hating the way her
stomach had suddenly turned to liquid. Was he deliberately reminding her of a potent sexuality which
had once blown her away?

She became aware that her heart was pounding like mad and that her cheeks had grown hot. She might not like him. She might consider him the most controlling person she'd ever met—but that didn't stop her from wanting him in a way she'd never wanted anyone else. Didn't seem to matter how many times she tried to block out what had happened, or tried to play it down—it made no difference. All they'd shared had been one dance and one kiss—but it had been the most erotic experience of her life and she'd never forgotten it. It had made every other man she'd met seem as insubstantial as a shadow when the fierce midday sun moved over it. It had made every other kiss seem about as exciting as kissing your teddy bear.

She ran her gaze over him, wishing he were one of those men who had developed a soft paunch in the intervening years, or that his jaw had grown slack and jowly. But not Niccolò. No way. He still had the kind of powerful physique which looked as if he could fell a tree with the single stroke of an axe. He still had the kind of looks which made people turn their heads and stare. His rugged features stopped short of being classically beautiful, but his lips looked as if they had been made with kissing in mind—even if their soft sensuality was at odds with the hostile glitter in his eyes.

She hadn't seen him for ten years and ten years could be a lifetime. In that time she'd achieved a notoriety she couldn't seem to shake off, no matter how much she tried. She'd grown used to men treating her as an object—their eyes fixed firmly on her generous breasts whenever they were talking to her.

In those ten years she'd seen her mother get sick

and die and had woken up the day after the funeral to realise she was completely alone in the world. And that had been when she'd sat down and taken stock of her life. She'd realised that she had to walk away and leave the tawdry world of glamour modelling behind. She had reached out to try something new and it hadn't been easy, but she had tried. She was still trying—still dreaming of the big break, just like everyone else. Still trying to bolster up her fragile ego and hold her head up high and make out she was strong and proud, even if inside she sometimes felt as lost and frightened as a little girl. She'd made a lot of mistakes, but she'd paid for every one of them—and she wasn't going to let Niccolò da Conti dismiss her as if she were of no consequence.

And suddenly, she was finding it difficult to do 'calm', when he was staring at her in that contemptuous way. A flicker of rebellion sparked inside her as she met his disdainful gaze.

'While you, of course, are whiter than the driven snow?' she questioned sarcastically. 'The last thing I read was that you were dating some Norwegian banker, who you then dumped in the most horrible way possible. Apparently, you have a reputation for doing that, Niccolò. The article quoted her as saying how cruel you'd been—though I guess that shouldn't have really surprised me.'

'I prefer to think of it as honesty rather than cruelty, Alannah,' he answered carelessly. 'Some women just can't accept that a relationship has run its natural course and I'm afraid Lise was one of them. But it's interesting to know you've been keeping tabs on me all this time.' He gave her a coolly mocking smile. 'I

guess single billionaires must have a certain appeal to
women like you, who would do pretty much anything
for money. Tell me, do you track their progress as a
gambler would study the form of the most promising
horses in the field? Is that how it works?'

Alannah tensed. Now he'd made it sound as if she'd
been *stalking* him. He was trying to make her feel
bad about herself *and she wasn't going to let him.*
'Now who's flattering themselves?' she said. 'You're
best friends with the Sultan of Qurhah, aren't you?
And if you go out for dinner with royalty, then the
photos tend to make it into the tabloids—along with
speculation about why your date was seen sobbing
outside your apartment the following morning. So
please don't lecture me on morality, Niccolò—when
you know nothing of my life.'

'And I would prefer to keep it that way,' he said. 'In
fact, I'd like to keep you as far away from any member of the da Conti family as possible. So why don't
we get down to business?'

She blinked at him, momentarily disconcerted.
'Business?'

'Sure. Don't look so startled—you're a big girl
now, Alannah. You know how these things work. You
and I need to have a little talk and we might as well
do it in some degree of comfort.' He waved his hand
in the direction of the cocktail cabinet which stood
at the far end of the glittering hotel suite. 'Would
you like a drink? Don't good-time girls always go for
champagne? I can't guarantee a high-heeled shoe for
you to sip it from, but I can vouch for an extremely
good vintage.'

Don't rise to it, she told herself, before fixing a

weary smile to her lips. 'I hate to challenge your stereotype, but I'm not crazy about champagne and even if I was I certainly wouldn't want to drink it with you. That might imply a cordiality we both know doesn't exist. So why don't you say whatever it is you're determined to say? And then we can end this conversation as quickly as possible so that I can concentrate on fitting Michela's wedding gown.'

He didn't answer for a moment, but instead leaned back against one of the giant sofas and looked at her, his arms folded across his broad chest. Yet for all his supposedly casual stance, Alannah felt a chill of foreboding as his eyes met hers. There was a patina of power surrounding him which she hadn't noticed in that long-ago nightclub. There was a hardness about him which you didn't find in your average man. Suddenly he looked formidable—as if he was determined to remind her just who she was dealing with.

'I think we both know a simple way to resolve this,' he said softly. 'All you have to do is step out of the spotlight right now. Do that and there will be no problem. Michela is about to marry a very powerful man. She is about to take on an important role as a new wife. In time, she hopes to have children and her friends will be role models to them. And…'

'And?' she questioned, but she knew what was coming. It was crystal clear from the look on his face.

'You are not an appropriate role model,' he said. 'You're not the kind of woman I want fraternising with my nephews and nieces.'

Her heart was beating very fast. 'Don't you dare judge me,' she said, but her voice wasn't quite steady.

'Then why not make it easy for yourself? Tell Michela you've changed your mind about acting as her bridesmaid.'

'Too late!' Forcing herself to stay strong, she held up her palms in front of her, like a policeman stepping into the road to stop the traffic. 'I've made my own dress, which is currently swathed in plastic in my room, waiting for me to put it on just before noon tomorrow. I'm wearing scarlet silk to emphasise the wedding's winter theme,' she added chattily.

'But it's not going to happen,' he said repressively. 'Do you really think I would let it?'

For a moment Alannah felt another shimmer of doubt flicker into the equation. The quiet resolution of his voice scared her and so did the forthright expression in his eyes. Somehow he was making her feel...vulnerable. *And she wasn't going to let that happen.* Because she didn't do vulnerable. Not any more. Vulnerable got you nowhere. It made you fall down when life landed one of its killer punches and think you'd never be able to get back up again. It made you easy prey to powerful predators like Niccolò da Conti. 'How wicked you make me sound,' she said.

'Not wicked,' he corrected silkily. 'Just misguided, out-of-control and sexually precocious. And I don't want any publicity generated by the presence of *Stacked* magazine's most popular pin-up.'

'But nobody—'

'Michela has already mistakenly tried to tell me that nobody will know,' he interrupted impatiently. 'But they will. The magazines you stripped for have become collectors' items and back issues now change hands for thousands of dollars. And I've just been informed that a film of you has made its way onto YouTube, raising your public profile even further. It doesn't matter what you wear or what you don't wear—you still have the kind of body which occupies a fertile part of the male imagination. Men still look at you and find themselves thinking of one thing— and only one thing.'

Alannah tried not to cringe, but unfortunately his words struck home. Clever, cruel Niccolò had— unwittingly or not—tapped into her biggest insecurity. He made her feel like an object. Like a *thing*. Not a woman at all, but some two-dimensional image in a magazine—put there simply for men to lust over.

The person she was now wouldn't dream of letting her nipples peek out from behind her splayed fingers, while she pouted at the camera. These days she would rather die than hook her thumbs in her panties and thrust her pelvis in the direction of the lens. *But she'd needed to do it, for all kinds of reasons. Reasons the uptight Niccolò da Conti wouldn't understand in a million years.*

'You were *notorious*, Alannah,' he continued. 'And that kind of notoriety doesn't just go away. It sticks like mud.'

She looked at him in despair. He was telling *her* that? Didn't he realise that she'd been living with the consequences of that job ever since? No, of course he didn't. He saw what he wanted to see and no more— he didn't have the imagination to put himself in someone else's shoes and think what their life might be like. He was protected by his wealth and position and his arrogance.

She wanted to go up and shake *him* and tell him

to think outside the box. To wipe that judgemental look from his face and to start seeing her as a person, instead of someone who'd once behaved rashly. She could see exactly why Michela had been so scared of him when they'd been at school together. Was it any wonder that the Italian girl had rebelled from the moment he'd dropped her off at the exclusive Swiss finishing school where Alannah's mother had worked as school matron?

'The most important thing for me,' she said slowly, 'is that Michela wants me there. It's her day and she's the bride. So, short of tying me up and kidnapping me—I intend to be there tomorrow.'

'Unless we come to some kind of mutually beneficial arrangement,' he said.

'Oh?' She tilted her head. 'Tell me more.'

'Oh, come on, Alannah.' He smiled. 'You're a streetwise woman. You've been around. There must be something in your life that you'd...*like*.'

'Something in my life that I'd like?' she repeated. 'You mean like a cure for the common cold, or an alarm that doesn't make you want to smash the phone every time you hear it?'

'Very amusing. No, nothing like that.' He paused, and his black eyes glittered. 'I am a very wealthy man—and I'm willing to make it worth your while to tell Michela that you've changed your mind.'

She stared at him in disbelief.

'Let me get this straight,' she said. 'You're offering me *money* to stay away from your sister and not be her bridesmaid?'

'Why not?' He gave a cold smile. 'In my experience, if you want something badly enough you can usually get it. The tricky thing is negotiating the right price—but that is something I should imagine you're very good at.'

'But that's…bribery.'

'Try thinking of it as common sense,' he suggested softly.

She was shaking her head. 'You know, Michela used to tell me how unbelievably controlling you were,' she said. 'And part of me thought she might have been exaggerating. But now I can see that every word was true.'

'I am not seeking your approval of my character,' he clipped out. 'Just think why I'm making you this offer.'

'Because you're a control freak?'

'Because Michela means everything to me,' he said, and suddenly his voice grew harsh as he re-membered how he'd fought to protect his sister from the sins of their father. *And their mother.* He thought of their flight from Sicily—his mother pregnant with Michela and not knowing what lay ahead. Niccolò had been only ten, but he had been the one everyone had relied on. He had been the man around the house. And it was hard to relinquish that kind of role or those kinds of expectations…

'Michela is the only family I have left in the world and I would do anything for her,' he ground out.

'Except give her the freedom which a woman of her age has the right to expect?' she retorted. 'Well, I'm *glad* she's had the courage to stand up to you. To maybe make you realise that you can't keep snapping your fingers and expecting everyone else to just leap to attention. I'm not going anywhere until after the wedding. Better deal with it, Niccolò.'

Their gazes clashed and Niccolò felt the flicker of something unknown as he returned her stare. Oh, but she was a one-off. She took defiance to a whole new level and made it seem erotic. She made him want to take her in his arms and dominate her—to show her that he could not and would not be thwarted. He took a step towards her and a primitive surge of pleasure rippled over him as he watched her eyes darken. Because she still wanted him, he realised. Maybe not quite as much as he wanted her—but the desire he could read in her eyes was unmistakable.

And couldn't desire be the most powerful weapon of all? Didn't sex give a man power over a woman who wanted it?

'Why don't you think about what I've said?' he suggested. 'So that by the time I see you at the pre-wedding dinner later, you'll have had the sense to change your mind about my offer.'

Her eyes narrowed. 'But...'

He raised his eyebrows. Suddenly, she didn't look quite so defiant. Suddenly she looked almost unsure of herself. 'But?'

'I...' She shrugged her shoulders. 'It's just that... well, Michela said you were probably going to skip the dinner and that we wouldn't see you until tomorrow. Something to do with a business deal. Some new apartment block you've recently built in London.'

'Is that what she said?' He smiled. 'Well, not any more. I've decided business can wait, because something much more important has come up.' There was a pause as he looked at her and suddenly it was easy to forget the pressing needs of his billionaire clients and friends. 'What is it they say? Keep your friends close but your enemies closer. And I want you *very* close for all kinds of reasons, Alannah. You'd better believe that.'

CHAPTER TWO

ALANNAH PULLED UP the zip of her cocktail dress and stared at her pale-faced reflection in the mirror. She'd tried deep breathing and she'd done a quick bout of yoga, but her hands were still trembling and she knew why. Slipping on a pair of high-heeled shoes, she felt a wave of self-recrimination washing over her.

She thought about the things Niccolò had said to her earlier. The way he'd insulted her and looked down his proud, patrician nose. He'd been judging her in the most negative way possible, but that hadn't stopped her wanting him. She shuddered. Where was the self-respect she'd worked so hard to get back? She wondered what had happened to the cool, calm Alannah who wasn't going to let him get under her skin. How had he managed to puncture her self-possession with nothing more than a heated ebony gaze, which reminded her of things she'd rather forget?

Because memory was a funny thing, that was why—and sometimes you had no control over it. It flipped and jerked and jumped around like a flapping fish on the end of a hook. It took you to places you didn't want to visit. It could make ten years seem like a minute, or a minute seem like an hour.

It could put you back inside the skin of the person you'd once been.

And suddenly she was a teenager again. Seventeen years old and about to break the rules. Off to a party wearing the make-up which her Swiss finishing school strictly forbade, when really she should have been tucked up in bed in the dormitory. Wearing a tiny little micro-mini because she had been young and carefree—because back then she hadn't realised that a woman's body could become her enemy, instead of her friend...

By rights, someone like her shouldn't have been a pupil at the exclusive all-girls academy, tucked high in the beautiful mountains of Switzerland. She wasn't rich. She wasn't well-connected. She was just the illegitimate daughter of a single-parent mother who happened to be Matron at the fancy boarding school. And while this meant that Alannah got herself a great education, her 'charity' status meant that most of the girls simply tolerated her.

Michela da Conti was different. She was the only one who had held out the hand of genuine friendship—maybe because they had something in common, despite their rich-girl/poor-girl pairing. Alannah had spent her life rebelling against her super-strict mother while Michela had known real tragedy in her short life, plus she wanted to escape the strictures of her controlling brother, Niccolò.

Their youthful rebellion usually stretched no further than going out for illicit under-age drinks in one of the nearby bars after lights-out, or hanging out of the dormitory window, trying to inhale cigarettes without being sick.

But one night they heard about a party. A glitzy twenty-first birthday celebration for one of Niccolò's godsons—which was being held in one of the neighbouring mountain valleys.

'And we're going!' declared Michela excitedly.

Alannah remembered frowning. 'But what about your brother? Won't he be there?'

'You're kidding.' Michela had given a smile of satisfaction. 'Apparently, he's miles away in some obscenely expensive resort in Barbados, with his latest ghastly supermodel girlfriend. So we're safe.'

Alannah remembered walking into the crowded room, where coloured lights were flashing and music was blaring out loudly. Her borrowed silver minidress was clinging to her body like honey and she was getting lots of requests to dance, but she turned down every one because all the boys seemed too loud and too brash to be interesting.

She did her best to enjoy herself. She sipped a soft drink and admired the snowy view. Found a sleeping kitten on her way back from the loo and spent an enjoyable ten minutes stroking its furry tummy and wishing she could go home. When eventually she went back into the main room to find Michela to suggest they got a cab back to school, she couldn't find her anywhere. So she went and stood in a quiet corner of the room, losing herself in the shadows while everyone else partied—and that was when she saw him.

Him.

She had never forgotten that moment. It was like being struck by something with no sense of warning that it was coming. As if a velvet sledgehammer had hit her very hard. She was aware that he was tall and his hair was as black as the night sky. His eyes were black too—even from this distance she could see that. He was dressed in a dark suit, which made him look outwardly sophisticated, but she could sense something *primitive* about him. There was something predatory in the gleam of his eyes, which should have scared her as he began to walk towards her, with a sense of purpose in his step.

But she wasn't scared.

It was the most illogical thought she'd ever had, but at that moment she felt as if she'd been waiting all her life for him to arrive, and here he was.

Here he was.

He looked her up and down—as if it was his right to study a strange woman as he might study a car he was thinking of buying. But surely no car would make him smile like that—a smile which seemed to come from somewhere deep inside him, one that pierced her heart and made her knees feel as if they might have difficulty supporting her.

'I think you need to dance,' he said.

'I'm not a very good dancer.'

'That's because you've never danced with me. So come here and let me teach you how.'

Later, she would remonstrate with herself at the eagerness with which she fell into his arms. At the way she let him slide his hands around her back as if she'd known him for years. His hand moved to her hair and he started stroking it and suddenly she wanted to purr as loudly as that kitten had done earlier.

They said very little. The party was too loud for conversation and, anyway, it didn't seem to be conversation which was dominating Alannah's thoughts right then. Or his. Words seemed superfluous as he pulled her closer and, although the music was fast, they danced so slowly that they barely moved. Their bodies felt as if they were glued together and Alannah almost wept with the sheer pleasure of it all. Did he sense her enjoyment? Was that why he dipped his mouth to her ear, so that she could feel the warmth of his breath fanning her skin?

'You,' he said, his velvety voice underpinned with an accent which she recognised as Sicilian, 'are very beautiful.'

Wasn't it funny how some people you just seemed to spark off? So that she—inexperienced and raw as she was—didn't respond in a conventional way. She didn't blush and tell him she wasn't beautiful at all—but instead came out with something which sounded almost slick.

'And you,' she cooed back, looking straight into his black eyes, 'are very handsome.'

He smiled. 'A perfect match, then?'

She tipped her head back. 'Aren't you getting a little ahead of yourself?'

'Probably.' He leaned forward, so that her face was bathed in the dark spotlight of his gaze. 'Especially as we haven't even kissed. Don't you think that's a shocking omission, my beauty? So shocking that I think we ought to remedy it right now.'

She remembered the way her heart had crashed loudly against her ribcage. The way her mouth had dried with anticipation and the words had just come tumbling out of her mouth. 'Who says I'm going to kiss you?'

'I do.'

And he did.

In that shadowy corner of some anonymous house in the Swiss mountains, while outside flakes of snow floated past the window like big, white feathers, he kissed her.

He kissed her so intensely that Alannah thought she might faint. He kissed her for so long that she wanted him never to stop. It was like that pile of bone-dry sticks she'd once built on a long-ago holiday to Ireland—she remembered the way they'd combusted into flames the moment her aunt had put a match to them. Well, it was a bit like that now.

She was on fire.

His thumb brushed over her breast and Alannah wriggled with excitement. Because surely this was what she had been made for—to stand in this man's arms and be touched by him. To have him look at her as if she were the most beautiful woman in the world. He deepened the kiss to one of added intimacy and as he pushed his thigh between hers the atmosphere suddenly changed. It became charged. She could feel the flood of liquid heat to her groin and the sudden, almost painful hardening of her nipples as they pushed insistently against his chest. His breath was unsteady as he pulled away from her and there was a primitive emotion on his face which she didn't recognise.

'We'd better think about moving somewhere more comfortable,' he said roughly. 'Somewhere with a bed.'

Alannah never had a chance to reply because suddenly the mood was broken by some kind of commotion at the door. She felt him tense as Michela burst into the room with snow melting on her raven hair, and the guilty look on her friend's face when she saw Niccolò told its own story.

It was unfortunate that Michela was surrounded by the miasma of sickly-sweet marijuana smoke—and even more unfortunate when Niccolò's discreet enquiries the next day yielded up the information that both girls were already on a formal warning from the school. A small matter of the building's elaborate fire-alarm system having been set off by the two of them hanging out of a dormitory window, smoking.

Alannah would never forget the look of passion dying on Niccolò's face, only to see it being replaced with one of disgust as he looked at her. She remembered wanting to wither beneath it.

'You are my sister's friend?' he questioned incredulously. 'Her *school friend*?'

'Y-yes.'

'How old are you?'

'Seventeen.'

All the colour drained from his face and he looked as if she'd hit him. 'So Michela associates with a *puttana*, does she?' he hissed. 'A cheap little tart who puts out for strangers at parties.'

'I d-don't remember you objecting,' she stammered, stung into defending herself, even if deep down she felt she had no real defence to offer.

'No man objects when a woman offers herself to him on a plate like that,' he snapped.

The following day he had withdrawn Michela from the school and shortly afterwards the head teacher had summoned Alannah and her mother to her office. The head had clearly been furious at the prospect of having to say goodbye to Niccolò da Conti's generous donations to the school. She had told Alannah that her behaviour was unacceptable and her mother had pre-empted the inevitable expulsion by offering up her resignation.

'I'm not having my girl scapegoated by some rich financier,' she'd said fiercely. 'If you're going to heap all the blame on her, then this is not the kind of school for her.'

Of course, that was not an end to it—merely the beginning of a nightmare which put the whole Niccolò incident to the back of her mind.

But she'd never grassed up Michela and Michela had remained loyal to her ever since.

Her thoughts cleared and she saw her friend looking at her in the dressing-table mirror, her face still glowing from her pre-wedding facial, and Alannah sighed as she met Michela's questioning gaze. 'Maybe it would be better if I just bowed out, if it's going to cause a massive row between you and your brother. I'll just stand at the back like everyone else and throw rose petals. I can live with that.'

Michela glared as she put her hairbrush down.

'And let Niccolò have his own way? I don't think so. You've been the best of friends to me, Alannah—and I want you there. In fact, it'll probably do Niccolò good on all kinds of levels. I've never heard *anyone* speak to him the way you do.' She smirked. 'Nobody else would dare.'

Alannah wondered what Michela would say if she realised how much of her reaction to her powerful brother was bravado. That her feelings for him were... *complicated*. Would she be shocked if she knew the truth? That she only had to look at him to want to rip the shirt from his body and feast her eyes on all that silken olive flesh? That somehow he brought out a wildness in her which frightened her. Which she knew was wrong. And not only wrong…she knew only too well that those supposedly seamless sexual fantasies were nothing but an illusion.

She forced a smile. 'Okay, if you insist…it'll be business as usual. In which case, we'd better get going. I know it's traditional for the bride to keep her groom waiting on the big day, but not on the eve-of-wedding dinner!'

They took the elevator down to the iconic Midnight Room, where a large clock was set permanently at the witching hour. It was a spectacular party room designed by Emma Constantinides, the hotel owner's wife—and had won countless industry prizes since its opening. Circular tables had been set for dinner and the dark velvet ceiling was punctured with tiny lights, so that it resembled a star-filled sky. In the silvery light from hundreds of candles, people in evening dress stood drinking champagne as the scent of dark blue hyacinths wafted through the air.

A roar of delight greeted the bride-to-be's appearance and Alannah leaned forward to whisper in Michela's ear as people began to surge towards them. 'You go and sparkle,' she said. 'Anything you need me to check?'

Michela shook her head. She had already spotted Lucas on the opposite side of the room, talking to his mother. 'No. You go and sparkle too,' she said. 'And for goodness' sake, have a very large cocktail before we sit down to dinner. You look completely washed out, Alannah.'

But Alannah refused a drink. A drink on an empty stomach was a recipe for disaster and hers was already in knots. All she had to do was to get through the next thirty-six hours without crumbling, and surely she could do that.

And then she looked around the room and saw Niccolò—and every empowering thought flew straight from her mind as her gaze focused on him.

He was standing talking to a blonde whose sequined dress left little to the imagination and Alannah found herself thinking that he didn't seem to have a problem with *that*. The woman was gazing up at him and nodding intently, as if nothing but pearls of wisdom were falling from those cruel and kissable lips. There were other women clustering nearby, too—as if he were a dark shark and they were all hungry little pilot fish, just waiting for whatever scraps he cared to leave for them.

He lifted his head as if he had sensed her watching him—glancing across the room to where she stood. And suddenly it was too late to look away. His gaze captured hers and held it and it felt as if some fierce dark light were piercing through her skin. She felt sensitive. Exposed and raw. Terrified he would see through to the dark mass of insecurities hidden beneath her cool exterior, she tried to look away, but she couldn't. *She couldn't.* He seemed to be drawing her in by the force of his formidable will.

Desperately, she tried to compose herself. To concentrate on something other than how beautifully the dark suit caressed his hard body, but she failed at that, too. Instead she found herself staring at the snowy edge of his dinner-shirt and the way his olive skin gleamed like burnished gold above it.

He bent his head to say something to the blonde, who turned to look at her, and Alannah thought she saw faint surprise clouding the other woman's eyes. Had her uncomfortable stance given her away—making the woman guess that she was the outsider here?

She forced herself to turn away to talk to some of the other guests, who seemed genuinely charmed by her English accent, and for a while she allowed herself to relax before the bell rang for dinner. But a glance at the seating plan showed her that she was next to Niccolò—*of course she was,* for hadn't Michela made it clear that she wanted the two of them to get along better? She wondered when her friend was going to realise that it simply wasn't going to happen. Or at least, not in this lifetime. Her heart began thumping painfully as she made her way towards the top table.

She felt his presence behind her even before his shadow fell over the table. The palms of her hands were clammy and the race of her heart was thready, but somehow she managed to fix a wide smile to her lips as she turned to look at him.

'Niccolò!' she said brightly.

'Just the person you wanted to sit beside, right?'

'How did you guess?' Solely for the benefit of the other guests, she maintained that brittle rictus of a smile. 'You were right at the top of my list.'

But Alannah tensed as he leaned forward to kiss her on both cheeks, just as he would have done to any other female guest. She wondered if any other female guest would have reacted the way she did, with a pulse which was threatening to rocket out of control and a desire to tip her head up so that his mouth would meet hers, instead of grazing the innocent surface of her cheek. She found herself longing to reach up to touch that hard, chiselled jaw and to feel it scrape against her fingertips. She wanted to press her lips against his ear and kiss it. And how crazy was that? How could you want a man so much when you didn't even *like* him?

Stop it, she told herself as he pulled out her chair with an exaggerated courtesy, which seemed to be at odds with the mockery gleaming from his eyes. Did he know what kind of effect he had on her? Did he realise that her legs were weak and her breasts growing heavy? He sat down next to her and she could smell his warm, male flesh—as subtle and spicy as sandalwood—and all she wanted to do was to breathe it in. Reaching out, she picked up her champagne flute and took a gulp.

She could feel him watching as she drank the cold, fizzy wine but the champagne tasted as sour as a remedy you might take for an upset stomach. She put down her glass and looked at him, because they couldn't go on like this. Not with a whole day and a half to get through.

'I think Michela has sat us together deliberately,' she said.

He raised his eyebrows. 'Because?'

'I think she's hoping that we're going to declare some sort of truce.'

'Why—are we engaged in some sort of battle?'

'Please don't be disingenuous, Niccolò. You know we are. We've done nothing but argue since we reconnected.' She shrugged. 'And while that seems to be what you seem to want—I'd prefer it, and your sister would prefer it, if we could manage to be non-confrontational. At least, in public.'

Niccolò met her denim-blue eyes and gave a small dissenting shake of his head—thinking how wrong she'd got it. Because battle was the last thing he wanted. His needs around Alannah Collins were much more fundamental. He might even have contemplated a more conventional route by asking her out on a date, if she hadn't been the kind of woman he despised.

Yet there was nothing of the precocious teenager or sexy glamour model about her tonight. The image she presented was almost *demure*. Her navy silk dress was high-necked and the hemline showed nothing more than an couple of inches of slender knee. A small, glittering brooch in the shape of a fluttering moth was her only jewellery. Her most magnificent assets—the breasts which had once so captured the imagination of the British public—were only hinted at and certainly not on show. All he could see was the occasional glimpse of a soft curve as the material brushed against them. He swallowed. Was she aware that it was just as provocative to conceal something, as to reveal it?

Of course she was.

Trading on her own sexuality had been her stock-in-trade, hadn't it? She knew everything there was to know about how to pull in the punters and leave them slavering for more.

Shaking out his napkin, he placed it in his lap and scowled, recalling the first time he'd seen her at his godson's birthday party.

He remembered looking in amazement at the silver dress, which had clung to her curvy body like melted butter, and thinking that he'd never seen anyone looking quite so alluring. Had he been frustrated? Too long without a woman? Unlikely. All he knew was that he hadn't been able to tear his eyes away from her.

The look which had passed between them had been timeless. The lust which had overwhelmed him had been almost tangible. He had never experienced anything like it in his life—not before, nor since. The hardness at his groin had been almost unbearable as he had danced with her. Something elemental had caught him in its grip and he'd felt almost...*lost.* The dance had been simply a formality—paving the way for their first kiss. He had kissed her for a long time, tempted by a need to pull her into a dark and anonymous corner and just *take* her. And even though he detested being out of control...even though his own history had warned him this was not the way to go— it hadn't been enough to deter him from acting on it.

He had been just about to drive her back to his hotel, when there had been some sort of commotion by the door. He remembered turning to see Michela giggling as she'd entered the room, accompanied by a group of boys. His *sister.* Large flakes of snow had been melting on her raven hair and her look of guilt when she had seen him had told its own story.

And that was when Niccolò had discovered that Alannah Collins wasn't some twenty-something party guest, but the teenage best friend of his only sister. A wild-child who had been threatening to ruin Michela's reputation and bring shame on the da Conti name, after he'd spent years meticulously dragging it from the mud.

Was it any wonder that he despised her?

Was it any wonder that he despised himself, knowing what he had nearly done to her?

What he still wanted to do to her.

He leaned back in his chair, paying little attention to the plates of smoked salmon which were being placed in front of them. 'Did you ever tell Michela what happened between us?' he questioned suddenly.

She stiffened a little before turning to look at him, her eyes narrowing warily. 'But nothing did happen.'

'Oh, come on.' He gave a harsh laugh. 'It might as well have done. It would have done, if my sister hadn't arrived. I've never had a dance quite so erotic as the one I had with you. It was a dance which was headed straight for the bedroom.'

'Oh, for heaven's sake—'

'Does Michela realise that you would have spent the night with me if she hadn't turned up when she did?'

'You can't know that.'

'Yes, I can. And so can you. Why don't you try being honest with yourself for once, Alannah?' He leaned forward and his voice roughened. 'I know enough about women to realise when they want a man to make love to them—and you were screaming out to have me do it to you that night.'

'Really?' She took a nervous sip of her drink.

'And you've avoided answering my question,' he persisted. 'What exactly did you tell Michela?'

There was a pause. 'I didn't tell her anything.'

'Why not?'

Alannah shrugged, reluctant to admit the truth—that she'd been too ashamed of her own reaction to want to acknowledge it to anyone and certainly not to her best friend. That she'd felt dirty and cheap. Michela had warned her that her big brother was a 'player'. That he changed his women nearly as often as he changed his shirts. She remembered the two of them agreeing that any woman who went out with a man like him was *sad*. But she'd nearly been one of those women, hadn't she? Because he was right. If Michela hadn't walked in right then, she would have…

Briefly, she let her eyes close. She'd been so in thrall to him that he probably could have taken her outside and taken her virginity pressed up against a cold and snowy tree. She had certainly been up for going back to his hotel with him.

She opened her eyes and looked at him. 'Why not? Because even though Michela has always thought you a total control freak, she absolutely idolised you—and I knew you were the only family she had. It wasn't for me to disillusion her by telling her that you'd been hitting on her best friend.'

'Hitting on her best friend?' He gave a cynical smile. 'Oh, please. Unfortunately, I didn't realise I was dealing with *jailbait* at the time. You kept that one crucial fact to yourself.'

'Is that why you got me expelled?' she said, without missing a beat.

He shook his head. 'I didn't mention your name when I withdrew Michela from the school.'

Her eyes narrowed. 'Are you serious?'

He shrugged. 'There was no need. I thought I was removing Michela from your bad example—what I didn't realise was that you were going to continue the friendship behind my back.'

Alannah ran her fingertip down over her champagne glass, leaving behind a transparent stripe in the condensation. 'But all that happened a long time ago,' she said slowly.

'I guess it did.' He leaned back in his chair. 'And since your role seems to be non-negotiable, I guess I'm just going to have to be nice to you.'

'Is that possible?'

'Me being nice?' He watched the golden flicker of candlelight playing on her pale skin. 'You don't think so?'

'Not really. I think it would be like someone hand-rearing a baby tiger and then expecting it to lap contentedly from a saucer of milk when it reaches adulthood. Naïve and unrealistic.'

'And nobody could ever accuse you of that.'

'Certainly not someone with as cutting a tongue as you, Niccolò.'

He laughed, his gaze drifting over fingers which he noticed were bare of rings. 'So what has been happening to you in the last ten years? Bring me up to speed.'

Alannah didn't answer for a moment. He didn't want to know that her life had imploded like a dark star when her mother had died and that for a long time she had felt completely empty. Men like Niccolò weren't interested in other people's sadness or ambition. They asked polite questions at dinner parties because that was what they had been taught to do— and all they required was something fairly meaningless in response.

She shook her head at the waitress who was offering her a basket heaped with different breads. 'I'm an interior designer these days.'

'Oh?' He waited while the pretty waitress stood close to him for slightly longer than was necessary, before reluctantly moving away. 'How did that happen? Did you wake up one morning and decide you were an expert on soft furnishings?'

'That's a very patronising comment.'

'I have experience of interior designers,' he said wryly. 'And of rich, bored women who decide to set themselves up as experts.'

'Well, I'm neither rich, nor bored. And I think you'll find there's more to the job than that. I studied fashion at art school and was planning to make dresses, but the fashion world is notoriously tough— and it's difficult to get funding.' Especially when you had the kind of past which meant that people formed negative judgements about you.

'So what did you do?'

'I worked for a big fashion chain for a while,' she continued, pushing her fork aimlessly around her plate. 'Before I realised that what I was best at was putting together a "look". I liked putting colours and fabrics together and creating interesting interiors. I spent a few years working for a large interiors company to gain experience and recently I took the plunge and set up on my own.'

'And are you any good?' he questioned. 'How come I've never heard of you?'

'I think I'm good—have a look at my website and decide for yourself,' she said. 'And the reason you haven't heard of me is because there are a million other designers out there. I'm still waiting for my big break.'

'And your topless modelling career?' he questioned idly. 'Did that fall by the wayside?'

Alannah tried not to flinch, terrified he would see how much his question had hurt. For a minute back then she'd actually thought they were sticking to their truce and talking to each other like two normal human beings. 'This is you being "nice", is it, Niccolò? Behaving as if I was something you'd found on the sole of your shoe?'

His eyes didn't leave her face. 'All I'm doing is asking a perfectly legitimate question about your former career.'

'Which you can't seem to do without that expression of disgust on your face.'

'Wouldn't anyone be disgusted?' he demanded hotly. 'Isn't the idea of a woman peddling her flesh to the highest bidder abhorrent to any man with a shred of decency in his bones? Although I suspect the end-product must have been spectacular.' There was a pause before he spoke. 'Alannah Collins *shaking her booty.*'

His last few words were murmured—and Alannah thought how unexpected the colloquialism sounded when spoken in that sexy Sicilian accent of his. But his words reminded her that what you saw wasn't necessarily what you got. Despite his cosmopolitan appearance and lifestyle, Niccolò da Conti was as traditional as they came. His views and his morals came straight from another age. No wonder his sister had been so terrified of him. No wonder she'd gone off the rails when she had been freed from his claustro-phobic presence and judgemental assessment.

'Those photographs were stills,' she said tonelessly. 'I never *shook* anything.'

'Ah, but surely you're just splitting hairs.' He gave a dangerous smile, his finger idly circling the rim of his untouched champagne glass. 'Unless you're try-ing to tell me that cupping your breasts and simulat-ing sexual provocation for the camera while wearing a school uniform is a respectable job for a woman?'

Alannah managed to twist a sliver of smoked salmon onto the end of her fork, but the food never made it to her mouth. 'Shall I tell you why I did that job?'

'Easy money, I'm guessing.'

She put the fork back down. Oh, what was the point? she thought tiredly. He didn't *care* what had motivated her. He had judged her—he was still judg-ing her—on the person she appeared to be. Someone who had danced too intimately with a stranger at a party. Someone who had gone off the rails with his beloved sister. Someone who had discovered that the only way to keep hope alive had been by taking off her clothes...

Who could blame him for despising her—for not realising that she was so much more than that?

She dabbed at her lips with her napkin. 'On second thoughts, I don't think polite interaction is going to be possible after all. There's actually too much his-tory between us.'

'Or not enough?' he challenged and suddenly his voice grew silky. 'Don't you think it might be a good idea to forge some new memories, Alannah? Something which might cancel out all the frustrations of the past?'

Alannah stiffened. Was he suggesting what she *thought* he was suggesting? Was he *flirting* with her? She swallowed. And if he were? If he were, she needed to nip it in the bud. To show him she respected herself and her body.

She slanted him a smile. 'I don't think that's going to happen. I think we need to avoid each other as much as possible. We'll support Michela all the way and try not to let our mutual animosity show, but nothing more than that. So why don't you do me a favour and talk to the woman on your other side? She's been trying to get your attention since you first sat down and she's very beautiful.' She picked up her wine glass and took a sip, her eyes surveying him coolly over the rim. 'I'm surprised you hadn't noticed that, Niccolò.'

CHAPTER THREE

IT WAS THE worst night he'd had in a long time, or maybe it was just that Niccolò couldn't remember ever losing sleep over a woman before. He lay tossing and turning in the king-size bed of his hotel room, trying to convince himself that Alannah had been right and the less time they spent together, the better. But every time he thought about distancing himself from those denim-blue eyes and that pouting, provocative mouth he felt an uncomfortable ache deep inside him.

What was the matter with him?

Kicking away the rumpled sheet, he told himself she wasn't his kind of woman—that she represented everything he despised in a sometimes trashy and disposable society.

Abandoning all further attempts to sleep, he dealt with his emails and spoke to his assistant in London, who informed him that Alekto Sarantos was still unhappy with the interior of the penthouse suite. The Greek billionaire had let it be known that the apartment's design was too 'bland' for his tastes and, despite a close association going back years, he was now considering pulling out of the deal and buying in Paris instead. Niccolò silently cursed his temperamental friend as he terminated the phone-call and wondered how soon he could decently leave after the wedding to return to work.

Pulling on his gym gear, he went for a run in Central Park, where the bare trees were etched dramatically against the winter sky. Despite his restless night and the fact that little was in bloom, his senses seemed unusually receptive to the beauty which surrounded him on this cold winter morning. There were ducks and gulls on the lakes and woodpeckers were tapping in the trees. Other runners were already out pounding the paths and an exquisite-looking blonde smiled hopefully at him, slowing down as he approached. But he didn't even bother giving her a second look. Her eyes were glacial green, not denim blue—and it was that particular hue which had been haunting his sleep last night.

The run took the edge off his restlessness, even if it didn't quell it completely, and after he'd showered and dressed he found a series of increasingly frantic texts from his sister queuing up on his smartphone. The final one was followed by a wobbly voicemail message, demanding to know where he was.

He went along the corridor and knocked at her door—stupidly unprepared for the sight of Alannah opening the door, even though he'd known she was sharing a suite with his sister. He felt almost *high* as he looked at her and could feel the aching throb of longing which stabbed at his groin. She was wearing a denim shirt-dress which matched her eyes and a tiny ladybird brooch which twinkled red and black on the high collar. For a moment it occurred to him that she was dressed as sedately as a schoolteacher and he watched as a complicated series of expressions flitted across her face as she looked at him, before producing a smile which was clearly forced.

'Hi,' she said.

'Hi.' He tried his own version of that fake smile. 'Sleep well?'

She raised her eyebrows. 'You're here to enquire how I slept?'

No, I'm here because I'd like to take your panties down and put my tongue between your thighs. He shrugged. 'Michela has been bombarding my phone with texts. Is she here?'

'She's...' cocking her head in the direction of one of the closed doors behind her, she pulled a face '...in the bathroom.'

'Is something wrong?'

'She's broken a nail.'

He frowned. 'Is that supposed to be some kind of a joke?'

'No, Niccolò, it's not a joke. It's the finger her wedding ring will go on and everyone will notice. To a bride who's just hours away from the ceremony, something like this is nothing short of a catastrophe. I've called the manicurist, who's on her way up.'

'First World problems,' he said caustically. 'So everything is under control?'

'Well, that depends how you look at it.' She met his gaze and seemed to be steeling herself to say something. 'Her nerves aren't helped by the worry that you're going to lose your temper at some point today.'

'What makes her think that?'

'Heaven only knows,' she said sarcastically, 'when you have a reputation for being so mild-mannered and accommodating. Could it have something to do with the fact that you and I were at loggerheads through-out dinner last night, and she noticed?'

He raised his eyebrows. 'So what does she want us to do—kiss and make up?'

'Hardly,' she snapped. 'That might be stretching credibility a little too far.'

'Oh, I think I could manage to put on a convinc-ing enough performance,' he drawled. 'How about you?'

So she *hadn't* been imagining it last night. Alan-nah stiffened. He really *was* flirting. And she was going to have to put on the performance of a lifetime if she wanted to convince him that it wasn't working.

She raised her eyebrows. 'So can I tell Michela that you're planning to be a good boy today? Do you think you're a competent enough actor to simulate enjoyment and behave yourself for the duration of the wedding?'

'I don't usually have to simulate anything—and I've never been called a *good boy* in my life,' he an-swered softly. 'But if Michela wants reassurance that I'm going to behave myself, then tell her yes. I will be extremely virtuous. And I will be back here at three, to take you both down to the wedding.'

Alannah gave a brief nod and her cool, careful smile didn't slip until she had shut the door on him, though her pulse was pounding loudly.

At least an air of calm had descended by the time the manicurist arrived to repair the tattered nail and the mood was elevated still further as Alannah helped Michela slide into her delicate white gown. Because this was *her* territory, she reminded herself fiercely.

She was proud of the dress she'd made for the bride and she wasn't going to let Niccolò da Conti whittle away at her confidence.

Her movements became sure and confident as she smoothed down the fine layers of tulle and soon she felt like herself again—Alannah Collins, who was living life according to her own rules, and ignoring the false perceptions of other people.

But the moment Niccolò arrived all that composure deserted her. She was aware of his piercing gaze as he watched her adjusting the floral circlet which held Michela's veil in place and it was difficult to keep her fingers steady. She could feel his dark eyes moving over her and the only comfort she got was by reminding herself that after this day was over, she need never see him again.

So why did that make her heart plummet, as if someone had dropped it to the bottom of a lift-shaft?

'You look beautiful, *mia sorella*,' he said, and Michela gave a smile of delight as she did a twirl.

'*Do* I?'

'Indeed you do.' His voice was indulgent. 'Lucas is a very lucky man.'

'Well, I have Alannah to thank for my appearance,' said Michela brightly. 'She's the one who made the dress. It's gorgeous, isn't it, Niccolò?'

Alannah wanted to tell her friend to stop trying so hard. To tell her that she and her brother were never going to achieve anything more than a forced civility. But she maintained the fiction necessary to soothe the bride's frazzled nerves by smiling at him in what she hoped looked like a friendly way.

'It is indeed a very beautiful dress,' he agreed

softly, his eyes gleaming out a silent message which she didn't dare analyse.

Alannah tried to relax as she handed Michela her bouquet and the three of them made their way to the Pembroke's celebrated wedding room, where the assembled guests were waiting. A harpist began to play and Alannah saw the sudden look of tension which hardened Niccolò's features into a grim mask as he gave his sister away to be married.

Maybe he just didn't like weddings, she thought.

She tried not to stare at him as the vows were made and to ignore the women who were clearly trying to catch his eye. And after the rings had been exchanged, Alannah tried to be the best guest she possibly could. She chatted to the groom's sister and offered to suggest some new colour schemes for her house in Gramercy Park. After the wedding breakfast, she took time to play with several of the frilly-dressed little girls from Lucas's huge extended family. And when they were all worn out, she lined them all up to twist their long hair into intricate styles, which made them squeal with delight.

By the time the tables had been cleared and the band had struck up for the first dance, Alannah felt able to relax at last. Her duties had been performed to everyone's satisfaction and the wedding had gone off without a hitch. Drink in hand, she stood on the edge of the dance-floor and watched Michela dancing in the arms of Lucas—soft white tulle floating around her slender body and a dreamy smile on her face as she looked up at her new husband.

Alannah felt her heart contract and wished it wouldn't. She didn't want to feel *wistful,* not today—

of all days. To wonder why some people found love easy while others seemed to have a perpetual struggle with it. Or to question why all that stuff had never happened to her.

'How come I always find you standing alone on the dance-floor?'

Alannah's heart clenched at the sound of Niccolò's Sicilian accent, but she didn't turn round. She just carried on standing there until he walked up to stand beside her.

'I'm just watching the happy couple,' she said conversationally.

He followed the direction of her gaze and for a moment they stood in silence as Lucas whirled Michela round in his arms.

'Do you think they'll stay happy?' he asked suddenly.

The question surprised her. 'Don't you?'

'If they are contented to work with what they've got and to build on it, then, yes, they have a chance. But if they start to believe in all the hype...' His voice grew hard. 'If they want stardust and spangles, then they will be disappointed.'

'You obviously don't rate marriage very highly.'

'I don't. The odds against it are too high. It's a big gamble—and I am not a gambling man.'

'And love?' she questioned as she turned at last to look at him. 'What about love?'

His mouth hardened and for a moment she thought she saw something bleak flaring at the depths of his black eyes.

'Love is a weakness,' he said bitterly, 'which brings out the worst in people.'

'That's a little—'

'Dance with me,' he said suddenly, his words cutting over hers, and Alannah tensed as his fingers curled over her bare arm.

They were a variation on the words he'd spoken all those years ago. Words which had once turned her head. But she was older now and hopefully wiser—or maybe she was just disillusioned. She no longer interpreted his imperious command as masterful—but more as an arrogant demonstration of the control which was never far from the surface.

She lifted her face to his. 'Do I get a choice in the matter?'

'No.' Removing the glass from her hand, he placed it on the tray of a passing waitress, before sliding his hand proprietorially around her waist and propelling her towards the dance floor. 'I'm afraid you don't.'

She told herself that she didn't have to do this. She could excuse herself and walk away. Because he was unlikely to start behaving like a cave-man by dragging her onto the dance-floor—not with all his new in-laws around.

Except that she left it a split second too long and suddenly it was too late for objections. Suddenly, she was on the dance-floor and his arms were round her waist and the worst thing of all was that she *liked* it. She liked it way too much.

'You can't do this, Niccolò,' she said breathlessly. 'It's over-the-top alpha behaviour.'

'But I just can't help myself,' he said mockingly. 'I'm an over-the-top alpha man. Surely you knew that, Alannah.'

Oh, yes. She knew that. A block of stone would

have known that. Alannah swallowed because his hands were tightening around her waist and making her feel there was no place else she would rather be. She told herself it would cause a scene and reflect badly on both of them if she pulled away from him. *So endure it. One dance and it will all be over.*

She tried to relax as they began to move in time with the music and for a while they said nothing. But it wasn't easy to pretend that it meant nothing to be wrapped in his arms again. Actually, it was close to impossible. His body was so hard and his arms were so strong. His unique scent of sandalwood and raw masculinity seemed to call out to something deep inside her—to touch her on a subliminal level which no one else had even come close to. She could hear the thunder of her heart as he lowered his head to her ear and even his voice seemed to flood over her like velvety-dark chocolate.

'Enjoying yourself?' he said.

She swallowed. 'I was before you forced me into this farce of pretending we have a civilised enough relationship to be dancing together.'

'But surely you can't have any complaints about what we're doing, *mia tentatrice*. Aren't I behaving like a perfect gentleman?'

'Not with…' Her words tailed away, because now he had moved his hands upwards and his fingers were spanning her back. She could feel their imprint burning through the delicate material of her bridesmaid dress and her throat constricted.

'With what?'

'You're holding me too tightly,' she croaked.

'I'm barely holding you at all.'

'You are a master of misinterpretation.'

'I am a master of many things,' came the silken boast, 'but misinterpretation wouldn't have been top of my list.'

She looked up from where she had been staring resolutely at his black tie and forced herself to meet the mocking light in his eyes. 'Why are you doing this?' she whispered.

'Dancing with you? Isn't it customary for the brother of the bride to dance with the bridesmaid at some point—particularly if both of them are single? Or were you holding out for the best man?'

'I'm not holding out for anyone. And I don't remember telling you I was single.'

'But you are, aren't you? And if you're not, then you might as well be.' He met her eyes. 'Because you are responding like a woman who hasn't been touched by a man for a very long time.'

She was tempted to snap back at him with indignation, but how could she? Because he was right. It *was* a long time since she had been touched by a man. It was a long time since she had danced with a man too, and it had never felt like this. Not with anyone. *It had only ever felt like this with him.*

'I don't understand what it is you want,' she said. 'Why you're dancing with me. Taunting me. Trying to get underneath my skin. Especially when you don't even *like* me—and the feeling is mutual.'

He pulled her closer. 'But not liking doesn't stop us *wanting*, does it, Alannah? Desire doesn't require affection in order to flourish. On the contrary, sometimes it works better without it. Don't you find that, *mia tentatrice*?' He stroked a reflective finger along her waist. 'That sex can be *so* much more exciting when there is a frisson of animosity between a man and a woman?'

Her skin still tingling from the lazy caress of his finger, she pulled away from him, trying to focus on the presumptuous things he was saying, rather than the way her body was reacting. 'Stop it,' she said weakly.

'But you haven't answered my question.'

'And I don't have to. Just as I don't have to stand here and take any more provocative comments. My duty dance is over.' With a monumental effort, she pulled away from him. 'Thanks for reminding me what a consummate player you are, Niccolò. And thanks for reminding me that ten years might have passed but you don't seem to have changed. You still treat the opposite sex as if—'

'I wouldn't generalise if I were you,' he interjected and now his voice was edged with steel. 'Because you have no idea how I treat women. And believe me when I tell you that I've never had any complaints.'

The sexual boast was blatant and Alannah suddenly felt as if her skin were too tight for her body. As if her flesh wanted to burst out of her bridesmaid dress. Her breasts were tingling and she knew she had to get away from him before she did something she regretted—or said something she would never live down. 'Goodnight, Niccolò,' she said, turning away and beginning to walk across the dance-floor. 'I think we can officially declare our truce to be over.'

Niccolò watched her go and felt frustration mount inside him, along with an even greater feeling of disbelief. She had gone. She had walked away with her head held high and her shoulders stiff and proud, and all his hunter instincts were aroused as he watched the retreating sway of her silk-covered bottom.

He swallowed.

He had played it wrong.

Or maybe he had just read her wrong.

She had been right. He didn't particularly like her and he certainly didn't *respect* her. But what did that have to do with anything? He still wanted her in a way he'd never wanted anyone else.

And tomorrow she would be gone. Leaving New York and going back to her life in London. And even though they lived in the same city, their paths would never cross, because their two lives were worlds apart. He would never know what it was like to possess her. To feel those creamy curves beneath his fingers and her soft flesh parting as he thrust deep inside. He would never know what sound she made when she gasped out her orgasm, nor the powerful pleasure of spurting his seed deep inside her. She might be the wrong type of woman for him on so many levels— but not, he suspected, in bed.

Still mesmerised by the sway of her bottom, he began to follow her across the dance-floor, catching up with her by one of the bars, where she was refusing a cocktail.

She barely gave him a glance as he walked up beside her.

'You're not leaving?' he said.

'I can't leave. At least, not until Michela has thrown her bouquet and driven off into the night with Lucas. But after that, you won't see me for dust, I promise.'

'Before you make any promises—I have a proposition you might like to hear.'

'I don't need to hear it,' she said flatly. 'I wouldn't need to be a genius to work out what you might have in mind, after the things you said on the dance-floor and the way you were holding me. And it doesn't make any difference.' She sucked in a deep breath and met his gaze. 'I'm not interested in having sex with you, Niccolò—got that?'

Niccolò wondered if she knew how blatantly her nipples were contradicting her words—but maybe now wasn't the time to tell her.

'But what if it was a business proposition?' he questioned.

Her eyes narrowed. 'What kind of business proposition?'

He looked at the waxy white flowers which were woven into her hair and he wanted to reach out and crush them between his fingers. He wanted to press his lips on hers. He wanted to undress her and feast his eyes on that soft, creamy body. In a world where he had managed to achieve every single one of his objectives, he suddenly recognised that Alannah Collins had been a residual thorn in his flesh. A faint but lingering memory of a pleasure which had eluded him.

But not for much longer.

He smiled. 'You said you were an interior designer and suggested I have a look at your website, which I did. And you *are* good. In fact, you are very good. Which means that you have a skill and I have a need,' he said.

Her mouth thinned into a prudish line. 'I don't think that your needs are the kind I necessarily cater for.'

'I think we're talking at cross purposes, Alannah. This has nothing to do with sex.' He slanted her a thoughtful look. 'Does the name Park View ring any bells?'

'You mean that enormous new apartment block overlooking Hyde Park which has been disrupting the Knightsbridge traffic for months?'

'That's the one.'

'What about it?'

'It's mine. I own it. I built it.'

Alannah blinked. 'But it's the most…'

'Don't be shy, Alannah,' he said softly as her voice tailed off. 'One should never be shy when talking about money. It's the most expensive building of its kind in the world—isn't that what you were going to say?'

She shrugged. 'I fail to see how your property port-folio could possibly interest me.'

'Then hear me out. A friend of mine—a brilliant Greek named Alekto Sarantos—is about to complete one of the penthouse apartments.'

She lifted her hand to adjust a stray petal on her headdress. 'And is there a problem?'

'*Sì*. Or at least—he certainly seems to think there is.' A note of irritation entered his voice. 'The prob-lem is that Alekto doesn't like the décor, even though it has been overseen by one of the most popular de-signers in the city.'

'Let me guess.' She raised her eyebrows. 'Cream walls? Bowls of big pebbles lying around the place? Lots of glass and neutral-coloured blinds?'

He frowned. 'You must have seen photos.'

'I don't need to, but I'd recognise a bandwagon

anywhere—and every interior designer in the business seems to be jumping on it. Presumably this friend of yours doesn't do bland and that's why he doesn't like it.'

'No, Alekto doesn't do bland—in fact, he is the antithesis of bland. He described the décor to my assistant as a "tsunami of beige" and unless I can transform the place to his satisfaction before the Greek new year, then he says he'll pull out of the deal and go to Paris instead. It has become a matter of pride for me that he chooses London.' He gave a hard smile. 'And maybe that's where you could come in.'

'Me?'

'You want a break, don't you? I don't imagine they get much bigger than this.'

'But…' Somehow she managed to keep the tremble of excitement from her voice. 'Why me? There must be a million other designers itching to accept a job like this.'

His gaze swept over her like an icy black searchlight—objective, speculative and entirely without emotion.

'Because I like your style,' he said unexpectedly. 'I like the way you dress and the way you look. I always have. And if you can satisfy my exacting friend with your designs—then the job is yours.'

Alannah felt ridiculously thrilled by his praise, yet she didn't want to be thrilled. She wanted to feel nothing. To give nothing and take nothing. She met his dark gaze. 'And the fact that you want to go to bed with me has nothing to do with your offer, I suppose?'

He gave a soft laugh. 'Oh, but it has everything to do with it, *mia sirena*,' he said. 'As you said yourself, there are a million interior designers out there, but your desirability gives you a distinctive edge over your competitors. I cannot deny that I want you or that I intend to have you.' His black eyes gleamed. 'But I wouldn't dream of offering you the job unless I thought you were capable of delivering.'

CHAPTER FOUR

'NICCOLÒ WILL SEE you in just a moment, Alannah.' The redhead sitting outside Niccolò's office wore a silk blouse the colour of the lilies on her desk and when she smiled her lips were a neat coral curve. 'My name's Kirsty, by the way—and I'm one of Niccolò's assistants. Take a seat over there. Can I get you a coffee? Some tea perhaps?'

'No. I'm fine, thanks.' Carefully putting down her mood-boards, Alannah sank onto a seat, wondering if any of her reservations showed in her face. Whether her nerves or sick dread were visible to the impartial observer.

Ever since she'd left New York, she had listed all the reasons why she should say no to Niccolò's offer of work and during the cramped flight she had checked them off on her fingers. He was arrogant. Tick. He was dangerous. Double tick. He was also completely unapologetic about wanting to take her to bed. Only he hadn't even said *that* in a flattering way. He'd made it sound as if she was just something he needed to get out of his system. Like an itch. Or a fever. She bit her lip because his attitude brought too many memories flooding back. She hated men who regarded a woman as some kind of *object*, so surely self-respect and pride should have made her turn his offer down, no matter how lucrative?

But he was offering her work—legitimate work. His proposition had been like a cool drink when your throat was parched. Like finding a crumpled ten-pound note in your jeans before you washed them. She thought about the scarcity of jobs in her highly competitive field, and the ridiculously high mortgage on her tiny bedsit. She couldn't *afford* to turn him down—which was why she'd spent all weekend coming up with ideas she thought might appeal to a Greek billionaire who didn't like beige. And through it all she had realised that this was the vital spring-board her career needed and she was going to grab at it with both hands.

She stared at the cream lilies on Kirsty's desk, try-ing to concentrate on their stark beauty, but all she could think about was the way Niccolò had stroked his finger over her when they'd been dancing at the wed-ding. Her heart began to pound. It had been an almost *innocent* touch and yet her response had been any-thing but innocent. The intensity of her feelings had shocked her. She had wanted him to peel the brides-maid dress from her body and touch her properly. She had wanted him to kiss her the way he'd done all those years before—only this time not to stop.

And that was the problem.

She still wanted him.

She had done her best to quash that thought when she'd emailed him some suggestions. And had attempted to ignore her spiralling feeling of excitement when his reply came winging into her inbox late last night.

These are good. Be at my offices tomorrow at 7p.m.

It hadn't been the most fulsome praise she'd ever received, but it was clear he considered her good enough for the job and that pleased her more than it should have done. And hot on the heels of professional pride came a rather more unexpected feeling of gratitude. She had stared at his email and realised that, no matter what his motives might be, Niccolò was giving her the chance to make something of herself.

So she'd better show him that his faith had not been misplaced.

A buzzer sounded on Kirsty's desk and she rose to her feet, opening a set of double doors directly behind her.

'Niccolò is ready for you now, Alannah.' She smiled. 'If you'd like to come this way.'

Alannah picked up her mood-boards and followed Kirsty into a huge and airy office, blinking a little as she looked around her, because she'd never been anywhere like this before. She gulped. It was...*spectacular*. One wall consisted entirely of glass and overlooked some of London's more familiar landmarks and Alannah was so dazzled by the view that it took a moment for her to notice Niccolò sitting there and to realise that he wasn't alone.

Her first thought was how at home he looked in the luxury of his palatial surroundings. Long legs stretched out in front of him, he was reclining on a large leather sofa in one corner of the vast office—and opposite him was a man with black hair and the bluest eyes she'd ever seen. This must be Alekto Sarantos, Alannah thought, but she barely noticed him. Despite his unmistakable gorgeousness, it was Niccolò who captured her attention. Niccolò whose outwardly relaxed stance couldn't quite disguise the tension in his powerful body as their gazes clashed and held. She could read the mockery in his eyes. *I know how much you want me,* they seemed to say. And suddenly she wished that the floor could swallow her up or that the nerves which were building up inside her would show her some mercy and leave her alone.

'Ah, Alannah. Here you are.' Black eyes glittered with faint amusement as he looked her up and down. 'Not jet-lagged, I hope?'

'Not at all,' she lied politely.

'Let me introduce you to Alekto Sarantos. Alekto—this is Alannah Collins, the very talented designer I was telling you about.'

Alannah gave an uncertain smile, wondering exactly *what* he'd said about her. They were friends, weren't they? And didn't men boast to their mates about what they'd done with a woman? She could feel her cheeks growing slightly warm as she looked at Alekto. 'I'm very pleased to meet you.'

'Do sit down,' he said, in a gravelly Greek accent.

Alannah saw Niccolò pat the space beside him on the sofa—and she thought it looked a bit like someone encouraging a dog to leap up. But she forced herself to smile as she sat down next to him, unwinding the vivid green pashmina which was looped around her neck.

Alekto turned his startling blue gaze on her. 'So…

Niccolò assures me that you are the person who can replace the existing décor with something a little more imaginative.' He grimaced. 'Although frankly, a piece of wood could have produced something more eye-catching than the existing scheme.'

'I'm confident I can, Mr Sarantos.'

'No. *Parakalo*—you must call me Alekto,' he said, a hint of impatience hardening his voice, before giving a swift smile. 'I always like to hear a beautiful woman saying my name.'

Beautiful? No woman ever thought she was beautiful and that certainly hadn't been the effect Alannah had been striving for today. She'd aimed for a functional, rather than a decorative appearance—tying her hair back in a thick plait to stop it being whipped up by the fierce December wind. She had wanted to project style and taste as well as hoping her clothes would be like armour—protecting her from Niccolò's heated gaze.

Her Japanese-inspired grey dress bore the high neckline which had become her trademark and the fitted waist provided structure. A glittering scarab beetle brooch and funky ankle-boots added the unconventional twists which she knew were necessary to transform the ordinary into something different. It was the detail which counted. Everyone knew that.

'If you insist,' she said, with another polite smile. 'Alekto.'

Niccolò raised his eyebrows. 'Perhaps you'd like to show *Alekto* what ideas you have in mind for his apartment, while he concentrates on your undoubted beauty,' he suggested drily.

Trying to ignore the sarcasm in his voice, Alannah

spread out the mood-boards she'd been working on and watched as Alekto began to study them. Squares of contemporary brocade were pasted next to splashes of paint colour, and different swatches of velvet and silk added to the textural diversity she had in mind.

'We could go either traditional or contemporary,' she said. 'But I definitely think you need something a little bolder in terms of colour. The walls would work well in greeny-greys and muted blues—which would provide a perfect backdrop for these fabrics and textiles and reflect your love of the sea.'

'Did Niccolò tell you that I love the sea?' questioned Alekto idly.

'No. I searched your name on the Internet and had a look at your various homes around the world. You do seem rather fond of sea views and that gave me a few ideas.'

'Enterprising,' Alekto commented, flicking through each page, before lifting his head. '*Neh*. This is perfect. All of it. You have chosen well, Niccolò. This is a huge improvement. You have pleased me, Alannah—and a woman who pleases a man should always be rewarded. I think I shall take you out for dinner tonight, to thank you.'

'I'm sure Alannah would love nothing more,' interjected Niccolò smoothly, 'but, unfortunately, she is already committed this evening.'

'Really?' Alekto raised dark and imperious brows. 'I'm sure she could cancel whatever it is she is *committed* to.'

'Possibly.' Niccolò shrugged. 'But only if you are prepared to wait for your apartment to be completed, my friend. Time is of the essence if you expect it to be ready for your new year party. Isn't that what you wanted?'

The gazes of the two men clashed and Alekto's eyes suddenly hardened with comprehension.

'Ah,' he said softly as he rose to his feet. 'Suddenly, I begin to understand. You have always been a great connoisseur of beauty, Niccolò. And since good friends do not poach, I shall leave you in peace.' His blue eyes glittered. 'Enjoy.'

Alekto's chauvinistic innuendo took Alannah by surprise but she reminded herself that she was simply working for him—she wasn't planning on having him as her friend. Keeping her lips clamped into a tight smile, she stood up to let him shake her hand, before Niccolò led him into the outer office.

She waited until the Sicilian had returned and closed the door behind him before she turned on him.

'What was that all about?' she questioned quietly.

'What?' He walked over to his desk, stabbing at a button on his telephone pad, so that a red light appeared. 'The fact that your designs pleased him? Alekto is one of the wealthiest men I know. You should be delighted. The patronage of a man like that is more priceless than rubies.' He looked at her, his eyes curiously flat and assessing. 'Who knows what kind of opportunities could now come your way, Alannah. Especially since he clearly finds you so attractive.'

'No, none of that!' She shook her head—hating the way he was looking at her. Hating the way he was talking about her. 'I don't care that he's rich—other than it means I will have a very generous budget to work with. And I don't care whether or not he finds me attractive. I'd like it if for once we could keep my looks out of it, since I'm supposed to be here on merit.' She stared at him. 'What I'm talking about is you telling him I was busy and couldn't have dinner with him tonight.'

'Did you want to have dinner with him?'

'That's beside the point.'

He slanted her a look. 'I'm not sure what your point is.'

'That I don't want you or anyone else answering for me because I like to make my own decisions. And...' she hesitated '...you have no right to be territorial about me.'

'No,' he said slowly. 'I realise that.'

She narrowed her eyes warily. 'You mean you're agreeing with me?'

He shrugged. 'For a man to behave in a territorial way towards a woman implies that she is his. That she has given herself to him in some way. And you haven't, have you, Alannah?' The eyes which a moment ago had looked so flat now gleamed like polished jet. 'Of course, that is something which could be changed in a heartbeat. We both know that.'

Alannah stiffened as his gaze travelled over her and she could feel her throat growing dry. And wasn't it crazy that, no matter how much her mind protested, she couldn't seem to stop her body from responding to his lazy scrutiny. She found herself thinking how easy it would be to go along with his suggestion. To surrender to the ache deep inside her and have him take all her frustration away. All she had to do was smile—a quick, complicit smile—and that would be the only green light he needed.

And then what?

She swallowed. A mindless coupling with some-one who'd made no secret of his contempt for her? An act which would inevitably leave him triumphant and her, what? *Empty*, that was what.

A lifetime of turning down sexual invitations meant that she knew exactly how to produce the kind of brisk smile which would destabilise the situation without causing a scene. But for once, it took a real effort.

'I think not,' she said, scooping up her pashmina from the sofa. 'I have a self-protective instinct which warns me off intimacy with a certain kind of man, and I'm afraid you're one of them. The things I re-quire from you are purely practical, Niccolò. I need a list of craftsmen—painters and decorators—who you use on your properties and who I assume will be available to work for me—and to work very quickly if we're to get this job in on time.'

The impatient wave of his hand told her that paint-ers and decorators were of no interest to him. 'Speak to Kirsty about it.'

'I will.' She hitched the strap of her bag further over her shoulder. 'And if that's everything—I'll get going.'

He nodded. 'I'll drive you home.'

'That won't be necessary.'

'You have your own car?'

Was he kidding? Didn't he realise that car parking costs in London put motoring way beyond the reach of mere mortals? Alannah shook her head. 'I always use public transport.'

'Then I will take you. I insist.' His eyes met hers

with cool challenge. 'Unless you'd prefer to travel by train on a freezing December night, rather than in the warm comfort of my car?'

'You're boxing me into a corner, Niccolò.'

'I know I am. But you'll find it's a very comfortable box.' He took his car keys from his jacket pocket. 'Come.'

In the elevator, she kept her distance. Just as she kept her gaze trained on the flashing arrow as it took them down to the underground car park, where his car was waiting.

He punched her postcode into his satnav and didn't say another word as they drove along the busy streets of Knightsbridge, where Christmas shoppers were crowding the frosty pavements. Alannah peered out of the window. Everywhere was bright with coloured lights and gifts and people looking at the seasonal displays in Harrods's windows.

The car turned into Trafalgar Square and the famous Christmas tree loomed into view and suddenly Alannah felt the painful twist of her heart. It was funny how grief hit you when you least expected it—in a fierce wave which made your eyes grow all wet and salty. She remembered coming here with her mother, when they were waiting for the result of her biopsy. When standing looking up at a giant tree on an icy winter night had seemed like the perfect city outing. There'd been hardly any money in their purses, but they'd still had hope. Until a half-hour session with a man in a white coat had quashed that hope and they'd never been able to get it back again.

She blinked away the tears as the car began to speed towards West London, hoping that Niccolò's concentration on the traffic meant he hadn't noticed. He reached out to put some music on—something Italian and passionate, which filled the air and made her heart clench again, but this time with a mixture of pleasure and pain.

Closing her eyes, she let the powerful notes wash over her and when she opened them again the landscape had altered dramatically. The houses in this part of the city were much closer together and as Niccolò turned off the main road a few stray traces of garbage fluttered like ghosts along the pavement.

'Is this where you live?' he questioned.

She heard the faint incredulity in his voice and realised that this was exactly why she hadn't wanted this lift. *Because he will judge you. He will judge you and find you wanting, just as he's always done.* 'That's right,' she said.

He killed the engine and turned to look at her, his dark features brooding in the shadowed light.

'It's not what I expected.'

Her question was light, almost coquettish. She wondered if he could tell she'd been practising saying it in her head. 'And what *did* you expect?'

For a moment Niccolò didn't answer, because once again she had confounded his expectations. He had imagined a pricey location—a fortified mansion flat bought on the proceeds of the money she'd earned from *Stacked* magazine. Or a cute little mews cottage in Holland Park. Somewhere brimming with the kind of wealthy men who might enjoy dabbling with a woman as beautiful as her.

But *this*…

The unmistakable signs of poverty were all around

them. The rubbish on the pavement. A battered car with its wing-mirror missing. The shadowy group of youths in their hoodies, who stood watching their car with silent menace.

'What happened to all your money?' he questioned suddenly. 'You must have earned—'

'Stacks?' she questioned pointedly.

His smile was brief as he acknowledged the pun. 'A lot.'

She stared down at her handbag. 'It was a short-lived career—it didn't exactly provide me with a gold-plated pension.'

'So what did you do with it?'

I paid for my mother's medical bills. I chased a miracle which was never going to happen. I chased it until the pot was almost empty though the outcome hadn't changed one bit. She shrugged, tempted to tell him that it was none of his business—but she sensed that here was a man who wouldn't give up. Who would dig away until he had extracted everything he needed to know. She tried to keep her words light and flippant, but suddenly it wasn't easy. 'Oh, I frittered it all away. As you do.'

Niccolò looked at the unexpected tremble of her lips and frowned, because that sudden streak of vulnerability she was trying so hard to disguise was completely unexpected. Was she regretting the money she had squandered? Did she lay awake at night and wonder how the hell she had ended up in a place like this? He tried and failed to imagine how she fitted in here. Despite all her attempts to subdue her innate sensuality and tame her voluptuous appearance, she must still stand out like a lily tossed carelessly into a muddy gutter.

And suddenly he wanted to kiss her. The streetlight was casting an unworldly orange light over her creamy skin, so that she looked like a ripe peach just begging to be eaten. He felt temptation swelling up inside him, like a slow and insistent storm. Almost without thinking, he found himself reaching out to touch her cheek, wondering if it felt as velvety-soft as it appeared. And it did. Oh, God, it did. A whisper of longing licked over his skin.

'What…what do you think you're doing?' she whispered.

'You know damned well what I'm doing,' he said unsteadily. 'I'm giving into something which has always been there and which is refusing to die. Something which gets stronger each time we see each another. So why don't we just give into it, Alannah— and see where it takes us?'

She knew it was coming. Of course she did. She'd been kissed by enough men to recognise the sudden roughening of his voice and opaque smoulder of his black eyes. But no man had ever kissed her the way Niccolò did.

Time slowed as he bent his face towards hers and she realised he was giving her enough time to stop him. But she didn't. How could she when she wanted this so much? She just let him anchor her with the masterful slide of his hands as they captured the back of her head, before he crushed his lips down on hers.

Instantly, she moaned. It was ten long years since he'd kissed her and already she was on fire. She felt *consumed* by it. Powered by it. Need washed over her as she splayed her palms against his chest as his tongue licked its way into her mouth—her lips opened greedily, as if urging him to go deeper. She heard his responding murmur, as if her eagerness pleased him, and something made her bunch her hands into fists and drum them against his torso—resenting and wanting him all at the same time.

He raised his head, dark eyes burning into her like fire. But there were no subtle nuances to his voice now—just a mocking question in an accent which suddenly sounded harsh and *very* Sicilian. 'Are you trying to hurt me, *bella*?'

'I—yes! *Yes!*' She wanted to hurt him first—before he had the chance to do it to her.

He gave a soft laugh—as if recognising his own power and exulting in it. 'But I am not going to let you,' he said softly. 'We are going to give each other pleasure, not pain.'

Alannah's head tipped back as he reached down to cup her breast through the heavy silk of her dress. And she let him. Actually, she did more than let him. Her breathless sighs encouraged him to go even further, and he did.

He kissed her neck as his hand crept down to alight on one stockinged knee. And wasn't it shameful that she had parted her knees—praying he would move his hand higher to where the ache was growing unbearable? But he didn't—at least, not at first. For a while he seemed content to tease her. To bring her to such a pitch of excitement that she squirmed with impatience—wriggling restlessly until at last he moved his hand to skate it lightly over her thigh. She heard him suck in a breath of approval as he encountered the bare skin above her stocking top and she shivered as she felt his fingers curl possessively over the goose-pimpled flesh.

'I am pleased to see that despite the rather staid outfits you seem to favour, you still dress to tantalise underneath,' he said. 'And I need to undress you very quickly, before I go out of my mind with longing. I need to see that beautiful body for myself.'

His words killed it. Just like that. They shattered the spell he'd woven and wiped out all the desire—replacing it with a dawning horror of what she'd almost allowed to happen.

Allowed?

Who was she kidding? She might as well have presented herself to him in glittery paper all tied up with a gift ribbon. He'd given her a lift home and just assumed...*assumed*...

He'd assumed he could start treating her like a pin-up instead of a person. Somewhere along the way she had stopped being Alannah and had become a body he simply wanted to ogle. Why had she thought he was different from every other man?

'What am I doing?' she demanded, jerking away from him and lifting her fingertips to her lips in horror. 'What am I *thinking* of?'

'Oh, come on, Alannah.' He began to tap his finger impatiently against the steering wheel. 'We're both a little too *seasoned* to play this kind of game, surely? You might *just* have got away with the outraged virgin scenario a decade ago, but not any more. I'm pretty sure your track record must be almost as extensive as mine. So why the sudden shutdown at exactly the wrong moment, when we both know we want it?'

It took everything she had for Alannah not to fly at him until she remembered that, in spite of everything, he was still her boss. She realised she couldn't keep blaming him for leaping to such unflattering conclusions, because why *wouldn't* he think she'd been around the block several times? Nice girls didn't take off their clothes for the camera, did they? And nice girls didn't part their legs for a man who didn't respect them.

'You might have a reputation as one of the world's greatest lovers, Niccolò,' she said, 'but right now, it's difficult to see why.'

She saw his brows knit together as he glowered at her. 'What are you talking about?'

Grabbing the handle, she pushed open the car door and a blast of cold air came rushing inside, mercifully cooling her heated face. 'Making out in the front of cars is what teenagers do,' she bit out. 'I thought you had a little bit more finesse than that. Most men at least offer dinner.'

CHAPTER FIVE

EVERY TIME NICCOLÒ closed his eyes he could imagine those lips lingering on a certain part of his anatomy. He could picture it with a clarity which was like a prolonged and exquisite torture. He gave a groan of frustration and slammed his fist into the pillow. Was Alannah Collins aware that she was driving him crazy with need?

Turning onto his back, he stared up at the ceiling. Of course she was. Her *profession*—if you could call it that—had been pandering to male fantasy. She must have learnt that men were turned on by stockings—and socks. By tousled hair and little-girl pouts. By big blue eyes and beautiful breasts.

Had she subsequently learnt as she'd grown older that teasing and concealment could be almost as much of a turn-on? That to a man used to having everything he wanted, even the *idea* of a woman refusing sex was enough to make his body burn with a hunger which was pretty close to unbearable. Did she often let men caress the bare and silky skin of her thigh and then push them away just when they were in tantalising reach of far more intimate contact?

Frustratedly running his fingers through his hair, he got out of bed and headed for the bathroom.

If she hadn't been such a damned hypocrite when she'd slammed her way out of his car last night, then he wouldn't be feeling this way. If she'd been honest enough to admit what she really wanted, he wouldn't have woken up feeling aching and empty. She could have invited him in and turned those denim-blue eyes on him and let nature take its course. They could have spent the night together and he would have got her out of his system, once and for all.

He turned on the shower, welcoming the icy water which lashed over his heated skin.

True, her home hadn't looked particularly *inviting*. It didn't look big enough to accommodate much more than a single bed, let alone any degree of comfort. But that was okay. His mouth hardened. Mightn't the sheer *ordinariness* of the environment have added a piquant layer of excitement to a situation he resented himself for wanting?

Agitatedly, he rubbed shampoo into his hair, thinking that she made him want to break every rule in the book and he didn't like it. The women he dated were chosen as carefully as his suits and he didn't do *bad girls*. His taste tended towards corporate bankers. Or lawyers. He liked them blonde and he liked them cool. He liked the kind of woman who never sweated…

Not like Alannah Collins. He swallowed as the water sluiced down over his heated skin. He could imagine *her* sweating. He closed his eyes and imagined her riding him—her long black hair damp with exertion as it swung around her luscious breasts. He turned off the shower, trying to convince himself that the experience would be fleeting and shallow. It would be like eating fast food after you'd been on a health kick. The first greasy mouthful would taste like heaven but by the time you'd eaten the last crumb, you'd be longing for something pure and simple.

So why not forget her?

He got ready for the office and spent the rest of the week trying to do just that. He didn't go near Alekto's apartment, just listened to daily progress reports from Kirsty. He kept himself busy, successfully bidding for a new-build a few blocks from the Pembroke in New York. He held a series of back-to-back meetings about his beach development in Uruguay; he lunched with a group of developers who were over from the Middle East—then took them to a nightclub until the early hours. Then he flew to Paris and had dinner with a beautiful Australian model he'd met at last year's Melbourne Cup.

But Paris didn't work and neither did the model. For once the magic of the city failed to cast its spell on him. Overnight it had surrendered to the monster which was Christmas and spread its glittering tentacles everywhere. The golden lights which were strung in the trees along the Champs Élysées seemed garish. The decorated tree in his hotel seemed like a giant monument to bad taste and the pile of faux-presents which rested at its base made his mouth harden with disdain. Even the famous shops were stuffed with seasonal reminders of reindeer and Santa, which marred their usual elegance.

And all this was underpinned by the disturbing fact that nothing was working; he couldn't seem to get Alannah out of his mind. *Even now.* He realised

that something about her was making him act out of
character. There were plenty of other people whose
style he liked, yet he had hired her without reference
and only the most cursory of glances at her work.
Governed by a need to possess her, he had ignored all
reason and common sense and done something he'd
sworn never to do.

He had taken a gamble on her.

He felt the icy finger of fear whispering over his
spine.

*He had taken a gamble on her and he never gam-
bled.*

He ordered his driver to take him to the towering
block which rose up over Hyde Park. But for once he
didn't take pride in the futuristic building which had
been his brainchild, and which had won all kinds of
awards since its inception. All he could think about
was the slow build of hunger which was burning away
inside him and which was now refusing to be silenced.

His heart was thudding as he took the elevator up
to the penthouse, his key-card quietly clicking the
door open. Silently, he walked through the bare apartment, which smelt strongly of paint, and into the main
reception room where he found Alannah perched on
a stepladder, a tape measure in her hand.

His heart skipped a beat. She wore a loose, checked
shirt and her hair was caught back in a ponytail. He
didn't know what he'd been planning to say but before he had a chance to say anything she turned round
and saw him. The stepladder swayed and he walked
across the room to steady it and some insane part of
him wished it would topple properly, so that he could

catch her in his arms and feel the soft crush of her breasts against him.

'N-Niccolò,' she said, her fingers curling around one of the ladder's rungs.

'Me,' he agreed.

She licked her lips. 'I wasn't expecting you.'

'Should I have rung to make an appointment?'

'Of…of course not,' she said stiffly. 'What can I do for you?'

His eyes narrowed. She was acting as if they were strangers—like two people who'd met briefly at a party. Had she forgotten the last time he'd seen her, when their mouths had been hot and hungry and they'd been itching to get inside each other's clothes? Judging from the look on her face, it might as well have been a figment of his imagination. He forced himself to look around the room—as if he were remotely interested in what she was doing with it. 'I thought I'd better see how work is progressing.'

'Yes, of course.' She began to clamber down the ladder, stuffing the tape measure into the pocket of her jeans. 'I know it doesn't look like very much at the moment, but it will all come together when everything's in place. That…' Her finger was shaking a little as she pointed. 'That charcoal shade is a perfect backdrop for some of the paintings which Alekto is having shipped over from Greece.'

'Good. What else?' He began to walk through the apartment and she followed him, her canvas shoes squeaking a little on the polished wooden floors.

'Here, in the study, I've used Aegean Almond as a colour base,' she said. 'I thought it was kind of appropriate.'

'Aegean Almond?' he echoed. 'What kind of lunatic comes up with a name like that?'

'You'd better not go into the bathroom, then,' she warned, her lips twitching. 'Because you'll find Cigarette Smoke everywhere.'

'There's really a paint called Cigarette Smoke?'

'I'm afraid there is.'

He started to laugh and Alannah found herself joining in, before hurriedly clamping her mouth shut. Because humour was dangerous and just because he'd been amused by something she'd said it didn't mean he'd suddenly undergone a personality transplant. He had an *agenda*. A selfish agenda, which didn't take any of *her* wishes into account and that was because he was a selfish man. Niccolò got what Niccolò wanted and it was vital she didn't allow herself to be added to his long list of acquisitions.

She realised he was still looking at her.

'So everything's running according to schedule?' he said.

She nodded. 'I've ordered velvet sofas and sourced lamps and smaller pieces of furniture.'

'Good.'

Was that enough? she wondered. How much detail did he need to know to be convinced she was doing a good job? Because no matter what he thought about her past, he needed to know she wasn't going to let him down. She cleared her throat. 'And I've picked up some gorgeous stuff on the King's Road.'

'You've obviously got everything under control.'

'I hope so. That is what you're paying me for.'

Niccolò walked over to the window and stared out at the uninterrupted view of Hyde Park. The wintry trees were bare and the pewter sky seemed heavy with the threat of snow. It seemed as if his hunch about her ability had been right. It seemed she was talented, as well as beautiful.

And suddenly he realised he couldn't keep taking his anger out on her. Who *cared* what kind of life she'd led? Who cared about anything except possessing her? Composing his face into the kind of expression which was usually guaranteed to get him exactly what he wanted, Niccolò smiled.

'It looks perfect,' he said. 'You must let me buy you dinner.'

She shook her head. 'Honestly, you don't have to do that.'

'No?' He raised his eyebrows in mocking question. 'The other night you seemed to imply you felt short-changed because I'd made a pass at you without jumping through the necessary social hoops first.'

'That was different.'

'How?'

She lifted her hand to fiddle unnecessarily with her ponytail. 'I made the comment in response to a situation.'

'A situation which won't seem to go away.' His black eyes lanced into her. 'Unless something has changed and you're going to deny that you want me?'

She sighed. 'I don't think I'm a good enough actress to do that, Niccolò. But wanting you doesn't automatically mean that I'm going to do anything about it. You must have women wanting you every day of the week.'

'But we're not talking about other women. What if I just wanted the opportunity to redeem myself?

To show you that I am really just a...what is it you say?' He lifted his shoulders and his hands in an exaggerated gesture of incomprehension. 'Ah, yes. A regular guy.'

'Of course you are.' She laughed, in spite of herself. 'Describing you as a regular guy would be like calling a thirty-carat diamond a trinket.'

'Oh, come on, Alannah,' he urged softly. 'One dinner between a boss and his employee. What's the harm in that?'

Alannah could think of at least ten answers, but the trouble was that when he asked her like that, with those black eyes blazing into her, all her reservations slipped right out of her mind. Which was how she found herself in the back of a big black limousine later that evening, heading for central London. She was sitting as far away from Niccolò as possible but even so—her palms were still clammy with nerves and her heart racing with excitement.

'So where are we going?' she questioned, looking at the burly set of the driver's shoulders through the tinted glass screen which divided them.

'The Vinoly,' Niccolò said. 'Do you know it?'

She shook her head. She'd heard about it, of course. Currently London's most fashionable venue, it was famous for being impossible to get a table though Niccolò was greeted with the kind of delight which suggested that he might be a regular.

The affluence of the place was undeniable. The women wore designer and diamonds while the men seemed to have at least three mobile phones lined up neatly beside their bread plates and their gazes kept straying to them.

Alannah told herself she wasn't going to be intimidated even though she still couldn't quite believe she'd agreed to come. As she'd got ready she had tried to convince herself that exposure to Niccolò's arrogance might be enough to kill her desire for him, once and for all.

But the reality was turning out to be nothing like she'd imagined. Why hadn't she taken into account his charisma—or at least prepared herself for a great onslaught of it? Because suddenly there seemed nothing in her armoury to help her withstand it.

She had never been with a man who commanded quite so much attention. She saw the pianist nodding to him, with a smile. She saw other diners casting surreptitious glances at him, even though they were pretending not to. But it was more than his obvious wealth which drew people's gaze, like a magnet. Beneath the sophisticated exterior, he radiated a raw masculinity which radiated from his powerful body like a dark aura.

They sat down at a discreet table but suddenly the complex menu seemed too rich for a stomach which was sick with nerves. Alannah found herself wishing she were eating an omelette at her own kitchen table rather than subjecting herself to a maelstrom of emotions which were making her feel most peculiar.

'What are you going to have?' asked Niccolò as the waiter appeared.

The words on the menu had blurred into incomprehensible lines and she lifted her gaze to him. 'I don't know. You order for me,' she said recklessly.

He raised his eyebrows before giving their order but once the waiter had gone he turned to study her, his black eyes thoughtful. 'Are you usually quite so accommodating?'

'Not usually, no.' She smoothed her napkin. 'But then, this isn't what you'd call *usual*, is it?'

'In what way?'

'Well.' She shrugged. 'You made it sound like a working dinner, but it feels a bit like a date.'

'And what if we pretended it was a date—would that help you relax a little more?'

'To be honest, it's been so long since I've been on a date that I've almost forgotten what it's like,' she said slowly.

He took a sip of water which didn't quite disguise the sudden cynicism of his smile. 'I find that very difficult to believe.'

She laughed. 'I'm sure you do—given your apparent love of stereotypes. What's the matter, Niccolò—doesn't that fit in with your image of me? You think that because I once took off my clothes for the camera, that I have men queuing up outside the bedroom door?'

'Do you?'

'Not half as many as you, I bet,' she said drily.

They were staring at one another across the table, their eyes locked in silent battle, when suddenly he leaned towards her, his words so low that only she could hear them.

'Why did you do it, Alannah?' he questioned roughly. 'Wasn't it bad enough that you were kicked out of school for smoking dope and playing truant? Why the hell did you cheapen yourself by stripping off?'

The waiter chose precisely that moment to light the

small candle at the centre of the table. And that short gap provided Alannah with enough time for rebellion to flare into life inside her.

'Why do you think I did it?' she demanded. 'Why do people usually do jobs like that? Because I needed the money.'

'For what?' His lips curled. 'To end up in a poky apartment in one of the tougher ends of town?'

'Oh, you're so quick to judge, aren't you, Niccolò? So eager to take the moral high ground, when you don't have a clue what was going on in my life and you never did! Did you know that when my mother handed in her notice, she never found another job to match that one—probably because the reference the school gave her was so grudging. Did you know that they got all their clever lawyers to pick over her contract and that she lost all her rights?'

His eyes narrowed. 'What kind of rights?'

'There was no pension provision made for her and the salary she got in lieu of notice was soon swallowed up by the cost of settling back in England. She couldn't find another live-in job, so she became an agency nurse—with no fixed contract. I had to go to a local sixth-form college to take my exams and at first, I hated it. But we were just beginning to pick ourselves up again when…'

Her voice tailed off and his words broke into the silence.

'What happened?' he demanded.

She shook her head. 'It doesn't matter.'

'It *does*.'

Alannah hesitated, not wanting to appear vulnerable—because vulnerability made you weak. But wasn't anything better than having him look at her with that look of utter *condemnation* on his face? Shouldn't Niccolò da Conti learn that it was wise to discover all the facts before you condemned someone outright?

'She got cancer,' she said baldly. 'She'd actually had it for quite a long time but she'd been ignoring the symptoms so she didn't have to take any unnecessary time off work. By the time she went to see the doctor, the disease was advanced and she was scared,' she said, swallowing down the sudden lump in her throat. They'd both been scared. 'There was nobody but me and her. She was only a relatively young woman and she didn't want...' The lump seemed to have grown bigger. 'She didn't want to die.'

'Alannah—'

But she shook her head, because she didn't want his sympathy. She didn't *need* his sympathy.

'Our doctor told us about an experimental drug trial which was being done in the States,' she said. 'And early indications were that the treatment was looking hopeful, but it was prohibitively expensive and impossible to get funding for it.'

And suddenly Niccolò understood. Against the snowy tablecloth, he clenched his hands into tight fists. *'Bedda matri!'* he said raggedly. 'You did those photos to pay for your mother to go to America?'

'Bravo,' she said shakily. 'Now do you see? It gave me power—the power to help her. The thought of all that money was beyond my wildest dreams and there was no way I could have turned it down.' *No matter how many men had leered in her face afterwards. No matter that people like Niccolò judged her*

*and looked down their noses at her or thought that
she'd be up for easy sex because of it.* 'My unique
selling point was that I'd left one of the most exclusive Swiss finishing schools under rather ignomini-
ous circumstances and I guess I can't blame them
for wanting to capitalise on that. They told me that
plenty of men were turned on by girls in school uniform, and they were right. That's why that issue became their best-seller.'

Alarmed by the sudden whiteness of her face, he
pushed the wine glass towards her, but she shook her
head.

'It wasn't narcissism which motivated me, Niccolò—or a desire to flash my breasts like the exhibitionist you accused me of being. I did it because it's
the only way I could raise the money. I did it even
though I sometimes felt sick to the stomach with all
those men perving over me. But I hid my feelings
because I wanted to bring a miracle to my mother,
only the miracle never happened.' Her voice wavered
and it took a moment or two before she could steady
it enough to speak. 'She died the following spring.'

She did pick up her glass then, swilling down a
generous mouthful of red wine and choking a little.
But when she put the glass back down, she had to
lace her fingers together on the table-top, because she
couldn't seem to stop them from trembling.

'Alannah—'

'It's history,' she said, with a brisk shake of her
head. 'None of it matters now. I'm just telling you
what happened. I used the rest of the money to put
myself through art school and to put down a deposit
on a home. But property is expensive in London.

That's why I live where I do. That's why I chose to live in one of the "tougher" parts of London.'

Niccolò put his glass down with a hand which was uncharacteristically unsteady as a powerful wave of remorse washed over him. It was as if he was seeing her clearly for the first time—without the distortion of his own bigotry. He had judged her unfairly. He saw how she must have fought against the odds to free herself from a trap from which there had been no escaping. He'd fought against the odds himself, hadn't he? Though he realised now that his own choices had been far less stark than hers. And although he hated the solution she had chosen, he couldn't seem to stop himself from wanting to comfort her.

'I'm sorry,' he said huskily. 'For what happened and for the choices you had to make.'

She shrugged. 'Like I said, it's history.'

'Your mother was lucky to have a daughter like you, fighting for her like that,' he said suddenly. He found himself thinking that anyone would be glad to have her in their corner.

Her head was bent. 'Don't say any more,' she whispered. 'Please.'

He stared down at the plateful of cooling risotto which lay before him. 'Alannah?'

'What?'

Reluctantly, she lifted her head and he could see that her eyes were unnaturally bright. He thought how pale and wan she looked as he picked up his fork and scooped up some rice before guiding it towards her mouth. 'Open,' he instructed softly.

She shook her head. 'I'm not hungry.'

'Open,' he said again.

'Niccolò—'

'You need to eat something,' he said fiercely. 'Trust me. The food will make you feel better. Now eat the risotto.'

And although Alannah was reluctant, she was no match for his determination. She let him feed her that first forkful—all warm and buttery and fragrant with herbs—and then another. She felt some of the tension seep away from her, and then a little more. She ate in silence with his black eyes fixed on her and it felt like a curiously intimate thing for him to do, to feed her like that. Almost *tender*. Almost *protective*. And she needed to remember it was neither. It was just Niccolò appeasing his conscience. Maybe he'd finally realised that he'd been unnecessarily harsh towards her. This was probably just as much about repairing his image, as much as trying to brush over his own misjudgement.

And he was right about the food. Of course he was. It *did* make her feel much better. She could feel warmth creeping through her veins and the comforting flush of colour in her cheeks. She even smiled as he swopped plates and ate some himself while she sat back and watched him.

He dabbed at his lips with a napkin. 'Feel better now?'

'Yes.'

'But probably not in the mood to sit here and make small talk or to decide whether or not your waistline can cope with dessert?'

'You've got it in one,' she said.

'Then why don't I get the check, and we'll go?'

She'd assumed he would take her straight back to

Acton but once they were back in the car he made the driver wait. Outside, fairy lights twinkled in the two bay trees on either side of the restaurant door, but inside the car it was dark and shadowy. He turned to study her and all she could see was the gleam of his eyes as his gaze flickered over her face.

'I could take you home now,' he said. 'But I don't want the evening to end this way. It still feels…unfinished.'

'I'm not in the mood for a nightcap.'

'Neither am I.' He lifted his hand to her face and pushed back a thick strand of hair. 'I'm in the mood to touch you, but that seems unavoidable whenever you're near me.'

'Niccolò—'

'Don't,' he said unsteadily. 'Don't say a word.'

And stupidly, she didn't. She just sat there as he began to stroke her cheek and for some crazy reason she found that almost as reassuring as the way he'd fed her dinner. Was she so hungry for human comfort that she would take anything from a man she suspected could offer nothing but heartbreak?

'Niccolò—'

This time he silenced her protest with the touch of his lips against hers. A barely-there kiss which started her senses quivering. She realised that he was teasing her. Playing with her and tantalising her. And it was working. Oh, yes, it was working. She had to fight to keep her hands in her lap and not cling onto him like someone who'd found themselves a handy rock in a rough sea.

He drew away and looked into her face and Alannah realised that this was a Niccolò she'd never seen before. His face was grave, almost…assessing. She imagined this was how he might look in the board-room, before making a big decision.

'Now we could pretend that nothing's happening,' he said, as calmly as if he were discussing the mar-kets. 'Or we could decide to be very grown-up about this thing between us—'

'Thing?' she put in indignantly, but his fingers were still on her face and she was shivering. And now the pad of his thumb had begun to trace a line across her lower lip and that was shivering, too.

'Desire. Lust. Whatever you want to call it. Maybe I just want to lay to rest a ghost which has haunted me for ten long years, and maybe you do, too.'

It was his candour which clinched it—the bald truth which was her undoing. He wasn't dressing up his suggestion with sentimental words which didn't mean anything. He wasn't insulting her intelligence by pretending she was the love of his life or that there was some kind of future in what he was proposing. He was saying something which had been on her mind since Michela's wedding. Because he was right. This *thing* between them wouldn't seem to go away. No matter how much she tried, she couldn't stop want-ing him.

She wondered if he could read the answer in her eyes. Was that why he leaned forward to tap briefly on the glass which separated them from the driver, before taking her in his arms and starting to kiss her?

And once he had done that, she was left with no choice at all.

CHAPTER SIX

HE DIDN'T OFFER her a coffee, nor a drink. He didn't even put the lamps on. Alannah didn't know whether Niccolò had intended a slow seduction—but it didn't look as if she was going to get one. Because from the moment the front door of his Mayfair apartment slammed shut on them, he started acting like a man who had lost control.

His hands were in her hair, he was tugging her coat from her shoulders so that it slid unnoticed to the ground and his mouth was pressing down on hers. It was breathless. It was hot. It was...*hungry*. Alannah gasped as he caught her in his arms. He was burying his mouth in her hair and muttering urgent little words in Sicilian and, although her Italian was good, she didn't understand any of them. But she didn't need to. You wouldn't have to be a linguist to understand what Niccolò was saying to her. The raw, primitive sounds of need were international, weren't they?

He placed his hands on either side of her hips and drew her closer, so that she could feel the hard cradle of him pressing against her. He kissed her again and as the kiss became deeper and more urgent she felt him moving her, until suddenly she felt the hard surface of the wall pressed against her back and her eyelids flew open.

He drew back, his eyes blazing. 'I want you,' he said. 'I want to eat you. To suck you. To bite you. To lick you.'

She found his blatantly erotic words more than a little intimidating and momentarily she stiffened— wondering if she should confess that she wasn't very good at this. But now his palms were skating over her dress to mould the outline of her hips and the words simply wouldn't come. She felt his hand moving over her belly. She heard him suck in a ragged breath of pleasure as he began to ruck up her dress.

'Niccolò,' she said uncertainly.

'I want you,' he ground out. 'For ten years I have longed for this moment and now that it is here, I don't think I can wait a second longer.'

Niccolò closed his eyes as he reached her panties and impatiently pushed the flimsy little panel aside, because she was wet. She was very wet. He could detect the musky aroma of her sex as he slid his fingers against her heated flesh and began to move them against her with practised ease.

'Niccolò,' she whispered again.

'I want to see your breasts,' he said, moving his shaking fingers to the lapels of her silky dress and beginning to unbutton it. Within seconds two luscious mounds were revealed—their creamy flesh spilling over the edge of her bra. He narrowed his eyes to look at them. *'Madre di Dio,'* he breathed, his fingertips brushing over the soft skin. 'In the flesh it is even better. You have the most beautiful body I have ever seen.'

And suddenly he knew he really couldn't wait a second longer. Besides, she seemed more than ready for him. He felt as if something had taken hold of him and made him into someone he didn't recognise. As if this wasn't him at all but an imposter who'd entered his body. Unsteadily, he unzipped himself and he wanted to explode even before he positioned himself against her honeyed warmth.

She went very still as he entered her and for a moment he paused, afraid that he might come straight away—and when had *that* ever happened? But somehow he managed to keep it together, drawing in a deep breath and expelling it on another shuddering sigh as he began to move.

One hand was spread over her bare bottom as he hooked her legs around his hips and drove into her as if there were no tomorrow. As if there had been no yesterday. Her nails were digging into his neck as he kissed her, but he barely noticed the discomfort. He tried to hold back—to wait for her orgasm before letting go himself—but suddenly it was impossible and he knew he was going to come.

'Alannah!' he said, on a note of disbelief—and suddenly it was too late.

Wave after wave took him under. His frame was racked with spasms as he gasped out her name, caught up in a feeling so intense that he thought he might die from it. It felt like the first orgasm he'd ever had. He closed his eyes. The only orgasm he'd ever had. And it wasn't until his body had grown completely still that he noticed how silent and how still she was.

He froze.

Of course she was.

Remorse filled him as she put her hand against his chest and pushed him away. And although withdrawing from her succulent heat was the last thing he felt like doing he could see from the tight expression on her face that she wanted him to. And who could blame her?

There had been no answering cry of fulfilment from her, had there? He had given her no real *pleasure*.

With a grimace, he eased himself from her sticky warmth, bending to pull up his trousers before carefully zipping them up. 'Alannah?'

She didn't answer straight away—she was too busy fastening her dress, her fingers fumbling to slide the buttons back in place. He went to help her, but her voice was sharp.

'Don't.'

He waited until she'd finished buttoning and whatever little insect brooch she was wearing was surveying him with baleful eyes, before he lifted her chin with his finger, so that their eyes were locked on a collision course. 'I'm sorry,' he said.

She shook her head. 'It doesn't matter.'

'It does.' He heard the flatness in her voice. 'I'm not usually so…out of control.'

She gave a wry smile. 'Don't worry, Niccolò. I won't tell anyone. Your reputation is safe with me.'

His mouth hardened and his body tensed. It was her cool response which made something inside him flare into life—a feeling of anger as much as desire. A feeling set off by wounded male pride and an urgent need to put things right. This had never happened to him before. He was usually the master of control. He had always prided himself on his lovemaking skills; his ability to give women physical pleasure—even if he could never satisfy them emotionally.

A shudder of comprehension made his blood run cold.

Did he really want her to walk away thinking of him as a selfish lover? As a man who took, but gave nothing back? Was that how he wanted her to remember him?

'Let's hope you don't have to,' he said, his voice full of sudden resolution as he bent down to slide his arm behind her knees and then lifted her up.

'What...what the hell do you think you're doing?' she spluttered as he began to carry her along the wide corridor.

'I'm taking you to bed.'

'Put me down! I don't want to go to bed. I want to go home.'

'I don't think so,' he said, kicking open his bedroom door and walking over to the vast bed, before setting her down in the centre of the mattress. His knees straddling her hips, he began to unbutton her dress, but she slapped his hand away and he realised that his normal methods of seduction weren't going to work with her. Come to think of it, nothing felt remotely normal with her—and right now, this felt a million miles away from seduction.

He smoothed the tousled hair away from her face, staring down into the reproachful belligerence of her blue eyes, before slowly lowering his head to kiss her.

It wasn't a kiss, so much as a duel.

For a few seconds she held back, as if he were kissing some cold, marble statue. She lay there like a human sacrifice. He could sense her anger and frustration, so he forced himself to take it slowly—so slowly that it nearly killed him. He explored her lips with a thoroughness which was new to him—until he felt he knew them almost better than his own. And as she gradually opened them up to him—when she had relaxed enough to let his tongue slide inside her mouth—it felt like one of the most intimate acts he'd ever taken part in.

Her hands reached for his shoulders and he took the opportunity to press his body close to hers, but the shudder of delight as their bodies crushed against each other was entirely new to him. And still he took it slowly—still feasting on her lips until he was certain that her own desire was strong enough to make her wriggle against him with a wordless message of frustration.

He didn't speak. He didn't dare. Something told him that she didn't want him to undress her and he suspected that doing so would shatter a mood which was already dangerously fragile. His hands were trembling as they slid beneath her dress to reacquaint themselves with the hot, moist flesh beneath her panties. He heard her give a little moan—a sound of pleasure and submission—and his heart hammered as he unzipped himself and tugged her panties down over her knees.

He was only vaguely aware of the awkward rumpling of their unfastened clothing, because by then he was caught up with a hunger so powerful that he groaned helplessly as he slid inside her for a second time. It felt… For a moment he didn't move. It felt out of this world. He looked down to see an unmistakable flare of wonder in her eyes as he filled her, but just as quickly her dark lashes fluttered down to veil them. As if she was reluctantly granting him access to her body—but not to her thoughts.

He moved slowly. He kept her on the edge for a long time—until she was relaxed enough to let go. She wrapped her legs and her arms around him and held him close and Niccolò thought he'd never been quite so careful before. He'd learnt a lot about women's bodies during a long and comprehensive sexual education, but with Alannah it became about much more than technique.

Her body began to change. He could feel the tension building until it was stretched so tightly that it could only shatter—and when it did, she made a series of gasping little sighs, before she started to convulse helplessly around him. He was dimly aware of the groan he gave before he too let go, his every spasm matching hers, and he could feel her heart beating very fast against his as his arms tightened around her.

He must have fallen asleep, because when he next became aware of his surroundings it was to feel her shifting out from under him. His fingers curled automatically around her waist. 'What are you doing?' he questioned sleepily, moving his head so that her lips were automatically redirected to his and his voice was indistinct as his tongue slid into her mouth. 'Mmm?'

She let him kiss her for a moment before putting distance between them. He felt her lips ungluing themselves from his as she moved away.

'It's late, Niccolò—and this is a school night.'

He knew what she was doing. She was giving him

the opportunity to end the evening now, without either of them losing face. He wondered if this was what she normally did—give into a hot and mindless lust without much forethought, before following it up with a cool smile as if nothing had happened?

Without much forethought.

The words struck him and imprinted themselves on his consciousness. Suddenly he went hot and then cold as he realised their implication and he stared at her with growing horror.

'You know what we've just done?' he questioned and there was a note in his voice he'd never heard before.

She tilted her chin, but he could see the way she had instinctively started to bite her lip. 'Of course. We've just had sex. Twice.'

His fingers dug into her forearms, his voice suddenly urgent. 'Are you on the pill?'

He saw the exact moment that it registered. That would be the moment when her blue eyes widened and her lips began to tremble.

'We...' she whispered. 'We've...'

'Yes,' he completed grimly. 'We've just had unprotected sex.'

She swallowed. 'Oh, God,' she breathed. 'What are we going to do?'

He didn't answer at once. It was pointless to concentrate on the anger and frustration which were building up inside him, because he could see that harsh words of recrimination would serve no useful purpose. His mouth hardened. He should have known better. How could he have failed to take contraception into account?

'I think that there is only one thing we can do,' he said. 'We wait.'

'I…guess so.'

He frowned as he noticed that her teeth had started to chatter. 'You're shivering. You need to get into bed.'

'I don't—'

'I'm not listening to any objections,' he said emphatically. 'I'm going to undress you and put you to bed and then I'm going to make you tea.'

She wriggled. 'Why don't you go and make the tea and I'll undress myself?'

He frowned, and there was a heartbeat of a pause. 'Alannah, are you *shy*?'

She attempted a light little laugh, which didn't quite come off. 'Me? Shy? Don't be ridiculous. How could I possibly be shy when I've exposed my body to the harsh glare of the camera?'

Placing his palms on either side of her face, he stared down into her wide blue eyes. 'But stripping for a camera is a very anonymous thing to do,' he said slowly. 'While stripping for a man is intensely personal.'

She pulled a face. 'Stick with the day job, Niccolò—I don't think analysis is really your thing.'

Niccolò frowned. No, it wasn't his thing at all. Normally he ran a million miles from trying to work out what was going on in a woman's head. But most women weren't perplexing enigmas, were they? They didn't answer one question and immediately make you want to ask them a hundred more.

'You're shy,' he repeated. 'Are you going to tell me why?'

Alannah stifled a sigh as she looked at him, because telling Niccolò anything was the last thing she wanted. His lovemaking had left her feeling soft and vulnerable enough to have her defences weakened. And she wasn't stupid. She might despise the men who persisted in thinking of her as nothing but a body—yet surely that was the main attraction for Niccolò, no matter how much he might try to deny it. Wouldn't he be disappointed to discover the mundane truth about her?

Because iconic glamour models were supposed to typify sexuality, not belong to a band of women who had always found sex rather overrated until now.

'Yes, I'm shy,' she admitted grudgingly. 'I don't really like men looking at my body. I'm hung up about it. I hate being thought of as nothing but a pair of gravity-defying breasts. That's probably why I'm not usually able to relax very much. Why my sex life has been…'

Her words tailed off as she became aware that she'd said too much and she braced herself as she waited for him to distance himself, like a man who thought he'd bought a racy sports-car—only to find that he'd landed himself with a second-hand model which kept breaking down.

'Why your sex life has been, what?' he prompted softly.

She pulled a face. 'You really want me to spell it out for you? Isn't your ego healthy enough already without the added boost of me telling you how good you are in bed?'

He took her hand and lifted it to his lips, unable to hide his slow, curving smile of satisfaction. 'Am I?'

'You know you are.' She pulled her hand away. 'I'm sure I'm not the first woman to tell you that.'

'No, but you're the first woman who is such a mass of contradictions that you have my head spinning. You have a wildness...'

'Niccolò—'

He silenced her with a long kiss and when he finally raised his head, it was to subject her to a look of narrow-eyed thoughtfulness. 'I think we've done the subject to death for tonight,' he said. 'You're tired and so am I, and you're right—it *is* a school night. Bedtime,' he added firmly.

'I'm not sure,' she said.

'Well, I am. Relax, *mia tentatrice*.'

He was unbuttoning her dress again and suddenly Alannah had no desire to stop him. She lay there as he slid the silky garment from her body until she was left in just her hold-ups and her bra and, automatically, her palms moved towards her breasts—to protect them from his seeking gaze. But to her surprise he wasn't even looking at her breasts. He was sliding down her hold-ups as impersonally as if he'd been undressing a child who had been caught in a storm. Even her bra was removed with nothing but deft efficiency, so that she was naked and snuggled beneath the warm duvet almost before she'd realised it.

She blinked as he captured her in that searing ebony gaze.

'Now...was that so traumatic?' he questioned silkily.

She shook her head. 'I wasn't expecting...' Her words tailed off.

'You thought I would be unable to resist drooling

as I ogled your breasts? That you find yourself surprised by my sensitivity?'

'Something like that,' she mumbled.

He smiled, the pad of his thumb trailing a path over her bottom lip and causing it to tremble. 'You and me both,' he said drily, before getting up to let himself quietly out of the room.

While he was gone, Alannah took the opportunity to look around what was one of the most impersonal bedrooms she'd ever seen. There were no photos on display. No real hints as to what kind of man Niccolò really was. She knew his parents were dead—but there was no misty-eyed memorial of their wedding day. She remembered Michela clamming up whenever anyone had asked her about her folks—and hadn't she been a bit like that herself if people wanted to know about *her* father? It had seemed too crass to tell them the truth. *Oh, my mother was fresh out of Ireland and she had her drink spiked...*

She hadn't found out the whole story until three days before her mother had died. That Bridget Collins had woken up in her dingy hostel room with a splitting headache and vague, shifting memories of what had happened the night before—as well as a terrible soreness between her legs. She'd never seen the man again and the shame of it was that she didn't even know his surname. Nine months later Alannah had been born and her mother's over-protectiveness had kicked in.

Alannah stared at the photograph opposite the bed—a smoky, atmospheric monochrome study of a brooding Mount Vesuvius. If she'd known all that stuff before...if she'd been able to make sense of why her mother had been so unbelievably strict with her—would it have changed anything?

Probably not. And even if it had—it was all irrelevant now. Because you could never go back. You could never wipe out the things you'd done. Everyone knew that.

She was almost asleep by the time Niccolò returned, carrying a tray of camomile tea. Her eyelashes fluttered open as he sat down and the bed sank beneath his weight.

'This will help you sleep,' he said.

She didn't think she needed any help, but she drank the flower-filled brew anyway and then settled back down against the bank of pillows while Niccolò gently stroked her hair.

She wriggled her bare toes and stretched out her body and at that precise moment she didn't think she'd ever felt quite so blissfully content. Until a dark memory flickered into her mind like an evil imp—reinforcing the disturbing thought that they hadn't remembered to use protection....

CHAPTER SEVEN

'ANYONE WOULD THINK,' said Niccolò slowly, 'that you were trying to avoid me.'

Alannah looked up to find herself caught in the spotlight of a pair of ebony eyes, which cut into her like dark twin lasers. Winter light was flooding into the main reception room of the still bare Sarantos apartment, emphasising its vast and elegant dimensions. She had been there all morning, sitting on the newly upholstered window seat and sewing tassels onto a cushion, but the sight of the Sicilian standing in the doorway made her suspend her needle in mid-air.

She tried to compose herself and to say the right thing. Just as she'd been trying to do the right thing, ever since she'd crazily decided to have sex with him. She needed to treat what had happened as a one-off, and keeping their relationship on a purely professional footing was the only sane solution.

For both of them.

She put the needle down and pushed her empty coffee mug along the floor with the tip of her sneaker. 'Of course I'm not trying to avoid you,' she said lightly. 'You're my boss—I wouldn't dare.'

'Is that so?' He walked towards her. 'So why wouldn't you have dinner with me last night?'

'I explained that,' she protested. 'I had to travel to Somerset to buy some paintings and the man who owned the shop was just about to close up for the holidays, so it was the only day I could go. And then on the way back, there were loads of leaves on the line so the train was delayed. Didn't you get my voicemail message?'

'Oh, yes, I got your voicemail message,' he said impatiently. He stood looking down at her, feeling perplexed and more than a little frustrated. This had never happened to him before. Usually he had to barricade his bedroom once a woman had been granted access to it—he couldn't remember a lover ever being so reluctant to return. His mouth tightened. 'But the fact remains that on Tuesday we had sex and I've barely seen you since.'

She shrugged. 'That's just the way it's worked out. You're employing me to get this apartment done in a hurry and that's what I'm trying to do. That's my primary role, isn't it? You're not paying me to keep appearing at your office door and haunting you.'

Niccolò felt his mouth dry. He wouldn't mind her appearing at his office door. She was making him think of a few very creative uses for his desk… He swallowed. 'Am I going to see you later?'

Alannah sucked in a breath, trying not to be flattered at his persistence, but it wasn't easy. Because she had been dreading this meeting. Dreading and yet longing for it, all at the same time. Ever since she'd slipped out of his Mayfair apartment on Tuesday she'd told herself that it would be safer to stay away from Niccolò and not pursue the affair any further. She liked him. She liked him way more than was sensible for what she was sure he'd only ever intended to be a casual hook-up. And she didn't do casual. Just as she didn't do the kind of affair which would end up with her getting her heart smashed into a hundred little pieces.

'You're my boss, Niccolò,' she said.

'I haven't lost sight of that fact, *mia tentatrice*. But what does that have to do with anything?'

'You know very well. It's…unprofessional.'

He gave a soft laugh. 'You don't think we might already have crossed that boundary when you lay gasping underneath me for most of the night?' He narrowed his eyes. 'And on top of me at one point, if my memory serves me well.'

'Stop it,' she whispered, feeling colour flooding into her cheeks. 'That's exactly what I'm talking about. It blurs the lines and confuses things. I'm trying to concentrate on my work and I can't when you—'

'Can't stop wanting a rerun?'

'A rerun is what you do with movies. And it's a bad idea.'

'Why?'

She sighed. 'What happened last week was…' Her words tailed off. How best to describe it? The most amazing sex she'd ever had? Well, yes. She had certainly never realised it could be so intense, or so powerful. But there had been another blissful side to that night which was far more worrying. She'd realised that she could get used to waking up with Niccolò lying asleep beside her, his arms wrapped tightly around her. Just as she could get used to thinking about him at odd moments of the day and wishing he were there to kiss her. And those kind of daydreams would get her nowhere.

Because where would that leave her when the whole thing imploded? She'd just be another heart-broken woman crying into her gin and tonic, trying to resist the urge to send him a 'casual' late-night text. She would run the risk of making herself vulnerable and she wasn't going to let that happen. She felt a new resolve steal over her. 'A mistake,' she said.

'A mistake,' he repeated.

'Maybe that's a bad way to put it. It was obviously very enjoyable.' She pushed the cushion away and forced herself to face the truth, no matter how un-palatable it was. 'But the fact remains that you don't really like me. You told me that.'

He smiled. 'I like you a lot more now.'

'You described what you felt for me as, and I quote—"a wildness". You made me sound like a mild version of the bubonic plague.'

'I don't think any plague feels quite like this—ex-cept maybe for the fever in my blood when I close my eyes at night and find it impossible to sleep because I can't get you out of my mind.' His eyes gleamed. 'And you look incredibly beautiful when you're being defiant. Do you do it because you know how much it turns me on?'

'It's not defiance for the sake of it,' she said. 'It's defiance for a reason. I'm not doing it to try to entice you.' She forced herself to say it. To put the words out there instead of having them nagging away in-side her. 'This relationship isn't going anywhere. We both know that.'

'So you're not pregnant?'

His words completely shattered her fragile façade and she stared at him, her heart pounding. During the day, when she was busy working, it was easy to push that thought to the back of her mind. It was at night-time when it became impossible. That was when the fear flooded through her body as she tried to imagine just how she would cope with having Niccolò da Conti's baby. That was when she had to fight to stop herself imagining a downy little black head, glugging away contentedly at her breast.

'I don't know,' she said. 'It's too early to do a test.'

'Which means we may be about to be parents together, *sì*? I think that constitutes some sort of relationship, don't you?'

'Not the best kind,' she said.

'Maybe not. But I need to know that if you are pregnant—*if you are*—whether I am the only man in the frame who could be the father.' His black eyes burned into her, but he must have seen her flinch because his voice softened by a fraction. 'Is that such an unreasonable request?'

She met his gaze, telling herself that in the circumstances he had every right to ask. But that didn't make it hurt any less and some of that hurt came spilling out.

'Yes. You are the only man in the frame. Did you think that because of my previous line of work that there would be a whole load of contenders?' She shook her head in despair. 'You really are fond of stereotypes, aren't you, Niccolò? Well, for your information, there isn't. If you really must know, I could count my previous lovers on one hand and still have

some fingers free—and there's been no one in my life
for the last three years.'

Niccolò let out the breath he'd been holding, unprepared for the powerful hit of pleasure which flooded
through his body in response to her words. *He was
the only man in the frame. There had been no one
else in her life for the past three years.*

He stared at her, his eyes taking in the way she
was illuminated in the harsh winter light. Her thick
hair looked blue-black, like the feathers of a raven.
He swallowed. *Dai capelli corvini.*

In her jeans and loose shirt she shouldn't have
looked anything special, but somehow she looked unbelievably beautiful. Against her hair, her skin was
creamy and her pallor emphasised the dramatic blue
of her eyes. A little brooch in the shape of a dragonfly glittered on her lapel and suddenly he found himself envying the proximity of that worthless piece of
jewellery to her body.

What if there were a baby?

His mouth hardened.

He would cross that bridge when he came to it.

The shrill sound of the doorbell shattered the silence.

'That'll be one of the painters,' she said. 'He rang
up to say he'd left his keys behind.' Rising to her
feet, she walked over and picked up a shoal of silver
keys from where they lay on another window seat. 'I
won't be long.'

Alannah was aware of his eyes burning into her as
she left the room. Her shoes were squeaking as she
went to open the front door where one of the paint-
ers stood. There were four of them in total and they'd

been working around the clock—and although she'd stopped short of making cups of tea for them, she'd been friendly enough. This one had plaster dust in his hair and he was grinning.

She forced a smile as she held out the clump of keys. 'Here you go, Gary.'

But after he'd taken them and shoved them into his dust-covered jeans, he caught hold of her wrist. His big, calloused fingers curled around her skin and his face had suddenly gone very pink. 'I didn't realise you were *the* Alannah Collins,' he said suddenly.

Her heart sank as she snatched her hand away because she knew what was coming next. She wondered if it would be better to call his bluff or to slam the door in his face. But there were only a few days of the project left and it *was* nearly Christmas...why alienate one of the workforce unless it was absolutely necessary?

'Will there be anything else?' she questioned pointedly. 'Because I have work to do.'

'The schoolgirl,' he said thickly. 'With the big—'

A figure seemed to propel itself out of nowhere and it took a moment for Alannah to realise it was Niccolò and he was launching himself at Gary with a look of undiluted rage on his face.

Grabbing hold of the workman's shirt collar, he half lifted him from the ground and shoved his face very close.

'Che talii bastardu?' he spat out. *'Ti scippo locchi e o core!'*

'Niccolò!' protested Alannah faintly, but he didn't seem to be listening.

'How dare you speak to a woman like that?' he demanded. 'What's your name?'

The man blanched. 'G-Gary.'

'Gary what?'

'G-Gary Harkness.'

'Well, take it from me that you won't ever work in this city again, Gary Harkness—I shall make sure of that.' Releasing the shirt collar, Niccolò pushed him away and the man staggered a little. 'Now get out of here—get out before I beat your worthless body to a piece of pulp.'

Alannah didn't think she'd ever seen anyone look so petrified as the workman turned and ran down the corridor towards the elevator.

She lifted her gaze to Niccolò and met the furious blaze firing from his eyes as he clicked the door shut.

'What was that you said to him in Sicilian?'

'I asked him what he was looking at.' He paused as he steadied his breath. 'And I told him I would wrench out his eyes and his heart.'

Alannah gulped. 'You don't think that was a lit-tle…over the top?'

'I think he's lucky he didn't end up in hospital,' he ground out and his jaw tightened as he stared at her. 'How often does that happen?'

'Not much. Not these days.' She shrugged as she began to walk back into the main reception room, aware that he was following her. Aware that her heart was pounding. This wasn't a conversation she usu-ally had—not with anyone—but maybe Niccolò was someone who needed to hear it. She turned to look at him. 'It used to be a lot worse. People only ever seemed able to have a conversation with my breasts—

'or think that I would instantly want to fall into bed with them.'

Guilt whispered over his skin and Niccolò swallowed down the sudden dryness in his throat. Because hadn't he done something very similar? Hadn't he judged her without really knowing the facts and assumed a promiscuity which simply wasn't true?

'And I did the same,' he said slowly.

Her gaze was fearless. 'Yes, you did.'

'That was why you suddenly froze in the hallway of my house when I was making love to you, wasn't it?' he questioned suddenly.

His perception was nearly as alarming as the realisation that the conversation had taken an even more intimate twist. Despite her determination to stay strong, Alannah couldn't prevent the rush of heat to her cheeks. 'Yes,' she said quietly.

She started to turn her head away, but suddenly he was right there in front of her and his fingers were on her arm. They felt good on her arm, she thought inconsequentially.

'Tell me,' he urged.

It was hard to get the words out. Baring her soul wasn't something she normally did—and she had never imagined herself confiding in Niccolò da Conti like this. But for once his gaze was understanding and his voice was soft and Alannah found herself wanting to analyse the way she'd reacted—not just because he'd asked, but because she needed to make sense of it herself. 'I just remember you saying something about my body being even better in the flesh and I started to feel like an object. Like I wasn't a real person—

just a two-dimensional image in a magazine, with a staple in her navel. Like I was *invisible*.'

'That was not my intention,' he said slowly. 'I think I found myself overwhelmed by the realisation that I was finally making love to you after so many years of thinking about it.' There was a pause as he looked at her. 'Do you think you can forgive me for that, *mia tentatrice*?'

She studied him, and the flicker of a smile nudged at her lips because it was strange seeing him in this conciliatory mood. 'I'll think about it.'

Niccolò pulled her into his arms and she didn't object. She didn't object when he bent his head to kiss her either. Her breath was warm and flavoured with coffee and he wanted to groan with pleasure. She tasted as good as he remembered—in fact, she tasted even better—and there seemed something awfully decadent about kissing her in the near-empty apartment. This wasn't the kind of thing he usually did between meetings, was it? His heart skipped a beat as his fingertips skated over her breast, feeling it swell as he cupped it, and he heard her breath quicken as he began to unbutton her shirt.

It pleased him that she let him. That she really did seem to have forgiven him for his out-of-control behaviour of the other night. That she was relaxed enough not to freeze again.

He deepened the kiss, rubbing at her taut nipple with his thumb, and she gave a little sigh of pleasure. He kissed her for a long time until she was squirming impatiently and kissing him back. Until he forced himself to pull away from her, his voice unsteady as he looked into the darkening of her denim eyes and he felt a rush of triumph fuse with the headiness of sexual hunger.

'I would like to lay you down on the bare floor and make love to you, but I am short of time and must go straight from here to a meeting. And I don't feel it would do my reputation much good if I walked in so dishevelled.' He grimaced as he remembered that time in the hallway of his apartment, when he had shown all the finesse of a teenage boy. 'And I am aware that perhaps you like your lovemaking to be a little more slow and considered.'

'I...thought I did.'

He heard the reluctance in her voice but noticed she was still gripping tightly onto his arms. Her lips were trembling, even though she was biting down on them in an effort to stop it—and he realised just how turned on she was.

'Of course...' He moved his hand down to the ridge of hard denim between her legs. 'I probably do have enough time for other things. Things which you might enjoy.'

'Niccolò,' she said breathlessly.

'What do you think?' he said as he edged his middle finger forward and began to stroke her. 'Yes, or no?'

'Y-yes,' she gasped.

'Keep still,' he urged—but to his delight she didn't obey him. Or maybe she just couldn't. Her head was tipping back and suddenly she didn't look remotely shy...she looked *wild*. Beautiful. He felt her thighs part and heard her moaning softly as he increased the relentless pressure of his finger.

She came very quickly, tightening her arms around

his neck and making that shuddering little crescendo of sighs with which he'd become so familiar on Tuesday night. As he kissed her again her fingers began to claw at his shirt, as if she wanted to tear it from his chest, and for a moment he thought about changing his mind and taking her in the most fundamental way possible.

Temptation rushed over him in a dark wave. Impatiently, his hand strayed to the belt of his trousers, until some remaining shred of reason forced him to play out the ensuring scene. What did he have in mind? Rushing into his meeting with his shirt creased and a telltale flush darkening his skin? Using Alekto's apartment to have sex with a woman—wouldn't that be kind of *cheap*? On every single level, it wouldn't work—but that didn't make it any easier to pull away from her.

She started buttoning her shirt back up with trembling fingers and he walked over to the window to compose himself, willing his frustration to subside.

Outside, a light flurry of snowflakes was whirling down and he felt a sudden sense of restlessness. He thought about the impending holiday and what he would be forced to endure, because one thing he'd learned was that unless you were prepared to live in a cave—it was impossible to ignore Christmas. Already there was a glittering tree which he'd been unable to ban from the main reception of his offices. He thought about the horrendous staff party he'd been forced to attend last night, with those stodgy mince pies they were so fond of eating and several drunken secretaries tottering over to him with glassy smiles and bunches of mistletoe.

He turned round. Alannah had finished buttoning up her shirt, though he noticed her hands were shaking and her cheeks still flushed.

'What are you doing for Christmas?' he questioned suddenly.

'Oh, I'm wavering between an invitation to eat nut roast with some committed vegans, or having an alternative celebration all of my own.' She glanced over his shoulder at the snowflakes. 'Like pretending that nothing's happening and eating beans on toast, followed by an overdose of chocolate and trash TV. What about you?'

He shrugged. 'I have an invitation to ski with some friends in Klosters, but unfortunately my schedule doesn't allow it. I hate Christmas. What I would really like is to fast-forward the calendar and wake up to find it was the new year.'

'Oh, dear,' she said softly.

His eyes met hers and another wave of desire washed over him. 'But since we are both at a loose end, it seems a pity not to capitalise on that. We could ignore the seasonal madness and just please ourselves.'

She opened her eyes very wide. 'Are you asking me to spend Christmas with you, Niccolò?'

There was a pause. 'It seems I am.' He gave a cool smile. 'So why don't you speak to Kirsty and have her give you one of my credit cards? You can book us into the best suite in the best hotel in the city—somewhere you've always wanted to stay. Forget the nut roast and the beans on toast—you can have as much caviar and champagne as you like.' He gave a slow smile as he touched his fingertips to her raven hair. 'Maybe I can make some of your Christmas wishes come true.'

* * *

Alannah felt like taking her sharpest pair of scissors and snipping the small square of plastic into tiny pieces. She thought about what Niccolò had said to her. Make her wishes come true. *Really?* Did he honestly think that staying in a fancy hotel suite was the sum total of her life's ambition, when right now her biggest wish would be to tell him that she didn't need his fancy platinum credit card and she'd rather spend Christmas day alone than spend it with him?

Except that it wouldn't be true, would it? She might *want* it to be true, but it wasn't. Why else would she be sitting hunched in front of her computer, about to book a two-night break in a London hotel? She wondered what had happened to her determination to forget the night she'd spent with him and maintain a professional relationship.

She bit her lip. It had been shattered by Niccolò's resolve—that was what had happened. She had been lost the moment he'd kissed her. A single touch had been enough to make all her good intentions crumble. All her silent vows had been a complete waste of time—because she'd gone up in flames the moment he'd taken her in his arms.

She remembered the way his fingertip had whispered over the crotch of her jeans and her face grew hot. She hadn't been so shy then, had she? He'd soon had her bucking beneath him, and he hadn't even had to remove a single item of clothing. And still in that dreamy, post-orgasmic state she had agreed to spend Christmas with him.

That was something it was hard to get her head round. There must be millions of things he could be doing for the holiday—but he wanted to spend it with her. *Her*. Didn't that mean something? Her mouth grew dry. Surely it *had* to.

She stared at the credit card, which Kirsty had crisply informed her had no upper limit. Imagine that. Imagine having enough money to buy whatever you wanted. *The best suite in the best hotel.* How fancy would a hotel have to be for Niccolò not to have seen it all before, and be jaded by it? She ran through a list of possibilities. The Savoy. The Ritz. The Granchester. London had heaps of gorgeous hotels and she'd bet that he'd stayed in all of them. Had constant exposure to high-end affluence helped contribute to his inbuilt cynicism?

She was just about to click onto the Granchester when something made her hesitate. Perhaps it was a desire to shift him out of his comfort zone—away from the usual protective barriers which surrounded him. He had knocked down some of her defences, so why shouldn't she do the same with him? Why *shouldn't* she try to find out more about the real Niccolò da Conti?

She thought of a fancy hotel dining room and all the other people who would be congregated there. People who had no real place to go, who just wanted the holiday to be over. Or even worse—the wink-wink attitude of Room Service if they started asking for turkey sandwiches and champagne to be brought to their room.

An idea popped into her mind and it started to grow more attractive by the minute. She stared at the long number on the credit card. She might not have much money of her own, but she did have her imagination. Surely she was capable of surprising him with something unexpected. Something simple yet meaningful, which would incorporate the true meaning of Christmas.

His power and privilege always gave him an edge of superiority and that couldn't be good for him. An expensive tab in a smart hotel would only reinforce the differences between them. Wouldn't it be great to feel more like his *equal* for a change?

Because what if she *was* pregnant? She was going to have to get to know him better, no matter what the outcome. Her heart gave a painful lurch as she waited for that intrusive yet strangely compelling image of Niccolò da Conti's baby to subside.

She waited a minute before typing *cute Christmas cottage* into her browser. Because cute was exactly what she needed right now, she told herself. Cute stood a chance of making a cynical man melt so you might be able to work out what made him tick. Scrolling down, she stared at the clutch of country cottages which appeared on the screen.

Perfect.

CHAPTER EIGHT

THE FLURRIES WERE getting stronger and Niccolò cursed as he headed along the narrow country lane.

Why could nothing ever be straightforward? Glancing in his rear-view mirror at the swirl of snowflakes which was obscuring his view, he scowled. He'd given Alannah a credit card and told her to book a hotel in town and she'd done the exact opposite—directing him to some godforsaken spot deep in the countryside, while she went on ahead earlier.

Well, in terms of distance he wasn't actually *that* far from London but he might as well be in middle of his friend Murat's Qurhahian desert for all the sense he could make of his bearings. The sudden onset of heavy snow had made the world look like an alien place and it was difficult to get his bearings. Familiar landmarks had disappeared. The main roads were little more than white wastelands and the narrow lanes had begun to resemble twisting snakes of snow.

Glancing at his satnav, he could see he was only four minutes away, but he was damned if he could see any hotel. He'd passed the last chocolate-boxy village some way back and now an arrow was indicating he take the left fork in the road, through an impenetrable-looking line of trees.

Still cursing, he turned off the road, his powerful headlights illuminating the swirling snowflakes and turning them golden. Some people might have considered the scene pretty, but he wasn't in the mood for pretty scenery. He wanted a drink, a shower and sex in exactly that order and he wanted them now.

Following the moving red arrow, he drove slowly until at last he could see a lighted building in the distance, but it looked too small to be a hotel. His mouth hardened. Something that small could only ever be described as a cottage.

He could see a thatched roof covered with a thick dusting of snow and an old-fashioned lamp lit outside a front door, on which hung a festive wreath of holly and ivy. Through latticed windows a woman was moving around—her fall of raven hair visible, even from this distance. His hands tightened around the steering wheel as he brought the car to a halt and got out—his shoes sinking noiselessly into the soft, virgin carpet.

He rang the bell—one of those old-fashioned bells you only ever saw on ships, or in movies. He could hear the sudden scurrying of movement and footsteps approaching and then the door opened and Alannah stood there, bathed in muted rainbow light.

His body tensing, he stepped inside and the door swung violently shut behind him. His senses were immediately bombarded by the scene in front of him but, even so, the first thing he noticed was her dress. Who could fail to notice a dress like that?

It wasn't so much the golden silk, which skimmed

her curves and made her look like a living treasure, it was the scooped neck showing unfamiliar inches of creamy skin and the soft swell of her breasts. She had even positioned the glittery grasshopper brooch so that it looked poised to hop straight onto her nipple. Had she started to relax enough to stop covering her body up in that old puritanical way? he wondered.

But even this wasn't enough to hold his attention for long. His gaze moved behind her, where a fire was blazing—with two wing chairs on either side. Sprigs of holly had been placed above the paintings and, yes, there was the inevitable sprig of mistletoe dangling from the ceiling. On a low table a bowl was filled with clementines and in the air he could scent something cooking, rich with the scent of cinnamon and spice. But it was the Christmas tree which jarred most. A fresh fir tree with coloured lights looped all over the fragrant branches from which hung matching baubles of gold.

He flinched, but she didn't seem to notice as she wound her arms around his neck and positioned her lips over his. 'Merry Christmas,' she whispered.

Like a drowning man he fought against her feminine softness and the faint drift of pomegranate which clung to her skin. Disentangling her arms, he took a step back as he felt the clutch of ice around his heart.

'What's going on?' he questioned.

She blinked, as if something in his voice had alerted her to the fact that all was not well. 'It's a surprise.'

'I don't like surprises.'

Her eyes now held a faint sense of panic. Was she realising just how wrong she'd got it? he wondered grimly. He could see her licking her lips and the anger inside him seemed to bubble and grow.

'I thought about booking a hotel in London,' she said quickly. 'But I thought you'd probably stayed in all those places before, or somewhere like them. And then I thought about creating a real Christmas, right here in the countryside.'

'A *real* Christmas,' he repeated slowly.

'That's right.' She gestured towards a box of truffles on the table, as if the sight of chocolate were going to make him have a sudden change of heart. 'I went online at Selfridges and ordered a mass of stuff from their food hall. It was still much cheaper than a hotel. That's a ham you can smell cooking and I've bought fish too, because I know in Europe you like to eat fish at Christmas. Oh, and mince pies, of course.'

'I hate mince pies.'

'You don't…' Her voice faltered, as if she could no longer ignore the harsh note of censure in his voice. 'You don't *have* to eat them.'

'I hate Christmas, full stop,' he said viciously. 'I already told you that, Alannah—so which part of the sentence did you fail to understand?'

Her fingers flew over her lips and, with the silky dress clinging to her curves, she looked so like a medieval damsel in distress that he was momentarily tempted to pull her into his arms and blot out everything with sex.

But only momentarily. Because then he looked up and saw the Christmas angel on top of the tree and something about those gossamer-fine wings made his heart clench with pain. He felt the walls of the tiny cottage closing in on him as a dark tide of unwanted emotion washed over him.

'Which part, Alannah?' he repeated.

She held out the palms of her hands in a gesture of appeal. 'I thought—'

'What did you think?' he interrupted savagely. 'That you could treat me like your tame puppet? Playing happy couples around the Christmas tree and indulging in some happy-ever-after fantasy, just because we've had sex and I asked to spend the holidays with you, since we were both at a loose end?'

'Actually,' she said, walking over to the blaze of the fire and turning back to stare at him, 'I thought about how soulless it might be—having a corporate Christmas in some horrible anonymous hotel. I thought that with the kind of life you lead, you might like some home cooking for a change.'

'But I don't *do* home. Don't you get that?' he questioned savagely. He saw a small, rectangular present lying on the table and realised he hadn't even bought her a gift. *It wasn't supposed to be that kind of Christmas.* He shook his head. 'I can't stay here, Alannah. I'm sorry if you've gone to a lot of trouble but it's going to be wasted. So pack everything up while I put out the fire. We're going back to town.'

'No,' she said quietly.

His eyes narrowed. 'What do you mean...*no*?'

'You go if you want to, but I'm staying here.'

There was a pause. 'On your own?'

Alannah felt a sudden kick of rebellion as she met the incredulity in his eyes. 'You find that so surprising?' she demanded. 'You think I'm scared? Well, think again, Niccolò. I live on my own. I've spent pretty much the last seven years on my own. I don't need a man to protect me and look after me—and I certainly don't want to drive back to London with someone who can misinterpret a simple gesture with your kind of cynicism. So go to your anonymous hotel and spend the next few days splashing your cash and telling yourself how much you hate Christmas. I'll be perfectly happy here with my chocolate and mulled wine.'

His black eyes glittered. 'I'm telling you now that if you're calling my bluff, it won't work. I'm not staying here, but I'm not leaving without you, either.'

'I'm afraid you don't have a choice,' she said, walking across to the cocktail cabinet and pouring herself a glass of wine with a trembling hand. 'Like I said, I'm not going anywhere—and I don't imagine that even you are macho enough to drag me out by my hair. So leave. Go on. Just *leave*!'

Silently, they faced each other off before he pulled open the door and a fierce gust of wind brought a great flurry of snowflakes whirling into the room, before it slammed shut behind him.

Alannah didn't move as she heard the sound of his car starting up and then slowly pulling away on the snowy path. Her fingers tightened around her wine glass as she wondered how she could have judged him so badly. Had she thought that, because he'd murmured soft words in Sicilian when he'd been deep inside her, he'd lost the elements of ruthlessness and control which defined him?

Or was he right? Had she been naïve enough to imagine that a homespun meal might make him crave an intimacy which extended beyond the bedroom?

Her heart pounded.

Yes, she had.

Walking over to the sink, she threw away the wine, washing out the glass and putting it on the side to dry. She drew the curtains on the snowy darkness of the night and switched on the radio, just in time to hear the traditional Christmas service being broadcast from King's College, Cambridge. And as soon as the sound of carols filled the room she felt tears spring to her eyes, because it was so heartbreakingly beautiful.

She thought about the nativity scene—the helpless little child in a manger, and briefly she closed her eyes. She'd got it so wrong, hadn't she? She had taken him as her lover and ignored all the warning bells which had sounded so loudly in her ears. She had conveniently forgotten that everything was supposed to be on *his* terms and she'd tried to turn it into something it wasn't. Something it could never be. What had she been thinking of? She'd even bought herself a new and more revealing dress to send out the silent message that he had liberated her from some of her inhibitions. And she was almost as grateful to him for that as she was about the job he'd given her.

But he had thrown the offer back in her face.

She was cold now and ran upstairs to find a sweater, her heart contracting painfully as she looked around the bedroom. She had thought he would be charmed by the antique iron bedstead and the broderie-anglais linen. She'd imagined him picking up that old-fashioned jug and studying it—or telling her that he liked the view out into the snow-covered woods at the back of the house. She had planned to run him a bath when he arrived, and to light some of the scented candles she'd had delivered from London. She had pictured washing his back. Maybe even joining him, if he could persuade her to do so. She'd never shared a bath with anyone before.

What a fool she was, she thought viciously, dragging a mismatched blue sweater over the golden dress, and shaking her hair free. It wasn't as if she'd had no experience of life and the cruel lessons it could teach you. Hadn't she learnt that you had to just accept what you were given—warts and all? She should have taken what was already on the table and been satisfied with that. But she had been greedy, hadn't she? Niccolò had offered her something, but it hadn't been enough. She had wanted more. And still more.

The sound of the front door clicking open and closing again made her heart race with a sudden fear which made a mockery of her defiant words to Niccolò. Why the hell hadn't she locked it after he'd left— or was she hoping to extend an open invitation to any passing burglar? Except that no self-respecting burglar would be out on a snowy Christmas Eve like this. Even burglars probably had someone to share the holiday with.

'Who is it?' she called.

'Who do you think it is? Father Christmas?'

The sardonic Sicilian voice echoed round the small cottage and Alannah went to the top of the stairs to see Niccolò standing in the sitting room, snow clinging like frozen sugar to his black hair and cashmere coat. He looked up.

'It's me,' he said.

'I can see that. What happened?' she questioned

sarcastically as she began to walk downstairs. 'Did you change your mind about the mince pies?'

He was pulling off his coat and snow was falling in little white showers to the ground. She reached the bottom stair just as the poignant strains of 'Silent Night' poured from the radio. Quickly, she turned it off, so that all she could hear was the crackling of the fire and the sound of her own heartbeat as she stared at him. 'Why did you come back?'

There was a pause. His black eyes became suddenly hooded. 'It's a filthy night. I couldn't face leaving you here on your own.'

'And I told you that I would be fine. I'm not scared of the dark.' *I'm much more scared of the way you make me feel when you kiss me.*

'I'm not about to change my mind,' he said. 'I'm staying, and I need a drink.'

'Help yourself.'

He walked over to the bottle she'd opened earlier. 'You?'

A drink would choke me. 'No, thanks.'

She went and sat by the fire, wondering how she was going to get through the next few hours. How the hell did you pass the time when you were stuck somewhere with someone who didn't want to be there? After a couple of moments Niccolò walked over and handed her a glass of wine, but she shook her head.

'I said I didn't want one.'

'Take it, Alannah. Your face is pale.'

'My face is always pale.' But she took it anyway and drank a mouthful as he sat down in the other chair. 'And you still haven't really told me why you came back.'

Niccolò drank some of his wine and for a moment he said nothing. His natural instinct would be to tell her that he didn't have to justify his actions to her. To anyone. But something strange had happened as he'd driven his car down the snowy lane. Instead of the freedom he'd been expecting, he had felt nothing but a heavy weight settling somewhere deep in his chest. It had occurred to him that he could go and stay in a hotel. That if the truth were known, he could easily get a flight and join his friends and their skiing party. He could pretty much get a plane to anywhere, because the hosts of the many parties he'd declined would have been delighted if he'd turned up unexpectedly.

But then he'd thought of Alannah. Curled up alone by the fire with her raven hair aglow, while beside her that corny Christmas tree glittered. All that trouble she'd taken to create some sort of occasion and he'd just callously thrown it back in her face. What kind of a man did that? He thought of how much he'd anticipated making love to her again. How he'd spent the day aching to possess her and wanting to feel her arms wrapped tightly around him. What was *wrong* with him?

He put down his glass and his face was sombre as he turned to look at her.

'I came back because I realised I was behaving like an idiot,' he said. 'I shouldn't have taken it out on you and I'm sorry.'

Alannah sensed that sorry wasn't a word which usually featured highly in his vocabulary, but she wasn't letting him off that lightly. Did he think that a single word could wash away all the hurt he'd inflicted? 'But you did.'

'Yes. I did.'

'Because you always have to be in charge don't you, Niccolò?' she demanded, her anger starting to bubble up. 'You decided how you wanted Christmas to play out and that was it as far as you were concerned. What *you* want is paramount, and everyone else's wishes can just go hang. This is exactly what happened at Michela's wedding, isn't it? Niccolò wants it this way—so this is the way it must be.'

'That was different.'

'How?' she demanded. 'How was it different? How did you ever get to be so damned…*controlling*?'

The flames were flickering over his brooding features and illuminating his ebony hair, so that it glowed like fire-touched coal.

'How?' He gave a short laugh. 'You don't have any ideas?'

'Because you're Sicilian?'

'But I'm not,' he said unexpectedly. 'I'm only half Sicilian. My blood is not "pure". I am half Corsican.' He frowned. 'You didn't know that?'

She shook her head and suddenly his almost swashbuckling appearance made sense. 'No. I had no idea. Michela never really talked about that kind of thing. Boarding school is about reinvention—and escape. About painting yourself in the best possible light so that nobody feels sorry for you. All we knew was that you were unbelievably strict.' She put her glass down. 'Although you did used to take her to the Bahamas for Christmas every year, and we used to get pretty jealous about that.'

'She never told you why?'

'I knew that your parents were dead.' She hesitated. 'But nobody wants to talk about that kind of stuff, do they?'

Niccolò felt his mouth dry. No, they didn't. They definitely didn't. And when death was connected with shame, it made you want to turn your back on it even more. To keep it hidden. To create some kind of distance and move as far away from it as you could. He'd done that for Michela, but he'd done it for himself, too. Because some things were easier to forget than to remember.

Yet even though she was doing her best to disguise it, Alannah was looking at him with such hurt and confusion on her face that he felt it stab at his conscience. All she'd done was to try to make his Christmas good and he had thrown it back in her face in a way she didn't deserve. He'd given her a lot of stuff she didn't deserve, he realised—and didn't he owe her some kind of explanation?

'Mine was a very…unusual upbringing,' he said, at last. 'My mother came from a powerful Sicilian family who disowned her when she married my father.'

She raised her eyebrows. 'Wasn't that a little… dramatic?'

He shrugged. 'Depends which point of view you take. Her family was one of the wealthiest on the island—and my father was an itinerant Corsican with a dodgy background, who worked in the kitchens of one of her family hotels. It was never going to be thought of as an ideal match—not by any stretch of the imagination.' His gaze fixed on the flames which danced around one of the logs. 'My father was completely uneducated but he possessed a tremendous charisma.' He gave a bitter laugh. 'Along with a massive gambling addiction and a love of the finer things in life. My mother told me that her parents did everything in their power to prevent the marriage and when they couldn't—they told her she would only ever be welcome if she parted from him. Which for a strictly traditional Sicilian family was a pretty big deal.'

Alannah stared at him. 'So what did she do?'

'She defied them and married him anyway. She loved him. And she let that *love*—' His voice took the word and distorted it—so that when it left his lips it sounded like something dark and savage. 'She let it blind her to everything. His infidelity. His habitual absences. The fact that he was probably more in love with her inheritance, than with her. They took the boat to Italy when my mother was pregnant with me and we lived in some style in Rome—while my father flew to casinos all over the world and spent her money. My mother used to talk to me all the time about Sicily and I guess I became a typical immigrant child. I knew far more about the place of my birth than I did about my adopted homeland.'

Alannah leaned forward to throw another log on the fire as his words tailed off. 'Go on,' she said.

He watched the flames leap into life. 'When I was old enough, she used to leave me in charge of Michela so she could go travelling with him. She used to sit in casinos, just watching him—though I suspect it was mainly to keep the other women at bay. But he liked the attention—the idea that this rich and wealthy woman had given up everything to be with him. He used to tell her that she was his lucky charm. And I guess for a while that was okay—I mean, the situation certainly wasn't perfect, but it was bearable. Just that beneath the surface everything was crumbling and there was nothing I could do to stop it.'

She heard the sudden darkness in his voice. 'How?'

Leaning his head back against the chair, he half closed his eyes. 'My mother's inheritance was almost gone. The rent on our fancy apartment in Parioli was due and the creditors were circling like vultures. I remember her mounting sense of panic when she confided the bitter truth to me. I was eighteen and working towards going to college, though something told me that was never going to happen. My father found out about a big tournament in Monaco and they drove to France so that he could take part in it.' There was a pause. 'It was supposed to be the solution to all their problems.'

She heard the sudden break in his voice. 'What happened?'

'Oh, he won,' he said. 'In fact, he cleaned up big time. Enough to clear all his debts and guarantee them the kind of future my mother had prayed for.'

'But?' She sensed there was a *but* coming. It hung in the air like a heavy weight about to topple. He lowered his head to look at her and Alannah almost recoiled from the sudden bleakness in his eyes.

'That night they celebrated with too much champagne and decided to set off for Rome, instead of waiting until the morning. They were driving through the Italian alps when they took a bend too fast. They hit the side of the mountain and the car was destroyed.' He didn't speak for a moment and when he did, his words sounded as if they had been carved from stone.

'Neither of them would have known anything about it. At least, that's what the doctors told me.'

'Oh, Niccolò,' she breathed. 'I'm so sorry. Michela told me they'd died in a car crash, but I didn't know the background to the story.'

'Because I kept as much from her as I could. The post-mortem was inconclusive.' His voice hardened. 'Determining the level of alcohol in a…cadaver is always difficult. And no child should have the shame of knowing her father killed her mother because he was on a drunken high after winning at cards.'

She thought how *cold* he sounded—and how ruthless. But that was his default position, wasn't it—and wasn't it somehow understandable in the circumstances? Wasn't much of his behaviour explained by his dreadful legacy? 'You still must have been devastated?' she ventured.

He gave a bitter laugh. 'Do you want the truth? The real and shocking truth? My overriding emotion was one of relief that my father had won so big and that somehow the money got to me intact. It meant that I could pay the rent and clear the debts. It meant that I could send Michela away to school—at thirteen she was getting too much for me to handle. And it meant that I could live my own life. That I could capitalise on his win and make it even bigger. And that's what I did. I bought my first property with that money and by the end of that first year, I had acquired three.'

Alannah nodded. It was funny how when you joined up the dots the bigger picture emerged. Suddenly, she realised why he'd always been so strict with his sister. She saw now that his own controlling nature must have developed as an antidote to his father's recklessness. Financial insecurity had led him to go on and make himself a colossal fortune which nobody could ever bleed away. His wealth was protected, but in protecting it he had set himself in a world apart from other men.

'And did this all happen at Christmas?' she questioned suddenly. 'Is that why you hate the holidays so much?'

'No. That would have been neat, wouldn't it?' He gave a wry smile. 'It's just that Christmas came to symbolise the bleak epicentre of our family life. For me, it was always such an empty festival. My mother would spend vast amounts of money decking out the rooms of our apartment, but she was never there. Even on Christmas Eve she would be sitting like some passive fool on the sidelines while my father played cards. Supposedly bringing him luck, but in reality—checking out that some buxom hostess wasn't coming onto him.'

She winced at the phrase, but suddenly she could understand some of his prejudice towards her, too. For him, buxom women in skimpy clothes were the ones who threatened his parents' relationship. Yet in the end, his puritanical disapproval of her chosen career had done nothing to destroy his powerful lust for her, which must have confused him. And Niccolò didn't do confusion. She'd always known that. Black and white, with nothing in between.

'To me, Christmas always felt as if I'd walked onto a stage set,' he said. 'As if all the props were in place, but nobody knew which lines to say.'

And Alannah realised that she'd done exactly the same. She had tried to create the perfect Christmas.

She'd bought the tree and hung the holly and the mistletoe—but what she had created had been no more real than the empty Christmases of his past.

'Oh, Niccolò—I'm sorry,' she said. 'I had no idea.'

He looked at her and some of the harshness left his face. 'How would you have done? I've never talked about it. Not to anyone.'

'Maybe some time, it might be good to sit down and discuss it with Michela?' she ventured.

'And destroy her memories?'

'False memories are dangerous. And so are secrets. My mother waited until she was dying to tell me that her drink had been spiked and she didn't even know my father's name. I wish she'd shared it with me sooner. I would have liked to have let her know how much I admired her for keeping me.'

His eyes narrowed. 'She sounds an amazing woman.'

'She was.' His words pleased her but she felt vulnerable with his black eyes looking at her in that curiously assessing way. In an effort to distract herself, she got up and went to look out of the window. 'I'm afraid the snow shows no sign of melting?'

'No.'

She turned round. 'I suppose on a practical level we could take down all the decorations if that would make you feel better—and then we could watch that programme on TV which has been generating so much publicity. Have you heard about it? It's called "*Stuff Christmas*".'

Without warning, he rose from the chair and walked over to her, his shadow enveloping her and suddenly making her feel very small. His ebony gaze flickered over her and she saw that the bitterness in his eyes had been replaced by the much more familiar flicker of desire.

'Or we could do something else, *mia fata*,' he said softly. 'Something much more appealing. Something which I have been aching to do since I walked back in here. I could take you upstairs to bed and make love to you.'

His features were soft with lust and Alannah thought she'd never seen him looking quite so gorgeous. She wanted him just as she always wanted him, but this time her desire was underpinned with something else—something powerful and inexplicable. A need to hold him and comfort him, after everything he'd told her. A need to want to reach out and protect him.

But he'd only told her because of the situation in which they found themselves and she needed to face the truth. He wanted her for sex—*that was all*—and she needed to protect her own vulnerable heart. Maybe it was time to distance herself from him for a while. Give them both a little space.

But by then he was kissing her and it was too late to say anything. Because when he kissed her like that, she was lost.

CHAPTER NINE

SLOWLY, NICCOLÒ LICKED at the delicious rosy flesh of Alannah's nipple until eventually she began to stir. Raising her arms above her head, she stretched languorously as the silky tumble of her hair rippled over the pillow like a black banner.

'Niccolò,' she murmured, dark lashes fluttering open to reveal the sleepy denim eyes beneath.

He gave a smile of satisfaction as she somehow turned his name into a breathy little sigh—a variation of the different ways she'd said it throughout the night. She had gasped it. Moaned it. At one point she had even screamed it—her fingernails clawing frantically at his sweat-sheened body as she'd bucked beneath him. He remembered her flopping back onto the pillow afterwards and asking if was it always like this. But he hadn't answered her. He hadn't dared. For once there had been no words in his vocabulary to describe a night which had surpassed any other in his experience. He had come over and over again... in her and on her. And this time he'd remembered to use protection. Hell. Even doing *that* had felt as if it should be included in the pages of the Kama Sutra. He swallowed as he felt the renewed jerk of desire just from thinking about it. No orgasm had ever felt more powerful; no kisses that deep.

He was still trying to work out why. Because he had allowed her to glimpse the bleak landscape of his past—or because he had waited what seemed like a whole lifetime to possess her? He gave another lick. Maybe it was simply that he was discovering she was nothing like the woman he'd thought her to be.

'Niccolò?' she said again.

'Mmm?'

'Is it morning?'

'I think so.' His tongue traced a sinuous path over the creamy flesh and he felt her shiver. 'Though right now I don't really care. Do you?'

'I don't...' He could hear the note of dreamy submission in her voice. 'I don't think so.'

'Good.' He moved his tongue down over her body, feeling himself harden as it trailed a moist path to her belly. But the anatomical significance of that particular spot suddenly began to stab at his conscience and the thought he'd been trying to block now came rushing into his mind. *Was* she pregnant? He felt the painful contraction of his heart until he reminded himself that was a possibility, not a fact—and he only ever dealt with facts. There was nothing he could do about it right now—so why not continue tracking his tongue down over her salty skin and obliterating the nagging darkness of his thoughts with the brief amnesia of pleasure?

He wriggled down the bed and knelt over her, his legs straddling her as he parted her thighs and put his head between them. The dark triangle of hair at their apex was soft and for a moment he just teased at the curly strands with his teeth. She began to writhe as he flickered his tongue with featherlight accuracy against her clitoris, and the fingernails which had begun to claw restlessly at the sheet now moved to grip his shoulders.

She tasted warm and wet against his mouth and her urgent little cries only increased when he captured her circling hips and pinned them firmly against the mattress, so that he could increase the unremitting pressure of his tongue. He could hear her calling his name out. He could feel her spiralling out of control. And suddenly he felt her begin to spasm helplessly against his mouth.

'N-Niccolò!' she breathed. 'Oh, Niccolò.'

His mind and his body were at such a fever-pitch of hunger that he couldn't speak and, urgently, he reached for a condom and eased himself into her slick warmth.

He groaned. She felt so *tight*. Or maybe it was because he felt so big—as if he wanted to explode from the moment he thrust inside her. As if he wanted to come, over and over again. And yet surely she had drained every seed from his body, so that there was nothing left to give?

It seemed she had not. He drove into her until he didn't know where he ended and she began. Until her back began to arch and her eyes to close—each exquisite spasm racking through his body as time seemed to suspend itself, leaving him dazed and breathless.

The silence of the room was broken only by the sound of his own muffled heartbeat.

'I don't know how much more pleasure I can take,' she said eventually and he felt her face pressing against his shoulder.

He turned his head and blew a soft breath onto her cheek. 'Don't you know that you can never have too much pleasure, *mia tentatrice*?'

But Alannah wrinkled her nose as she stared up at the ceiling because she didn't agree. You could. You definitely could. There was always a snake in the garden of Eden—everyone knew that. She thought about all the things he'd confided in her last night. Her heart had softened when she'd heard his story. She'd felt so close to him—and flattered that he had trusted her enough to tell her all that stuff about his past. But that was dangerous, too. If she wasn't careful she could start weaving hopeless fantasies about something which was never intended to last.

She looked over at the window where bright light was shining against the closed curtains. And she realised that it was Christmas morning and last night he'd wanted to leave. She watched as he got out of bed and walked over to the window to pull back the curtains and she blinked as she gazed outside. Thick snow lay everywhere. Branches and bushes were blanketed with the stuff. Against a dove-grey sky the world looked blindingly white and not a sound could be heard and Alannah knew she mustn't let the fairy-tale perfection of the scene in front of her blind her to the reality of their situation.

She put her hands beneath the duvet, her warm belly instinctively recoiling from the icy touch of her fingers.

'We haven't really discussed what's going to happen if I'm pregnant.'

The words hung and shimmered in the air, like the baubles on the unwanted Christmas tree downstairs.

He seemed to choose his words carefully, as if he was walking through a minefield of possibilities.

'Obviously, if such a situation arises—then I will be forced to consider marrying you.'

Alannah did her best not to recoil because he made it sound like someone being forced to drink a bitter draught of poison. She didn't say anything for a moment and when she did, she chose her words as carefully as he had done.

'Before you do, I think there's something you should take into account,' she said quietly. 'Gone are the days when women could be forced to marry against their will—because there's a baby on the way. If I *am* pregnant, then I want my baby to have love— real love. I would want my baby to put contentment before wealth—and satisfaction before ambition. I would want my baby to grow up to be a warm and grounded individual—and, obviously, none of those things would be possible with you as a cynical role model. So don't worry, Niccolò—I won't be dragging you up the aisle any time soon.'

She had expected anger, or a righteous indignation—but she got neither. Instead, his expression remained cool and non-committal. She almost thought she saw a flicker of amusement in those ebony eyes.

'Have you finished?' he said.

She shrugged, wishing she didn't want him so much. 'I guess.'

'Then I'll make coffee.'

He didn't just make coffee. After a bath which

seemed to take for ever to fill, Alannah dressed and
went downstairs to find him deftly cracking eggs into
a bowl with one hand.

He glanced up. 'Breakfast?'

She grimaced. 'I don't know if I can face eggs.'

'You really should eat something.'

'I suppose so.' She sat down and took the cup of
coffee he poured for her and, after a couple of minutes, a plate of scrambled eggs was pushed across the
table. She must have been hungrier than she'd thought
because she ate it all, before putting her fork down and
watching while he finished his own. She thought how
he could even make eating look sexy. *Keep your mind
fixed on practicalities,* she told herself. 'We ought to
investigate the roads,' she said. 'Maybe we can dig
ourselves out.'

'Not yet.' His eyes were thoughtful as they sur-
veyed her over the rim of his coffee cup. 'I think we
should go for a walk. You look as if you could do with
some colour in your cheeks.'

'That's what blusher is supposed to be for.'

He smiled. 'There's a cupboard below the stairs
packed with boots and waterproof jackets—why don't
we go and investigate?'

They found coats and wrapped up warm and as
Niccolò buttoned up her coat Alannah kept reinforcing the same mantra which had been playing in her
head all morning. That none of this meant anything.
They were just two people who happened to be alone
at Christmas, who happened to enjoy having sex with
each other.

But the moment they stepped out into the snow, it

was impossible to keep things in perspective. It felt as if nature were conspiring against her. How could she not be affected when it felt as if she'd been trans-planted into a magical world, with a man who made her feel so *alive*?

They walked along, their footsteps sinking into the virgin tracks, and she was surprised when he took her hand as they walked along. Funny how something so insignificant could feel so meaningful—especially when she thought about the many greater intimacies they'd shared. Because holding hands could easily masquerade as tenderness and tenderness was shot with its own special kind of danger...

As occasional stray flakes drifted down on their bare heads they talked about their lives. About the reasons he'd come to live in London and her summer holidays in Ireland. She asked how he'd met Alekto Sarantos, and he told her about their mutual friend Murat, the Sultan of Qurhah, and a long-ago skiing trip, when four very alpha men had challenged each other on the slopes.

'I didn't realise you knew Luis Martinez,' she said. 'That *is* Luis Martinez the world-champion racing driver?'

'Ex world champion,' he said, a little testily—and Alannah realised how competitive the four friends must have been.

He told her he hated litter and cars which hogged the middle lane of the motorway and she confided her dislike of drugs and people who ignored shop as-sistants by talking on their mobile phones. It was as if they had made an unspoken decision to keep the conversation strictly neutral and, unexpectedly, Alannah found herself relaxing. To anyone observing them, they probably looked like an ordinary couple who'd chosen to escape the mad rush of the city to create a dream holiday for themselves. And that was all it was, she reminded herself fiercely. A dream.

'Are you finding this...impossible?' she said. 'Being stuck here with this manufactured Christmas everywhere, when last night you were desperate to leave?'

He kicked at some snow, so that it created a powdery white explosion before falling to the ground. 'No,' he said eventually. 'It's easier than I imagined. You're actually very good company. In fact, I think I enjoy talking to you almost as much as I enjoy kissing you.' His eyes gleamed. 'Although, on second thoughts...'

She turned away, blinking her eyes furiously because kindness was nearly as dangerous as tenderness in helping you to distort reality. But he was getting to her—even though she didn't want him to. Wasn't it funny how a few kind words had the power to make everything seem different? The world suddenly looked bright and vivid, even though it had been bleached of colour. The snow made the berries on the holly bushes stand out like drops of blood and Alannah reached up to bend back a tree branch, watching as it sent a shower of snow arcing through the air, and something bubbled up inside her and made her giggle.

She turned around to find Niccolò watching her, his eyes narrowed against the bright light, and her mouth grew dry as she saw an instantly recognisable hunger in their black depths.

'What…what are we going to do if it doesn't melt?' she said, suddenly breathless.

He leaned forward to touch a gloved finger to her lips. 'Guess,' he said, and his voice was rough.

CHAPTER TEN

HE MADE LOVE to her as soon as they got back—while her cheeks were still cold from the snowy air and her eager fingers icy against his chest as she burrowed beneath his sweater. Alannah lay on the rug in front of the fire, with her arms stretched above her head, wearing nothing but a pair of knickers. And all her shyness and hang-ups seemed like a distant memory as he trailed his lips over every inch of her body.

His fingertips explored her skin with a curiously rapt attention and she found herself reaching for him with a sudden urgency, drawing in a shuddering breath as he eased into her and letting the breath out again like a slow surrender as he lowered his mouth to hers. She loved the contrast of their bodies—his so olive-skinned and dark against her own milky pallor. She liked watching the flicker of flames gilding his flesh and the way his limbs interlocked so perfectly with her own. She loved the way he tipped his head back when he came—and made that low and shuddered moan of delight.

Much later, he pulled his sweater over her head and set about cooking lunch, while she curled up on the sofa and watched him, and suddenly she felt relaxed.

Really and properly relaxed. The cushion behind her back was soft and feathery and her bare toes were warm in the fire's glow.

'It seems *weird*,' she said as he tipped a pile of clean vegetables from the chopping board into a saucepan, 'to see you in the kitchen, looking like you know exactly what you're doing.'

'That's because I do. It isn't exactly rocket science,' he answered drily. 'Unless you think cooking is too complicated for a mere man and that women are naturally superior in the kitchen?'

'Women are naturally superior at many things,' she said airily. 'Though not necessarily at cooking. And you know what I mean. You're a billionaire businessman who runs an international empire. It's strange to see you *scraping carrots*.'

Niccolò gave a soft laugh as he grabbed a handful of fresh herbs, though he recognised that she'd touched a nerve. Just because he *could* cook, didn't mean he did—and it was a long time since he'd done anything like this. Yet wasn't there something uniquely *comforting* about creating a meal from scratch? He'd cooked for his sister in those early days of loss but as she'd got older his responsibilities towards her had lessened. When he had sent her away to school, only the vacations had required his hands-on guardianship. But he had enjoyed his role as quasi-parent and he'd made sure that he carried it out to the best of his ability—the way he tackled everything in his life.

He remembered the trips to the famous Campagna Amica market, near the Circus Maximus. He had taken Michela with him and shown the sulky teenager how to select the freshest vegetables and the finest pieces of fruit. And all the stall-owners had made a fuss of her—slipping her a ripe pear or a small bunch of perfect grapes.

When Michela had finally left home, he had filled every available hour with work—building up his property portfolio with a determination to underpin his life with the kind of security he'd never had. And as his wealth had grown, so had his ability to delegate. These days he always ate out, unless a woman was trying to impress him with her culinary repertoire. His Mayfair fridge was bare, save for coffee and champagne. His apartment was nothing but a base with a bed. It wasn't a home because he didn't *do* home. But as he squeezed lemon juice over the grilled fish he realised how much he had missed the simple routine of the kitchen.

He glanced up to find Alannah still watching him, her bare legs tucked up beneath her. His sweater was much too big for her and it had the effect of making her look unbelievably fragile. Her black hair was spilling down over her shoulders and her blue eyes were shining and something about that almost innocent look of eagerness made his heart contract.

Deliberately, he turned away, reaching for a bottle of prosecco and two glasses. *She's just someone you're trying to get out of your system,* he reminded himself grimly.

His face was composed by the time he handed her a glass. 'Happy Christmas,' he said.

They drank prosecco, lit candles and ate lunch. Afterwards, he made love to her again and they fell asleep on the sofa—and when they awoke, the candles were almost burnt down and outside the starry sky was dark and clear.

Alannah walked over to the window and he wondered if she was aware that her bare bottom was revealed with every step she took.

'I think the snow might be melting,' she said.

He heard the unmistakable note of disappointment in her voice and something inside him hardened. Did she think they could exist in this little bubble for ever, and pretend the rest of the world wasn't out there?

He insisted on loading the dishwasher and making tea to eat with their chocolate. Because any kind of activity was better than sitting there letting his mind keep working overtime.

But action couldn't permanently silence the nagging thoughts which were building inside him and he thought about what she'd said earlier. About putting contentment before wealth and satisfaction before ambition. About not wanting to drag him up the aisle.

Because that was not a decision she alone could make. And if there *was* a baby, then surely there was only one sensible solution, and that solution was marriage.

His jaw tightened. Obviously it was something he'd thought about, in the same way that the young sometimes thought about getting old—as if it would never happen to them. He liked children—and was godfather to several. Deep down, he'd recognised that one day he wanted to be a father and would select a suitable woman to bear his child.

He'd imagined she would be blonde and slightly aloof. Maybe one of those American women who had been brought up on milk and honey and could trace their roots back over generations. The type who kept their emotions on an even keel. The type who didn't believe in fairy tales. The type he felt safe with. It wasn't their trust funds which excited him, but the satisfaction of knowing that they would unknowingly welcome the son of a Corsican bandit into their rarefied drawing rooms.

He stared across the room at Alannah. In no way was she aloof; he had never seen a woman looking quite so accessible. Even with her fingers wrapped chastely around a mug of herb tea, she looked...wild. He felt his throat dry. She touched something deep inside him, something which felt...*dangerous*. Something which took him to the very edges of his self-control. She always had. She spoke to him as nobody else did. She treated him in a way which no one else would dare try.

But the fact remained that she had a background even more unsettled than his own. He had already taken a gamble on her—but surely there was no need to take another. He might not have learnt many lessons at the knee of his father, but one thing he knew was that the more you gambled—the greater your chance of losing. The most sensible thing he could do would be to walk away from her. To keep on walking, without looking back.

He swallowed. Yet if she carried his child—he could walk nowhere. What choice would he have other than to stay with her? To tie himself to someone who no way fitted the image of the kind of woman he wanted to marry. Two mismatched people united by a single incident of careless passion. What future was there in that?

She looked up and her expression grew wary.

'Why are you frowning at me?'

'I didn't realise I was.'

'Actually, frowning isn't really accurate. You were glaring.'

'Was I?' He leaned back in his chair and studied her. 'I've been thinking.'

'Sounds ominous,' she said.

'You do realise that despite all your words of rebellion this morning—I'm going to marry you if you're having my baby?'

Her creamy skin went pink. He saw her fingertips flutter up to touch the base of her neck.

'What…what made you suddenly think of that?'

He saw the flare of hope in her eyes and knew he mustn't feed it, because that wasn't fair. He had a responsibility to tell her the truth and the last thing he wanted was her thinking he was capable of the same emotions as other men. He mustn't fool her into thinking that his icy heart might be about to melt. His mouth hardened. Because that was never going to happen.

'I suddenly realised,' he said slowly, 'that I could never tolerate my son or daughter growing up and calling another man Father.'

'Even though I am the last kind of person you would consider marrying under normal circumstances.'

He met her eyes—but hadn't he always been completely honest with her? Wouldn't she see through a placatory lie to try to make her feel better? 'I guess.'

She put her cup down quickly, as if she was afraid she was going to spill it. 'So this is all about possession?'

'Why wouldn't it be? This child is half mine.'

'*This child* might not even exist!' she choked out. 'Don't you think we ought to wait until we know, before we start having arguments about parental rights?'

'When *can* you find out?'

'I'll do the test when I get back to London,' she said, jumping up from the sofa and dabbing furiously at her eyes with shaking and fisted hands.

The warm and easy atmosphere of earlier had vanished. And how.

Alannah stormed upstairs to splash cold water onto her face and to try to stem the hot tears from springing to her eyes, and yet all she could feel was a growing sense of frustration. She didn't *want* to be like this. She couldn't blame him for what he'd said, just because it didn't fit in with her fantasies. He was only being straight with her. So maybe this was a wake-up call to start protecting herself. To start facing up to facts.

Their fairy-tale Christmas was over.

She went back downstairs and turned on the TV, giving an exaggerated sigh of relief when she heard the weatherman announce that a warm weather front was pushing up from Spain, and the snow was expected to have thawed by late morning.

'Great news,' she said. 'London here we come.'

Niccolò watched as she stomped out of her chair to throw away the untouched mince pies and chocolates and every attempt he made to start a conversation was met with a monosyllabic response. He realised that he'd never been given such cool treatment by a woman before.

But that didn't stop them having sex that night. Very good sex, as it happened. Their angry words momentarily forgotten, he reached for her in the darkness with a passion which she more than matched. In a room washed silver by the full moon, he watched as she arched beneath him and called out his name.

He awoke to the sound of dripping outside the window to find the weatherman's predictions had been accurate and that the snow was melting. Leaving Alannah sleeping, he packed everything up, made a pot of coffee, then went along the lane to find his car.

By the time he drove back to the cottage, she was up and dressed, standing in the middle of the sitting room, clutching a mug—her face pale and her mouth set. He noticed she'd turned the tree lights off and that the room now looked dull and lacklustre.

'Christmas is over,' she said brightly, as if he were a stranger. As if she hadn't been going down on him just a few sweet hours before.

'What about the tree?'

'The woman I hired the cottage from supplied it. She said she'll take it away.'

'Alannah—'

'No,' she said quietly. 'I don't want any protracted stuff, or silly goodbyes. I just want to get back to London and finish up the job you've employed me to do.'

Niccolò felt a flicker of irritation at her suddenly stubborn and uncompromising attitude, but there didn't seem to be a damned thing he could do about it. She was almost completely silent on the journey back as the car slushed its way through the unnaturally quiet streets and, for some reason, the passionate opera he usually favoured while driving now seemed completely inappropriate.

He drove her to Acton and parked up outside her

home, where most of the small nearby houses seemed to be decked with the most garish tinsel imaginable. Someone had even put an inflatable Santa in their cramped front yard.

'Thanks for the lift,' she said, as she reached for the door handle.

'Aren't you going to invite me in?'

She gave him a steady stare. 'Why would I do that?'

'Maybe because we've been sleeping together and I might like to see where you live?'

Alannah hesitated and hated herself for that hesitation. She wondered if secretly she was ashamed of her little home and fearful of how judgemental he might be. Or was it simply an instinctive reaction, because she was unwilling to expose any more of herself to him?

'Okay, come in, then,' she said grudgingly.

'Grazie,' came his sardonic reply.

It was shiveringly cold as she unlocked the door. She'd turned the heating down low before the taxi had arrived to take her to the cottage and now the place felt like an ice-box. Niccolò stood in the centre of her small sitting room as she adjusted the thermostat, looking around him like a man who had just found himself in a foreign country and wasn't quite sure what to do. She wondered how he managed to make her furniture look as if it would be better suited to a doll's house.

'Would you like a guided tour?' she said.

'Why not?'

The cramped dimensions meant she needed to be vigilant about tidiness and Alannah was glad there were no discarded pieces of clothing strewn around her bedroom and that the tiny bathroom was neat. But it still felt excruciating as she led him through an apartment in which she'd tried to maximise all available light in order to give an illusion of space. She'd made all the drapes herself from sari material she'd picked up at the local market, and the artwork which hung on the walls was her own. A friend from college had feng-shuied every room, there were pots of herbs lined up on the window sill in the kitchen, and she found the place both restful and creative.

But she wondered how it must seem through Niccolò's eyes, when you could practically fit the entire place into his downstairs cloakroom back in Mayfair.

They walked back into the sitting room and, rather awkwardly, she stood in front of him. He really did seem like a stranger now, she thought—and a terrible sense of sadness washed over her. How weird to think that just a few hours ago he was deep inside her body—making her feel as if she was closer to him than she'd ever been to anyone.

'I would offer you coffee,' she said. 'But I really do want to get on. If Alekto is going to have the apartment ready for his New Year's Eve party, then I need to get cracking.'

'You're planning to work *today*?'

'Of course. What did you think I'd be doing?' she questioned. 'Sobbing into my hankie because our cosy Christmas is over? I enjoyed it, Niccolò. It was an… interesting experience. And you're a great cook as well as a great lover. But you probably know that.'

She made a polite gesture in the direction of the door but he suddenly caught hold of her wrist, and all pretence of civility had gone.

'Haven't you forgotten something?' he iced out, his eyes glittering with unfeigned hostility.

She snatched her hand away, swallowing as she met his gaze. 'No, I haven't. It's not the kind of thing you can easily forget, is it? Don't worry, Niccolò. I'll let you know whether I'm pregnant or not.'

CHAPTER ELEVEN

'I'M NOT PREGNANT.'

Alannah's voice sounded distorted—as if it were coming from a long way away, instead of just the other side of his desk—and Niccolò didn't say anything—at least, not straight away. He wondered why his heart had contracted with something which felt like pain. Whether he'd imagined the cold taste of disappointment which was making his mouth bitter. He must have done. Because wasn't this the news he'd been longing for? The only sane solution to a problem which should never have arisen?

He focused his eyes to where Alannah sat perched on the edge of a chair opposite him and thought how pale she looked. Paler than the thick white lanes through which they'd walked on Christmas Day, when the snow had trapped them in that false little bubble. Her blue eyes were ringed with dark shadows, as if she hadn't been sleeping.

Had she?

Or had she—like he—been lying wide-eyed in the depths of the night, remembering what it had felt like when they'd made love and then fallen asleep with their limbs tangled warmly together?

He flattened the palms of his hands flat on the surface of his desk. 'You're sure?'

'One hundred per cent.'

He wondered why she had chosen to tell him here, and now. Why she had come to his office after successfully negotiating a ten-minute slot in his diary with Kirsty. And Kirsty hadn't even checked with him first!

'Couldn't you have chosen a more suitable time and place to tell me, rather than bursting into my office and getting my assistant to collude with you?' he questioned impatiently. 'Or is it just a continuation of your determination to keep me at arm's length?'

'I've been busy.'

That was usually *his* excuse. He leaned back in his chair and studied her. 'You won't even have dinner with me,' he observed coolly.

'I'm sure you'll get over it,' she said lightly.

His gaze didn't waver. 'I thought you said you'd enjoyed our "experiment" over Christmas—so why not run with it a little longer? Come on, Alannah.' A smile curved his lips. 'What harm could it do?'

Alannah stared at him. What *harm* could it do? Was he serious? But that was the trouble—he was. Unemotional, cynical and governed by nothing but sexual hunger—Niccolò obviously saw no reason why they shouldn't continue with the affair. Because it meant different things to each of them. For him, it was clearly just an enjoyable diversion, while for her it felt as if someone had chipped away a little bit of her heart every time she saw him. *It was being chipped away right now.*

She had chosen his office and a deliberately short

appointment in which to tell him her news in order to avoid just this kind of scene. She'd actually considered telling him by phone but had instinctively felt that such a move would have been counterproductive. That he might have insisted on coming round to confront her face to face and her defences would have been down.

It was bad enough trying to stay neutral now— even with the safety of his big oak desk between them. Sitting there in his crisp white shirt and tailored suit, Niccolò's face was glowing with health and vitality and she just wanted to go and put her arms around him. She wanted to lean on him and have him tell her that everything was going to be okay. But he didn't want a woman like her leaning on him and anyway— she was independent and strong. She didn't need a man who could never give her what she wanted, and what she wanted from him was love. *Join the queue,* she thought bitterly.

'You haven't *done* anything,' she said. 'You haven't made or broken any promises. Everything is how it's supposed to be, Niccolò. What happened between us was great but it was never intended to last. And it hasn't.'

'But what if…?' He picked up the golden pen which was lying on top of the letters he'd been signing and stared at it as if he had never really seen it before. He lifted his gaze to hers. 'What if I wanted it to last—at least for a little while longer? What then?'

Alannah tensed as fear and yearning washed over her—yet of the two emotions, the yearning was by far the deadlier.

'And how long did you have in mind?' she questioned sweetly. 'One week? Two? Would it be presumptuous to expect it might even continue for a *whole month*?'

He slammed the pen down. 'Does it matter?' he demanded. 'Not every relationship between a man and a woman lasts for ever.'

'But most relationships don't start out with a discussion about when it's going to end!' She sucked in a breath and prayed she could hold onto her equilibrium for a while longer. 'Look, nothing has changed. I'm still the same woman I always was—except that I have you to thank for helping me lose some of my inhibitions. But I still don't know who my father was and I still have the kind of CV which would make someone with your sensitive social antennae recoil in horror. Appearances matter to you, Niccolò. You know they do. So why don't you just celebrate the fact that you had a lucky escape and that we aren't going to be forced together by some random act of nature.' She rose to her feet. 'And leave me to finish off Alekto's apartment in time for his party. The caterers are arriving tomorrow, and there are still some last-minute touches which need fixing.'

'Sit down,' he said. 'I haven't finished yet.'

'Well, I have. We've said everything which needs to be said. It's over, Niccolò. I'm not so stupid that I want to hang around having sex with a man who despises everything I stand for!'

'I don't despise what you stand for. I made a lot of judgements about you and some of them were wrong.'

'Only *some* of them?' she demanded.

'Why can't you just accept what I'm offering? Why do you have to want more?'

'Because I'm worth it.' She hitched the strap of her handbag over her shoulder. 'And I'm going now.'

He rose to his feet. 'I don't want you to go!' he gritted out.

'Tough. I'm out of here. *Ciao.*'

And to Niccolò's amazement she picked up her handbag and walked out of his office without a backward glance.

For a moment he stood there, stunned—as the door slammed behind her. He thought about rushing after her, about pulling her into his arms and kissing her and *then* seeing whether she was so damned certain their relationship was over. But that would make it all about sex, wouldn't it? And sex had always been the least troublesome part of this equation. Besides, Kirsty was buzzing through to tell him that his eleven o'clock had arrived, so he was forced to concentrate on listening to what his architect was saying, rather than on a pair of stubborn pink lips he still wanted to crush beneath his own.

By seven o'clock that evening, he decided that Alannah had been right. Better to end it now, before she got in too deep—because it wouldn't be fair to break her heart as he had broken so many others. She would start falling in love with him. She would want more from him than he was capable of giving. Better they both recognised his limitations now.

He glanced up at the clock again. Maybe he should start as he meant to go on. Dinner with someone new would surely be the way to go. A civilised dinner with someone who didn't get under his skin the way she did.

He flicked through his address book, but none of the long list of names excited him enough to pick up the phone. He had his driver drop him home and worked in his study until way past midnight. But still he couldn't sleep. He kept remembering when Alannah had spent the night with him there and, even though the linen had been laundered, he thought he could still detect the unique scent of her skin on his sheets. He thought about the cottage. About the tree-lights and the snow. About that unreal sense of quiet satisfaction as he had cooked her Christmas lunch. The way they had fallen asleep on the sofa after they'd made love. Hadn't that been like the closest thing to peace he'd felt in a long, long time?

And that was all make-believe, he told himself fiercely. As insubstantial as Christmas itself.

He lay and watched the luminous numbers on his clock changing slowly and just before his alarm was due to go off a text arrived from Alekto Sarantos.

Don't be late for my party! Beautiful women and a beautiful apartment—what better way to see in the new year? A

Niccolò stared blankly at the screen of his mobile phone, telling himself that a party was exactly what he needed, and didn't Alekto throw some of the best parties he'd ever been to? But just the thought of it left him cold. Tugging on his running gear, he got ready for the gym and wondered why his eyes looked so shadowed and haunted.

But deep down, he knew exactly why.

'It is *spectacular.*' Alekto Sarantos smiled as he looked around the main reception room, his blue eyes gleaming. 'You have transformed my apartment, Alannah—and you have worked against the clock to get it done in time for my party. *Efkaristo poli*. I thank you.'

Alannah smiled back, even though just smiling seemed to take a massive effort these days. It was true that the place *did* look pretty amazing—especially when she thought back to the sea of beige it had been before. The woman who had made the curtains had got very excited about it and she had told someone, who had told someone else. Even during the short period between Christmas and new year, word had soon got round in an industry which survived by constantly seeking out new ideas and new faces. Already Alannah had received a phone call from one of the big interior magazines, asking if they could do a photo shoot there. She doubted whether Alekto would agree, since she got the idea he was very hot on privacy. Still, she could *always ask* him. And even if he didn't give his permission, she sensed that she had turned a corner—because this was the big break she had been waiting for. *And she had Niccolò to thank for it*.

Security and creative fulfilment were lying within her grasp. So why did it all feel so empty? Why was she having to force herself to look and sound enthusiastic about something she'd always dreamed of?

She sighed. She knew *exactly* why. *Because she'd made the fundamental mistake of falling in love with a man who had never offered her anything but sex.*

'I hope you're coming to my new year's party?' Alekto was saying. 'You really ought to be the guest of honour, after what you've achieved here. Unless, of course, you have already made plans?'

Alannah glanced out at the late afternoon sky, which was now almost dark. The only plans she had made were to buy the TV guide and turn up the central heating, while she waited for Big Ben to chime in a new year she couldn't seem to get worked up about. She thought about getting dressed up for a party attended by Alekto Sarantos and his glamorous friends, and how any sane person would leap at such an opportunity.

But what if Niccolò was there?

Her heart pounded. The possibility was high. It was more than high. They were best mates, weren't they? She shook her head. 'It's very sweet of you— but I think I'll just have a quiet evening in,' she said.

'Up to you.' Alekto shrugged. 'But if you change your mind…'

Alannah went home, bathed and washed her hair— before pulling on her dressing gown and a pair of slouchy socks and switching on the TV. She flicked channels. Crowds of people were already flocking into Trafalgar Square, even though it was still early. People were being interviewed, swigging from beer bottles and giggling—and Alannah suddenly saw herself as a fly on the wall might see her. A woman sitting on her own at nine o'clock on New Year's Eve, wearing a dressing gown and a pair of old socks.

What had she become?

She swallowed. She had become a cliché, that was what. She had fallen in love with someone who had always been out of reach. And yet, instead of accepting that and holding her head up high and just getting on with her life, the way she'd always done, she had caved in. She was like some sort of mole, liv-

ing in darkness—cowering inside her own safe little
habitat, because she was afraid to go out. It was the
worst night of the year to be home alone—especially
if your stupid heart was heavy and aching—and yet
here she was. *Mole.*

What was she so worried about? That she might
see Niccolò with another woman? Surely that would
be the best of all possible outcomes—it would remind
her of how easily he could move on. It would make
her accept *reality*, instead of chasing after rainbows.

Tearing off her slouchy socks, she pulled out the
gold dress she'd worn at Christmas and slithered into
it. Then she slapped on a defiant amount of make-up,
her highest heels—and a warm, ankle-length coat.
People were milling outside pubs as she made her
way to the station and more snow was falling as she
caught the underground and got out at Knightsbridge.

It was much quieter in this part of town. There
were few revellers out and about around here—this
was the world of the private, rather than the street
party. But by the time she reached Park View other
partygoers were milling around in the foyer and the
party atmosphere was contagious. She shared the elevator up to Alekto's apartment with several stunning
women and a man who kept surreptitiously glancing
at his phone.

The elevator pinged to a halt and the door to the
penthouse was opened by a waitress dressed as a fla-
mingo, a tray of exotic-looking cocktails in her hand.
Alannah went off to hang up her coat and then wan-
dered along the corridors she knew so well, back towards the sitting room. It was strange seeing the place
like this—full of people—when she had only ever

seen it empty. Most of the furniture she'd installed had been pushed back against the walls to maximise the space—but the room still looked spectacular. Even she could see that. The colours worked brilliantly—providing the perfect backdrop for Alekto's extensive art collection—and she was particularly proud of the lighting.

In spite of everything, she knew Niccolò would be pleased with her work. He might regret some things, but he would never regret giving her the job and she should take pride in that. A horrible dark pain washed over her, only this time it was underpinned with reproach. She wasn't supposed to be thinking about Niccolò. Wasn't that going to be her one and only new year resolution? That part of her life was over. She had to cut her losses and move on. And it was a waste of time to wonder what it would have been like if she *had* been pregnant. Or to dwell on that irrational and sinking sense of disappointment when she had stared at the test result and it had been negative.

A woman masquerading as a bird of paradise offered her a drink and Alannah took one, but the sweet concoction tasted deceptively powerful and she put the glass down as Alekto Sarantos came over to talk to her.

'You made it, then,' he said, with a smile. '*Thavmassios.* If I had a Euro for every person who has asked me who is responsible for the design of this apartment, then I would be a very rich man.'

'But I thought you *were* a very rich man,' she said, and he laughed, before giving her a thoughtful look. 'I might have some work for you in Greece, if you're interested?'

Alannah didn't even need to think about it. 'I'd be very interested,' she said immediately, because a different country might be just what she needed. What was it they said? A new year and a new start.

'Why don't you call my office on Monday?' he suggested, pulling out a business card and handing it to her.

'I will,' she said, putting it into her handbag as he walked away.

'Alannah?'

A familiar voice curled over her skin like dark velvet and she turned to see Niccolò standing there. His hair and shoulders were wet with melting snow and he was wearing a dark cashmere coat, which made him stand out from all the other guests. Alannah stiffened as his shadow fell over her and her heart began to hammer as she looked up into his shuttered features.

The knot of tension in her stomach grew tighter. But she had come here tonight to hold her head high, hadn't she? Not to hang it in shame. Nor to waste time wishing for something which could never be.

'Niccolò,' she said coolly. 'Fancy seeing you here.'

'What were you saying to Alekto?'

'That's really none of your business.'

'You do know he is world-famous for breaking women's hearts?'

'Why, has he lifted the crown from you?' she questioned acidly. 'And what are you doing still wearing your overcoat?'

'Because I have driven halfway across London looking for you,' he growled.

She frowned. 'Why?'

'Why do you think?' he exploded. 'I went round to your apartment, only you weren't there.' He had spent the afternoon psyching himself up, making careful plans about what he was going to say to her. He had decided to surprise her, because he…well, because he wanted to—and that in itself was uncharacteristic. He had naturally made the assumption that she would have been home alone, only when he'd got there Alannah's apartment had been shrouded in darkness and his heart had sunk. The sight of all those empty windows had suddenly seemed like a metaphor for his life and they had confirmed the certainty which had been growing inside him for days.

Instinct had made him pull out his telephone to speak to Alekto and his hunch was proved right. His friend had coolly informed him that, yes, Alannah *had* been invited to the party and although she'd told him she wasn't coming, she seemed to have changed her mind. In fact, she had just walked in, looking like a goddess in a spectacular golden dress.

Niccolò had turned his car around and driven from Acton, getting snarled up in the new-year traffic—his nerves becoming more and more frayed as an unfamiliar sense of agitation nagged away at him. And now he was here standing in front of her and nothing was as he thought it would be. He had not intended to launch into a jealous tirade because he'd seen her being chatted up by one of the world's biggest players.

Wasn't he supposed to be a 'player' himself?

His mouth hardened.

Not any more.

He was in a roomful of some of the most beautiful

women in the world and yet he could see only one. One who was staring at him with hostility and suspicion and, in his heart, he knew he couldn't blame her.

So why the hell was he demonstrating an arrogance which might cause her magnificent pride to assert itself, and tell him to take a running jump? He needed to keep her onside. To placate her. To make her realise why he had come here. *And to make her realise that it was the only possible solution.*

'I need to talk to you,' he said.

'Talk away.' She gave a careless shrug. 'I'm not stopping you.'

'In private.'

'I'd prefer to stay here, if you don't mind.'

'Unfortunately, *tentatrice*, I do mind.'

Without warning, he caught hold of her hand, his fingers enclosing her hammering pulse as he led her through the throng of partygoers until they had reached one of the bedrooms. He shut the door, just as she shook her hand free and glared at him.

'What do you think you're doing?' she demanded. 'You can't just waltz up to someone in the middle of a party and *manhandle* them like that! You can't just drag a woman from a room because you've decided you want a private word with her. Oh, sorry—I'd forgotten.' She slapped her palm against her brow. 'You can—and you do. Well, you might be Tarzan but I am not your Jane. I don't *do* Neanderthal and I don't *do* arrogant men who think they can just blaze into other people's lives doing exactly what they want. So will you please step aside and let me pass?'

'Not until you've heard me out,' he said, as a strange sense of calm washed over him. 'Please.'

She looked at him for a moment before pointedly glancing at her watch. 'You've got five minutes.'

Niccolò sucked in a breath but for a moment he couldn't speak. His calmness seemed to be deserting him as he realised that this wasn't going to be easy. He was going to have to do something unheard of—something he had instinctively always shied away from. He was going to have to pull out his feelings from the dark place where he'd buried them and he was going to have to admit them. To her. And even when he did, there was no guarantee that it might not be too late.

He looked into the wary blue of her eyes and his heart pounded. 'I need to ask your forgiveness,' he said. 'For all the unjust accusations I hurled at you. For my bull-headedness and my lack of compassion. For taking so long to realise the kind of woman you really are. Strong and proud and passionate and loyal. I've missed you, Alannah, and I want you back. Nobody talks to me the way you do, or makes me feel the way you do. Nobody else makes my heart skip a beat whenever I see her. I want to spend the rest of my life with you. To one day make the baby we didn't have this time. I want to make a real home—with you. Only with you.'

She took a step back, as if she'd just seen a ghost, and she started shaking her head. 'You don't want me,' she said in a hoarse voice. 'You only think you do, because I'm the one who walked away and that's probably never happened to you before. You want someone respectable, who is as pure as the driven snow—because that's the sort of thing you care about. Someone *suitable*. You didn't want me as bridesmaid because you were worried about what other people would think. Because you're hung up on appearances and how things look from the outside, no matter what you say.'

'I used to be,' he said savagely. 'But you have made me realise that appearances and social position don't matter. It's what's underneath which counts. And you have everything that counts. You are soft and smart and funny. You are kind and caring and talented. You didn't even smoke dope at school, did you— even though you were accused of it?'

Startled by this sudden conversational twist, Alannah narrowed her eyes suspiciously. 'Did Michela tell you that?'

He shook his head. 'She didn't have to. I worked it out for myself. I think you may just have covered up for my sister all this time.'

'Because that's what friends do,' she said fiercely. 'That's called loyalty.'

'I realise that now,' he said. 'It's just taken me a long and very circuitous route to get here. But I don't want to talk about the past any more… I want to concentrate on the future.'

He reached within the pocket of his snow-covered overcoat and pulled out a little box. 'This is for you,' he said, and his voice was slightly unsteady.

Alannah watched as he opened it and she was shamefully aware of a sinking sense of disappointment as she looked inside. Had she really thought it was an engagement ring? Was she really that fickle? Because glittering against the background of dark velvet was a brooch shaped like a little honey-bee. Its back was covered with yellow, black and white stones and she found herself thinking that she'd never seen anything so sparkly. She looked up at him, still disorientated.

'What's this?' she said.

'You collect insect brooches, don't you? They're diamonds. The black ones are quite rare. It's for you,' he said again. 'Because I didn't buy you a Christmas present.'

But Alannah felt a terrible lump in her throat as she began to blink her eyes rapidly. 'You just don't get it, do you?' she whispered. 'The brooches I have are all worth peanuts. I wear them because my mother gave them to me—because they *mean* something to me. I don't care if they're diamonds or paste, Niccolò. I don't care how much something is *worth*.'

'Then what if I tell you this is worth what I feel for you, and that is everything. *Everything*.' He moved closer. 'Unless you want me to go to a flea-market to find you something cheaper? Tell me, Alannah—are you going to set me a series of challenges before you will accept me?'

She almost laughed, except that now hot tears were springing to her eyes and she couldn't seem to stop them. 'I don't know what I'm going to do,' she whispered. 'Because I'm scared. Scared because I keep thinking this is all a dream and that I'm going to wake up in a minute.'

'No, not a dream,' he said, taking the brooch from the box and pinning it next to the little grasshopper which already adorned her golden dress. 'I bought you this because I love you. This is the reality.'

Her lips parted. 'Niccolò,' she said again, and now her voice was shaking. 'If this isn't true—'

He halted her protest by placing his finger over her lips. 'It *is* true. It has always been true. The first time I set eyes on you, I was hit by a thunderbolt so powerful that I felt as if you'd cast some kind of spell on me. And that spell never really faded. I love you, Alannah—even though I've been running away from the idea of love all my life. I saw what it did to my mother. I saw it as a weakness which sucked the life from everything in its path. Which blinded her even to the needs of her children.'

She bit her lip. 'I can understand that.'

He sensed her absolution, but he was not finished. 'But what I feel for you does not feel like weakness. I feel strong when I am with you, Alannah. As strong as a mountain lion. As if I could conquer the world.'

She let him put his arms around her and her head rested against his chest. 'That's funny, because right now I feel as weak as a kitten.'

His black eyes burned into her as he gently levered her face up so that she was looking directly at him. 'The only thing I need to know is whether you love me?'

'Of course I love you.' The words came tumbling out as if she'd been waiting all her life to say them. She thought about the first time she'd seen him, when they'd just clicked. It had been a thunderbolt for her, too, and she had never been able to forget him. She thought about how empty her life seemed when he wasn't there. He wasn't the man she'd thought him to be—he was so much more. 'I think I've always loved you.'

'Then kiss me, my beautiful Alannah,' he said softly. 'And let me show you my love.'

Slowly and tenderly, he traced his fingertip along the edges of her lips before lowering his head towards hers and Alannah's heart filled up with so much happiness that she felt as if she might burst with it.

EPILOGUE

'I USED TO think you hated weddings.'

Niccolò looked down into Alannah's face as he closed the door to their honeymoon suite, and smiled at her. 'I did. But that was before I found the woman I wanted to marry. Now it seems that I'm their biggest fan.'

'Mmm. Me, too.' She looped her arms around his neck. 'You did like the dress?'

'You looked beautiful. The most beautiful bride in the world. But then, you could wear a piece of sacking and I still wouldn't be able to tear my eyes away from you.'

'Oh, Niccolò.' She slanted him a look from between her lashes. 'Whoever would have guessed that beneath that cynical exterior beat the heart of a true poet?'

'It's true,' he said, mock-seriously. 'Though I must be careful not to lose my edge. If my competitors find out how much I'm softening, then I will soon be toast in the world of finance.'

'You?' She laughed easily. 'Yeah, sure. Like *that's* ever going to happen!'

He began to unzip her dress. 'Are you tired?'

'Not a bit. Even though it's been a very long day.'

She closed her eyes as the costly gown pooled to the ground around her feet. She had thought he would want a quiet wedding—something discreet, even a little hushed-up. Hadn't she thought he'd want to keep the risk of press interest to a minimum, despite his protestations that her past no longer bothered him? Probably. But once again he had surprised her. It was funny how love had the power to change people and to alter their views on what was important. He had told her that he was going to announce their engagement to the world's press and then he had gone out and bought her an enormous sapphire ring, which he said was the closest colour he could get to the denim-blue of her eyes.

Predictably, some of the old photos from *Stacked* magazine had made an appearance in the papers—but suddenly, they didn't seem to matter. It was slightly surreal to hear Niccolò echoing his sister's words—*and believing them*—by saying really they were very tame in comparison to a lot of the stuff you saw in contemporary music videos.

'I am proud of you, *tentatrice*,' he had murmured, crumpling the newspaper into a ball and hurling it into the bin. 'Proud of all you have achieved and how you have kept your dignity intact. Most of all, I am proud that you have consented to be my wife.'

And she had smiled. 'Oh, darling.'

The wedding was held in London's oldest Italian church, in Clerkenwell, and there was a stellar number of guests. A fully recovered Luis Martinez was there—as was the Sultan of Qurhah, Murat 'the Magnificent'. And naturally, Alekto Sarantos was at his dazzling best, even though he was barely visible through the sea of eager women who were clamouring round him. Michela was matron of honour—her silk gown cleverly hiding the beginning of a baby bump.

With Alannah's encouragement, Niccolò had told Michela the truth about their parents' death—and the admission had brought brother and sister much closer. Because secrets were always more dangerous than the truth, as he'd learned.

Alannah shivered with pleasure as Niccolò lifted her out of the discarded wedding dress and carried her over to the bed, wearing nothing but her underwear, sheer stockings and a pair of very high, white stilettos. As he undressed her she thought about the inhibitions which had once crippled her and which now seemed like a distant memory.

Tomorrow they were flying to the island of Niccolò's birth. He had only been back to Sicily once, after his mother's death—when he had been full of youthful rage and bitterness about the rejection she had suffered at the hands of her own family. But time had mellowed him and Alannah had helped him get some perspective. His maternal grandparents were dead—but he had cousins and uncles and aunts living there. A whole new family for them to get to know. And she was excited about that, too—looking forward to a big, extended family after so many years on her own.

He moved over her, his face suddenly very serious as he brushed her hair away from her cheek. 'Thank you,' he said softly.

She took his hand and kissed it. 'For?'

'For loving me. For being you.'

For being you. He didn't want anyone else, she had come to realise. He just wanted her exactly as she was, with no changes or modifications. He didn't want to rewrite her past, or pretend it hadn't happened, because her past had made her the woman she was today. And he loved that woman.

Alannah sighed.

Just like she loved her man.

* * * * *

COMING SOON!

We really hope you enjoyed reading this book.
If you're looking for more romance
be sure to head to the shops when
new books are available on

Thursday 21st November

MILLS & BOON

LET'S TALK
Romance

For exclusive extracts, competitions and special offers, find us online:

- **f** MillsandBoon
- **X** @MillsandBoon
- **◉** @MillsandBoonUK
- **♪** @MillsandBoonUK

Get in touch on 01413 063 232

MILLS & BOON

THE HEART OF ROMANCE

A ROMANCE FOR EVERY READER

MODERN
Prepare to be swept off your feet by sophisticated, sexy and seductive heroes, in some of the world's most glamourous and romantic locations, where power and passion collide.

HISTORICAL
Escape with historical heroes from time gone by. Whether your passion is for wicked Regency Rakes, muscled Vikings or rugged Highlanders, awaken the romance of the past.

MEDICAL
Set your pulse racing with dedicated, delectable doctors in the high-pressure world of medicine, where emotions run high and passion, comfort and love are the best medicine.

True Love
Celebrate true love with tender stories of heartfelt romance, from the rush of falling in love to the joy a new baby can bring, and a focus on the emotional heart of a relationship.

HEROES
The excitement of a gripping thriller, with intense romance at its heart. Resourceful, true-to-life women and strong, fearless men face danger and desire - a killer combination!

From showing up to glowing up, these characters are on the path to leading their best lives and finding romance along the way – with plenty of sizzling spice!

To see which titles are coming soon, please visit

millsandboon.co.uk/nextmonth

MILLS & BOON
MODERN
Power and Passion

Prepare to be swept off your feet by sophisticated, sexy and seductive heroes, in some of the world's most glamorous and romantic locations, where power and passion collide.

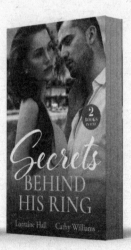

GET YOUR ROMANCE FIX!

Get the latest romance news,
exclusive author interviews, story
extracts and much more!

blog.millsandboon.co.uk